THE GRAVESTONES' SECRETS

CAROLYN S. WILLIFORD

TABLE OF CONTENTS

Chapter One 11
Chapter Two 49
Chapter Three 89
Chapter Four 121
Chapter Five 161
Chapter Six 199
Chapter Seven 233
Chapter Eight 265
Chapter Nine 299
Chapter Ten 335
Just a few musings from Carolyn 377

To Craig
I still think our love story is the best, ever.

THE GRAVESTONES' SECRETS

30 of July, 1587

To You, My Future Children, My Descendants,
 If our Merciful and Gracious God deigns to allow this lowly soul's survival, one knows I can merely pretend and hope that you will one day come to be. I only imagine you reading this poor Seaman's attempts to describe what cannot be adequately put into words. I am desirous of leaving behind something, some proof of my life, physical evidence that I lived, and not only lived, but crossed the Sea even while in constant and grave peril, arriving in a World that is far beyond what one could imagine.
 I would also tell of our Island in this New World, and the plant that grows upon it looking like oats, nearly as tall as I and bowing gracefully like a young maiden before the Queen. I would have you watch how the sand shifts and flows in obeisance to the Sea, and then one is simply compelled to grasp it in the hands, to see the whitish color and feel how fine it is! And I would show you the creatures in this World—of the great and vast variety of fowl and odd Sea creatures and fish and beasts, nearly all providing

victuals, and many the like of which never before upon my curious tongue.

This New World is a wondrous land indeed, for such a thing as Savages come in tree boats down the River, men as curious of us as we of them, and we Christian men must meet and have doings with them. With much pointing and gesturing we are able to talk of many needs, and our discourse must prove beneficial if we Colonists are to survive in this strange and unknown World.

And lastly, I would tell you of my cherished Catherine, my love left behind—the delight of my life!—and how we speak to each other in our minds. There is much to share with you, so that these encounters may not be forgotten, not lost in this New World!

  Your Ever Faithful Servant,
  Mauro

MAY 1997

CHAPTER ONE

It's the smell that assaults me first. That all-too-familiar stench of rank, decaying earth—and I feel the involuntary gag reflex kick in. Calming myself, I swallow it back down. But then my feet start to slip in the slimy muck beneath them and the distraction is enough to encourage nausea to move through me like waves pushing against the shoreline. Panic beckons, but still, cowardly, I refuse to open my eyes. There's no need for me to look; I know exactly where I am. Frantically, I grip the edge with my toes, finding precious little security in the muck that squishes between them. *You have to be still!* my mind screams, and instantly, I freeze. If I can't control every muscle's movement… if I give in to my terror…I'll lose my balance. And tumble even farther down into this foul hole.

My mind searches for answers in the darkness. *Why am I here again? What is it you want from me, God?* Risking one quick look, I glance down, only to gasp in terror of the abyss of inky gloom below me.

There is no bottom, a disembodied voice pronounces. *If you fall in, no one would ever find you. Not even God.* Tears fill my eyes, and I feel them start to slide down my cheeks. *You'll never feel God down there. He's certainly not going to catch you, and who knows? He might be the one who pushed you in!*

And then, when my despair feels smothering, like I'm about to suffocate, I awake. Jerking upright in bed, I gasp for air like one who's just broken to the surface after nearly drowning. I sit there panting, greedily breathing in gulps of air until my mind can finally regain control. *It's all right. You're home, safe in your own bed*, I tell myself. *Whatever that terrifying hole represents—it's not real, Julia. It's obviously symbolic of something you fear, but it simply doesn't exist. And it never will.*

-Jules! You all right? Is it the nightmare? Again?

I lie back, easing down into the comforting hollows of my lumpy mattress and pillows. Still feeling the lingering insecurity—the familiar by-product of my nightmare.

-Jules?

-Yes, I'm here, Guy. Why do I repeatedly torture myself with that nightmare? No. Don't answer that. It was a rhetorical question.

There's just a fraction of a beat before he responds. And I know I've hit a sore spot.

-You've made it clear you don't want my advice on this, Jules.

I tug the covers over my head. Childlike—oh, I'll give you that. And especially since that's not gonna make a dent in the volume of Guy's voice in my head. Stubbornly, I remain silent.

-I still think this is all partly related to your mom's death, Jules. The fact that you feel so much regret mixed in with your sadness. Something is *off* there, because you shouldn't—

-Guy!

-Okay, my bad. I think we'd better leave this for another time. Until you're...

-More agreeable? Sanguine? Submissive to yet another demand in my life?

-O-kay. Correct mood read on my part. Later, Jules.

He was gone then, that quickly. And also that quickly, I am instantly remorseful. What on earth compelled me to be so...caustic?

When, once again, like a caring big brother, Guy was only trying to help?

I role over onto my back, flopping one arm across my face. It's the blasted nightmare that started everything. What on earth must I do to make to make it *stop*? I've never seriously entertained the idea of seeing a counselor, but maybe Guy's right. Maybe I *should* talk with someone. But is a counsellor necessary? I could talk with my dad. Or maybe *not*. Uncle Ollie? And then I shake my head. As if! Add this onto...well, my other "issues"? Better yet: *The Issue*. Because it's all part of the One Big Problem in Dad's mind. And though Uncle Ollie's generally dodged getting into all that with Dad, if I put yet another thing out there...this weird. Nothing good's gonna come from me trying to explain this new wrinkle.

You, Julia, I lecture myself, *are certifiably insane. Or possess the emotional intelligence of a three-year-old. Possibly both.*

I roll back over onto my stomach to pour out my heart to God. The *Why's?* and *Please just help me's!* tumble out yet again like a cascading waterfall, and though I hear no audible answers, a bit of calm descends on my soul and mind. *"Pour out your heart to God"* the Psalmist says. That, I do. And one thing more too: I claim the reassurance that my God is with me. That I can trust him. And that I am most assuredly his child—insane or not. Nightmares or no.

And then I launch into that old repetitive justification in my mind: I am *not* insane. Though at one time my parents and teachers thought exactly that. Neither am I delusional, though I clearly hear a voice speaking inside my head, and have heard that voice, for as long as I can remember. And it's not gibbering nonsense, either, or a voice that tells me to do weird stuff. But how to make anyone understand and believe me? Considering no one can hear him but *me*?

It appears I can't help myself, and so once again I rehearse my defense as though I'm standing before a courtroom: I hear this definitely recognizable voice inside my head, talking specifically to me. Some call it mental telepathy, but that seems too vacuous a description, too empty of emotion to explain what Guy and I share. It goes deeper than that, to the core of our very self-awareness: From the very beginning of when I was first conscious of me...I was also just as conscious of *him*. So we talked, which meant that when he spoke to me, I answered. And then he responded to me. It's as simple as that.

Not so much to my concerned parents, however. Because once I was around five or so, I'd be sitting by myself somewhere—or sometimes with my parents and extended family—and I'd answer a question this inward voice had posed to me. Only I'd answer—out loud. So how was I supposed to know that was odd or different? For as long as I can remember, that was just the way it was, so I assumed *everyone* heard an inward voice that you laughed with, complained to, discussed nearly everything with (though some things have always been and definitely remain off limits) and enjoyed an intimate soul mate connection to. It wasn't until I started catching my parents' horrified looks that I began to realize this was a unique situation.

A huge part of the problem is that I absolutely know that Guy is a real person, yet another soul with this unique ability to mind talk. I've never doubted that he's a living, breathing, functioning human being on this earth; nor has Guy (according to him) doubted that I'm the same. Needless to say, I can't prove it—none of it. Eventually I realized I couldn't do anything to convince people it's real, either. Not that I didn't try! But I instinctively *know* that one day Guy and I will meet face to face. That I will touch him, I'll look into his eyes, and I'll put a face with the voice I've heard in my head for the last nearly twenty-four years.

Life changed irrevocably, however, when I turned six years old and excitedly looked forward to starting first grade. Mom—I'm sure out of protective instincts—insisted that I give up my imaginary friend. So I tried, I seriously did. But when my teacher caught me chattering away at the back of my class one day—and there was no one near to be chattering away *to*—she called my parents. Sigh. Who then decided that I needed a battery of doctors and tests.

Physical blood tests and brain scans were first, and once they discovered all those were normal, they marched me off to numerous psychiatrists and psychologists—who could drive a sane person nearly batty if she was normal to begin with. I met with psychiatrists who had me coloring ("Draw a picture of your family, Julia, including your special 'friend'"), and answering endless lists of questions. To settle once and for all if I simply had a wildly creative imagination with an imaginary playmate. Or was a classic schizophrenic.

And the doctors! First there were the kind ones who were condescending and fawned over me. What, did they think I was *the case* who was going to allow them to write *the book* (and eventually, *the screen play*) that would make their careers? I saw vacant look/lack-a-personality doctors who were determined to find the correct diagnosis, fit me into a familiar slot and fix me. Easy as putting a new battery in the flashlight—a perfect illustration since they were convinced I was dim. As in dim-witted, I mean.

And then there were some totally unique characters too: Like the bushy-eyebrowed (I remember staring at them in terror, wondering if bugs lived there) and pop-bottle-thick glasses doctor who squinted at me and inquired, "Does your daddy do strange things?" I was interested what question he was going to ask next, but I was yanked out of that office so quickly—Dad pulling on Mom and Mom yanking on me—I swear we left a cloud of dust in our wake. But seriously, this "doctor/cure quest" went on for months until two major events changed everything.

I just…stopped. Decided to "go underground," so to speak. Young as I was, I realized I had to live with two unresolvable facts: Guy's voice was *not* going to be silenced. He was as much a part of my life as the beat of my heart. I couldn't imagine him away, wish him away, or turn a deaf ear when his voice completely by-passed my ears! And besides. I didn't want to. Somehow that whole decision brought me into a closer relationship with God too, even at that young age. I'm convinced I leaned into God and needed him in a way most children never do. So even as I realized my unique reality would ultimately make me more of a loner, I gained the beginnings of a deeper relationship with my God.

Secondly, I accepted that *no one* was ever going to believe me—not even my parents. They might eventually accept my quirks and love me the best they could, but I accepted that no one else would. So I changed course and fully committed to… lying. "My imaginary friend is gone!" I announced to my parents and Uncle Ollie. And then I vowed to never reveal one more word that Guy spoke to me. Or tell another soul about him. I kept that promise until Melissa.

I grew up in southern Wisconsin, bastion of the average, normal American home life. Land of Swedes, blond hair, homemade rye bread and Lutfisk (ugh). Okay, so to most people lutefisk is not normal, but in Swede country, it definitely is. Enter Melissa Harrison, fresh from Los Angeles, California, land of Hollywood and New Age. Needless to say, she was different from us cheeseheads.

Our first conversation went something like this:

"Me an you're gonna be friends." Melissa had approached me on the playground where I sat under the slide, hiding out in its shade. She peered down at me through unevenly cut bangs that hung in her eyes, making her blink repeatedly. Melissa had stated this friend thing as fact, which rather startled me. "I can tell you're different. So'm I. We match good."

I slowly stood up so that we were eye to eye. I figured she needed to see me up close if our friendship had a reasonable chance past five minutes. Which was doubtful, in my experience. Why would she be any different from all the others who gave me a wide berth? Already I'd learned to be wary of strangers *and* supposed friends. I decided to lay it all on her and get this over with, fast.

"Just so you know…I have this friend I call Boy. He talks to me and I answer him. He's inside my head." I watched Melissa's eyes widen. She leaned in closer.

"Is he nice?" She'd raised one eyebrow, and her voice carried the edge of a co-conspirator.

I shrugged. "Sure. Unless we're angry."

"What happens then?"

"I argue with him!"

Her entire body smiled—which is what happens when Melissa really likes something: It's never only her mouth turning up at the corners, but instead a whole production that travels from her face clear down to her toes as a series of excited little wiggles and ticks passes from limb to limb. "Oooh, way cool. Wish I had a friend who talked in my head." She glanced towards our teacher who happened to be watching us intently; Melissa nonchalantly motioned towards the swings. We turned and walked farther away from Mrs. Andreson, the spy. "Me and you need a little privacy." Melissa briefly looked over her shoulder, making a face that indicated adults were akin to aliens. "They just don't get us, do they?" she asked, knowingly.

"Get us?"

"Understand us. Get it?"

Now I smiled back. And that's when I knew Melissa was right: We were destined to be friends. Best friends. "No, they don't."

We both giggled like the wise first graders that we were.

Melissa whole-heartedly agreed with my decision to keep my mouth shut about the voice inside my head. "They're adults, and adults are kooky. 'Cause they don't have good eyes." To my puzzled expression, she continued to explain, "They only see easy stuff. Me and you? *We* see the fizzy stuff."

"Fuzzy stuff?"

"No, *fizzy* stuff. Like pixie dust and fairies and monsters under the bed. But adults don't, right? So we keep secret the stuff that adults can't see so they don't believe us. The fizzy stuff." She looked at me knowingly.

I nodded. Because I did understand—sort of. Most of all, as I recall, because I really wanted to.

"Pinkie swear with me." She held out her little finger and I put mine up to hers to entwine them together. "So what's he look like?"

"Um, well. Like a boy, I guess."

Notice how even my recollection of that first encounter with Melissa reveals how passive and uncreative I can be? When I first became aware of the voice inside my head, I called him *You*. Even as a toddler, he objected to that original name. When he blurted out (I remember it sounded just like that in my mind—like he'd erupted in a fit of toddler rage), *I'm not a* You; *I'm a boy!* So I started calling him simply *Boy*.

And I had absolutely no idea what he looked like—the thought to do so hadn't yet even crossed my mind.

Anyone else appreciate the irony here? My parents and teachers and doctors all thought I was incredibly creative to have this imaginary friend in my head when actually I never had the innate ability to make up one bit of it. Seriously, wouldn't you assume I could come up with a better name than *Boy*? When I was rehearsing my name and address for first grade, I unwittingly let it leak to Guy that my name was Julia Anne Johnson. But he's always been reticent, coyly refusing to tell me his real name. When we reached middle school age, however, he groused, "I'm not a little boy anymore, Jules. I'm a pretty big guy now, for your information." My witty response? I called him *Guy*. Oh yeah, I'm creative all right. As creative as a slug.

After Melissa asked what Boy looked like, I realized I also hadn't inquired where he lived, what kind of house he lived in, what his family was like. I wasn't mature enough to understand this as a 6-year-old, but I truly took him and his entire perspective on the world for granted. He was so much an extension of me that I didn't yet know how to separate us out as two independent people. It was like I had two pairs of eyes, and I gazed out at the world through not only my eyes, but Boy's as well. Except that I clearly didn't take in many specifics through his "window."

I suppose it was inevitable—with this kind of an inward relationship constantly developing—that as Guy and I grew closer, it became more and more awkward to make friends with my peers. I can't blame the girls at church and school for judging me odd and standoffish and preoccupied. Because it's true: I was all those things. Only Melissa could accept me for what I was, and eventually, she really was my rescuer. Because Melissa eventually became the bridge to our other classmates, enabling me to finally be somewhat accepted into the adolescent world. I would never be popular—no way that was going to happen. Instead, I moved warily and protectively through that world, content to remain more of an observer than actual participant. They'd judged me harshly in the past, and would find me even more so if they knew...well, it wouldn't be pretty at all if they really knew.

As Melissa and I grew into adulthood together, she went through a phase when she researched mental telepathy like a fiend, reading everything she could find on the internet. As expected, she discovered a multitude of doctors and scientists out there who declared it all a sham of parlor tricks. And as you would also assume, Melissa was gratified to also uncover a good number of doctors and scientists who granted telepathy legitimacy, grouping it with other "unexplained abilities of the brain we simply can't yet explain or understand." Sometimes I'd read one of the articles she found particularly interesting, but they left me feeling depressed, frustrated or even angry. My daily reality was quite clear: Guy existed. And we talked in our minds. Ultimately, any positive *or* negative comments were mere chaff. Melissa eventually came to pretty much the same conclusion, and I've never doubted that she would defend me *and* my sanity to the death. I'm blessed that she loves and accepts me unconditionally, weird "abilities" and all. And that makes me love her all the more.

Psychiatrists, however—goodness, would they ever have a field day with the likes of me. They'd quickly surmise that my "dysfunctional inner life" has affected me in other ways too. As in I tend to get totally *stuck*—my recurring inability to make decisions. I successfully completed my K-3rd grade teaching degree at the local university, but currently there are no open fulltime teaching positions anywhere in this county—maybe the whole mid-west, for all I know. So for the time being I'm filling a maternity leave—a job one of my professors thankfully recommended me for—but obviously has a built-in time limit. Then what? Dad says if I put half the drive and effort I have for triathlons into my career I'd have other options. "If you could simply find the ability to speak up for yourself!" Dad constantly tells me. But honestly, what good would that do anyway when my future feels about as thrilling as kissing sleazy Eddie Murphy, the loser set to inherit the cheese factory here in the town of Sundhamn? Don't even get me started on my so-called love life.

I'd finally drug myself out of bed and visited the bathroom when I heard the sound of nails hitting the wood floor, staccato clicks that always made me smile. Moppit—my medium-sized mound of floating hair, otherwise known as a dog—stood in the middle of the hallway, looking up at me, ears up and tail wagging.

She was aptly named, and I have to grant credit for that to Guy. Moppit looks exactly like the dogs they tend to use in the musical *Annie*, so I'd planned to name my adopted mutt—my creativity at its zenith—Sandy. Guy had scoffed. And yes, I heard exactly that sound in my head.

-That's the best you can do? he'd teased.

I'd gotten defensive. And then, though I dissed his choice, eventually began calling her the name Guy called her all the time. He was insufferably smug for a while when he realized I'd given in.

Moppit ran over to the cupboard where I kept her food—nails clicking across the floor again as she bounces in her excitement—and switches her gaze from me to the cupboard and back again several times. Anyone who thinks dogs don't clearly communicate hasn't observed Moppit when it's time to eat.

I'd just poured a cup of coffee when the phone rang. I took a small sip before answering, "Hello?"

"Julia, I know exactly what you need to do. Come out here. Right away."

I laughed. "No good morning, eh? Right to the point!" Typical Melissa communication, at warp speed, just like she lives life: No need for a greeting, easing into a subject, or a build-up. I always feel like I've jumped into the middle of an on-going conversation with her, even if we haven't spoken for days. Sometimes I'm clueless about what she's chattering away about for several minutes.

"Don't laugh, Julia! I'm serious."

"Aren't you just always?! Oh, Mel. You know I can't come right now. I've a commitment. I'm teaching, for crying out loud. I can't jeopardize this position because I'm hoping it will lead to a fulltime position. Next year, actually."

"Excuses, always excuses." I could see her shaking her head and drumming her manicured fingers. "I have an interview for you out here."

"What?" I plopped onto the recliner, while Moppit followed, immediately making use of the available lap. "What kind of interview? I can't just—"

"There you go again with the excuses! Why not? Fly out here next weekend. I've lined up an interview with a friend of mine. He's the superintendent of a huge district, a genuine VIP. Met him at a gala last week."

I snickered. "Okay, now I'm getting it. You have a date with him this weekend, too, no doubt."

Melissa's turn to chuckle. "He also happens to be a very handsome VIP."

"Why am I not surprised?" Moppit nudged my arm and I got the hint; I stroked the fur on her tummy while she stretched out contentedly. "Mel, you're a dear. And I really appreciate your efforts—honestly I do. But I have responsibilities here."

It sounded like she was slamming things around in a pique, and it would be entirely like Melissa to do just that. I could hear a blender start up when she grumbled, "Yes, I know. Miss Responsible—that's our Julia. It's just that I miss you terribly. So when this opportunity presented itself—" Her voice trailed off, and she sounded genuinely disappointed.

"I know. I miss you too." After graduating from college, my still loyal and best friend moved back to California and immediately enrolled in Stanford's law school. Her "summa cum laude" J.D. led to a job at a prestigious firm where she's become the passionate lawyer I always knew she'd be. But honestly, she's perfect for the Hollywood scene too. Don't get me wrong as I love this about her: Melissa is the yin to my yang because she's such the drama queen. Emotional? Oh my, off the charts. But when you're apparently stunted emotionally, like I am, you don't just tolerate someone like Mel. In some respects, I pretty much encourage her to act as my substitute. To *feel life* for me. Generally works out well for both of us, actually.

When Melissa is able to provoke me into finally *doing* something, she's like the expert skier attacking double diamond slopes, while I'm the novice skiing in slow, wide arcs from one side of the bunny hill to the other. And when I end up stalled in one of my "stuck modes"? I drive her insane. I don't especially like it either, for crying out loud, but my current dilemma isn't due to my reliance on Guy….or my dad's handling of my mom's death when I was twelve years old…or Mel's observation that I've failed miserably at having a serious relationship with a person of the opposite sex.

"I'm desperately lonely for you, Julia. You have no idea!"

"To the point you can't bear going on that date with good-looking Mr. Superintendent?" I teased.

She re-started the blender—I assumed Mel was in the healthy fruit and yogurt smoothie fan club—and then shouted over the noise, "I'll ignore that. And just this *once* I had hopes you'd surprise me and do something—something totally unlike you. Like hop a plane and come out here for a serious interview. You know, jumping out of your comfort zone wouldn't be totally impossible, Julia." I tried to get a word in then, but Mel wasn't having it. "Let me guess. Bet I can tell you exactly what you're planning to have for breakfast."

"That's not—"

"One of those boring yogurt cups—most likely plain vanilla. One piece of wheat toast and two eggs. Since you're swimming later, of course. Am I right?"

"Melissa, I—"

"See! You're so…so…utterly *predictable*, Julia! When are you going to really start living? Take some risks? Experience life?"

I sighed. "Mel, darling. I'd love to come out there if it weren't for my dad. I can't leave him, you know that. Please tell me you understand."

Now it was Melissa's turn to sigh. "Yes, I do. Can't blame me for giving guilt manipulation a good try, though, can you?"

"If anyone in the whole world could tempt me to pull up stakes and move all the way across the country to California, it would be you, Melissa Linne." I let that sit a moment, pausing to let Melissa's angst dissipate. "Seriously, Mel. I miss you too, so much. Say, what about this idea: I could fly out after school's out. Wouldn't that be fun?"

"No hedging. No backing out. You'd really come?"

"Absolutely. I have this gut feeling that I need to check out this new man. Since he just might be *the one*."

She laughed. "He is delicious, I must admit. And for your information, he's taking me out tonight. *And* this weekend."

I could feel her smiling all the way from California—that entire body thing she does. "So I have a date tonight too." I stopped for a couple beats, teasing Mel to think outside the box. "With my dad."

"Whatever. You didn't fool me for one second, Julia. Give the darling my greetings. And call me Sunday. We need to talk more about this trip, okay? Ciao."

"We are definitely on for Sunday. Bye, Mel." I shake my head and take a deep breath. Mel often has that effect on me: Like I've just run an emotional mini-marathon.

I moved about the kitchen, pulling two eggs, butter and a yogurt cup from the fridge. Thought to myself, *It's not plain vanilla, so there, Melissa. Ran out of vanilla yesterday, so it's strawberry for today*. Gotta take your wins where you can, I always say.

After consuming my predictable breakfast and throwing some dirty clothes into the washer, I started packing my duffle bag for a swim at the fitness club. Glancing into the mirror in my bedroom provoked an instant frown. "Bor-ing," I announced to my reflection, since there was nothing even remotely remarkable in your basic category of physical beauty. And I am the complete opposite of Melissa, who grew up to be drop-dead gorgeous. When the two of us walked around campus we were definitely noticed, but that was due to Melissa. She's your classic Swedish blond: Hair that glints like gold in the sun; gorgeous ivory complexion; long, willowy legs; high, defined cheekbones and bright blue eyes. Though she moved here from California, Melissa's heritage is solidly Swedish; how could she not be when her grandmother's maiden name was Gustafson? And that means she has the coloring of pretty much everyone else around this part of Wisconsin.

You would think I'd have that same classic coloring, but that's not the way my family's gene pool worked out. Instead, I'm the total opposite of Melissa and the Swedish look in every way. First of all, I have ink-black, perfectly straight hair, coupled with an olive complexion. No ivory skin for me, and definitely no peaches and cream. The prerequisite dark brown eyes are also part of the package.

Dad tells me I take after his paternal grandmother, and the photographs I've seen of Grandmother Johnson—as much as you can make out in a grainy black and white photo—seem to agree with Dad's assessment. But she is truly the *only one* in our family tree with dark hair and eyes; everyone else has the blond hair and blue eyes of your typical Swede. What possessed my particular gene alignment to fixate on Grandmother Johnson, I have no earthly idea.

I used to dream of being tall enough to jump hurdles with ease. Cursed again. My short legs—people politely describe me as petite, but I think of my legs as length challenged—can actually go fairly fast. But they certainly don't extend. And the word *petite* only feels like a polite euphemism for *shrimp*, in my opinion.

I have a straight, unremarkable nose, high cheekbones and fairly generous lips. Besides a good-sized birthmark on the back of my left shoulder, I have three unremarkable scars—one from the playground monkey bars (the time I hit my head and got five stitches ended my daredevil days on the bars) and another from a bike accident (a hands-free fall meant I never did that trick again either; can you tell I became a cautious kid?). I've also got a funny looking raised scar next to my left pinky finger—from a forceps birth, I was told. When trying to remember something, I have a tendency to nervously rub that small patch of uneven skin.

I also have one other idiosyncrasy: I hiccup at odd times, like during the romantic scenes of a movie. My friends are wiping away delicate tears and I'm trying to silence loud, guttural noises, which can be totally embarrassing. Sometimes I do the same thing when I'm anxious or tense or feeling ill-at-ease. It's like my wiring for emotions and automatic non-verbal responses got crossed at birth or something. And only Guy would find my hiccupping endearing.

As for my personality, people describe me as so shy that I can be hard to get to know. After all those horrendous childhood tests and condescending doctors, years of desperate-for-answers parents and classmates who judged me either a bit quirky or downright odd…well, I learned to go totally silent about Guy and wall myself off. For protection. Only Melissa can coax me to poke my head out of my shell, but when she's over two thousand miles away…

My parents, Liam and Annie Johnson, really did the best they could with what they were given. Namely, quirky and odd *me*. It wasn't their fault they had no idea what to do with a child who had a telepathic, invisible friend! They worked hard to give me a stable, loving home life, demonstrating how to have a personal relationship with God. And yet it feels like my life has these gaps—deep canyons with no bridges available. I stand at the edge of one of those cliffs and suddenly, I'm stymied. Rather than risk falling, I simply stop, paralyzed by insecurities.

Later, when I'm swimming and concentrating on *stroke and stretch, pull the water, turn my head to breathe in…breathe out… then stroke and stretch, breathe in…flip, breathe out while pushing off the wall, breathe in…lap twenty-two…*

-Jules. Where are you? At the pool?

Only Guy calls me Jules. I do love that.

-Yes. It's Friday. Remember I always swim Fridays? Can't talk now or I'll lose lap count.

-Let me count for you so we can talk a bit. Trust me?

-That's a loaded question! Wouldn't put it past you to make me swim extra laps.

-Ha. Tempting. What lap are you on?

-Just turning at twenty-three...

-Gotcha. I swear your voice sounds like you're talking under water.

-I *am* talking to you when I'm under water!

He paused, and I jumped into the silence. When you have no non-verbals to take your cues from, those in between moments can be difficult. Misconstrued. It's one of the areas where our mind talking has proved problematic.

-You've got an agenda today, I can tell. What's up?

-Need to warn you. One of those intuitive times again.

That's another thing Guy and I share: An innate sense when something is about to happen to the other. We're not clairvoyants or anything remotely like that. But we always give each other a heads-up when we sense a surprise is around the corner. He sounded unusually concerned.

-Not a good sense, I take it?

-No, sorry. Hoping I'm wrong this time. Really hoping.

The lingering memories of the nightmare coupled with Guy's warning cloud my thinking. God, what now? I could feel a sense of foreboding come over me like the thick fog of an early morning.

-Why does everything have to be so hard right now? Is it possible for your *life* to be out of sorts?! Because mine sure feels that way.

Guy chuckled. I would bet that he's shaking his head now too, searching for the right response.

-So your life is...what, now? Cranky? Love your powers of description, Jules.

-What lap am I on?

-Twenty-five.

-Liar! I *knew* you'd do that!

-Okay...really, it's lap twenty-six.

-Guy!

-Okay, okay. It's actually and absolutely twenty-seven. I swear.

-And I swear you lost count. You know I make myself take the lowest number....

-Hey, I need to run. Just remember. When you need me later, Jules, I'll be here, okay? That's all. I'm right here.

-Oh, Guy. I know. It's just...

-Just remember.

-Thanks, Guy.

So many times I've wondered, *Where does Guy live? And what does he look like?* Though he discovered I live in Wisconsin (since I slipped years ago and gave him my full name, he's clearly done some research), I have no idea if he's in South Africa or South Carolina, though I do sometimes pick up the hint of a twang. And when the only name you have for someone is *Guy*, your abilities to sleuth hover right at zero. My nemesis Mr. Sherlock Holmes, however, tricked me into giving him a fairly good description of my appearance about a year ago. Fell right into his trap, naïve innocent that I am. But ironically, though I know how Guy feels and thinks about practically everything, I remain ignorant about even the very basics like his hair and eye colors. As for the sound of his voice, I hear him quite clearly in my head. But could that be like when you hear your own recorded voice played back to you? How it sounds so different because you're used to hearing it through your head? I suppose it's possible I wouldn't even recognize Guy's voice if I heard him for real.

Speaking of voices…explaining how I separate out Guy's voice from the Holy Spirit's was tricky to explain even to Melissa. She asked, incredulously, "But don't you ever get them mixed up?" Actually, I don't. *Ever*. Because I don't hear God's voice like Guy's when we're mind talking. Guy's is clearer and more present—present as *in this world*. That word *present* doesn't begin to describe what it's like to hear Guy's voice in my head, but there is literally no word in the English language that comes close. The Other, God's voice, is no less influential or powerful. Or less present, either, but in a different way altogether.

The only way I could attempt to explain the difference is to say that God's voice is more like a movement over my soul. It's a sensing—really a pushing at the core of who I am and what I should be and do. As deeply as Guy knows me, there are thoughts, feelings and needs that go only to God. There's simply no doubt at all who clearly has known me better than *anyone* else since that evening around our youth group's campfire when I knew I needed Him like no other. When Jesus came into my heart that night, God's domain wouldn't be limited to merely the allowed sections of my mind and heart. Instead, God knows *all* of me, to the very depths of my soul.

Laps completed (heaven only knows how many laps I did today), I run some errands before heading home, using the driving time to pray. If my life is truly out of sorts, however, then my prayer life is near disaster. Do I talk with God? Oh, absolutely.

All the time! But why does it feel more like I'm striving with him than anything else? At this stage of life, I relate far too much to Jacob, the Angel wrestler, unfortunately.

Absolute truth? I want God to be fully in control of my future. That's good, right? So I wait, cautiously, allowing God to work as I read my bible and pray. Melissa says that's just an excuse to put off making decisions, that I'm only fooling myself by waiting for God's will to become blatantly obvious. I just want to *get it right*. The future feels so cloudy now. Evasive, even. I don't understand why God can't somehow clearly point out what he wants me to do. I'm not asking for a pillar of fire like the Israelites had, but something, *anything* that would give clear direction.

Later, arms loaded with swim gear and bags of groceries, I kick the door open with a foot (a habit which has considerably weakened the lock's screws), nearly tripping over Moppit in the process. "Hey, how's my girl? Hungry?" I plopped my duffel on the floor and bags on the counter, bending down to ruffle Moppit's wiry fur and accept a few slobbery kisses under my chin. "My day's been a bit rough. Yours?" She looked up at me with ears stiffened forward, eyes wide and bright, pink tongue hanging out. "That good for you, huh? I'm jealous. Good time spying on the neighborhood, I presume?"

I moved to pull back the shade and peer out the front window, searching for signs of life across the street or down the block. From what I could tell, watching everyone and everything (squirrels were considered special enemies and therefore due extensive observation) was Moppit's favorite activity while I was gone.

As if on cue, she jumped up onto her favorite viewing spot on the back of the old couch that served as the focal point in my apartment's main room. That room also contained a clunky TV perched on an old coffee table, an end table with a study lamp from my dorm room and a dilapidated recliner that looked like a Goodwill reject. The faded and worn plaid material smells like my dad's aftershave (which is a plus, in my opinion), and it still reclines—though getting it back upright requires applying some kung-fu moves to the footrest. Still, the down position is worth the hassle since that transforms it into perfect form for TV watching. Aftershave scent included.

Moppit's worn the couch's fabric nearly threadbare due to her favorite viewing perch, and there's also a recognizable indentation from her daily idiosyncrasies. As if cued for demonstration, she made three circles and lay down, nose pointed towards the house directly across the street. I follow Moppit's gaze, not really seeing what's out there since my focus had drifted back to Guy. He really does try to help, the best possible to the extent a voice in your head can. The intimacy I know with him is equal to or even better than what twins share, from what I've read. He's the one I go to for testing nearly every idea, thought, and impression. If God is the Rock who defines me and all that I am, then God has given me Guy to help pencil in the edges. I realize it's not God's or Guy's fault that, the older I get, the hazier those edges feel. And it's certainly not anyone's fault but mine that I'm paralyzed by my indecision.

I tell myself I'll get past this stalemate soon and a great job teaching third graders, my favorite age to teach, will simply land in my lap—then I'll know without doubt it's God's will. Next I'll marry the man of my dreams, settle down to lead a totally normal life and have three adorable kids. Who will look just like their dad: blond, peaches and cream complexions, blue eyes. The Wisconsin ideal. Hey, I admitted I might be stuck, but that doesn't mean I can't still dream.

Stroking Moppit's fur, I felt insecurity wash over me again, and just as suddenly, I remembered how Guy had warned me before my mother's imminent death. Ironically, I'd been sitting on the floor stroking our dog Bailey when his voice had tip-toed into my consciousness. At first I assumed he felt guilty about something, noting the cautious way he'd approached me. *You've done something, haven't you?* I asked, teasingly. *I can feel your guilt, you coward.*

But I had it all wrong. It wasn't guilt I'd sensed in Guy: It was his reluctance to tell me what he knew. That something awful was coming. He had no idea what, but he was worried about me. And he hated being the bearer of bad news.

I'd argued with him, but it was one of those times when even I knew my arguing was senseless. Like insisting that it's not going to storm when the ugly dark clouds are churning and rolling over each other, just to the west. The humidity starts to push up against you in such a way that you feel a headache coming on, and you have to swallow to release the pressure in your ears. As soon as Guy started talking, I knew a storm was brewing. Oh, I had no idea it would be my mom who'd be caught up in that firestorm, and I certainly had no second sight about a drunk driver walking out of the local bar at that very moment. Staggering towards his car, climbing in and driving off towards a violent meeting with my mother's little compact Honda Civic.

I shivered. All those horrible feelings – the insecurity, the pain, the helplessness – all of it came rushing back.

I don't like reflecting on that time, since it felt like I lost not only my mom, but for too long, like I lost my dad, also. Understandably, he'd been locked away in his own pain—pain like a tsunami of grief that engulfed and nearly drowned everything in its path—including me. I didn't seek his help because I instinctively knew that it wasn't….that I couldn't. No, *shouldn't*. Because Dad had to take care of himself. And months later, when he did reach out to me, it was because Uncle Ollie stepped in. "Do something, Liam," he'd snapped, "before you lose your daughter too."

Thanks to Uncle Ollie, eventually Dad and I were able to form some semblance of a home together, minus Mom. Our communication improved. To this day we still rarely talked about mom, but at least mentioning her wasn't taboo. Dad touched me more; he made an effort to actually be present when he pulled me into a hug. And slowly but surely we developed a new life—re-configured routines for just the two of us, and a good many that included Uncle Ollie. But the scars from those years are there still. And everyone who has a scar knows the skin will always be more sensitive there. And never as resilient as it once was.

God, I pleaded silently, *what now? Who now? Please don't take Guy from me.* Followed by a quick jab of guilt that my first concern had been Guy, and not my dad.

-Guy, you there?

No answer. Of course there were times when one of us was busy. Sleeping was a possibility, though an urgent call could easily wake the sleeper. Sometimes we'd choose to ignore the other for whatever reason, but that didn't happen often. There's also the "busy now but I'll be back to you soon" type of response, but it was rare that a request like the one I'd just sent out went unanswered. Since Guy had just said he'd be there for me when I needed him, I gave it one more try.

-Hey. Got a minute?

I sighed. *No sense being obnoxious,* I reasoned. If he did hear me, he could tell by my tone that it's truly not an emergency. Yet?

I reach out to pet Moppit and absent-mindedly ask, "That where the action was today?"

She looked up at me knowingly.

"I get the feeling you're holding out on me, but we'll get to your secrets later. For now, I would think you'd be hungry." Moppit's next move was the reason there was yet another section of cushion that looked awful: Jumping off the back of the couch—and therefore shredding another area of the fabric—she literally launched herself out onto the middle of the wood floor.

I poured a heaping cup of food into her bowl, stepping back to watch her obvious pleasure for a few moments. *Moppit's life is so basic, so scripted and controlled and uneventful. There's a lot to envy about that*, I thought to myself, sighing.

After a trip outside with Moppit, I gave myself a quick perusal in the bathroom mirror before grabbing my keys.

Moppit's tail wagged furiously, and she looked up at me.

"Okay, I guess you can go. Dad smiles more when you're around. Come on—we'll surprise him."

So on a whim, I dumped Moppit in the front seat with me, where she spent the entire time with front paws on the door handle, gazing out the passenger window. She rarely barked and never nervously traipsed back and forth across the seat like many dogs would in a car. However, Moppit did leave nose prints smeared all over the glass, and she was downright demanding about access to what she considered *her* window. Front seat passengers, be forewarned.

With good intentions, I decided to leave the radio off, electing to use my time to think about the fascinating story of Esther. I was currently reading about her, and had just dug into the chapter on Mordecai's response to Haman and his plot to kill all the Jews. Quite frankly, the chapter was nagging at me in a way that I couldn't quite put my finger on. Whenever that happened with Scripture, I'd sleep on it, re-visit it again, sensing there was something I was missing. I'd had several nights to sleep on this one, but for right now, whatever was hidden still eluded me.

I turned into the strip mall that housed a salon, a dentist's office, a UPS store and lastly, Luigi's, Dad's and my favorite restaurant in town. It's not known for being fancy, but the chef who runs it—Bob VanHaven, whom I assume hasn't a drop of anything remotely Italian in his veins—is one fine chef. When

I pulled into the parking lot, I noted Dad's sweet white (not a speck of dirt on it, anywhere) Lexus LS400, parked right next to the sidewalk. Either he'd come early, or he'd lucked out in finding that space just as another customer left. My bet was on the early arrival, however, assuming he'd already downed a glass of wine and some garlic rolls.

"Okay, Moppit. Knock yourself out watching people." She gave me a bored glance and turned right back to her sentry position. The window? Already a lost cause. *Remember, Julia: Wash car tomorrow.*

Opening the ornate wooden door of Luigi's, I was greeted with the steady hum of contented voices and background music, something Italian themed, of course. I recognized Andrea Bocelli's beautiful tenor and smiled in appreciation. Scanning the dimly lit room, I caught Dad's eye; he would never raise his voice or even think to wave in my direction. One of the servers, Jenny, a friend from school days, hustled by and threw over her shoulder, "The usual to drink?"

"Yeah, thanks, Jenny. That would be great." I greeted Dad and gave him the expected kiss on his cheek. Just a quick peck, nothing too personal or affectionate in public, though we wouldn't be much more demonstrative in private, truthfully. We just weren't a family that practiced that sort of thing. Except for Uncle Ollie, who, in many ways, makes me wonder if he might be a foundling, he's that different from the rest of the Johnson clan.

"You're looking exceptionally dapper tonight," I said, and noted his pleased smile. As usual, he had on a crisply starched white shirt; tonight he'd also added a corduroy vest. And though Dad had a tendency to nag about the time I spent training for triathlons, he also was very much into fitness. The fitted vest showed off his still trim waist, and for the age of sixty-eight—with a full head of thick white hair and good posture at 6'4"—Liam Johnson could still turn female heads.

"Flattery will get you dessert." He finished the last sip of his wine—I'd obviously guessed right—and the tell-tale crumbs on his bread plate affirmed my other assumption. His bright blue eyes sparkled in the light from the Tiffany lamp hanging above us.

"Are you going to behave tonight and order something that your cardiologist approves of?"

"Now see…there goes your desert offer right out the window."

"Excuse me for caring about you and a healthy heart!"

"You're too late anyway. Already told Jenny I'd like tonight's specialty pasta from the Early Bird. According to her, people are saying its homemade sausage is outstanding."

I shook my head at him in resignation while quickly perusing the Early Bird—though that was unnecessary. Dad and I knew the entire menu by heart, and he could've easily guessed what I'd choose. "I think I'll just go with pasta and marinara sauce."

"What a surprise. All these terrific options, and you're choosing that, again?"

Jenny placed a glass of the house red before me and then refilled Dad's before looking expectantly at me. "Want to hear tonight's special?"

"I hear it's exceptional."

"It's to die for. Baked fettuccini with sausage and bacon." She stared at me, one eyebrow up, pen poised and ready. "Absolutely gooey with cheese."

I was pretty sure *gooey* hadn't been part of Bob's description for Jenny to use with customers. "Tempting, but I think I'll stick with my usual."

Leaning towards me, Jenny raised both eyebrows now. "You know. The—"

"Spaghetti marinara. Cheese on the side. You and *Rain Man*: Fish sticks and green Jell-o on Fridays." Since when are servers allowed to be sarcastic? She ignored my scowl and turned to my dad. "Mr. Johnson? Bet you're not gonna let me down. The special, right?"

Dad handed her his menu. "Absolutely. And thanks for the refill of wine."

I waited a moment for Jenny to be out of earshot before I commented, "Gotta appreciate living in small towns, huh? Even the servers are comediennes. And for the record, I despise Jell-O."

"Have to agree with you there." Settling back comfortably into his seat, Dad held his wine glass before him and stared into the deep red. He swirled it around in his glass. "Your grandparents wouldn't be pleased if they could see us now. Not only am I drinking wine, but worse yet—I've condoned you doing so too. Your grandmother especially would've been outraged."

I grinned and took a sip. "What about Mom?"

"Oh, your mother wouldn't have been overly happy with me either, I'm afraid." Shifting in his chair, putting the glass back onto the table, Dad took a deep breath. Like he was preparing a speech.

I looked at him expectantly, but he remained silent. "Something you wanted to bring up?"

"I saw your high school English teacher today."

"Oh? Which one?"

"Mrs. Holub. Wasn't she your favorite?"

"Yeah, she was. Definitely the 'tough as nails but you learned a lot' variety."

"Don't you credit her with your desire to be a teacher?"

"Uh-huh." I nodded at him, encouragingly, I hoped. Thinking he was having a tough time getting to the point, whatever that was. "Ran into her at the post office. I was buying stamps."

I leaned forward and raised my eyebrows. Whatever Dad needed to say, I figured it had to be important, as awkward as he was acting. And due to the round-about way we were getting wherever it was we were going.

"Made me think about purpose and goals. What you want from life. What's important."

Now we're finally getting somewhere, I thought.

"Here's your salads and more garlic bread, right out of the oven," Jenny said, placing the heavenly-smelling basket and our plates on the table. "Wine okay?" We both nodded and she moved on to the next table of newly arrived customers. We could hear her voice carrying, enticing them with a repeat of "The special tonight is to *die* for."

I looked back to Dad and we automatically bowed our heads for him to say grace, and then I patiently waited for him to pick up the conversation where we'd left off as we helped ourselves to the delicious bread and salads. Dad's and my conversations were never an animated talk fest; there was no striving or need to fill every moment with words. Instead, we were both comfortable with stretches of silence, easing into topics. And we allowed the conversation to ebb and flow, go at its own pace, even if it meant we actually talked about very little over the course of a meal. So I leisurely enjoyed much of my salad before nonchalantly inquiring, "You were saying? Something about what's important?"

"Yes, I was. About goals and what you want out of life." Dad picked a cherry tomato out of his salad and put it onto mine. It was part of a standard agreement between us: Tomatoes were mine. All cucumbers were his. "I believe you have another tri coming up, right?"

"Always is. I'm registered for the second week in June. Hudson, Illinois."

"Even though I've teased you about your ambition and teaching, Julia, you know I'm proud how you train and compete." He took the time to pause a moment and look me in the eye.

"Well, thanks, Dad. I guess I assumed that was true. But it's still nice to hear it."

"Your mother would've been proud too, for sure."

"You think?" Mom wasn't one to exercise, to put it mildly. I never saw her run anywhere. Watched her ride a bike for about an hour, and that was a tandem, with Dad. And swimming? Any depth above her waist caused panic. Heaven knows how she kept her fears from being transferred to me, but she did, and I applaud her for it. At the same time, except for when she was eating, I rarely saw her sitting down—and even then she'd be busy doing something like sewing on a button, reading her bible, writing a letter or paying bills. I guess my mom simply chose to exercise in her own way, on her own terms.

"Oh, absolutely. You know she wasn't much into sports—watching or competing. But she would've appreciated how you set goals. And for having the discipline and work ethic to follow through."

I loved it when he talked about Mom. It wasn't often, and like other conversations, he never, ever gushed. But any bits of information Dad passed along were pieces of gold, pure treasure. "Do you think she would've gone to some of my races?"

"Most definitely."

What was left unsaid was that Uncle Ollie attended more races than Dad did. I knew it was because Uncle Ollie had retired pretty young, was independently wealthy and suddenly single, since Aunt Susan died one month before his official retirement. (That was yet another source of some contention between God and me: Aunt Susan's dying right when she and Ollie had so much to live for.) Dad, on the other hand, would most likely never completely retire. He still worked part-time for the same company he'd been employed by since graduating from college: An employee-owned dairy that had managed to grow and adapt and continue to turn a good profit after all these years. Naturally, Uncle Ollie had more free time to travel to my triathlons, in state or out.

"Your mom. Well, she had major goals in her life too, and she—"

"Here you go." Jenny interrupted at a pivotal time again, putting our entrees onto the table; Dad and I hurriedly pushed our yet unfinished salads out of the way. That was the problem with small town restaurants around here, along with small town servers. Dad and I would've preferred more time to linger over our salads, but what are you going to do? "You're gonna love it. Everybody does." Jenny stood there, smiling at my dad, hands on hips. It did smell wonderful, but Dad refused to take the bait. Jenny finally caught on. "Well, enjoy!"

I knew Jenny's ill-timed disruption would mean I'd have a problem getting Dad back on topic. It felt like we were playing a game of chicken for a while; each of us was stubbornly remaining silent, finishing our salads before digging into our entrees, silently daring the other to attempt re-starting the conversation. Suddenly I realized who would be the real loser if one of us— namely, me—didn't push this along.

"Tell me more about Mom. What were some of her life's goals?" To my complete surprise and delight, Dad immediately jumped right back in.

"She'd intended to be a teacher."

"Seriously. But she never went to college."

"Yes, she did. For two years."

I put down my fork then. *How could I have not known this?* "She never—neither of you ever told me that."

Dad glanced up at me, calmly said, "So I'm telling you now."

"When did she go to school? And why did she drop out?"

Now Dad put down his fork. "You know we were thirty-one and thirty-five when we married. Your mom always wanted to get a college education so she could teach, but hadn't been able to afford it. So after we married, I encouraged her to go."

"Dad, that's wonderful. I'm so happy you did that for her. But why didn't she finish?"

He sighed and folded his hands on the table before him. Looked down for several moments before somberly replying, "She'd miscarried for the second time. And then was convinced the only way she'd have a healthy baby was if she quit school." Dad looked up at me, and the softening around his eyes nearly did me in. "You were more important to her than…than anything else, Julia. More than finishing school. More than teaching. Above everything else, she wanted *you*."

I reached across the table to lightly touch his arm. "I never knew about the miscarriages. That had to be so hard. For both of you."

He reached for his fork, began picking through the pasta to find more chunks of the perfectly spiced sausage. "More so for your mom. She'd always wanted a house full of children."

"Really? I can't picture her with more than me. How self-centered that is." Other thoughts raced through my mind: How I assumed I alone was the center of her world, even before she had me. The news she'd wanted more than…well, just me, but also wanted an education and to teach school? How incredibly self-focused I'd always been to assume, so much—in actuality, so little—about her.

"Julia, there's much more you don't know. And I've come to realize—"

"Dessert?" Dad and I turned to look up at Jenny with barely disguised irritation, hoping she'd get the hint. "I guess you're not quite ready yet, huh? I'll just grab up these salad plates for you and get out of your hair." She chirped happily the entire time, seemingly clueless.

This time, I wasn't about to waste precious time. "You've come to realize what, Dad?"

"Well, she needed to set her priorities. You know. Decide what was most important to her. But allow God to maybe change things around a bit how that would work out." He was hedging. And we both knew it.

"So, how did God change things around?"

"I thought that would be pretty clear. We had *you* in our lives."

I narrowed my eyes at him, but though Dad was one to send hints, he never took them himself. Or rarely did. Whatever, he clearly intended to ignore me this time. It was also clear our discussion about Mom and goals and me was over.

"Speaking of cars."

Dad had the uncanny ability to switch gears in a heartbeat, often leaving his companion a bit stunned. I scrunched up my entire face into my very best *"Say what?"* look. "We weren't speaking about cars, Dad."

"Were so. You said you were going to Hudson in June. When's the last time you had your oil changed?"

I shrugged my shoulders, frustrated at Dad's avoidance. "Honestly, I don't have the foggiest."

"Now see. That's exactly my point."

So I closed my eyes and shook my head, resigned. "Okay. So what *do* you want to talk about now?"

"I thought that was obvious: I want to talk about your car, Julia. If you're driving to Hudson next month, I imagine you're going to need an oil change beforehand. How 'bout we switch cars tonight and I'll get that done for you?"

I polished off the last bite of my pasta, wiping my mouth carefully, hoping there were no telltale signs of basil left behind in my teeth. "Thanks, Dad. That would be really helpful."

"Glad to do it."

"I brought Moppit along with me tonight, though. So my car's most likely not going to be as clean as yours." I gave him an apologetic look. "Um...I know for sure there's dog slime on the passenger window. Can you live with that?"

He smirked. "My car's *most likely* not as clean as yours?" he parodied.

I laughed. "Okay. Point taken. My car's *never* as clean as yours, especially considering the dirty coffee cups in the console. Next to the used tissues, gum and candy bar wrappers. And the stack of useless announcements the school sent around last week that I tossed into the back seat. Might be other stuff back there too, and it could be so covered in green mold it's not easily identified. To say nothing of the dog hair." I pointed a finger at him before I added, "You know you enjoy taking Moppit on a road trip as much as I do."

"That dog can do little wrong in my book." He leaned back in his chair to scan the restaurant. "Where's that server when you need her, anyway?" He picked up his glass and, smiling back at me as he drank the last sip, sighed contentedly.

Moppit was over-the-top delighted to see him; as he switched her from my car to his, she wiggled in his arms, pink tongue providing a dozen sloppy kisses under his chin. And then he gave me a quick hug. The kind of hug that generally feels like an afterthought, but you learn to appreciate the closeness that you're offered.

"I see you've got a full tank. Thanks, Dad."

"And I presume yours is just below a quarter?" To my shrugged shoulders and second apologetic look that night, he merely shook his head. "I'll give you a call when the maintenance's done."

"Maintenance? I thought it only needed an oil change?"

"Oh, I'll just have them check out a few things while it's in. Won't hurt."

I reached out to squeeze his arm. "Thank you, Dad. I really appreciate all you do to take care of me. Still."

"No big deal. Just good sense to take care of a car." He tapped the door lock. "Doors locked? Seat belt's buckled, I see."

"I'm good to go. Talk with you soon."

I honked and waved as I pulled out, watching him in the rearview mirror as he climbed into my considerably older Toyota Camry, now a rust-colored shade of medium blue due to the layer of dust all over it. I pulled the scrunchie from my ponytail and ran a hand through my freed "Rachael cut" mane (*Friends* being a favorite show of mine, of course). *Might as well make use of driving a Lexus while I've got it,* I thought to myself. *Attract a little attention, if I can.* Grinning at my reflection in the rearview mirror and mostly, my own conceit, I'd just pulled out onto the main highway when Guy broke into my thoughts.

-Jules, you there?

-Yup. Just finished an enjoyable and yet somewhat frustrating dinner with my dad.

-How so?

-He was hinting all around something important he wanted to say to me, Guy. But it's like he chickened out. Left me feeling...kind of *defrauded*, actually.

I was trying to put my jumbled thoughts into words when I glanced up into the rearview mirror and noticed one of those huge SUV's suddenly appear out of nowhere. It was gaining on me, coming fast.

-Wow. The guy behind me is in quite the hurry. He's gotta be going close to eighty!

-Give him a wide berth, Jules.

-I will, but I need to revise that estimate. Ninety, maybe?

The cautious plurality in me immediately took over: I intentionally slowed and eased over to the right berm, giving the black behemoth ample room to pass me. Making it clear I wanted him to do that rather than ride my tail.

-Jules? What's happening now?

-Just give me...what on earth?

The SUV intended to pass me all right, because he nearly flew across the double yellow line and came alongside. But then he suddenly jerked to the right, ramming into my back door and causing me to jump. My front wheels skidded left from the collision, and I had just instinctively pulled the Lexis back to the right when the SUV rammed me again, hitting much closer to my door this time. Panic-stricken, reacting reflexively, I jerked the steering wheel sharply to the right to get away from the threat and promptly plowed into the ditch, missing two huge trees by mere inches. At some point, I must've screamed, because Guy was now screaming back at me.

-Jules! Are you all right? What happened? *Talk to me, Jules!*

THE GRAVESTONES' SECRETS

10 of August, 1587

To My Descendants,
We Adventurers have learned more of this New World, and it is with much concern that I report of such to you. We have been diligent in our work in repairing the fort built and later abandoned by one Captain Lane, the first Governor of our fair Virginia. I have learned that Governor Lane, for what reasons we do not know—whether out of self-preservation or with intended aggressive engagement—attacked neighboring Savages, killing their king, a Chief Wingina. After much discouragement and despair, the Governor and his men abandoned their efforts in this New World, whereupon fifteen Brave Souls remained here to hold the fort.
 That leads me to my worrisome epistle to you, for it has been made known to us that these fifteen Souls came to a violent end, and by the hands of vicious murderers. Were these the very same afore-mentioned Savages, avenging the death of their king? We cannot know, but we proceed with great caution in our dealings with them.
 We have Chief Manteo with us, whom many had the great pleasure of meeting in London. As the king of a Tribe

farther south of our settlement, we can only hope and continue to trust he rules over a more peaceful People, those with which we have already had much exchange of information and goods. Even Chief Manteo is aggrieved with concern for those violent Savages, and we go about our work with much foreboding.

Even as I worry for our safety, my mind conversation with my beloved Catherine was of joyful provision to this man's Soul, and I am eternally grateful for God's provision in that regard.

Yours, forever,
Mauro

CHAPTER TWO

For a few moments, I just sat there—in shock, I suppose. I clutched the steering wheel with a death grip, breathing like I'd just finished a triathlon. Then, along with Guy's yelling in my head, I heard knocking, and another insistent male voice at my window.

"Miss, are you all right?"

Who to answer first? I asked myself. But years of hiding my ability to mind talk meant I shifted into instinctual reactions: I hit the button for the window. "I'm okay. Shaken up, but yeah. I'm fine." I thought of Moppit, and had a moment of panic again. But she'd only been knocked to the floor, and upon discovering someone who might provide attention, she immediately jumped into my lap and stuck her head out the window, begging to be petted.

He kindly obliged, rubbing Mops' ears, and gave me a once-over too, his eyes quickly skimming from my head downward. "I don't know what that idiot was doing, but that was the worst job of passing another car I've ever seen. What a moron. You seem okay, but should I call 911? I've got a cell phone."

"Um, yes. Please. That would be helpful. Obviously I need to report that driver—whatever he was trying to do indeed." I rummaged around in my purse for a tissue, stalling for time, knowing I had to answer Guy before he went berserk. He'd been yelling at me through the entire conversation with this kind stranger, and though I was good at talking to Guy and another person simultaneously, I wasn't skilled at multi-tasking in my present harried state of mind. I also didn't want the good Samaritan to think I had a concussion or anything. Just let him catch me responding to a disembodied voice and I'd be off in an ambulance for a brain scan in a heartbeat.

-*Guy, I'm okay.* Honestly. I'm fine. Some idiot side-swiped me, didn't even bother to stick around. Now I'm sitting in a ditch, talking with a kind man who stopped to help. I'll get back to you later, okay?

-You sure you're okay?

-I'm still shaking. It scared me, yeah, absolutely. But I'm fine. Later?

-Sure. But if you don't signal me soon.

-I know. I won't forget.

"You sure you're all right, miss? You seem a little...hazy."

I glanced up at him, catching the typical look of a man who's more intimidated by the contents of a woman's purse than a pit of poisonous snakes. I pulled out a tissue and smiled up at him, granting him my very best *I'm completely fine* look—right before I blew my nose, providing a good honk to fill the silence.

While we waited for the police to arrive, the kind man tested my door for me, helped me out (I was admittedly a bit wobbly), and though the back passenger and driver's door were damaged, at least they both *mostly* worked. Fortunately, we didn't wait long for the police officer to arrive, and after my rescuer and I had both given our accounts of what happened—we were both slack in our descriptions, able to recall only that it was a big, dark, fast SUV, one of those with the equally dark tinted windows—my good Samaritan and the policeman helped push me out of the ditch.

The officer pressed quite a bit when I explained the part about the SUV hitting my back door, and then ramming me a *second* time by crashing into my door. "Are you sure he hit you twice, miss?" he asked. "Because accidently hitting you once and then leaving the scene—that's a common thing we see all the time. But hitting you twice? That appears intentional. And a completely different animal." He looked me over like I was the prize pig at the fair, judging if I was worth the inflated price the 4-H kid was asking. "*Ninety*, you said?"

"Excuse me?"

"You said he appeared to be going ninety miles per hour."

"Oh, yeah. Could easily have been that fast."

"Then I'm thinkin' the fool was completely out of control. Drivers of some of those blasted SUV's....like steerin' the Queen Elizabeth..."

We agreed about the driver's skills, I took a deep breath and thanked him again, and then slowly pulled out onto the highway. Very slowly, feeling insecure suddenly like it was an unwanted companion breathing on the back of my neck.

The side of Dad's beautiful Lexus was now dimpled, to put it euphemistically. *Wouldn't you know it?* I thought to myself. *I have Dad's car, for what? A whole five minutes and this happens?* I sighed at the thought of telling Dad, explaining how the guy hadn't even stopped, yet intuitively knowing he'd only be relieved I hadn't been hurt. *One thing at a time. There's another man in your life who's waiting for an explanation.* I knew I'd put Guy off as long as I could.

-Hey. News flash. I have frayed nerves and a slightly mangled car. Correction: My dad has a slightly mangled car.

He was there instantly, obviously waiting for me, and probably a good bit frustrated too.

-Jules, finally. I've been so worried. What took so long? Did you go to the hospital? What did the police say? Did they catch the idiot driver?

-Guy, one question at a time, okay? I'm just a bit...frazzled. I honestly don't think I can remember more than one thing at a time right now.

-So did they catch him? Let's start there as I'd like to strangle the creep.

-No, and I imagine there's slim to no chance they ever will. The nice man who stopped to help didn't see any more than I did. A dark-colored SUV—that's it for our combined impressive ability to recollect details.

-Not even a guess at a license plate number?

-Nope. I was too busy trying to keep my car from hitting trees. Very big trees.

We were both silent a moment, hedging, I think. That's a tricky thing with mind talking—the need to mull over something when you're in the middle of a conversation. It takes some finessing. I ended the impasse by stating the obvious.

-At least I'm over and done with the doom of your premonition.

And then Guy was silent again. Not a good sign in any language, verbal or non.

-Guy? That jerk forcing me off the road was what you sensed coming, right?

-I'm sure of it.

Fudging is a universal form of communication too.

I'd just opened the door to my apartment when I heard the phone ringing.

-Guy, I need to go. We'll talk later, once I'm in my pj's, okay?

-You're not going out again tonight, are you?

-Absolutely not. I'm thinking Dad might want to come over to check out the damage to his car. But I'm staying put, and like I said—into my pj's ASAP.

I grabbed the handset, assuming it was my dad. "Hello? Dad?"

"Julia. No, darling girl. It's Uncle Ollie here. I'm so sorry to tell you this over the phone, but you'll want to come right away, sweet. Your father's been in an accident, I'm afraid."

I instantly felt like I'd been punched in the stomach. "Oh no. Where is he?"

"At Mercy Hospital, in the ER."

"I just walked in. Um," I glanced around the room, my mind going blank and then focusing, desperately trying to think clearly. "I need to feed Moppit and take her outside. But I'll be there as fast as I can, Uncle Ollie."

"Your dad's likely headed for surgery soon. Drive safely, Julia dear. But yes. Come as quickly as you can."

—

Once I was behind the wheel again I felt my eyes fill with tears. I struggled to get my emotions in check, knowing I'd be in the ditch again if I let myself get out of control. I prayed first, pleading with God that Dad would be okay, and then called out to Guy. Explaining what little I knew, blinking back the stubborn tears and wiping at my runny nose.

-You knew, didn't you, Guy?

-I'm sorry. It was so much like before, when your mom— you know, the sense that something equally hard for you was coming.

- Then will...do you think he'll be all right?

Once again, there was the pause before Guy answered. Like when you're talking to someone who's on a different continent, and there's that split second of silence in between your questions and responses. It's nothing, really, it's so insignificant. And yet, it's definitely noticeable.

-You know I have no idea, Jules, and that I'd love to tell you only what you want to hear.

-Oh Guy. I need you so much.

-I'm here, love. Always.

-But I mean *really* here. With me. Where I could touch you, clutch your hand, absorb your strength.

-Not yet. But one day.
-Promise?
-Promise.
-Will you be available later? If...if I need you?
-I'm a breath away, Jules, that's all.

I focused on picturing my endearing uncle—how much he resembled Dad in his build, height, and thick white hair. There was no denying they were brothers. The resemblance ended when it came to demeanor, however, for while my dad carried himself with a coiled, ready-to-spring urgency and a distinguished, business-like approach to nearly everything—from dealing with his secretary's typos to his daughter's need for a sympathetic ear concerning an irate school parent—Oliver approached most of life's challenges with an unhurried desire to understand and offer empathy to others. Amazingly, that translated into his physical features too: He had less sharp lines and angles on his face (Dad had the classically handsome deep lines that defined a masculine, square jaw; Oliver had a less angular jawline and only the barest hint of lines, even at his age), soft eyes that hinted at a constant twinkle, and lastly, a subtle incline of his head towards whomever he was speaking to or interested in. Which was just about everybody.

The best thing about Uncle Ollie, however, was his sense of humor and the accompanying huge grin, which made its appearance easily and often. Stretching almost from ear to ear, his smile was so wide that its presence instantly made Oliver resemble a mischievous boy. You couldn't help but smile back at him, it was that contagious. And for as long as I could remember, Uncle Ollie appeared to delight in making me laugh. Whether he cracked a corny joke; delivered a witty off-the-wall view of life; or whispered a snide remark (delivered dead pan) which was guaranteed to make me laugh out loud (especially when I definitely shouldn't), he knew I was always his best audience.

Tonight I intuitively knew I was going to depend on and need every facet of my uncle: his offers to help, his compassion, his understanding. And even that infectious sense of humor. Hopefully—once Dad was fine and we were reminiscing about this frightening day—we'd also chuckle over Uncle Ollie's light-hearted observations.

Lord, thank you for Uncle Ollie, I whispered in a quick but heart-felt prayer.

I handed Dad's blemished car over to the valet, not wanting to waste a moment's time searching for a parking spot. Eagerly reaching for the security of Uncle Ollie's embrace the moment I stepped into the ER waiting room, I looked up at him, attempting to read his face. His response was a manufactured relaxing of the muscles around his eyes and mouth, but it was far too contrived. Uncle Ollie was no actor; I gave him a squeeze on the arm for trying, but his failed attempt to calm my soul merely resulted in heightening my sense of panic.

We turned and rushed down the hallway, Oliver's hand at the small of my back, gently guiding. As he related the latest news on Dad, my senses were bombarded by the harsh glare of overhead fluorescent lighting; the urgency in the clipped voices of those all about us; and the antiseptic smell that clung to objects and everyone there—which would include me, even after I'd gone home, thinking I'd left the hospital and its effects behind.

"So what exactly are the doctors saying?"

"They've moved him to the ICU, and they're being stubbornly obtuse. Completely noncommittal. I get mumbling when I ask for more specifics."

I glanced at the people we skirted around. Tension hung in those small groupings like a blanketing rain, and I reflexively shrugged as though attempting to shake splattered raindrops off me. "What happened, Uncle Ollie? Do you know?"

"The doctors mentioned his having a heart attack. They're speculating that caused him to black out and drive off the road."

The coincidence was alarming, and I stopped in my tracks. I turned to look up at my uncle while simultaneously reaching out to grab onto his arm—partly to impress him with the urgency I felt, but mostly from a need to steady myself. "I was just in an accident too, Uncle Ollie. A hit and run. Some idiot forced me off the road into the ditch."

He reached out to me then, clutching both my arms in his strong hands. "Darling girl. You're all right?" He looked me over, briefly shifting his gaze from my head to toes. I nodded my head *yes*. "You called the police?" A nod *yes* again. "Get the license plate, I assume?"

I sighed. "No, unfortunately, I didn't. Nor did the one other guy who witnessed the whole thing. A nice man, but neither of us saw anything more than a dark SUV."

"It's certainly an uncanny coincidence that you both—but Julia, your father's heart attack caused his accident. Not some out-of-control bozo." He distractedly shook his head, protectively putting his hand under my elbow to guide me through the maze of hallways until we reached the Intensive Care Unit. Where we were met by locked doors and threatening signs. **RESTRICTED AREA. DO NOT ENTER. AUTHORIZED PERSONNEL AND GUESTS ONLY.**

Oliver pressed a button and calmly spoke into the intercom. "Oliver Johnson here. And I have my niece with me now. Julia. Liam Johnson's daughter."

An irritating buzz sounded (it was the companion to those signs, after all) and the doors magically opened. I immediately nearly ran right into Al Borland, Tim the Tool Man's companion on *Home Improvement*. No, obviously, not really, but he was a dead ringer for him, and especially with the world-weary Al-like gaze when Tim's presented him with yet another mess to fix.

The nurse fixed a disconcerted stare on me and asked, "Mr. Johnson's daughter, I assume?" and then began listing off succinct orders: "You have ten minutes. *Only* ten minutes. It will go fast, so make the most of it. At the same time, don't expect too much. He's heavily medicated. Do *not*—under any circumstances—over-excite him. Questions?"

I'd nodded, stupidly, like a bobble-head doll. But the nurse clearly wasn't expecting much of a response anyway as he merely motioned for me to follow him, guiding me towards a glass door. And then suddenly, I was looking down at my father. *Was it really my dad? Could this possibly be the same man I'd had dinner with less than two hours ago?*

His head was swathed in bandages, as was his right arm. Tubes ran everywhere—hooked to and connecting him to all sorts of beeping-blinking-humming-producing monitors—and he had an oxygen mask strapped over his face. My strong, vibrant and independent dad looked shriveled, reduced, and so very frail lying there, completely dependent upon hospital personnel and machines and medicines. His coloring was alarming too: He was so pasty that his skin blended right in with the white hospital sheets he lay on.

"Mr. Johnson? Your daughter's here, Mr. Johnson."

I flinched at the sound of the nurse's voice. Hadn't been aware he was still beside me, since I'd been absorbed by tunnel vision: All I could take in was Dad.

His eyes flickered open. It took him a few moments to focus and find me, and then—though I couldn't be certain because of the mask—I was pretty certain he attempted a smile.

Dad feebly raised his bandaged arm, signaling to the nurse— who promptly shook his head *no*. But this part of my dad, at least, was unchanged, for Dad gestured with more vehemence towards the oxygen mask, and the nurse relented to his request. Nurse Al muttered under his breath as he removed the mask.

"You have five minutes without this, Mr. Johnson, and that's all. And I'm instructing your daughter to put it back on *immediately* should you have any problems breathing during that time." He positioned his face mere inches from Dad's. "Agreed?" The nurse himself nodded, though the only visible response from his patient was one raised eyebrow. "Agreed."

The nurse threw me a determined stare (eyes now narrowed to slits), closed the door behind him, and disappeared.

"Apparently I'm not making him happy."

Dad's voice was raspy and frail, but I was so relieved to hear him I felt weak in the knees. I grasped one of his hands between my own—partly because I needed to touch him, but mostly to hide how badly mine were shaking—careful not to touch the areas already badly bruised from the attached IV. Or was that from the accident?

"Not surprising," I replied, smiling, attempting to match his humor. Anything to keep the mood light. "He doesn't strike me as Mr. Happy anyway."

"Julia. Mutilated your car. Awful of me."

I shook my head violently, an effort to convince him it wasn't worth a second of our valuable time together. But Dad clearly didn't intend to dwell on that, as he moved onto another subject immediately. He labored to swallow, and I think I swallowed right along with him in my subconscious attempts to help. I could feel his grip on my hands tighten.

"Julia, there's something. Things I need to tell you."

I smiled and waited, expecting the speech about how much he and Mom loved me. Preparing to tell him he didn't need to say those things as we'd have years to be together yet.

"What I was trying to tell you. Earlier tonight." He stopped, catching his breath. I motioned towards the oxygen mask, but he frowned, shook his head, and waved his other hand, dismissing the idea like an irritating fly had landed there. "About your mother's miscarriages. After she quit college. The classes she so enjoyed. There were more." A quick breath taken in between each statement.

Confused about what he was referring to, I asked, "She took more classes?"

"No. Suffered miscarriages. Too many. The doctor said…no more. No more attempts."

My thoughts raced. Trying to grasp his point, I ventured, "So, you're saying I must've been quite the surprise. A miracle, right?"

He avoided my eyes, looking away towards the multitude of colorful blinking screens.

"Dad?"

"Couldn't. Doctor said we dare not. Thought I would lose her. To despair."

I started feeling sick to my stomach, and a dull headache was beginning to form behind my eyes. Still, my conscious mind simply wouldn't go there and my thoughts rambled erratically, searching for an alternative reality to latch onto. *This is entirely too much like some bargain table novel,* I rationalized. *Who hears a death-bed confession besides a one-dimensional character, anyway? This simply isn't happening.*

"We started putting out feelers. To friends. A few agencies."

Now *my* breathing was labored. I could feel myself breaking out in a cold sweat. *Was* I *going to need the oxygen mask?* I wondered.

Dad coughed, and then glanced with a look of alarm towards the glass door. If the nurse was within earshot, we both knew our conversation would come to an abrupt end—an interruption I might welcome, actually. But he must've stepped away temporarily, so Dad muffled yet another cough the best he could. Taking a tenuous breath, he continued, "Finally got a response. Friend of a friend. That sort of thing, you know?"

I shook my head. "No, I don't know. Just spell it out, will you, Dad?" I knew my voice didn't sound particularly soft or kind. *Which is what you* should *use in an ICU,* I lectured myself. *Soft, kind responses from a loving daughter. Unless?* In the awkwardness of that tortuous moment, I couldn't seem to make myself apply the bandage of graced nuance.

"Oh, Julia. Should've told you. Earlier tonight. Better: Should've told you years ago. Couldn't. Your mother. She made me promise—"

Now I couldn't stop myself. "Don't blame this on Mom. After…everything. Don't. Just *don't*." I put one hand to my face, covering my eyes as if that pathetic maneuver could shield me somehow. Keep me from hearing what he was about to say—and what the cynical voice in my head was taunting: *Didn't you really always know? You're a reject, Julia. Why would you be surprised to hear that your birth parents didn't want you either? That's a total of four parents—four! And* not *one of them accepted and wanted the strange creature that you are.*

Just then Dad made a horrible sound, a deep-throated gasp, and I opened my eyes to discover his staring back into mine with the fragility of pure terror. Panicking, I reached out for him like he was falling. "Dad?"

Gulping like a drowning man struggling to keep his head above the water, Dad clenched his jaw, opened and closed his mouth twice as he fought to form coherent words and sentences. In a voice thick with sheer determination, his eyes boring into mine, he finally spit out, "Worried…Tennessee. You must never…*go*, Julia."

A single tear formed and ran down the grooved line in his cheek. He concentrated harder, gripping my hand so tightly I flinched, and he pulled his features into a near scowl of effort. The word "*Melungeon*" erupted from him, followed by "Only wanted. Protect you, Julia! And your letter. The letter's there.

In…in the safe. But don't—" he barely got out, before a violent cough cut him off. Dad surely sensed the nurse's approach, but he wasn't about to stop now, and I was paralyzed—I felt literally frozen in place, unable to move a muscle—by his cryptic message. I noticed the veins protruding on his forehead and he strained to lift his head a few inches off the pillow. "Julia. Please. Just…"

That time, the nurse was there instantly, cutting off whatever Dad had intended to say. "Mr. Johnson? Mr. Johnson, stop talking and stay with me now." Totally focused on his patient, he pushed me back out of the way.

Still, Dad was full of fight; he dodged and put up his hands to fend off the nurse's efforts to put on the oxygen mask.

"Julia, your mom and I. Love you. So much. Remember. *It was you we wanted.*"

The once-steady *blip! blip!* of the monitor went silent. I watched my dad fall limply against the bed and I blinked twice at the screen before my brain registered the flat line there. And then alarms sounded and the place erupted in an explosion of activity.

Personnel roughly pushed me aside and out of the immediate area before I could even think to protest. I vaguely registered that Uncle Ollie put an arm around me before four more people pushing a crash cart flew past us in the hallway. A couple doctors raced by us too, lab coats flying behind them. We could hear carts and paraphernalia scraped across the floor, people shuffling around, and raised voices in the sense of an orderly panic, if there is such a thing.

"Uncle Ollie?"

He pulled me even more tightly against him.

"Dad told me I was adopted." My voice sounded distant to me, as though it was coming from the opposite end of a long tunnel. "Now. He tells me *now*. It can't possibly…it can't be true." My tone sounded unnaturally flat, devoid of any emotion.

But I knew that inside me a current of emotions flowed like a river of turbulent rapids.

After a few minutes—how long was it? Truly, I have no sense of how much time passed during the pandemonium—all frantic activity came to an abrupt, painful stop. And now as one after another left Dad's ICU area, I received apologetic looks or completely averted faces as personnel shifted their eyes to the floor and silently moved on.

A young doctor paused before me. "I'm so sorry, Miss? Johnson is it?"

I nodded at him numbly, stupidly, mouth hanging open.

His eyes darted about the hallway as he attempted to look anywhere but into my eyes, apparently. Constantly shifting his weight from one foot to the other, he offered, "Nothing we could do. His heart was so badly damaged from the initial attack. Beyond repair, I'm afraid." Finally, he gathered the courage to meet my gaze, if only momentarily. "Do you have any questions for me?"

"Yes, as a matter of fact, I do." I can see his eyes widen in alarm. He's obviously picked up the odd tenor of my voice, and is expecting equally abnormal behavior. Fleetingly, the thought crosses my mind, *Wouldn't want to disappoint him.* "Could you just tell me who I am, please? Because I have no idea. Who I am."

His expression mirrors the perplexity in my voice. "Excuse me?"

"My niece is a bit, um, unraveled, shall we say?" dear Uncle Ollie offers.

And then nurse Al steps in, rescuing all of us, the dumbfounded doctor included. "Would you like to be with your father for a while?" Softened considerably from his earlier demeanor, the nurse is clearly making an effort, and fortunately there was a rational part of me that noted and appreciated that. "You and your uncle?" He looked at Oliver with raised eyebrows, telegraphing his request for Oliver's assistance with me—the fragile female who appeared to be tipping precariously over the edge of sanity.

Oliver still had me wedged tightly against his chest, and I could feel his breath on my hair as his chin rested atop my head. Wisely, he kept silent; my uncle knew me well. Recognizing that I'd pull myself together momentarily, stubbornly—and that I wasn't about to concede to the mantra of the weak little woman. "Yes. Yes, I would like that. Will you go with me, Uncle Ollie?"

"You know I will, darling girl. Anywhere."

In spite of my willful resolve, I probably would've fallen to the floor if not for my uncle's hold on me, for the difference in Dad now was stark. Put simply, *he* was gone. I'd never before taken in the gap between a living, breathing body with a soul—and one without that life force within. You would think I'd have noticed earlier at the many funerals I've attended, and especially at my mom's. But I was still young then, really, and oblivious to much of what happened, protectively shielded by family members. This time, however, I immediately realized what lay before me was an empty shell now. What made him my dad…Annie's husband…Oliver's brother…and Liam before his God…all of the spirit of *him* was simply no longer there. That distinct vacancy left a gaping hole in the universe. My universe.

I sat on the bed, easing my head onto Dad's chest. And then I let myself dissolve into hysterical sobbing, a nose dripping, hiccupping, heaving and messy wail, for when I cry hard—as I was right now—I'm not a dainty crier. I was barely aware of Uncle Ollie, fumbling through pockets until he found and offered a clean handkerchief (linen, freshly ironed, of course) for the downpour.

But even as I produced the devoted daughter's show of grief, I clearly heard the shameful accusation, *Why are you crying, really? For the dad that you'll miss? Or is this mostly about his painful revelation? Oh, you're heartbroken, all right. Because you learned you were a throw-away!*

But then I retaliated, pitching questions at God like darts. *Why, God? How could you let this happen? I lose my mom and then you take my dad too—like this? I earnestly pray for the courage to really let go, trusting you, and this is what you do?* I knew the judgments were unfair. Immature. Out of line from my understanding of God, his goodness and love. But I just couldn't stop the demands for answers that erupted from my pain—demands for him to explain himself. To justify this travesty.

I heard the whispers of responses in long-ago memorized passages of Scripture. Flashes of books studied, sermons heard, small group discussions. But I squashed the memories; instead, I was overwhelmed by the evidence of life's cruelty right before me. Past assurances and pleading with God—at least, at this point—were no match for the reality of Dad's empty shell, and the devastating news he'd left behind.

How could you, Dad? I threw at him in my mind. *How could you wait until, literally, the very last moments of your life to tell me I was adopted?*

The word *adopted* tasted bitter in my mouth, and I wanted to spit it out like grinds from the bottom of a cup of coffee.

I need you now to lead me through this…this total mess, Dad! I continued, railing in my mind still. *How can I—how can I possibly understand any of this without you here to help me? How totally unfair. Making me do this on my own.*

Uncle Ollie, evidently sensing my inner struggle, reached out to stroke my arm. Thankfully, he remained silent too, granting me whatever time I needed to walk through my last "conversation" with my dad.

Were you really so insecure about me, Dad? Was that why? 'Cause it doesn't matter at all to me whether or not you were my biological father. I loved you, completely. Always will. Can you somehow hear me still? You asked me to remember, so I'm asking that too. Remember I wanted you. I want you too, Dad. No matter what. Always.

My emotions were spent then. Guess I'd purged what I needed to, and was worn out. Like when I finish a three-hour run in hot, humid weather, and it's all I can do to make my wobbly legs get me to my car, they're so weak. While I continued to rest my head on Dad's chest—summoning the will for the energy to get up and out of this horrible glassed-in room—Guy came to me again.

-Sweet Jules. Has it...happened?

-It's my dad. He's...*gone*. I feel so alone, Guy. Abandoned.

-Oh, Jules. I'm so sorry. But you're never alone; your head knows that, even if your feelings don't just now. We've been down this road together before, Jules, remember? God's there with you, filling you inside. I'm with you too. And your uncle, bless him. You may feel alone, but it's not true, Jules. Not at all.

-Oh, but there's more I haven't told you yet. Feels like there's nothing beneath my feet. So what now? Where do I find what's real?

-Only God defines what's real, Jules. Security in anything else is mere illusion. Please, just let your uncle help you get through today. Tomorrow—well, tomorrow we'll handle whatever else you need to. Let's navigate one day at a time.

-Trite clichés? From you, Guy? Now? When I'm desperate for something real to hold onto?

-Jules, there's just nothing else but to gather up your faith and jump out into the void where trust lives. God's there. He'll catch you.

Startled by Guy's words, I react by jerking against Dad's chest.

"Julia, darling. Are you all right?" Uncle Ollie leaned down towards me, putting a hand protectively on my back.

"Yes. I'm fine."

And then Guy sends one last attempt at comfort.

-Ah, Jules. I'm a blundering fool. Can I simply say I love you?

Uncle Ollie gently squeezed my shoulder. "The nurse is back, darling girl," he said, barely above a whisper. "Are you finished here? Ready to go now?"

I looked up at Uncle Ollie, blankly. The transition from talking to Dad, switching to Guy and now back to my uncle was jarring. But my dad's body is far too real beneath me—and already beginning to go cold to the touch—to deny the present. "Almost," I mumbled, giving Dad one last kiss on the cheek, allowing my gaze to roam over his familiar features—his handsome face, his thick hair, even the stubborn cowlick that he battled daily. I'd inherited one just like it in nearly the exact same spot on my forehead.

Inherited? Not so much, Julia! my own voice mocked. I caught myself just before laughing out loud, with what would've sounded like a hysterical shriek. I cleared my throat and stood upright, pulling away physically and emotionally. Any tenderness I'd been feeling—nostalgia about the past, our past—melted away in the stark reality of Dad's last words like a splattered ice cream cone on a dirty sidewalk. I looked up at Uncle Ollie and nodded, allowing him to lead me from the room that had irrevocably changed my life forever.

There were forms to fill out, decisions to make before Uncle Ollie and I could leave the hospital. Fortunately, my mother's death had brought about one significant decision on my dad's part: He'd made plans. I knew his will was in order and he'd clearly expressed his wishes about his death and what was to follow, including organ donation before his cremation, which was also noted on his driver's license. For this much advance preparation, I was grateful. The paperwork forced me to function, keeping us busy until fairly late that night. By then, Uncle Ollie and I decided we needed to begin the dreaded duty of calling relatives and friends.

Adrenaline and several cups of strong coffee kept me going while we fulfilled responsibilities, but I discovered my energy was totally depleted once we placed the last call. I still needed to let Melissa know, but that call could wait. She was out on her special date, and there was no reason she had to know about my dad tonight.

I stretched my back, blinked a few times and rubbed tired eyes, noting how the cheap fluorescent lighting was pulsating like a flickering candle. When I couldn't contain a particularly loud yawn, Uncle Ollie volunteered to drive me home in Dad's car—he said a friend would help him get his car later—and I readily accepted. I knew how tired I was emotionally and physically, and besides, I was going to be a bit shaky behind the wheel for a while. The memory of that car running me off the road was still too vivid in my mind's eye.

Once we were in the car, I decided to hit Oliver point blank. Maybe the abruptness would shock him into a forthright and truthful answer. "Did you know?" *Et tu, brute?* I thought, but kept to myself. *Or did I?* Whatever words I actually voiced out loud seemed to be instantly absorbed by the interior of the car, for there was a profound silence for several moments.

"Julia, I do think it better to discuss this after you've had a good night's sleep."

So much for the *startle him into an honest answer* strategy. "It's a simple yes or no answer, Uncle Ollie. I think I've earned that much tonight, don't you?"

He sighed, refusing to look at me. You'd think that particular stretch of road was the toughest test of a driver's skill, he was that intent on keeping his eyes peeled ahead. "Your parents—"

"Yes or no. Please."

The slightest shake of his head, a signal of resignation. "Yes, I did know. But not until after the adoption was completed."

The sting of his words cut deep. "What does that mean? Would you have tried to stop it?" The telling pause before he spoke again was enough to alert me to the realization that I'd accidentally hit onto something.

"Julia, it's not—"

"What kind of adoption *was* it, anyway? What on earth was Dad blathering on about? I guess I assumed he was somewhat delusional at the time. Told myself to chalk it up to the drugs and his weakened state, I suppose, once you combine the trauma of a heart attack and an accident to boot. But now I'm wondering." Noting how uncomfortable my uncle had become—I could see the muscle flexing along his jaw line, and he was gripping the steering wheel with a tenaciousness much like Moppit's ferocious hold on his tug-of-war toy—my gut instincts switched from puzzled to horrified. "Oh geez. Don't tell me. It wasn't *illegal*, was it? Something done—under the table, shall we say?"

"No, no. Oh no. Nothing like that. Every part was done to the letter of the law and authorized by each party's lawyers."

"Then what is it?"

He shook his head. Released the steering wheel long enough to rub the back of his neck with one hand. "Just that you should've been told you were adopted years ago. I didn't approve of keeping it a secret, but your parents both swore me to it, Julia. In this, you must not blame me, agreed?" Now he did look over at me, seeking my eyes. My understanding. "They threatened I couldn't be with you if I wouldn't promise my silence!"

I nodded at him. "Not your fault, agreed. But go on."

"Just that."

Jaw muscle still flexing? *Check.* Hands back clenching at ten and two o'clock? *Check.* Eyes still keen to look only ahead, avoiding meeting mine? *Check.* Three strikes. "Uncle Ollie, I need the truth. Are you going to help me or not? 'Cause I'm going to find out, one way or another." He gave me a questioning glance, and in that one quick look I saw love, concern. And deep worry. I intentionally toned it down a bit, softening my voice. "Whatever the truth means, I have a right to hear it. *Please*, Uncle Ollie."

"Well, there were things about your adoption."

Silence again. Would I need to beg for every word to get the story out of him? "What *things?*"

He sighed. "I got only bits 'n pieces of the process, Julia. Your folks never told me the entire story, so all I know is what I've surmised and patched together. But there were…issues."

"Things. Issues. Uncle Ollie, I'm not going to stop badgering you until you spit out every little bit you know."

"Like a bulldog that way, just like your dad."

Sarcastically, "Whoever that is."

"No. We've got to agree on ground rules, Julia, and especially for this one: You are still Liam and Annie's daughter. You may biologically have the DNA of another couple, but Julia, they sacrificed for you. Liam and Annie poured themselves into you." He glanced my way with a look so reminiscent of my dad I sucked in my breath a moment. "We don't really need to re-hash nature versus nurture, do we? If you have any questions about taking after your father, then you should look at a replay of the colloquy with your dad as you lay with your head on his chest."

I thought bringing up that scenario was a cheap shot, but I had the good manners to keep that to myself—and to be duly embarrassed. "Oh. Well"—I waved a hand in dismissal, nonchalantly—"I was in shock."

"Whatever."

I glared at him. "Are you intentionally trying to get me off track, Uncle Ollie?" We pulled into my apartment building, but before he could climb out, I grabbed his arm. "Neither of us is moving until you give me an answer."

"Julia, darling. We're both so tired. I really did want to wait on this." He sighed and fiddled with the keys, finally conceding. "There were…irregularities."

"*What does that mean?*"

"Liam and Annie had to sign an agreement saying they wouldn't reveal where you were from or any specifics of your adoption until their deaths. And even at that, they were supposed to destroy most of the adoption papers once it was finalized." He shrugged his shoulders.

"Isn't that pretty standard? To keep details secret?"

"Not in this kind of an adoption."

"What do you mean, *this kind*?"

"They didn't use an agency."

"Not at all?"

He shook his head. "Just lawyers. But I always wondered a bit about both of them. It just all felt…what's the word I want?"

"Illegal. That's the word you're searching for."

"No, no, not that, Julia. I told you already. But it was as though there were other parties directing things, behind the scenes. Payments being made. Not from either set of parents—neither of them had that kind of money, and especially not your biological parents. I got the impression they were poor, Appalachian poor. It was all so strange, Julia."

"Uncle Ollie, I think Dad was trying to warn me about something. Something in Tennessee, maybe?" I realized my hand was still clutching his arm, only now my hand was white like I had him in a death grip. Embarrassed, I let go. "So tell me this: Was my adoption strange as in peculiar? Or strange as in *alarming* in some way?"

"I wouldn't use the word *alarming* exactly. But it seemed like something bigger was behind it all. And that something had a lot of money and power."

I swallowed. "How…strange. As in how much money and power?"

"Honestly?" He shrugged his shoulders. "I have no way of knowing. But my intuition always felt like it was pretty much unlimited."

I stared at him while he continued to play with the keys. I must've looked sensationally intelligent because I know my jaw hung open, dumbly.

Suddenly, like a soldier snapping to attention, Ollie reached out and gripped me tightly by the shoulders. Wide eyed, he admitted, "I've said too much. Oh darling girl, what a numbskull I am. Listen to me." Leaning in, he moved in to put his face mere inches from mine. I could see his jaw muscle twitching and his pupils constrict. "That was only a nosy man's musings—from years ago. I had no basis for those brash assumptions, and have even less basis now. *Seriously.*"

We heard a car pull in beside us, a friendly honk from the driver. Uncle Ollie and I both needed to shake ourselves out of this dream—or was it the beginning of a nightmare?—before we started undoing seatbelts, acknowledging my uncle's neighbor, Uncle Ollie's ride home.

We exchanged pleasantries, and the kindly gentleman offered his condolences to both of us.

Uncle Ollie put his arm around me, pulling me against his sturdy form. "Shall we plan on going to your dad's house tomorrow morning? Say, nine o'clock? Is that too early?"

"No, it's fine." I yawned, suddenly realizing how desperately I needed a good night's sleep. I was feeling woozy on my feet again.

"Oh, and your car. I'll see to it too."

"I'd completely forgotten about it. Where is it, do you know? Still in a ditch somewhere?"

"I got word it had been towed."

I leaned against the car door, feeling overwhelmed with the seemingly endless list of to-do's. The weight of it all felt like I needed to move a mountain, using only my bare hands. I motioned to the ugly dents in the Lexis, saying, "Need to get this car fixed too. But exactly where was my car towed, do you know?"

"I got the impression the police have it. But Julia, leave it to me. Please, put it out of your mind for now, okay? Listen. Why don't you stay with me tonight? I'd love to have you."

I shook my head. "You're dear to offer, but I know I'll sleep better in my own bed. And I need—well, I need some time by myself." I glanced up at him, seeking his understanding.

He nodded and guided me to the door, unlocking it and staying long enough to get Moppit and me settled. By the time he'd kissed me goodbye, I was desperate to get out of wrinkled clothes, into pajamas, and slip under the covers.

Where I stared at the ceiling and waited for sleep to take me away from a reality that I didn't want to deal with. My eyes had just started to fill with tears when I realized how much I needed Guy there with me.

-Guy?

It was clear he'd been waiting for me; he was there almost before I'd finished saying his name.

-How are you? What is it you need me to say to you, love?

-Oh Guy. I've lost...not just my dad, but *me*. My parents—at least, I thought they were my parents. But they aren't. My real parents.

-Jules?

-I was adopted, Guy.

He was quiet for a few moments. Taking it in, slowly, like I had. And then I realized that no, actually, he's purposefully hiding his thoughts from me. That's another thing we can sense, somehow. We both know we have that ability; thoughts one chooses to remain private, do so. But when we're in the midst of mind talking, we both can sense when one is intentionally withdrawing from the other. Concealing thoughts and feelings he or she doesn't want the other to know about.

 -What are you thinking, Guy? Let me in.

 -It wasn't anything. Just something I've wondered about. But that's not what you need from me now, my pulling into my own thoughts. I want to help you, Jules. Tell me how I can do that.

 -All I assumed I was? Based on a lie. I have no idea who I am. It feels like I'm in an earthquake and I can't find anywhere to stand that's safe and secure.

 -It's no lie, first and foremost, that you're a child of God. That hasn't changed, Jules.

 -No. But how could I not sense this—something this huge? I was misled by my parents. No, let's put it like it came down, shall we? I was intentionally *lied* to. Repeatedly. And all these years of prayer and feelings of intimacy with God. I've tried to be so real, totally vulnerable and transparent with him, Guy. Completely honest. That's what I've always sought in my relationship with God. And yet I had no hint I was adopted? What a farce. Feels like I was lied to by God too!

 -Jules, he's the only one who *didn't* lie to you. He can't, because that's against his very nature—any falsehood is. Don't blame him for what your parents did—and I have to believe they had their reasons. God alone supplies true security. As much as I want to provide that for you, I know he's the center we need to go to, the only place of total acceptance for each of us and all we are.

 -I just can't. Not yet. I think I'm too hurt, so I'm cowering.

 -He'll be there. When you're ready, Jules. He'll always be there to catch you.

 -Once again Guy's choice of words is startling, and I flinch at the uncanny connection to my nightmare. But even with that reminder, my eyes are suddenly so heavy, and I feel my body sinking into a foggy haze.

-I think maybe I could sleep now, Guy.
-Sleep now, love. If you need me when you wake—
-I know. You'll be here.

—

The fog is still with me as I begin to come awake, but it's notably heavy, sitting on my chest like a burden. *Dad.* Fully awake now, the truth of his death hits me, and I hug my pillow, allowing my mind to skim back through sweet memories. When I was ten and he took me on our first father-daughter date, both of us dressed up in church clothes for grown-up conversation at a local restaurant. He'd made me feel so special. And then there was the time he devoted an entire day to teaching me to ice skate. Such incredible patience he demonstrated, considering my ridiculously wobbly ankles. I'll never forget my first really good road bike, one Dad had saved for, secretly, for months. He'd endured bologna sandwiches instead of eating lunch out, day after day, week after week. *To this day, he still can't stand bologna,* I thought to myself, smiling.

And then I caught my error, again. It was so natural to think of him in the present tense; waves of realization for *what is* were sure to surprise me again, this day and beyond—the "natural" life transition of learning to live without someone much loved.

I closed my eyes again and offered up a quick prayer, a pathetic band aid for too many hurts that were festering just underneath. *God, I'm so completely lost. My head knows it's not really your fault, but still. Help me just get through this day, please? I need you so—need to feel you with me when I'm feeling so abandoned. Help me, God. Please, just remind me that you're here.*

I glanced over at the clock and quickly swung my feet onto the floor—nearly crushing Moppit in the process. "Oh, sorry,

Mops. You hungry?" She began her usual morning routine of spinning in circles while I pulled out clean clothes from my dresser and closet. "I'm coming. Can I visit the bathroom first? You're next, I promise."

By the time I arrived at Dad's condo, my hands were shaking and my stomach felt like I'd eaten a half-dozen corndogs and then ridden the tilt-a-whirl. I leaned back against the head rest, closed my eyes and sent up another urgent prayer. *God, help me do this. I need to; I know that. But...* Uncle Ollie interrupted by knocking softly on my window. I jumped and banged my knee against the steering column.

Seeing my grimace, he shook his head, saying, "Julia, darling. How inconsiderate of me. Are you all right?"

I opened the door and climbed out, ignoring the minor ache in my knee. "The only thing that's really hurting right now is my heart."

"This won't be easy. Going into your dad's home for the first time."

"I'm anxious about opening the safe, also. Feels rather ominous after yesterday's reveal." He put his arm around me, once again gently guiding me towards the inevitable while providing his unwavering support. "I can't tell you how much I appreciate you doing this with me."

"I wouldn't be anywhere else." He stopped, turning towards me and putting his hands on my shoulders. "I should tell you I spoke with the police earlier this morning. When I went to see about your car."

"What? What is it?"

"There's some evidence he was side swiped."

"But Dad had a heart attack. That's what caused the accident, right?"

Uncle Ollie sighed. "The driver's side of the car was dented. Appears they didn't pay much attention to it at first because the car had flipped all the way around; it was actually facing the wrong direction when the emergency crew arrived. They're still investigating, but they think someone clipped your dad *after* he had the heart attack, when he was spinning out of control. The police are wondering if it's someone with a record or was driving under the influence, maybe. Could even be whoever it was simply panicked and left the scene. But I wanted to alert you because of the coincidence, before we talk with the investigators later today. Give you a head's up, at least."

I turned to the damaged doors of Dad's Lexus and ran my hand along the ugly gashes. Rubbing a telltale streak of notable black paint on the Lexus' white, I said, "Quite the coincidence, huh? Both of us getting hit at nearly the exact same time." I glanced up at Uncle Ollie. "What did the police make of that? Anything?"

"No, nothing at all. I guess the rate of irresponsible drivers leaving the scene of accidents these days is rather alarming. Their only concern is the timing, actually: Whether the hit and run could have *caused* your father's heart attack, or if it happened *afterwards*. That call will be made by the police together with the forensic pathologist. If they rule the former scenario, however, it would turn their investigation into one of vehicular homicide."

I crossed my arms over my chest. "So, what color of paint did they find on my car?" He avoided my eyes. "Uncle Ollie?"

"There are more black cars on the road than probably any other color, Julia. Let's not make any inferences or conclusions based on that alone."

"Somehow I just knew you were gonna say *black*."

"Coincidence, Julia. Pure coincidence." I followed Uncle Ollie up the steps to the front door. "The police asked that we drop by the station later today since they have a few questions for you. I'm thinking in a week or so they'll sort all this out. Enough to provide rational answers for all our concerns."

I shook my head at him, whispering under my breath, "And pigs fly."

Dad had long ago given each of us spare keys for emergencies, but while I fumbled around in the vast reaches of my purse for mine (*how do things simply disappear in there?*), Oliver quickly produced his and unlocked the door.

I stepped in. And instantly stopped, causing Uncle Ollie to nearly run into me.

It felt like when you've held a sleeping baby, and your arms are so empty when you've just given him back to his mother. Or how a great room feels on a frigid winter day when the fire in the grate has completely gone out. It's not the kind of empty like a new house that's waiting to be filled with furniture and people and life itself. Instead, it's an emptiness that reminds and painfully highlights *what was once there*. What should be there. What's missing.

Uncle Ollie turned to look at me, his eyes soft and filling with tears. I felt my own eyes puddle—mostly in reaction to him, I think. Because even the emptiness of Dad's home was a reminder that right now, I was feeling more angry than sad. And then flustered and embarrassed by my cold reaction, I broke away from Uncle Ollie's gaze and started peeling off my jacket. It was one of those times, however, that my hands get stuck and I'm pulling and tugging and getting nowhere so that Uncle Ollie has to reach out to help me. When the clingy coat finally slipped from my arms, I coughed into my hand, a fake cough. The kind of exaggerated throat clearing people use to get through awkward situations, filling noteworthy voids. Uncle Ollie coughed too.

Ever patient and non-judgmental, however, dear Uncle Ollie gave me a raised-eyebrow look. "Ready?"

I nodded at him, a sigh escaping.

Years ago, it had seemed prudent to my dad to install a safe behind an oil landscape in his bedroom. Dad had to threaten me with grounding for a month to keep me from taking every one of my visiting friends into that room, proudly pointing out the genuine oil painting, and how the frame swung out on hidden hinges to reveal the locked door. "You totally defeat the reason for having a hidden safe if you show it off to everyone, Julia," he'd lectured, frustrated with my inability to recognize the requirement of secrecy. "Do not, under any circumstances, tell anyone. End of discussion."

What was I to do? I had to tell at least Melissa, and made her pinky swear she'd never tell another soul. As far as I knew, she hadn't. Melissa has her faults, but she can keep a secret.

All of this came rushing back to me in painful stabs as Uncle Ollie reached for the edge of the painting—a mountain scene with a rustic cabin; not bad considering Dad had purchased it solely for this purpose—and began turning the knob. It made the familiar clicks and the door to the safe swung open. I hadn't realized it, but I'd been holding my breath. Continued to do so until Uncle Ollie pulled out what I'd already known was in there: A white envelope with emergency money; Dad's will, life insurance policies and investment portfolios; and lastly, a velvet pouch with the few remaining pieces of Mom's jewelry Dad was saving for my wedding.

What came out next, however, were things I'd never seen before, causing me to sharply inhale: A large envelope labeled *Adoption*, printed with a red marker. And finally, the real kicker: a gun.

Even Uncle Ollie was surprised at that find; I'd heard him suck in his breath too. Once his initial shock was over, however, he cradled it in his hand like the expert he was. A trained marksman in the military, Oliver had been on official missions he still wasn't supposed to talk about. We both stared at the black handgun he cradled in his palm.

"You didn't know about that either, did you?"

He shook his head.

"And you're surprised." Not a question. A statement of fact. This time, Uncle Ollie solemnly nodded. "Why would he—"

"No idea, Julia."

"Could it somehow be related to my adoption? And what you said about—?"

"No sense speculating, Julia. Wasted time and more so, wasted emotional output."

I was annoyed, and as usual, not likely to keep my irritation to myself. "Uncle Ollie, I'm noticing a trend here. You keep—"

"Am not." He glanced up at me, eyes twinkling. We both laughed—my goodness, it felt good to release some tension—and I took a really deep breath for the first time since we'd walked into the house. "Julia, darling, Liam never mentioned this gun to me, either. Surprising, since I would've expected him to seek my opinion about what type to buy."

"What is it?"

"Smith and Weston semi-automatic nine millimeter."

"Translation, please?"

"Very efficient. Productive."

I looked up at him, mouth gaping open yet again before I realized and mentally told myself to close it. "You're scaring me."

"Sorry. Just giving the facts about the gun." Reaching into the very back of the safe, he pulled out a brochure that had been underneath. "Here's the proof of purchase; clearly Liam bought it new. But it's been used, Julia; most definitely been fired. Repeatedly." He leafed through the brochure and held up a card labeled Green Gun Club. "And this explains where."

"Dad was visiting a gun club? To practice shooting"—I grimaced and reached out gingerly to touch it—"this gun?"

"Apparently. Why, we may never understand." He placed it back in the safe, but pulled out yet another surprise—though it shouldn't have been. "Here's some ammunition, only a few shells left." He turned the box over in his hands before depositing it back in the safe and then checking all the corners for any other unexpected contents. Finding nothing more, he closed the door, and locked it. "Let's take the packets into the kitchen, shall we?"

I agreed and followed Uncle Ollie like a meek child. Until we walked into Dad's kitchen, and then felt like I'd been sucker-punched. There were clean dishes stacked by the sink. A grocery list—in Dad's familiar handwriting, of course—neatly jotted onto a sticky note was stuck to the refrigerator. Next to it was an article, cut out from the local paper, about the Packers winning the Super Bowl; it was just like Dad to leave that there, for months. *Need to celebrate this for a full year*, I could hear him announcing, with pride.

There was a basket of apples on the counter and even a vase of lilacs next to the window. Many of the individual, tiny flowers had fallen onto the counter, but their intoxicating smell still dominated the room, filling my nostrils. Flooding my soul. I instantly knew, from this moment on into the unknown future, that cloying scent would act like a vortex, forever pulling me right back to this time. To this kitchen and its inherent pain.

I reached out to clutch the counter a moment, I was that unsteady. I was afraid I'd begin sobbing again but won that battle: consciously blinking my eyes several times cleared the tears and then I set to work. Almost mechanically, I put away the dishes and wiped up the errant blossoms while Uncle Ollie laid out the various documents and packets from the safe. Realizing my mouth had gone desert dry, I retrieved two glasses, filled both with water, and placed one in front of Oliver. The other I put at my seat, my "assigned" place at the same wooden table for the past nearly twenty years.

I'd just turned to look for a snack of some sort when Oliver asked, "You going to join me, Julia? Or do you plan to clean out the refrigerator next?"

His question jolted me, but not in the manner I'm sure he intended. "I hadn't even thought of that. The frig. All the perishable stuff. I'll have to—"

"Julia, I know; I'm interrupting yet again, and my supposedly witty remark was anything but. We really do need to look over these things, and since my brother has proven to be one surprise after another, we must explore what's in this adoption packet."

I slid into my chair. "What? Other surprise? You've got me so flustered I can't speak in full sentences anymore."

"You just did."

"One and counting. Uncle Ollie, what *other* surprises?"

He sat back in his chair, staring at his folded hands resting on top of the adoption packet. "A strange discussion we had about two weeks ago. I wasn't going to tell you about it."

"But now you are."

"It wasn't long or drawn out. Instead, it was a quick exchange, rather like him. He asked me to promise him something." Oliver looked up at me. "Maybe he had a premonition? Made me promise I'd look out for you should something happen to him."

I searched my uncle's face. For more—actually, to gauge if he was leaving anything out. "That all?"

"Yes. The urgency in his voice surprised me, though. And that he felt compelled to ask me in the first place. I told him I thought that was understood, but he wouldn't settle for that answer. Pressed me to verbally promise him. I was rather insulted at the time, to tell you the truth."

I reached out to squeeze his arm. "I'm sure Dad was just feeling insecure. I bet that was more about *him* than you, Uncle Ollie."

He nodded. "The more I thought about it, the more I understood that. The timing with his latest doctor's appointment and all."

I sat up straighter and leaned closer towards him. "Doctor's appointment? He had one in the last couple of weeks?"

Uncle Ollie raised his eyebrows. "It was two weeks ago, Monday, I think. I just assumed you knew about it."

"You would assume wrong. Do you suppose the doctor said something to him that he didn't tell either of us?"

"Possible. But let's check his will and investments. Any recent updates could tell us all we need to know about that speculation." Oliver pulled out Dad's stock portfolio and his bank book; he handed those to me while he perused the will. I'd gone over all of them with my dad about eight months ago, and as Uncle Oliver and I compared notes, we saw nothing updated. No recent changes. Everything appeared to be just as it was the last time I'd viewed them with Dad. We set them aside, knowing we'd need to call our family's attorney as soon as possible. The best thing about Mr. Nilsson was how meticulous he was—to the point that he could be obsessive compulsive about everything being in perfect order. It was also the worst thing about Mr. Nilsson.

"Ready to tackle the adoption papers?"

"What if I said *no*?"

"Seriously?"

I shook my head. "We need to. I just don't think being ready for this is an apt description of my current state of mind."

"Agreed." He undid the metal fastener and lifted out several sheets.

As Uncle Ollie spread them out on the table before us, my first impression was how official most looked. Others, however, definitely did not. My gaze was first pulled to my official birth certificate, a piece of paper I recalled seeing before. "I remember

Mom taking this to school a couple times to register." We scanned the lines, looking for anything out of the ordinary.

"Here—this is significant," Oliver pointed out. "I did a bit of research on adoptive birth certificates. See, it lists your birth as August twenty-seven. But note the date this was filed: not until September twenty-nine. That means your parents"—he looked up at me, making a point to stare directly into my eyes—"and by that I mean *Liam* and *Annie*, didn't get you until you were over a month old." Moving his finger down the certificate, he said, "And look at this. Place of birth? It says Wisconsin. Interesting. I wonder if that's typical for this type of certificate? To put where the adoptive parents are living?"

I shrugged. "Guess we're going to need to do some research. Contact the attorneys they used. What's this?" I'd picked up the stapled sheath of papers with the heading of Garrett and Associates; underneath was a sealed envelope labeled *Confidential*. I looked over at my uncle, who raised his eyebrows. Suddenly feeling like I was about to break out in a cold sweat again, I handed it to him. "You open it."

In the same careful manner he opened all his Christmas presents (which drove me crazy as a child), Uncle Ollie slid his finger under the tape that had obviously been recently applied to an older, yellowing envelope. He tipped it over; out fell a second birth certificate, a paper with haphazard and sloppily written notes, a dog-eared (evidently well-read) paperback, and a battered piece of gold-colored jewelry in the shape of the letter *B*. My hand instinctively went to the bent *B*. Curious, I examined it, rubbing my thumb along the bottom, finding prickly stubs from three broken knobs. Evidently something had once been attached there. "Why on earth would Dad put this sad looking thing with my adoption papers? Suppose it's from my biological parents? Something they wanted me to have?"

Uncle Ollie eyed it and said, "Maybe this is why." He pushed the second birth certificate towards me, his finger just under the name *Blevins*. "Look at this. I do believe this must be your original birth certificate."

I took in the names, my gaze jumping from one to the next. *Mother*: Lucille Gibbons Blevins. *Father*: Jimmy John Blevins. My birth date was the same, August twenty-seven. Place of birth was listed as Rural Route something-or-other—I couldn't read the number because it was smudged—Collinsville, Tennessee. I looked up into Oliver's equally puzzled face. "Does this mean I was born in their *home*? Is that typical for Tennessee?"

"No idea, Julia. But that would be my guess too."

"And look at the certifier, Uncle Ollie." I slid my finger across the line and read out loud, "Midwife. *Midwife?* I was born in a home in Tennessee—a one-room shack, you think?—and a midwife attended." I pushed my chair back from the table, grabbed my glass of water and drank every bit of it. When I looked over at my uncle, he was still staring at the birth certificate, rubbing his chin. "What now?"

"It just doesn't make sense, that's all. Why this is in here." He ran a hand through his hair. "Remember I told you I had the impression the lawyers weren't doing everything quite… not quite…"

"*Legal.* That's the optimal word, Uncle Ollie, though you seem loathe to admit it. Truth is, Dad and Mom hired shady lawyers who did an illegal adoption."

Now it was my uncle's turn to grab his glass of water and down most of it. "No, Julia, that's not it. It's more like they skirted the edges of legalities. So everything would stand if tested in court. But just barely."

I picked up a page that began with the salutation *To him what reads this*, but after that clear beginning, the rest was nearly illegible because at some point it had gotten wet. The ink was smeared so that only portions of words were clear—*CRO*, all in caps, and another unrecognizable word followed by *Springs Creek*, which seemed like a odd name for a creek. One word in particular stood out, however, since it was repeated several times: *Melungeon*. "That's it!" I tapped my finger on it, excitedly. "That's the word Dad said, Uncle Ollie. *Melungeon*."

"Never heard of it—you? No? We're gonna be spending some time in the library."

"So you have no idea at all what it means?"

"I'd guess it has something to do with that area in Tennessee. Another town, maybe? Near where Collinsville is. But other than that? No, nothing."

"This isn't Dad's handwriting; I know that for sure."

"Never in his entire life did your father do anything even remotely that disorganized and messy. I'd swear on a bible in court to that."

"I'm positive Mom didn't write it either." Glancing up at Uncle Ollie, I saw him firmly shaking his head *no* before memory pushed at my consciousness. "Uncle Ollie, I'd forgotten. Dad also told me my letter would be there, in the safe." I held up the page with new appreciation. "This has to be it. The important letter he was trying to tell me about."

"I suspect so."

I swallowed, concentrating, trying to recall every word he'd said. Even more so, the urgency accompanying specific words. "He got so agitated, as if there was something he really wanted me to do." I chewed on my lip and then spit out, "He warned me about going to Tennessee."

"At this point of time, I can't imagine any rational reason why he'd want you to go there."

Brows drawn together in concentration, I searched the letter for other clues. "This part mentions something about ancestors.

What on earth?" I pointed to a particularly blurred line. "Does that say something about six fingers or am I seeing things here?"

Uncle Ollie squinted at it. Picked it up off the table and held it closer to his eyes. "Did your dad have a magnifying glass? That might help a good deal."

I located one in a desk drawer, but it wasn't until I reached for it that I realized I still clutched the gold *B* in my hand. "Here you go, Uncle Ollie." While he poured over what was still proving to be mostly undecipherable, I examined the *B* again. It was so bent and dented up that I doubted it could be worth much, if anything. Certainly, it was old, but the broken stubs were a puzzle. *What used to be there? Was this the sum total of all my biological family could leave to me?* I asked myself, rubbing the sad looking piece of jewelry between my fingers.

Uncle Ollie's voice pulled me back to the present. "Julia, this is not going to prove to be reliable information, I'm afraid." He held the magnifying glass so we could both better make out the handwriting. "Right after the word *Melungeon* here? There is indeed something about *six fingers* and more nonsense they describe as *mind talking*. Look, right here—I think it says, *There is those what can talk with 'something or other'*—I can't make out those words—*only by thinking on it*. Pitiful grammar, needless to say. But goodness." The scorn in his voice was thick as Luigi's lobster bisque soup. He waved one hand in the air, dismissively. "Six fingers. Mind talking. What's next? Levitating people? Who in his right mind would believe any of this?" His frustration apparent, Uncle Ollie tossed the letter back onto the table.

I couldn't help myself. I hiccupped.

THE GRAVESTONES' SECRETS

1 of September, 1587

My Descendants,
 Much has happened since my last correspondence to you, so there is much I have need to tell you, of great importance. On 18 of August, Ananias Dare and Eleanor, daughter of our own Governor John White, were delivered of a Daughter. We all were much overjoyed to hear the cry of this infant, seeing her birth as a blessed miracle and Sign to us from Our God. There was much celebration, such as we are able to do here, and the childe has been christened Virginia, as she is the first infant borne in the City of Raleigh, in Virginia, in this New World.
 We know Winter will soon be upon us, and even as we face grave fears for our survival in unknown and untested conditions, ten days after our Virginia's birthe, alas! Captain Fernandes set sail, abandoning us. Governor White deemed it necessary to join him, presumably to gather more supplies for our colony, and to bring those back to us forthwith. It was due to my Captain's persuasion that I joined this Adventure, and he has been a confidante and faithful friend. But I fear rising aggression between England—where my Catherine

lives—and my adopted Land of Spain has hastened Captain Fernandes's ill-timed departure, even as bitterly cold winds and dark clouds threaten. Governor White was loathe to leave, and only his Eleanor's reassurances bade him leave her and the childe, and his commitment to return from Britain with supplies such as we have desperate need of to survive here.

Some of our party have deemed it necessary to venture and explore westward of our expedition, as hostile natives continue to avail us much concern. Only our Almighty God knows what lies beyond into the vast Wilderness, but should we need to venture forth, we will do so protected by His Mighty Hand. Whilst we face such conditions as winter heaps upon us, however, we must needs stay together here, and support all as best we can whilst we look for and hope for Spring.

Some days, it is only mind talking with my precious Catherine, she who is the delight of my life, that sustains me.

Ever,
Your Mauro

CHAPTER THREE

To his great credit, Uncle Ollie graciously ignored my embarrassing faux pas and continued to pour out his love and support. I was thinking through the implications of my hiccup and what that might have inadvertently revealed (certainly Uncle Ollie remembers my childhood years with an invisible friend), when I caught up with his train of thought—somewhere in the middle of his conclusions about six fingers.

"…do think we can ignore every bit of that, don't you?"

"I'm sorry, Uncle Ollie. My mind wandered a little bit. What is it you think we can ignore?"

I did merit a look this time, one of pure incredulity. "Certainly you don't think there's any validity in searching for ancestors with six fingers and abilities in telepathy?" He made a scoffing sound. "I mean, honestly, Julia. We might as well widen our investigation to include zombies and Elvis Presley."

"My neighbor, Mrs. Fitzsimmons? She's convinced Elvis lives in South America."

"Is this the same neighbor who believes aliens once beamed her up into their space ship?"

"The one and only."

"I must remember her if I ever need a character witness." He gave me an exaggerated wink and I couldn't help smiling. We'd scattered all the documents and papers across the table, covering up the forgotten paperback. As we both began sorting the piles into some sort of organized order of importance, Uncle Ollie picked up the tattered book. "*The Melungeons: Mysterious People with a Mystifying History,*" he read out loud, and then flipped it over. An olive-complexioned, dark-haired and brown-eyed woman stared back at us—all the features I'd once assumed were part of the renegade ancestral branch of the Johnson gene pool.

Correction: *She* appeared to stare at *me*. And I gaped right back at her, transfixed, mouth open, holding my breath yet again.

Uncle Ollie glanced over at me, the hint of a frown pulling down the corners of his mouth. "Julia, darling, you look like a deer in headlights. Am I pushing you too far, too fast?"

I cleared my throat, searching for words, any words—since apparently any coherent thoughts were suddenly beyond me.

"Julia?"

I took the book from him and skimmed through the pages, taking in photo after photo. More women with deep brown eyes and matching dark hair. Olive complexions. High, prominent cheekbones. Whether these were my true ancestors or not was still unknown. But certainly, I resembled these people. "This is…I don't know. It's like my brain can't take it all in and sort through it. But it feels like I'm looking at a photo album. *Of my family.*"

Uncle Ollie must've been taken back too, for he also stared at the photos, silently.

"Your dad wouldn't have put this book in here without a reason. He wanted you to have it, and he's giving you a message. Exactly what that is, however—" He shrugged his shoulders and took the book back, flipping to the back cover again, reading out loud: "The Melungeons were a mixed race of people from the Cumberland area of central Appalachia, possibly Spaniards who had inter-bred with local Indians. But that's merely speculation, since proof for the Melungeons' origins remains elusive—and therefore, mystifying."

"Great. Just what we needed: another mystery."

Uncle Ollie reached out to pull me into another hug, and the solidarity of him was an instant comfort.

"Too many riddles and questions to solve in one day—and especially this day. I vote we wrap things up here, but before we go, maybe give the house a quick check? Make sure no windows are open, no plumbing leaks, nothing amiss?"

After sensitively asking if I could handle the upstairs by myself, he went down to the basement while I gave a quick perusal to the guest room, my old bedroom and bath, and finally, Dad's bedroom. I was determined to look at everything with a detached checklist perspective. *No emotional attachment. In 'n out in seconds*, I told myself.

So much for that goal since the first thing I noticed was Dad's clothes on a chair—freshly laundered shirt, pants with a sharp crease, argyle socks. All neatly laid out for him to put on the next day—which would never come for him. I held Dad's shirt up to my face to breathe in his scent when Guy broke into my thoughts.

-Jules? You all right?

-Define what you mean by *all right*.

-Yeah, okay. Ummm, are you able to do what you need to?

-Uncle Ollie and I meet with the funeral home director soon. I imagine I'll have some stories to tell you about that later. As for updates here, Uncle Ollie and I found nothing short of a mother lode in Dad's safe.

-What's that mean?

-I'll fill you in later. Too much to go into now.

-Anything else I can do?

-Show up? As in, come help me?

I can actually hear him let out his breath. And I can even sense him shaking his head.
  -You know I can't, as much as I want to.
  -I know. I just wish, that's all.
  -Oh, love. One day we'll discover our hiraeth.
  -What did you just say?
  -*Hiraeth.* It's a Welsh term I came across. Nothing remotely like it in English.
  -And it means—?
  -It's a longing for a place that's truly *home* in every sense of the word. For us as Christians, the ultimate hiraeth is heaven, of course. But even now we can long for a place because it's become so much a part of who and what we are that being separated from it causes pain.
  -Oh. I like that, Guy.
  -So you get what I'm describing?
  -I do. But—

A soft knock on the door interrupted us. Oliver leaned in the doorway. "Julia, darling. Just checking to make sure you're all right?"

"I'm fine, Uncle Ollie. I'll be right down after I put away these clothes."

Oliver nodded and then I could hear his footsteps padding down the hallway.
  -I have to go now, Guy.
  -I'll be here. Anytime you need me.

It'd been hard to keep secret from him, but I did *not* want Guy to know about the police investigation and the coincidence of Dad's and my accidents. At least, not yet, since he'd only press me for more information. Until I had more myself, there was no sense in dumping any uncertainties on him.

We'd scheduled an eleven o'clock appointment with a Mr. Truman at the Sundhamn Home of Eternal Rest. Dad had done all his pre-arrangements for cremation a year ago, dictating that the small memorial service he'd requested be held at our church; as a result, there really wasn't a lot to decide. I was busy fighting back tears when Mr. Truman began a hard sell for everything he possibly could, including: The Deluxe Loved One's Porcelain Vase, transportation by limo of said Deluxe Vase from funeral home to the church, and finally, he outlined the absolute "pinnacle of disposal of your loved one's ashes"—a private plane to scatter them over selected sites in the United States. I'd listened with something akin to fascination for the macabre, but clearly Uncle Ollie was a bit peeved.

"Is the Pirate's Lagoon at Disneyworld an option?" Oliver asked, managing to make his disapproval very clear.

Mr. Truman narrowed his eyes and frowned, Uncle Ollie raised his eyebrows expectantly, and I swallowed a chuckle. At least the threat of tears vanished, but the awkward pause of silence that immediately followed gave me an excuse to mumble something about needing to visit the ladies room. I'd let the guys haggle over this one.

Upon returning, I had no idea what all had transpired between the two. I did note that Mr. Truman's ego seemed rather subdued, probably because Uncle Ollie had declined each of the upgrades in my stead, settling on a more moderate urn. He'd also passed on the private plane delivery, since Dad's will directed exactly where he wanted his ashes scattered: Castle Rock Lake, our family's favorite vacation spot. Though I knew it would be difficult, putting Dad's ashes there would also feel exactly right.

Once we were safely out the door, Oliver *harrumphed*, quickly grabbing my full attention.

"What?"

"Haven't had that much pressure since a door-to-door salesman tried to sell me a laxative."

I couldn't stop the laugh that immediately erupted. "Pressure, eh? Uncle Ollie. There's no way I'm believing—"

"Absolutely true story! When I opened the door and frowned at him, the man contended my direct line was definitely plugged. Insisted his *guaranteed* formula would clean out that clogged line…"

His voice rambled on, but all I heard were garbled sounds. I was completely distracted by the huge lump in my throat—the harbinger of another major cry? Or simply evidence again of my deep love for not only my dad, but also for this man, his brother? I raised up on my tiptoes and kissed him on the cheek as he held open the car door for me. I interrupted him by asking, "Have I told you recently how much I love you? And how thankful I am for all the ways you've helped me in the past? And—?" I tried to get more out, to thank him for coming with me today, for deftly handling a pushy salesman and then making me laugh about it. But the lump made talking difficult, and Uncle Ollie, ever the sensitive gentleman, gave me a look that said he knew what I wanted to say. And so I didn't need to. Guy and I could carry on full conversations in a most unique way. But my uncle and I had always shared a special communication of our very own too.

We dropped off Uncle Ollie's car at his home—so he could take my car to the repair shop later—and grabbed lunch at the drive-thru before going to the police station. Once we'd covered the necessary introductions, the police officer assigned to our case, a Sergeant Whitman, got right down to business.

"I see here on the accident report that you didn't get the license plate number, right? Not even a guess for the first couple of letters?" The frumpy-looking officer peered over his reading glasses at me with haystack-like eyebrows and blood-shot eyes. He cracked his gum out loud, just like in the old cop movies.

"No, I was rather distracted at the time, trying to keep from hitting a tree." He continued to stare at me, clearly communicating that wasn't a sufficient answer. "I was busy concentrating on trying to keep from being killed, not read a license plate, okay?"

Sergeant Whitman cracked his gum again. Made another notation on the form. For all I knew he was writing *Hysterical dame fails to notice the obvious.*

"The reason my uncle and I are here is to pick up my car which you towed—"

"Now see. I'm confused. You say it's *your* car?"

"Yes, my dad was driving mine, while I took his. He was going to get the oil changed for me, actually. But back to what I was saying—"

"Now, miss. I'm still confused. I thought you said your dad's car was side-swiped."

"Yes, it is. Was. Side-swiped, that is." I took a deep breath. "*Both* cars are dented. My uncle and I are interested to find out if you think there's any connection between his accident and mine. Just seems pretty coincidental, you know? Because it was a black car that forced me off the road."

"Sez here, you said it was *dark*."

"There's very noticeable black paint on both doors of my Dad's car." To the sergeant's confused look, I added, "The car *I* was driving. Because my dad was driving mine." *Who's on first?* jumped into my thoughts, but I shook my head and squelched that in a heartbeat. "Didn't the responding officer write that down?" I peered at the papers scattered across his desk, trying to read upside down.

"Nope. Not on here. We'll hafta have someone take a look." Officer Whitman leaned back in his chair—which emitted a loud, protesting squeak—crossed his arms over an ample stomach and scrunched up one eye. "Been reading some of them sensationalist detective novels? What's his name? John King or something?"

I elected to let that pass. "I take it you don't think it was the same driver who ran my dad *and* me off the road?"

"Know of anybody who'd want to harm either of you?"

"No, not that I know of. But—"

"Either of you up to anything suspicious? Illegal? Like selling drugs?" He leaned forward again and held his pencil over the form like he was ready to jot down a confession.

I sat up straighter. "Of course not." I'd used my best indignant voice and Oliver *ha-rumph!*ed his agreement.

"We've got Doc Brown doing the path report. Yes, there are some concerns we might have us a vehicular homicide if the accident caused your dad's heart attack. But only by some fool runnin' your dad off the road 'cause he was DUI, most likely. Drunk versus intent of bodily harm—on both of you—those are two different things altogether, miss. Absolutely no reason to suspect that."

When he relaxed back into his chair for a second time, repeating the arms crossed and scrunched face routine, I realized we were done here. I held out my hand, thanking him for his time. Uncle Ollie followed suit, and after we'd collected the keys to my car, we exited as graciously and quickly as possible.

Before we went our separate ways—Uncle Ollie to take my car to the repair shop and I would go home to take care of Moppit and make some decisions—Uncle Ollie put an arm around my shoulders, giving me another of his reassuring hugs. "You okay to drive? I could take us both back to your apartment. Pick up your car here later."

"Uncle Ollie, you've been a dear to put up with me all day long. But I'm fine, truly I am. And I think you've earned a break, don't you?" He was shaking his head when I added, "And anyway, I've got so much to do that I need to make a list; otherwise I'll forget something important. And please don't let me forget to clean out Dad's refrigerator, okay?"

"Just read an article on remembering. It advised putting things in the positive. Instead of saying, 'Don't let me forget whatever,' you should say, 'Help me *remember* whatever.'"

"As in, help me remember to clean out Dad's refrigerator?"

"Exactly. Tell you what. I'll make a list too and we'll compare notes. Make sure we've covered everything that way. And I'll let you know how long your car will be in the shop. Once it's done, we'll get your dad's Lexus in."

"Dad's Lexus."

"Oh, Julia. Slipped out—I'm so sorry."

"Uncle Ollie, there's nothing to apologize for." I looked up at him and felt the tears gathering in my eyes again. "How can grief always be right there and yet sneak up on you at the same time? The ache for Dad"—I stopped a moment, needing to take a breath—"that ache is always there, gnawing at me. But still the sucker punch hits. The strange part about that? Generally, it's something inconsequential. Maybe that's why it catches me off guard."

Uncle Ollie pulled a handkerchief from his pocket and swiped at his nose. "How ironic. That very thing happened to me when we walked into the funeral home today. Your dad and I shared a moment when your Aunt Susan died. We didn't normally talk about things like relationships, how your dad felt about your mom or our relationship, mine with your aunt. Too uncomfortable—touchy-feely kind of thing for brothers, I s'pose?" He shifted awkwardly and sniffed loudly, then gave his nose a good honking blow. "But that day, well, that day we did. I'll never forget it."

I put my hand on his arm. "Tell me about it?"

"I'm not one to remember conversations word for word. But I recall most of that one. He said with your mom by his side, he was taller. Stronger. More courageous and godly. More everything he wanted to be, should be. He looked me right in the eye and said, 'You know the expression about being a better half? Annie wasn't just half, and she was more than better. She filled me, completed me. She was the best.' And then he added, 'I know you and Susan had that too.'" He blew his nose again, put the handkerchief back in his pocket and noticeably stood a little taller. "Couldn't have said anything more meaningful. And memorable."

We were both silent for a few moments. I don't know what Uncle Ollie was feeling or thinking. But as the tears flowed freely down my face, I savored every bit of that story.

"Will you need a ride home from the repair shop?"

"Nah. Ron's an old friend. He'll run me home."

"How can I ever thank you? For how much help you've been, already?"

"No thanks needed, darling girl."

I wanted to simply let my mind wander as I drove home, so I didn't allow myself to think about all I needed to do—though my obsessive need to make lists pulled at my conscience.

Instead, I indulged myself, allowing my imagination to create a small town in Tennessee. Complete with a family named Blevins and plausible, *logical* explanations why they'd given up their baby daughter for a secretive adoption. In the midst of so much murky information, however, I kept coming back to this core issue: Dad warned me not to go to Tennessee, and especially, it seemed, not to dig into anything related to my birth. And he appeared most adamant about not looking into the Melungeon mystery, for whatever reason. Whether there was an actual basis for his anxiety wasn't known yet, though I certainly couldn't entertain one viable reason why. Dad, Mom and I were small town, regular, run-of-the-mill nobodies. Not a whiff of anything about Liam or Julia Johnson would remotely interest John Grisham or James Patterson, despite Officer Whitman's implications. Nor could I imagine Lucille and Jimmy John Blevins being the grist for crime fodder. The only probable cause of a murder in my family might be that all of us would bore people to death. The defense would be justifiable homicide.

At some point, a bold idea flitted across my mind: a trip to Tennessee. I'd need to wait until Dad's memorial service was over (*Don't forget to call Pastor Stewart*, and then corrected myself per Uncle Ollie's advice: *Remember to call Pastor Stewart*), but was this something I'd really consider? My curiosity about all the riddles Dad left behind was drawing me like a magnet. And to Collinsville, Tennessee, specifically. And then I nearly start to hyperventilate when the magnitude of this idea begins to sink in. *What am I thinking? Me—the woman who can't make a decision if her life depended upon it—me, making this huge of a decision?*

And then the thought hits me: *Does my life depend upon this? If this "whatever" that Dad warned me about is truly dangerous, wouldn't I rather know what "it" is? Isn't it better to face the enemy that you're fully aware of, as opposed to an unknown entity?*

The pro's and con's come fast and furious now, a barrage banging around in my head like steel balls in a pinball game. But I soon realized it all funnels down into one huge question. *Is this the leap I need to make, God?* I wonder. *Is this what you want me to do?*

But any hint of a "yes" from God wasn't enough to erase the memory of the emotion I'd heard in Dad's voice. Worry. Fear. Even terror for me? I was hearing that and taking it to heart. "Be sensible, Julia," I whispered into the silence of the car. "There's nothing worth taking the risk of going to Collinsville, Tennessee. All those secrets? They're going to stay buried. Which is exactly where they belong."

—

-Guy?

-Jules. I was getting worried about you. So tell me: What's this mother lode you found at your dad's house?

-My adoption papers. And a ton of cryptic leads.

-Amazing. Start with the adoption info. What'd it say?

-I was born in Tennessee, Guy. In a town called Collinsville. I think I was actually born in a house—can you believe that? Attended to not by a doctor, but a midwife.

His split-second of silence was noteworthy, but I had no idea what that meant. Most likely just shocked by the incredible details of my birth—like I was.

-Interesting. But not unusual for that part of the country, I would think.

-Really? It'd be pretty much unheard of in Wisconsin.

-I suppose.

Was that a touch of defensiveness on his part? Maybe I have detected an accent and he does *live somewhere in the South?*

-What else?

-The dates line up. For my actual birthday, that is, though there's a noticeable gap. I wasn't adopted until I was about a month old. But here's the really interesting part, Guy: There was this scribbled letter full of clues, with peculiar leads. And the word *Melungeon* was there, several times. Ever heard of it?

-Okay, back up a second. What letter?

-It's obviously the letter Dad mentioned just before he... before he passed. He was insistent about it, saying, "your letter that's in there"—meaning in the safe. It's like somebody wrote the entire thing in the dark, Guy. Writing and grammar are atrocious. At some point it got saturated somehow, 'cause the ink's all smeared. It's nearly impossible to read except for a few phrases. And like I said, right in the middle of all that illegible mish-mash is the word *Melungeon*. Bet that's a new one for you.

-Actually, no.

-Seriously. Where'd you come across it?

-Some place. I don't know. School probably.

-Well, Uncle Ollie and I had never heard of it, but Dad left a book in the safe too. All about Melungeons. Fascinating information. But here's what's really interesting. One part of the letter you can make out mentions that Melungeons have the ability to mind talk—can you believe that? If that's for real, Guy, either one or *both* of us could be descendants of Melungeons! Oh, and talk about awkward. Things were a bit strange with my uncle for a moment there. I mean, I'm sure he remembers when I had all those tests done for hearing voices. My imaginary friend and all that—the way Mom and Dad interpreted our relationship. But he gave no indication that he connected my imaginary friend with the Melungeon mind talking. You think?

-Oh, I'd doubt that too, Jules. Didn't you stop talking about our communication when you were still a child? But it is interesting, I'll grant you that. We could also just be two people who communicate in a unique way, you know.

-Yes, but isn't this way more fun? To think of it as something from our genetic make-up?

-Sure. Whatever. What else did you find out?

-I look like them. The pictures of Melungeons in the book, I mean. I really do. It was disconcerting and yet...I can't tell you how—what was I feeling?—how *settling* to find possible ancestors that I actually resemble. In the midst of so much chaos in my life, it felt good to make some sort of connection, vague as it is.

-I get that, Jules. Wonderful for you, and especially right now.

-There was another weird fact about Melungeons too, though.

-Like what?

-Apparently another genetic trait is six fingers on one hand.

-You mean, six fingers on each hand?

-No idea. But that...that's certainly bizarre. And there was something else in the safe, Guy. I'm holding it right now.

-You sound intrigued.

-Yeah, I guess so. Wondering why a sad looking piece of broken jewelry would end up with my adoption papers.

-What is it?

-Nothing recognizable like a ring or bracelet or necklace. It's just a mangled letter *B*, but I'm guessing it was once a pendant. *I run my fingers along the B.* Yeah, maybe I can detect the slightest bump at the top, so I imagine it was a pendant. But what on earth does it signify?

-And why a *B*?

-My birth parents' last name was Blevins, so it's most likely related to that.

-Blevins?

-Yeah. Whatever, the *B* is awfully dinged up. Which brings me to my car. And Dad's car.

-I can hear the hedging in your voice already. What happened?

-No hedging; I'll just put it right out there. Both my dad and I were side-swiped by a black car. Within an hour of each other. What're the odds of that happening?

-I couldn't begin to—

-There's black paint on both cars, Guy. A hit and run both times.

He's silent for a few seconds, and I can't tell if he's skeptical. Or trying to keep me at arm's length from his worry.

-You and your dad anger the mob sometime recently?

-Very funny. I take it you're no more worried than the detective was?

-I think it's most likely just a major coincidence. Still, humor me a bit here, will you? Honestly, is there any reason we should take this seriously?

I hesitated, and that communicated way more than I'd intended.
-Okay, Jules. Spit it out.

-Well, it was one of the things Dad said. Again, just before. *I take a breath to keep my emotions in check, swallowing back the lump in my throat.* Actually, it was more how he acted than specifically what he said. He was insistent this letter and what it talked about—this Melungeon thing—was important in a way that made him suddenly intense. Really anxious for me, for some reason. I kind of think...well, telling me about all this evidently brought on his second heart attack, Guy.

I could feel my heart pumping. All this was still way too raw.

-Are you saying he indicated something was *dangerous*? Dangerous for *you*, Jules?

-He didn't *exactly* say that. But Guy—

-Jules, listen to me a minute. If this was *that* alarming to him, that it brought on a heart attack? You have to take precautions. Just don't go out alone at night for a while, okay?

-Seriously. Aren't you overreacting a bit?

-No. I'm not. Humor me, if only for a while here.

-Whatever. Besides school commitments, I really need to do something about Dad's condo, though Uncle Ollie did offer to help. So I can assure you I won't be out and about for any wild nights of partying. Like I usually do. Right.

-I can't...I can't lose you, Jules.

Tears threatened, a direct result of his sudden tenderness.

-And one more thing.

I scrambled to grab a tissue and blew my nose.

-Sorry. What else?

-I think you should leave this Melungeon thing alone.

I scoffed. And then could feel Guy react to my immediate defiance.

-It's the key, Guy, don't you get that? And listen to this: Right before we started talking, I read in the Melungeon book that one possible translation for the word *Melungeon* is, "*I am what I am.*" Remember I just told you I don't know who I am anymore, Guy. So do you have any idea what that expression means to me? *Melungeon* appears central to everything I want to discover about myself. Want I *need* to learn about *me*.

-But your dad—Jules, I really want you to leave this alone. Doesn't what your dad said—and our relationship—count for anything?

-That's unfair, Guy. Please don't couch it in those terms.

-I love you, Jules.

Instantly, he was gone, leaving me feeling even more alone than the last time. We quarreled like any couple in a relationship, but rarely as such opposites on an important issue—with no way to compromise, truthfully. Either I kept at this research. Or I completely ignored that infinitely curious chicken-scratched letter which Dad was so emotional about. *How on earth could Guy not expect me to follow those leads? He had no right to ask what he did*, I fumed. *He's got no basis, no facts, no reason to be so, so blasted bull-headed!*

Fortunately, I'd inadvertently (or subconsciously?) *not* told him about finding the gun. *Heaven knows how he would've ranted if he'd heard that*, I thought. *By all means, don't let that slip*, I lectured myself. Too late, again. *Put it in the positive, Julia: Remember to keep the gun a secret.*

—

Those last weeks of school were killers, stretching out so interminably that three weeks felt more like three years. And though the children were sky-high wired as they eagerly anticipated summer's arrival, I can't blame all of the attention deficit behavior on them. On the contrary, I think it was the teacher who needed a double-dose of Ritalin.

My scatterbrained thinking was a frequent culprit, resulting in disorganization in general. No amount of post-it notes were going to help, either, because emotional highs and lows on my part led to wild fluctuations in the children's behavior. After all, they were only a reflection of me and my instability. The fact that I could go totally brain dead at any given moment was a bit of a challenge too—even when the children were lined up and I was marching them off to the cafeteria. I still say I did not technically get lost. I merely made one wrong turn. So what if we ended up temporarily on the playground? The kids got their chicken nuggets in plenty of time.

I told our principal we could skip the end-of-year evaluation since I'd possibly be moving to California anyway. But Ms. Smith was gracious, saying she understood what a rough month I'd had and suggesting we chat in a few weeks. That it was still highly probable I'd be offered a contract for next year. That was a hopeful sign, but I wasn't holding my breath.

After waiting anxiously for the pathologist's report on Dad's death, it came back inconclusive. The police said they'd be filing it as an accident and a hit and run by someone who was most likely drunk, frightened, or already had too many penalty points on his or her license. Since there was simply no concrete evidence of foul play, they dropped their investigation. *Case closed*, as the expression goes.

Dad's memorial service went as well as could be expected. Melissa insisted on flying in, though she could stay only one night. But having the support of Uncle Ollie on one side of me and Melissa on the other made it bearable, at least. And what else can you say beyond that? Most of it is a blur in my memory anyway, except for the ambivalence that clung to me like a frightened cat, claws digging into a sweater. I dearly loved my dad, and I missed him dreadfully—the pain punched my gut at expected *and* totally caught-unawares moments. But allowing my emotions to show at the funeral? Not possible. I was propelled right back to Mom's memorial service: Back then, it seemed selfish for me to warrant attention when Dad was so completely despondent. I'd never once seen him cry before, so watching his whole body heaving with sobs? His emotions were…all-encompassing. Dad had suffered the greater loss, and I needed to make my presence small, to fade into the background.

Staring now at the picture of Dad that we'd put up front, I realized I wasn't going to be the expected loving, devoted daughter, seated in the front row, weeping piteously. I sniffed a few times and blew my nose, but as we stood to file out, I assumed our smattering of relatives—though not uttering a critical word in my presence—wouldn't have much good to say about me. Again. I wondered if they'd always viewed me as the black sheep, the dark one who never fit in with the flock of fair-skinned, blue-eyed blondes. Then you throw in the years when I chatted to an imaginary friend. They most likely thought I was simply being Julia—once strange, always strange, Julia. After all was said and done, maybe I merely provided what they actually expected?

Of course I had to bring home Dad's urn. At first I put it on my little kitchen table, where I sat and stared at it for about ten minutes. I don't know what I was expecting, but certainly something. *Anything.* Pulling up warm memories into my current state was evidently an effort beyond my capabilities, so instead, my mind went blank. My emotions, numb. Eventually I got up and after clearing a spot in the front closet, I put the urn up on the shelf. One thing I knew for certain: I wasn't ready to visit Castle Rock Lake. I needed answers that could only be found through research, and until I'd gathered the threads of my frayed existence, the urn was staying on the shelf. I closed the door, firmly.

Despite the police department's firm belief that Dad's and my accidents were merely a bizarre coincidence, I've developed a phobia: I'm paranoid about black SUV's. Whether I spy perfectly normal-looking, middle-aged drivers; young teens with hands at ten and two o'clock; even harried moms with a baby and a preschooler on board, a Labrador's head hanging out a back window and the bumper sticker that says *Warning! I brake for all yard sales*, it makes no difference. If I spot an SUV, first, I cower. Then I sneak stealthy looks at the driver and any tell-tale dented panels. Lastly, I make evasive maneuvers while speeding away. So far, I've avoided getting a speeding ticket.

Dad's condo is nearly ready to put up for sale. As always, Uncle Ollie has been true to his word and provided invaluable help. We've plowed through, sorted, sold, given away or absorbed just about everything the condo contained. I truly didn't need Dad's award plaques from his years at Dewdrop Dairy, Mom's collection of cow cream pitchers or various other "treasures." I've never been one of those sloppy sentimentalists who can't throw things away. For now, therefore, all the detritus I brought home from Dad's is confined to several boxes in a storage closet—including the plaques and pitchers. I check on those now 'n then to make sure they're not secretly multiplying in the dark.

I was thrilled to finally close the door (figuratively and literally) on school: I'd turned in final grades, left the room relatively clean, and loaded all boxed supplies into my (newly-repaired) car. I breathed a sigh of relief as I drove out of the parking lot for the last time and then headed to the fitness center, eagerly anticipating the positive feeling after a good workout in the pool.

As usual, my mind wandered as I counted laps, and I kept obsessing over recent conversations with Guy—we'd both been tip-toeing around the topic of my researching everything *Melungeon* and more importantly, what I'd do with that information. It's become the proverbial "elephant in the room," though in our case it's the "elephant in our minds," as I referred to it with Melissa. *But what* was *I going to do with this information?* I quizzed myself. I was going in circles and driving myself crazy, to what end?

I'd picked up a few groceries on my way home, so when I attempted to put my key into the front door lock, I was juggling not only the usual gym bag, purse, and groceries, but an additional large box of school supplies. I expected this balancing act to call for quite the coordinated feat, but I was surprised when my slightest weight against the door…pushed it wide open. It wasn't until then that I noticed the lock was completely demolished, and as I stood there a moment, paralyzed by the shock, Moppit came running out to hide and cower behind my legs. When I heard a noise coming from inside, that ended my temporary paralysis: I dropped everything I was holding—narrowly missing Moppit, thankfully, before I scooped her up into my arms—and bolted for the car.

Unfortunately, I'd dropped my keys with everything else (out of the corner of my eye I spotted apples rolling all over the porch), which meant I had no way to get *into* my locked car.

-Jules, are you okay? Why am I sensing you're in a panic again?

You can't let him know, I lectured myself. *He'll be rattled too and what good will that do either of us?*

-Nothing—I'm perfectly fine! Honest. Absolutely perfect.

I bolted for Mrs. Fitzsimmon's, right across the street. She was nuttier than a fruitcake, but since most of my neighbors were likely still at work, she was my best option. I rang the doorbell and then reached up to rap on the door—which immediately opened, startling me. "Oh! Mrs. Fitzsimmons—it's Julia Johnson. Remember me? I live right across the street and I think someone's broken into my house." I was doing this weird hop from one foot to another, which only made Mrs. F look at me like *I* was the nutcase. "Can you dial 9-1-1 for me? Please? Like...*now?*"

"I didn't see anyone go in. Are you quite sure?"

The first bizarre thought that went zinging through my brain? *So what's that mean? Does she watch my apartment all the time—like Moppit watches* her *house?*

"I'm pretty sure there's someone in there RIGHT NOW! Please—just call 9-1-1 and give the police my address, okay?"

-Jules?

-Later, Guy, k? Kinda busy here.

"Well, I suppose I could." She walks towards the kitchen where I can hear her punching buttons and then comes back with the handset, the long cord that connected to the wall stretched to its absolute limit. "Here you go—or I could possibly chat with them—"

I snatched it from her hand just as I heard the responder's voice.

"911. What's your emergency?"

"My apartment. It's been, I can't—*why on earth can't I be coherent?*—I think it's been broken into. And there might be someone...I think someone is still in there!"

"I'm here to help you, okay? First, are you somewhere safe? Because you need to be well away from your apartment just in case an intruder might be present."

The woman's voice is like a warm blanket on a freezing day, and I relax just a bit in response to her calming voice. "I'm at my neighbor's. Across the street."

"Okay. Good. What's your name?"

"Julia Johnson." *At least it was. Until recently,* I think to myself, but fortunately do not say out loud.

"Okay, Ms. Johnson, what's your address?"

Amazingly, I remember my address and can articulate it—until I realize Moppit's licking my chin like I've just eaten a melting ice cream bar. "Moppit, stop!"

"Excuse me?"

"Sorry. Just my dog. He was…never mind."

-Jules, I know you're evading me. But I'm worried you're in danger. Please…just tell me that you're okay. Jules?

My usual talent at juggling a conversation with Guy while talking with another is once again, nowhere to be found.

"An officer is in the area so he should be there soon. How did you first notice your apartment had been broken into?"

-Guy, I am perfectly okay. I promise you that—and I also promise I'll get back to you later.

"Ms. Johnson?"

"Sorry. I'm just a bit flustered." I close my eyes, concentrating.

"Understandable. So how did you first notice your apartment had been broken into?"

"The door. My lock. It's smashed and the door just…opened. And then I heard a noise inside."

"And you're sure you are in a safe place?"

As safe as alien-abducted Mrs. Fitzsimmons is, I think to myself, but out loud I respond, "Yes. I'm absolutely fine."

"Good. Just *do not under any circumstances* go back to your apartment; you need to be far enough away in case someone should come out that same front door. Do you have a back door?"

"Yes, I do! Do you think he'll go out that way?"

I can hear a siren close by and when I finally spot the police car, I let out a long sigh. *Had I been partially holding my breath this entire time?*

"I think I can hear the siren. Has the police officer arrived?" the responder asks.

"Yes, he's turning into the parking lot just now—and thank you! Thank you so much."

"That's what we're here for. Stay safe, Ms. Johnson."

I watch as a tall officer climbs out of his car, and he glances over at me as I shout out my name and wave at him. Offering a hurried, "Thanks, Mrs. Fitzsimmons!" to my helpful neighbor, she then starts to say something in response. But I shout back over my shoulder, "Sorry, need to run! Thanks again!" One more quick glance at her shows she's a bit perturbed at me, but I don't have time—or the urge—to soothe her feelings. At least, not today.

The officer is staring at the obvious evidence of the break-in: A gaping door with a smashed lock. The ripped grocery bag with apples all over the porch, purse, gym bag and toppled box piled in a heap only show evidence of my panic.

"Miss? Are you the one who called 911?"

I swear it takes every bit of control I can muster to collect my thoughts. And answer. "Um, yes. I'm Julia Johnson. Thanks for getting here so quickly!"

"Happened to be close by. I'm Officer Stan Kenney." He motions towards my door, leaning in to glance around. "Assume this is your apartment?"

I nod, and, feeling a wave of fear course through me again, I absentmindedly clutch Moppit tighter against my chest. But I've pushed the cuddling too far and she's not having it. With a strength that takes me by surprise, Moppit pushes off and leaps to the ground. She bolts past Officer Kenney and continues pell-mell into the apartment like she's on a mission. Her haste is comparable to when she hears the pantry door open, where I keep her dog food. I'm convinced she could hear the creak of that door in a hail storm, tornado or hurricane.

"Moppit! Come back here!" I yell. Like she's going to obey?

"*Stay here*," Officer Kenney commands, pointing at me, clearly communicating that I'm *not* to go after my errant dog. Pausing at the door a moment, one hand lightly touching his holstered gun, he cautiously looks inside and then disappears.

-Jules?!

-Oh, Guy—I'm sorry, I just haven't...it's a bit hectic here, that's all.

-Hectic? Why?

I'm fidgeting, bouncing nervously from one foot to the other again when I spot a second police cruiser turning into the parking lot.

-I've gotta go, Guy. I will get back to you later—promise! And I'm fine. I really am...just fine.

-I don't believe you, Jules.

I knew I wasn't going to fool him. But telling him this? Now? Impossible.

-Later, k? *There was nothing for it. He was going to be furious with me.*

This officer, a warm and friendly woman, introduces herself as Officer Zoe White. She's obviously been talking with Officer Kenney, as she kindly beckons for me to follow her into my apartment, adding, "It's safe, Ms. Johnson. Officer Kenney has given the all-clear." We step over the mess at the door and then gather in the kitchen, where the back door has been left wide open. Moppit has obviously run out back, still barking, furiously. Since I figure there's no way she's going to obey me at this point—and that Officer Kenney has already checked out back—I choose to ignore Moppit. For the time being.

Hesitantly, I take a few moments to scan the apartment, noting that the intruder has clearly given the whole place a quick search, leaving scattered objects in his wake. Pillows have been tossed, my desk drawers rummaged through in my office, and a quick peek at my bedroom shows that it's been rifled through also. Just as I assumed, the pantry door is indeed open, and my organized bins and boxes are anything but organized now. The dog food bin, however, has apparently not been touched. Moppit will be relieved.

"Pretty clear the intruder came in the front," Officer Kenney notes. "That lock looked to be pretty loose beforehand, I'm thinking?"

I sigh and nod my head. "It was on my list to fix." I knew Oliver was going to feel terrible that he hadn't gotten around to replacing it. But with Dad's death and two dented cars and everything else, I couldn't blame him a bit. But that made this break-in first and foremost a crime of convenience, the officers surmised. They explain how they've seen a rash of break-ins at apartment buildings in the area, and all were specifically targeted due to negligence of some sort—either a door was left unlocked or the lock was easily broken due to disrepair. The officers also decide I must've caught him not long after the intruder had broken in because the apartment hadn't been totally trashed.

"Seriously?" I look around me, dismayed at the mess. "This isn't 'trashed,' in your opinion?"

Officer White speaks up. "Honestly, I'm sure it looks pretty bad to you, but in our experience, this is relatively minor. But we need to know if anything is missing."

The officers begin a few duties—a bit of "detective work" as they term it, plus I have forms to fill out, including an inventory of missing items—when Moppit comes sauntering in, acting like the returning hero.

"She clearly didn't chase the intruder out of here," Officer Kenney explains, "but I don't doubt that she followed his exact path out this door and then down the fence line to the gate." He grinned at Moppit and reached down to rub behind her ears. "She was carrying on something awful right at the gate. Didn't wander out, but was certainly announcing the intruder had escaped that way. Didn't know you had a trained protector, did you?"

"Actually, I think she was more concerned about the intruder messing with her dog food than anything else," I add, but there's still a hint of pride for my little dog. The protector, eh?

We finish up about an hour later, and the good news is that, though it seems a bit insulting, I evidently have few valuable items that a home invader might want. The final tally? My office, bedroom and pantry are a bit of a wreck, but only one light bulb is broken from a fallen lamp and the sole missing item is one of my watches. Strange—though my jewelry box was clearly ransacked because all the drawers are opened—I had a much more expensive watch in plain sight that was left behind, as is all my other (relatively inexpensive) jewelry. My computer doesn't appear to have been touched—though I ask myself, *How could you tell?*—and my TV and small stereo system are both exactly where I'd left them. I could tell exactly what the officers were thinking when they asked about them, however: *No self-respecting thief would want to steal these.* And once again, I guess that's the good and the bad news for me. All in all, I fared pretty well, considering. Besides the general mess that I need to clean up, the officers conclude that it appears to be a minor case of breaking and entering.

So why do I feel so awful? And even more vulnerable—a weak in the knees *I-need-to-sit-down* kind of vulnerable? If I was a bit paranoid before, how much more so am I going to be now?

I'd held off yet another frantic inquisition from Guy while the officers were here, going over my apartment with a fine-toothed comb. I was trying to figure out what on earth I'd tell him as the police were finally leaving, climbing into their cars. But right at that moment, Uncle Ollie drove in. "Julia! Were those officers *here*? What's happened? Were you—are you—your door—I can't—?" One look at the lock and then the state of my apartment told him all he needed to know. With that, he put the box he was carrying onto the table and immediately reached for me, pulling me into one of those famous Uncle Ollie hugs. Where for the first time on this interminably long afternoon, I felt safe. I soaked up the security of being in his strong embrace, but unfortunately, Uncle Ollie's shirt soaked up my flood of tears.

When the tears had finally abated and I moved out of his arms, I gave my nose a good blow. And replied to his unspoken question, "I'm really okay, Uncle Ollie, and even though my apartment was broken into, it's—"

"Oh darling girl. *It's my fault!* I should've fixed that lock weeks ago! Can you ever forgive me?"

"Uncle Ollie, no, there's no need to forgive. I also knew that lock should've been fixed, so I'm equally guilty for procrastinating about repairing it. And who's responsible for its being broken in the first place? I've kicked that door with my foot almost every time I've come in here, making it work its way loose." I sighed and plopped down on the couch, motioning for Uncle Ollie to sit in the recliner. I figured Moppit would hop onto his lap, which she immediately did. I hoped he'd accept some consolation from her.

"You're staying at my place tonight. No arguments."

I sighed, a bit dramatically, I must admit. "I don't have the energy to argue with you, Uncle Ollie. Sleeping here tonight—truly going to sleep—would be an impossibility, I'm afraid. But I'll need to get past that at some point."

"What did the police have to say?"

I filled him in on all the details: What the intruder might've been looking for. What he took, explaining about the other break-ins in the area and how that provided a reasonable explanation for what happened here. And then I accidently let slip something I knew I should've kept mum about. "Going to need to swing by the grocery. Every single apple is too bruised to eat since I dropped them all when I was coming in the door…seeing the lock was broken…and then I heard someone…"

Uncle Ollie looked ashen and I instantly regretted my rambling. "I'm fine, Uncle Ollie—really! He was already on his way out so there was no possibility...and he's not that type of intruder. The police reassured me of that!"

If he'd looked depleted of energy seconds before, it was like a light just flicked back on behind his eyes. "Well, this is an interesting development." He popped up out of the recliner—unceremoniously dumping Moppit onto the floor, which clearly wasn't to her liking—to retrieve the box he'd placed on the table. Settling himself in the recliner once more, he removed the lid and set it aside. "Brought you all the contents of the safe—minus the gun and ammo, of course." He gave me a quick glance before drawing out the smeared letter. "Spent a good part of the day trying to decipher more of this, Julia. Goes without saying that I was frustrated over the letter *and* what we should do about it. Not like me to be so undecided, and honestly, I was still completely flummoxed driving over here. But now, there's one thing I'm convinced we *must* do. We need to take charge of this situation."

I looked at him expectantly, surprised that he'd come to any kind of a conclusion in this bungled mess that was supposedly my life these days. "We need to take charge? Exactly how?"

"I am definitely leaning towards a pro-active plan." He glanced around the room, nodding at the tossed pillows and general disorder. "Especially after....after *this*. I can't help but think it's all connected."

I frowned at him this time. "What are you implying?"

"This break in. Coincidental? An intruder taking only one inexpensive watch?" Dramatically, he held up the box. "*This right here* is what he was looking for. Good thing I had it with me, or every bit of this would've been gone."

He leaned forward, and the unblinking focus in his eyes startles me just a bit. *Is this what my uncle the sharp-shooter looked like? Am I seeing the intensity of the killer he once was still lingering there?* I could feel the hairs on the back of my neck stand up.

"I don't like staying put here, allowing these cowardly people—whoever they are—to manipulate us and our circumstances. I think *we* need to take control. We need to get to the bottom of this. And I am absolutely prepared to do so."

I opened my mouth. Shut it. And then met his glance, glare for glare.

"Uncle Ollie. Are you insinuating that we're going to Tennessee?"

"No, no, noooo. Not *you*, darling girl. *Me.* I intend to get to the bottom of this!"

-Jules! I've been picking up fear and panic from you all day. I've tried to be patient. But now your emotions are *over the top!* I will not be put off a moment longer. *What on earth is going on?*

THE GRAVESTONES' SECRETS

1 of March, 1588

My Descendants,
    It has been some time since I have taken pen in hand and written in this journal. If not for mind talking with my beloved Catherine, I believe I would have despaired because of all manner of hardships our colony has endured these last treacherous months. Winter arrived with angry vengeance, and we have known fierce winds, biting snow, and temperatures that have left us agape at the cold, wondering at Nature's fickle and ill treatment.
    Would that I could tell you our supplies of game and fish carried us through the winter. But such was our fate that those supplies dwindled all too quickly, and getting fresh game proved much more difficult than we could have foretold.
    Would that I could tell you our homes were warm, providing the shelter we needed to endure such a winter. But such was not our experience.
    Would that I could also tell you how all in our colony survived this first winter, but alas, that too is not a truthful telling. And yet, I can give word that our dear Babe Virginia

lives yet, and thrives! All told, we have lost seven of our colony of one hundred and eighteen Souls.

Need I say that my time here in this New World has changed this solitary man? I watch our young Ananias, Mistress Eleanor, and Babe Virginia with constant worry, as unforeseen enemies lurk everywhere. Such severe storms advance with little to no warning, and, as I bespoke earlier, the Savages also come and go, startling us with their sudden presence in our midst. Some are friendly, and for these we give our Great God eternal thanks. Others, however, give cause for fear, so we meet them with wariness and yet warm greetings such as we can grant, knowing we need have doings with them.

All this gives me courage in that I know not what each daybreak brings, but I rejoice in my Beloved Catherine, and I boldly profess my undying Love. That she is distant Cousin only floods me with more joy, as we can share our minds and hearts though an ocean lies between us, she in England, and this humble Servant Mauro, here in the New World.

As a mere Babe when my father was in secret spirited away from England, did anyone know the sacrifice would be for generations? Alas! In doing so, this one Truth is what mattered: My father's Life was spared, and my very existence is due to the bold daring of those committed to his Salvation!

Was that very same boldness in turn passed into my very mire as I yielded to Captain Fernandes' call, his pleading that I join this bold and grand Adventure? A journey in many ways equally perilous and secretive as my father's, likewise my only choice, and thus, my Salvation also? What other reason could take me this far from my Beloved Catherine?

I remain, forever, in God's Grace and Mercy,
Mauro

CHAPTER FOUR

Uncle Ollie and I simply stared into each other's eyes for a few seconds—rather like a child's stare-down contest. But there was no winning against the steely look on my uncle's face; I gave up that battle pretty quickly. And then I use the oldest female escape plan in the book: I excuse myself to flee to the bathroom.

-Guy, I'm sorry, I truly am. But you have to believe me that I had no time to get back to you until this very moment.

-You're not avoiding telling me something?

I hesitate for just a split second, but that was long enough.

-You *are* hiding something from me. And it must be pretty significant, considering the multitude of feelings I'm picking up from you today. Especially just now.

-Guy, I can't—

-Stop, Jules. Don't say anything until you're ready to tell me the truth—*all* of it.

The hurt in his voice is like a stone in my heart, and suddenly I'm miserable with weariness. *How do I handle this, God?* I plead. *I didn't want to burden Guy with more worry. But maybe I should pour out all—and let him process the best he can?* I splash water onto my face and then stare into the mirror as I pat my skin dry. *I don't want Uncle Ollie going to Tennessee without me. But the truth is, I'm terrified of facing the unknowns there,* I think to myself as I gaze at my alarmed reflection. *If Dad and I truly were intentionally sideswiped, and my apartment broken into because someone was looking for my letter and birth certificate*—then how does it make any sense for Uncle Ollie to charge right into the very heart of the problem? I lean into the mirror so that I'm inches from the mirror, and forcefully state: "I simply have to convince Uncle Ollie to just dig in here, doing research at the library. That's the smart thing to do, right, God?"

And then I have one of those times when God impresses a message on me. No, I didn't hear a voice. I'm not schizophrenic and it wasn't Guy talking and I have never claimed that God talks to me, Julia Johnson—or Julia Blevins, if I can believe that birth certificate—like I'm Abraham or Moses or Paul. But suddenly I sense that I need to trust God. And Uncle Ollie. The issue comes down to this: *What does that trust look like? Does it mean continuing to do research here? Or does it mean traveling to Tennessee? Was Dad's fear for my safety in Tennessee rational? Or was he overreacting in his weakened physical and mental state? Oh, God. I don't know what you want me to do!*

With one last glare at the totally confused image in the mirror, I open the door. Take a deep breath. And steel myself to face my uncle.

"Uncle Ollie," I announce as I go to stand before him, an ambivalent mix of determination and resignation, "I hate to admit that you could *possibly* be right. But as I try to sort this out in my mind, I don't see a clear path because I really don't know what Dad was trying to tell me. Or what he *would've* advised if he hadn't been so…ill." I plopped onto the sofa, putting elbows on my knees, and cupping my chin in my palms. "Dad's words were as muddy as the Rock River in the spring, Uncle Ollie. I'll admit—it was clear he was trying to warn me. But about what, exactly? It was all so disjointed! He was obviously on the verge of yet another heart attack, so how much of what he said can we take as…rational, and, and…well, *real?*" I hunched over, putting my forehead in my hands. "What a mess this is!"

I felt Oliver's hand on my head. When I looked up, his kind eyes were telegraphing waves of love and support. "Let's do this: We'll list what we know for sure. And then make a decision from there."

"Like….?"

"One: It's not clear that your dad's warning about going to Tennessee was warranted. Or rational. It still gives me great pause. But darling girl, I trust you and I'll abide by your decision: *You* must decide."

Only my Uncle Ollie would use a word like abide, I thought to myself, smiling up at him. "Not *we* must decide?"

"No, because I think that's part of what God wants to happen here, so I'm taking a step back. Truthfully, I would much prefer that you stayed here and just let me go. But I'm sensing that God's calling not only *you* to trust him, but me also—whether you stay. Or go. And I fully trust and support your ability to seek and know God's will in this decision."

I swallowed. Felt the weight sit on my shoulders like I struggled under a thousand-pound barbell. "Right. Okay, then. What else do we know for sure?"

"Secondly, we've set up this scenario assuming it's dangerous in Tennessee—as opposed to it being safe *here*."

I frowned. "Well, it hasn't been safe here, if we truly believe the two accidents and my break-in aren't coincidences."

"Exactly. Which brings me to number three: The police appear to believe all three *are* random and coincidental," Uncle Ollie mused, rubbing his chin. "Maybe we've watched too many crime movies?"

I nodded agreeably, but the jury was still out, in my opinion. "What else?"

"Fourth: If you want to truly get to the heart of the issue and discover your background and heritage—really see and experience where you're from—you can only do that in one place. Collinsville, Tennessee."

I lean back against the couch, staring at the ceiling. "I keep hearing that translation we discovered online for the word *Melungeon*—'*I am what I am.*' It's like this echo in my head. Because it confirms exactly what I want to do: Find *me*, Uncle Ollie. And isn't truly knowing where you come from part of that journey?"

"Absolutely, it is."

"You have one more point, don't you?"

I hear a low chuckle. "You're aware of that because you could pretty much state this one word-for-word yourself. It's about trust in God, Julia. Taking a leap of faith. The Bible's full of stories about those who took that leap. Abraham and Moses believed God. Mary believed she would deliver the Messiah. Peter—when he stepped out of the boat onto the water. That jump out into nothing but our belief in God? It's an inherent part of faith. *Growing* in our faith."

We were silent for a few moments, both so lost in thought that I could hear Moppit, lightly snoring. I noticed the steady hum of the refrigerator, and someone in the neighborhood was mowing their lawn. I took a deep breath and turned to face my uncle.

"Well. If I decide to do this, we might need to rent a parachute. If I'm going to make this jump, then I at least want a back-up."

Uncle Ollie laughed. "That would be *me*, darling girl." His eyes twinkled and the grin spread from ear to ear. "Go pack your over-nighter." Once again he hopped up out of the recliner with a surge of energy. He looked around the room and then pointed towards my office. "I can get busy putting some of this back in place, and then you can finish up tomorrow morning while I put on new locks." He immediately set to work, putting pillows back on the couch and stacking books and magazines. "Can't wait to tell you what I've learned about our upcoming adventure."

How could I not cherish this man? I thought to myself. And as frightened as I was of what awaited me in Tennessee, I knew I could face it—at least, I hoped so at this point—with Uncle Ollie by my side. He would keep me safe and defend me to the death. *That* was a given I could count on.

I was pulling my suitcase out from under my bed when I sat back on my heels a moment. And reached out to Guy.

-Hey. Are you there?

-Of course I am.

I hated hearing the hurt in his voice—pain that I caused. I don't know how that's possible for our mind talking. But the sharing goes so much deeper than simply the mere sound of a voice in my head, as it goes deeply into the marrow of my bones. Part 'n parcel of the very life principle of my blood, it would seem. I don't want to describe it as intimate, because Guy and I are… more like brother and sister. Only, closer? Maybe like what twins have? The words to explain us simply don't exist.

-I put off telling you something. About what happened today.

He's silent, waiting. Wondering how honest I will be?

-Guy, I didn't want you to worry about me. I'm okay—like I already assured you. But once I tell you this—

-Tell me what? What's happened now, Jules?

I sigh and then take a deep breath.

-My apartment was broken into. When I pushed open the door, I could hear someone.

-Oh my God, Jules. Do you know how dangerous—?

-Yes. I do. But whoever it was evidently went right out the back door. The police came quickly and they are insistent this was a crime of convenience. They've had several of these break-ins lately in apartments just like mine. And my front lock was clearly in bad shape, so the intruder simply took advantage of that.

-Do you believe the police?

-I want to.

-Uh-huh. And your uncle. What does he say?

-He did wonder if they were after my birth certificate. And that letter.

There's silence between us. But it's not empty.

-You have to do something about this, Jules.

-I know. I plan to. *And in that moment, I realize the decision is made. Guy would fight me about Tennessee, I know he would. So, for now, it's best that he doesn't know anything about our plans. Once I'm already there...then I'll tell him. This is best—all the way around. Best for me. And Guy.*

-But all decisions can wait until tomorrow. I'm taking my uncle's offer to sleep at his place. It's not safe here tonight, but it will be once Uncle Ollie's done!

-How's that? New lock?

-Yeah, but not just any lock. You know his military background—and the fact that he's good with anything mechanical. It will be equal to Ft. Knox, I'm thinking.

I can hear Guy letting out a deep breath. He's obviously feeling some relief, and that's a sure sign withholding our trip plans was the right thing to do.

-I know I can trust your uncle to do a great job.

Guy is pensive for a moment, and then he says, softly...

-Please don't leave me out of the loop, Jules. That only makes me worry more. Tell me you can relate to that?

-I get it, Guy. I really do. And now....now I need to get packed and off to Uncle Ollie's and to bed. Before I crash.

-Night, Jules. I hope you sleep well, love.

-Good night, Guy.

I did it: I managed to hold onto my emotions until we'd said good bye. But only *just*, as a new round of tears poured down my cheeks at my deception.

—

That next week, Uncle Ollie and I worked pretty much non-stop to get ready for our trip. Since he'd already done a good deal of research, he filled me in on what he'd already learned. We discussed travel plans first, deciding on the best route to Collinsville: Three interstates to a multi-lane highway and then a turn onto a smaller country road. Oliver thought it appeared to be a pretty easy drive until we reached the divided highway, and then that road would eventually dump us right into the Cumberland Mountain area. Which was only about twenty miles from the town of Collinsville, Tennessee.

Oliver secured lodging for us also, booking adjacent rooms at a motel. Which actually is the *only* hotel in Collinsville. I'm trying to temper my expectations. A plus to staying right there in town is that Collinsville is also the county seat, so any registries we would need should be right there at the county courthouse.

I spent a good amount of time doing more research at the library, but local records were patchy and scarce, to say the least. I learned Collinsville had suffered a major fire back in 1931 which destroyed several buildings in town, including most of the city hall building—where all official archives were stored, of course. What they did salvage wasn't in great shape since so much was thoroughly drenched from putting out the fire. And then the Great Depression meant they had precious little funding to do much of anything, let alone restore old records.

Guides for research advised that local churches might provide clues from their hand-written records—births, baptisms, marriages, that sort of thing. I knew also that graveyards were sometimes valuable sources for information that had long ago been lost from any written logs, since carved granite tends to outlast books vulnerable to mold, floods (which also happen frequently in Tennessee, I gathered, despite the work of the Tennessee Valley Authority) and as I'd already learned, fire.

Several months ago I'd watched a fascinating documentary on television about genealogy riddles that were sometimes solved only by reading the dates and messages on gravestones. However, that same documentary also vividly demonstrated how hunting down headstones could prove to be tricky, since they were also susceptible to inclement weather, the ravages of anything left to grow wild in the vicinity, and lastly, sinkholes. The last obstacle sounded ironic—and slightly unnerving, considering my nightmare.

In light of all those obstacles, Uncle Ollie and I expressed our hopes for a well-run library. We both knew an efficient librarian who took an interest in you and your research was worth his or her weight in gold. Right then, we committed to be on our very best behavior for her. Because in a small town in the South we deduced it would be a woman, most certainly. And we'd already nailed what she'd look like: Older, matronly, stern-faced but still friendly (although not overly so), efficient, and a veritable fount of knowledge. Since she'd been a resident there her entire life, it was a given she'd know exactly where every surviving, available document was stored. *Count on it*, we agreed. Right along with my absolute certainty that no trip to a cemetery would then be necessary. No ghosts or sinkholes would be addendums to *my* dreams!

Lastly, we agreed that we needed a convincing story—a credible reason why two northerners were in Collinsville to begin with. Uncle Ollie was insistent that being completely truthful could be potentially risky. "Seems prudent to not advertise exactly who you are," he pointed out. "We should avoid stating where we're from and your relationship to anyone there in Collinsville, Julia. We can be wisely cautious by merely leaving out details."

"Then what *do* we say? And especially when we start asking questions at city hall, the library and local churches too?"

"Well, we're close enough to Chicago to say we're from that area. That's rather nebulous but still the truth. And we're in Collinsville to research…say, how about your Aunt Susan's family tree? We'll tell people you're my niece, so there will be no connection between her and you other than by her marriage to me."

"And you think that'll sound believable?"

"Of course, it's believable, my dear. It's perfectly logical."

I winked at him. "You and Mr. Spock."

Guy and I talked several times a day, which of course meant that I left out pretty significant details constantly. I never actually lied to him, but I certainly wasn't forthcoming and became skilled at dodging his questions by changing the subject. He was suspicious and probed a few times, but I was able to distract him by blaming everything on my grief for my dad. And once I defaulted there, he let whatever go. My guilt at misleading him, however, hung in there like heavy fog on a humid morning.

Uncle Ollie and I slowly checked off everything on our to-do list: Oliver did indeed fortify my apartment so that the combined efforts of every branch of the military couldn't break in (maybe just a tad exaggerated); we stocked up on food for the trip; and we left Dad's condo in the care of a responsible realtor. Then we concentrated on stuffing every square inch of my car, packing first aid kits and items for contingencies (tools for repairs and possible archeological endeavors); our clothes (an assortment from casual to full hiking gear); personal items; and finally, all the paraphernalia Moppit would need, because naturally, she was going too. Trust me. *No trip* in the history of family adventures had *ever* had as much planning and time and prayer put into it as *this trip*.

On departure day at 5:00 a.m.—heaven knows why I ever agreed to that hour—Uncle Ollie climbed into the front passenger seat, Moppit staked out her position on his lap with paws on the door handle (I'd warned him repeatedly about that being her stipulated seat), and I settled in behind the wheel. With all the preparations and the multitude of discussions Oliver and I had shared, why was I nearly shaking with anxiety? Not one to miss any nuance or subconscious non-verbal, Uncle Ollie cleared his throat. A *noticeable* throat clearing.

"What?" I started up the car, thankful for its familiar hum.

"Shall we talk about your insecurity? And how it's one-hundred-percent logical?"

Of all the beginnings I could've imagined, I never suspected that one.

"Seriously? I've never viewed my insecurities as logical. And I don't think Dad did either, considering he was always pressing me to throw off my lack of confidence and make decisions in a timely manner."

"My brother was entitled to his view. I say you've had a few major obstacles thrown at you in your young life. Losing your mom? At that tender age?" He shook his head. "And then you throw in that you weren't allowed a space to grieve, Julia. The enormity of your dad's bereavement overshadowed anyone else's. Especially yours."

"I'm not following—what're you saying?"

"I knew the drill, darling girl. When Liam and I were growing up, it was like…Liam's emotions *demanded* attention." He paused a moment, reflecting. "I remember one year we both tried out for the basketball team. I made it, but that year, Liam didn't."

I glanced over and noted his jaw line, the muscle twitching there.

"His disappointment was so all-encompassing that my happiness was...lessened, and pretty much erased. Liam's emotions were generally like that: they could take over a room. A home. *Space.* And others' feelings? They were secondary to his."

He looked down at Moppit, absentmindedly rubbing her ears. But I could tell his thoughts were far from the dog who demanded his attention just then.

"So when your mom died, there was no allowing you to feel, darling girl. Because everyone else's grief was extinguished in the wildfire of your dad's emotions." He was quiet a few moments before adding, "I'm so sorry that happened to you, Julia. I couldn't prevent it, and I couldn't stop it. I felt so powerless. Watching it play out was torture."

Thinking that about my dad felt like breathing in foul air. "But Dad's loss *was* greater than mine, Uncle Ollie."

"Grief can't—shouldn't—be measured for validity. You lost your mom at twelve years old. I wish Liam could've shown the grace to allow space for *both* of you to grieve."

I glanced over at Oliver again, feeling embarrassed, and even *guilty* to entertain such thoughts. "I think I need time to mull this over a while."

"I want you to do exactly that, Julia. I intended to begin this conversation on our journey. Because it's key to so much more—your dad's death and how that's affected you. Then learning you were adopted. That has ripped away all that you've known and assumed about yourself. *Of course* you feel insecure, Julia. *How could you not?*"

"Don't you think most places where we want to put our security are only an illusion, though?" I asked.

"Absolutely. Money, possessions, education, health. They can rob you of life's greatest joys because they keep you from jumping out, in faith, into God's arms. *That's* the only place where permanent and real security is."

He pulled a fresh handkerchief from his shirt pocket and blew his nose, making the honking sound I could identify as his alone when I was a child. When the two of us were at the grocery store, he would be aisles away, squeezing cantaloupe in the produce section while I was staring through the glass at the bakery, debating which pastry to con him into buying. I could always locate him by the call of that honk. I was so focused on those memories that I had to pull myself back into the present.

He stuffed the handkerchief back into his pocket and said, "Your decision to go on this trip shows great courage, Julia. You've made one leap already. But get ready, as I'm sure there are more to come. That's a description of the Christ follower's life."

I stared off into the traffic ahead, avoiding meeting his eyes. "You described it as needing to *jump* into God's arms. Interesting choice of words."

"Sauntering, strolling, meandering, walking. Those words don't begin to embody what Jesus calls us to do. Yes, *jump* describes it rather well, I'd say." He winked and smiled at me, another of those huge boyish transformations that called out my own returning smile.

He'd stopped petting Moppit to rub a hand through his hair, and Moppit used the opportunity to assume her favorite road-tripping position once again: Front paws up on the arm rest, eyes peeled on the view, alert and ready for action.

"I'm afraid Moppit's going to drive you crazy before we get there."

"Oh, not at all. It appears I have a knack for finding compromise with any and all demanding females in my life. Isn't that right, Moppit?"

I laughed. And Moppit? She licked Oliver's chin.

—

When we stopped to get a burger for lunch, Uncle Ollie leaned across the table, and charged right into a sensitive subject. "About your biological parents. I assume you've given some thought to the possibility they might be still alive? And living in Collinsville?"

A flood of ambivalent feelings rushed through me. "I know it's possible. But I didn't think it very likely—"

"People born in these small towns don't often move away, Julia." He stirred his coffee, and I noted each *ding* of his spoon against the mug. "Could be they're still there. In the very same house."

I chewed my cheeseburger warily. Suddenly it seemed a bit grisly.

"You look like you're eating lemons instead of hamburger." He sipped his coffee, probably making the same face I'd just made. "Whew. This must be left over from yesterday. Or last week."

"A bit strong?"

"Let's just say if I'd brewed this first thing in the morning at home, it would wake up my neighbors."

I grinned at him, appreciating his attempt to add some levity. "Did you notice their ages on my birth certificate? They were awfully young when they had me. Like seventeen and sixteen."

"Also very typical for that section of the country at that time, I would imagine. But how do you feel about possibly meeting them?"

I shrugged my shoulders. "Told myself I'd think about all the 'what-ifs' when we were on our way there. Assumed I'd have plenty of time to stew on it. But now I find—well, let's just say I'm discovering it feels convenient to delay a lot of things."

Softly, he probed, "I can understand that. But when you're trying to figure out who you are? Not so helpful, maybe?"

"Hmmm, possibly." I put my hamburger back on my plate and cautiously lifted the bun to examine the patty. "I'll ponder that later too. Right now I need to investigate this mystery meat."

"Maybe it's one of those new plant-based burgers. An *implausiburger* or something like that."

I chuckled and then cut the burger in half to inspect the inside. "Implausiburger, eh? Pretty pleased with yourself, eh? Honestly, I think this is just your regular ole cheap, rubbery grade of hamburger. And doctoring it up with all the 'fixin's' isn't going to make it more palatable."

And then I changed the subject, deflecting to the weather and traffic. To his credit, Uncle Ollie tends to navigate gently through my denials and redirections. That skill alone made Oliver a wonderfully agreeable companion for a long road trip.

After lunch, Uncle Ollie took the wheel so I'd have a chance to rest. I'd just closed my eyes, however, when Guy popped into my head.

-Jules? Where are you?

-On a road trip. Busy in traffic right now. More later, k?

With all my might—and it was awfully hard when I was feeling insecure like this—I completely shut him out. Blocked out where we were headed, and why. He pestered me for quite a while but eventually gave up. For now, at least.

After that, I was convinced there was no way I'd rest much, but soon the gentle rhythm and low hum of the car lulled me into a deep sleep. I dreamed I was coming up the sidewalk of my biological parents' home—which turned out to be a modest but nice all-brick ranch—and was anxiously anticipating meeting them when I heard a dog barking. Turning to look, I saw my dad, who was waving and beckoning from a shed across the driveway. I ached to go to him, but hesitated because just at that moment, the door was opening. In excited anticipation, I watched the doorknob turn. And I saw—*my principal?*

I jerked awake, the stop'n go traffic of the divided highway not quite as soothing as the interstate. We had definitely entered another culture. Rubbing sleep from my eyes and blinking them several times, I was instantly taken by the area's obsession with billboards.

"*See Cumberland Gap! See Ruby Falls! Hike Lookout Mountain! Visit Historic Cumberland! See Rock City!* I read, emphasizing every exclamation point. "You get the feeling their marketers like expression?" I asked dryly.

The corners of Uncle Ollie's mouth turned down and his eyebrows scrunched together as he deadpanned, "Thank you for reading those to me, Julia. I had failed to notice the previous one-thousand two-hundred and eighty-six signs, thereby requiring your astute observational powers."

I grinned up at him. "Sorry. I promise to ignore the next two thousand, okay?" I stretched, reaching up and arching my back as I did so. "What time is it anyway? Three thirty?" Moppit—who'd slept along with me, sprawled across my lap—rolled over, conveniently exposing her pink tummy. I obliged and gave her a good rubbing. "I do feel rested. Want me to drive so you can take a break?"

"Nah. Actually, I'm rather enjoying this part of the trip. It's more interesting than the monotony of the expressway." He nodded towards the left. "Take a look over that way."

We'd driven out of a small town onto a terrain of wide curves around lush wooded hills, granting beautiful views. A busy creek ran parallel to the curving road, rushing over boulders, circling in eddies and pushing leaves and sticks around bends. Clustered on both sides of the stream were good-sized trees, their branches sometimes gracefully dipping down to touch the rushing waters. And everywhere farms dotted the landscape, aging clapboards surrounded by broken down equipment, rotting sheds and other outbuildings evidently still in use, and row upon row of crops in vibrant fields.

I felt a desire to fully take in the atmosphere of the countryside. *This is my genetic home,* I told myself. *You come from this. In some way, it's an inherent part of your DNA.*

I was enthralled by the beauty of the natural world here, but the slightest shift in any direction could provide incredible contrast. Oliver and I were silent as we were confronted with hard times and tougher living in homes no more than rough shacks. Precarious shelters held together with little more than a prayer, it appeared, and certainly any cold wind would be devastating to those inside. Though Tennessee winters weren't equal to Wisconsin's, an icy breeze would cruelly work its way through those crevices.

Mobile homes populated the area too. Balanced on cement blocks, they also appeared barely stable, tilting at awkward angles. But then maybe the accumulated clutter (bulging trash cans; discarded washers, refrigerators and sofas; broken toilets and sinks; rusty tools and tin cans) stuffed under, around and alongside the mobile homes were, ironically, somewhat of a support?

There were also neat-as-a-pin clapboard ranch homes with pick-ups or sedans parked beneath carports. Out back, we caught glimpses of diapers, men's shirts and clean sheets snapping in the breeze on clothes lines. Bicycles lay discarded on gravel driveways. Frilly curtains peeked out of sparkling windows. Gardens flourished and flowers bloomed around front porches that generally held gliders or rocking chairs.

What kind of house did Jimmy and Lucille Blevins live in? I wondered. *The wooden shack? A mobile home? Or one of these homey ranches?* I attempted to pry into windows, to seek out the people who lived and loved in this world that was so foreign to me. *God, who were they? What were they like—or maybe, what* are *they like?* I took a deep breath, and Uncle Oliver reached over to pat my arm.

We passed through more small towns, catching a bit of the flavor of each as we did so. Tiny custard or soft serve ice cream shops occupied a plot in nearly each one along with tired-looking general stores (advertising chewing tobacco and bait), farm stands, hardware stores, "Five and Dimes," and churches. Churches appeared to out-number all other buildings, and it seemed like nearly all had Vacation Bible School banners planted out front. Cracked cement bridges crossed an endless assortment of creeks, and often two to three men were hanging out at the local gas station (which looked like it came right out of the 1950's, except for the price)—with at least twice that many cars in various states of disrepair.

As we approached the Cumberland Mountain area, the rolling hills pushed higher; we were gaining in altitude. Then, just up ahead, we glimpsed the glory of the Gap: A nearly mile-long tunnel. I'd read up on the history and enlightened Uncle Ollie.

"This is so exciting, Uncle Ollie. The tunnel coming up? It's brand new—just opened for the first time last October." I sat up higher in my seat, not wanting to miss any of the fascinating scenery unfolding around us. "One of the main reasons they decided to build the tunnel? Besides the safety issue, I mean. They wanted to re-construct Cumberland Gap to the way it was when pioneers used it. The goal is for visitors to experience the Gap like it was in the late 1700's, so they're letting the topography and vegetation revert to what it used to be. There's something right about that, you know?"

"Interesting, and yes, I agree. So the tunnel is in a different location than the Gap?"

"Yes."

"Then we should go up to the Gap sometime. Explore a bit, eh?"

We entered the tunnel, and I pointed out the special lighting, how it allows drivers to adjust to the light inside. I explained that the nearly mile-long tunnel was difficult to build because they bored through so many differing types of rock. All too soon we were on the other side, but then looking down into the valley offered a magnificent view of the town below.

We grew silent as we drove the winding, narrow County Road 63. Moppit and I scanned the view outside the passenger window together. Well, as best we could, considering Moppit's wet nose meant a considerable portion of the window was smeared with her specialized goo. I had just begun scrubbing it with a dampened wipe when we rounded a bend. Just up ahead lay Collinsville.

I took a deep breath, eyes closed, and then slowly opened them. First impressions? It seemed disappointingly ordinary.

Uncle Oliver pulled over to the side of the road and turned off the car. We both silently studied the town a bit before he offered, "Not much to look at, is it?" Immediately apologetic, he clarified, "I mean, it's a town. A southern town, to be specific. Looks like it's got homes and banks and churches. Schools and parks. And stores." He shrugged his shoulders. "Don't know exactly what I was expecting, but what I mean to say is, it's rather ordinary as small towns go. And therefore, maybe not so intimidating?" He reached over to pat my arm again.

I nodded. "That's pretty much what I was thinking too." I pulled my arms against my chest, tucking my hands around the backs of my arms. "I guess I thought it would feel more, what? Strangely familiar, somehow? Maybe I'd have an intuition of some sort, I suppose. Like the town was calling out to me or something." Making a *pfww!* sound, I mumbled, "Silly, huh?"

"Not at all. You have much at stake here, darling girl. Much indeed." Starting up the car, he turned to me. "Let's get at it, shall we? Whatever is out there,"—Oliver waived one hand towards the scene below us—"we'll meet head on, together. You ready?"

"As I'll ever be." I wasn't about to admit it, but I was ever so glad Uncle Ollie was with me. Facing this alone? *Not possible.*

A beat-up truck pulled over beside us. I noted rifles in the rear window, two large tongues-hanging-out-slobbering dogs in the back, and the friendly eyes and smile of the driver as he leaned towards us and shouted out the open passenger window, "Y'all lost?"

Oliver returned his smile, saying, "Actually, we're headed to the Collinsville Motel. We'd be most appreciative if you could tell us how to get there."

"The mo-tel?" (Emphasis on the first syllable.) "I'm headin' right past. Foller me."

The two dogs in back—hunting dogs, no doubt—had been pacing back and forth, climbing up onto the wheel covers until they got a whiff of Moppit. At that point, they began furiously barking, jumping all over each other in their frantic attempts to get at him. To his credit, Moppit boldly barked right back. Safely from Oliver's lap, that is.

Our helpful pick-up driver wore a baseball cap, and as he slowly made his way through town, he braked constantly. We watched the bill of that cap going from right to left, left to right, and back again as he obviously perused everything and everyone we passed.

"It doesn't appear he's much into looking where he's going," I pointed out. "Awfully busy checking out what everyone in Collinsville is up to."

Uncle Ollie chuckled. "I expect that's the way of small towns," he said. "It's more about the *going to* a place than the *getting there*, I'm guessing."

When we saw the motel on the left, Oliver honked a *thank you* and was about to turn in when the pick-up stopped right in the middle of the road. A hairy, freckled arm popped out of the driver's side window, motioning for us to come up beside him. Uncle Ollie hesitated a moment, checking for traffic, but finally shrugged his shoulders and did as the man asked. I put my window down, allowing the nearly suffocating humidity of the hot, sticky day in Collinsville to punch up against our cooled air. And then I looked up into the whiskered face and gap-toothed grin of our friendly guide.

"Fancy car, that." He opened his door a crack to spit a brown wad of juice onto the pavement. "Right there's the mo-tel. I'm Bobby Harris, by the way." He tipped his cap. "Y'all kin to anyone round here?"

Simultaneously, Uncle Ollie and I both pretty much shouted, "*No*."

Now *that* was subtle. We exchanged chagrined looks and Bobby's eyebrows shot up. Hoping to cover our overplayed hand, I smiled at him, sweetly.

"Well, 'spect I'll be seein' you. Collinsville ain't like them big cities."

Gingerly, I reached out my hand to him and he grasped it in a firm handshake. "Thank you for your help. If everyone in Collinsville is this kind, we'll have a wonderful time."

"Oh, I 'spect so. Folks tend to hep folks round these parts."

I waved at him as he drove off, the bill of his hat still pointed in our direction.

"He was awfully kind, but it's a wonder that man doesn't have frequent accidents for how little he watches the road," Uncle Ollie mused.

"Didn't you notice his truck? Had at least one dent in every panel."

The Collinsville Motel was nothing fancy, but it was adequate and clean. After we'd settled in, freshened up and got Moppit fed and situated, we set out in search of the restaurant the manager heartily recommended: A Byrd in the Hand. I know, I know. Intentionally cute play-on-words restaurant names all but guarantee lousy food. (*Eats* being an exception to that rule.) But the manager was insistent Byrd's had "the best home-cooked food in the whole blessed county, includin' all yer fancy places up by the Gap. They ain't got nothin' on Mama Byrd's cookin'. And that's the gall-durn truth of it."

As we walked the two blocks to the restaurant, I looked up at Uncle Ollie and repeated, "Gall-durn?"

"No idea. But I kinda like the sound of it. Just might grow on me."

We'd just started across A Byrd in the Hand's parking lot when Guy prodded me again.

-Jules, where *are* you? What're you up to? I know you're—

-I'm with Oliver, and we're going to eat dinner. Someplace new we've never tried before. But I promise—I'll check in later.

Uncle Ollie opened the door and I walked into a restaurant décor that could've come right out of *Beautiful Homes and Gardens*. Chintz curtains matched the tablecloths, which were covered with glass so they were pristine still, lacking any stains. There was also a vase of freshly cut flowers on every table, and the arrangement of the tables gave the atmosphere a cozy, homey feel. The floor was a glossy tile that highlighted the natural red brick walls, on which real oil and watercolor paintings—by local artists, I assumed—were tastefully hung. But the best part was the mixture of tantalizing aromas wafting from the kitchen.

"Do I smell freshly baked biscuits?" Oliver asked.

"So maybe the manager wasn't exaggerating."

"Gall-durn," Uncle Ollie said, under his breath.

I was swallowing back a chuckle when a tall, trim, and decidedly interesting (as in *good* interesting) twenty-something host, menus in hand, slowly made his way to us from across the room. He greeted several other diners, calling out "Hey, Phillip!"

to one and allowing his hand to skim along the shoulders of an elderly woman—just before he leaned down and planted a kiss on her cheek. "Evenin', Miss Millie. Always a pleasure to see you." She shook her head, waving him off and chuckling. His height was such that, after nodding his head in greeting to us, he looked Oliver right in the eyes and asked, "A table for two, I assume? Right this way."

He had that southern twang to his speech, but it was refined; I'm betting he'd been to college, and up north somewhere. Broad shouldered, a straight nose and firm chin, jet-black eyes and long lashes, full head of short, dark brown hair with an obvious cowlick in front where he'd attempted a part. But it was the way he spoke and carried himself that made him attractive rather than the sum of his features: I sensed immediately he was comfortable in his skin, at ease with himself.

"Darling girl, he's asked if you'd like water?"

I immediately covered my mouth, fully expecting a hiccup. Fortunately, my quick reaction must've headed it off, but not so the ensuing blush. Though a dark-complexioned person like me doesn't redden as bright as those with fair skin, I could feel a flush coming on in a way that would still produce a noticeable glow. "Um, sorry. Yes, please," I mumbled.

"Anything else?"

"Yes, sure, but I need to look over the menu to—"

The server smiled at me, and the effect was much like Uncle Ollie's: It transformed his features instantly from man to boy. "Sorry. I meant anything else to drink?"

Can you blush on top of a blush? If it's possible, well, I did, and gangbusters. "Soda? What kinds do you have?"

"Oh, you mean Coke. We have Co-Cola, 7-Up, Orange, Root Beer. Some're diet. Hmmm. I think there's a couple Crème Sodas in the back too."

He looked at me expectantly, a puzzled expression passing over his face. And since I couldn't figure out what exactly he'd just conveyed, I blurted out the first thing that came to mind. "Coke, diet. Please."

"One Co-Cola." His gaze remained on mine just a beat longer than normal before shifting to Uncle Ollie. "And you, sir?"

"I'd love some coffee. Regular."

"Comin' right up. Any other questions?" He glanced quickly at both of us before offering, "Besides what's on the menu, we have one special tonight: stuffed peppers. They're fresh from the local Massengill farm, and guaranteed delicious."

I watched him walk back to the kitchen—he looked back at us, the perplexed look still there—before Uncle Ollie practically pounced on me. "What's the matter with you?" He had that grin thing going again.

"I couldn't figure out what he was asking. What's the deal with Coke and Co-Cola?"

"You didn't know everyone down here says *Coke* instead of *soda*?"

I shook my head, distracted by yet another young man coming out of the kitchen. If the first guy had addled me, this one had my full attention. They had to be brothers, they were so alike, but what the first one lacked in any way, this guy possessed in model-level perfection (firm *and* square jaw, no noticeable cowlicks in that glorious head of hair, and a smile that would light up a room). Suddenly my perspective of *Beautiful Homes and Gardens* switched to *GQ*, with this guy on the cover. He was that perfect.

"Good evening. I'm Brent, and I'll be servin' you all tonight."

Uncle Ollie pointedly looked towards the kitchen. "What happened to the other guy?" Leave it to my uncle to be subtle.

"Actually, E.A. generally works in the back. Or sometimes at the register." Brent cleared his throat. "My brother didn't realize I was here."

"Well, I thought he was doing a swell job."

Brent looked over at me, eyebrows raised, teasing grin forming; I gave him a slight smile in return and an even slighter shoulder shrug. *Did that convey sophisticated nonchalance?* I asked myself.

-Jules, where *are* you? Why am I sensing something strange going on?

-Told you, we're at a new restaurant that appears to be amazing. Gotta run, but we'll talk, I promise. *Later,* k?

Glancing up at Brent, I noticed he was watching me pretty closely—appraising, possibly?—eyebrows still raised. "Sorry. Um, I'd like the special, please."

Oliver handed over both our menus. "Make that two. Coffee coming for me?"

"Yes, sir. Brewin' a fresh pot as we speak."

Oliver rubbed his hands together. "Wonderful."

I watched Brent go towards the kitchen, glancing back at me once with a pensive look on his face still. When I knew we were clearly out of eyesight, I turned to drill Uncle Ollie. "So what's with *you*?"

"Beg pardon?"

"Why were you acting so snippy with Brent?"

But he merely gave me a look of total innocence and brushed me off, commenting on the creativity of the menu offerings from local sources. Seemed like only a few moments before Brent was pushing his way out of the hinged doors to the kitchen, heading our way with my Coke, a mug and a carafe of coffee. He served us with a flourish. "Mama's special brew, a concoction of select coffee beans. Have a sip and see if it's not the best coffee ever."

"Hmph," was all Oliver uttered before he blew into the mug and then ventured a taste. His eyebrows shot up and he took a bigger sip. "That *is* good coffee. You said your mother made it? She's the chef here, Mama Byrd?"

Brent nodded. "Myra Byrd," he offered, and held out an arm to motion around the entire room. "The three of us run this place. And I don't mind tellin' you, it's known round the whole county for the best cooking, plus the whole Cumberland area of Virginia, Kentucky, and Tennessee combined." Brent looked from me to Uncle Ollie and then back to me again. "Pretty clear you're visiting. Anything else I can tell you 'bout Collinsville you might be wantin' to know?"

"Well, actually, you can. My uncle and I are here to do some family tree research. I think we'll find resources here in town, no problem. But what about churches outside of town?" I hesitated, and then added, "Any chance some of them might have records we could look at? And any old cemeteries associated with those churches?"

Brent's eyes narrowed. "You all aren't some of those strange ghost hunting folks, are you?"

Oliver nearly choked on his coffee and I smiled. "No, just a couple of curious family members, researching my wife's ancestors," Uncle Ollie explained.

"Oh. You got kin from here, then?"

I started to elaborate when we heard a loud "*Psssst!*" coming from the door to the kitchen.

"Sounds like your dinner's about ready." Brent refilled Uncle Ollie's coffee mug again and as he walked away, threw back at us, along with an exaggerated wink, "Right formal 'round here, eh?"

I caught only a few words in the brothers' terse exchange—"flirting, other customers, work to do"—before the brother who seated us pulled Brent into the kitchen. Uncle Ollie and I met each other's eyes with the unspoken message,

"*Interesting—to be discussed later!*" We waited only a few minutes before Brent appeared again, bringing our meals, placing them before us with a flourish. Just looking at our plates was a culinary delight: Huge stuffed peppers overflowed with a delicious-looking filling, mashed potatoes oozed with dollops of butter on top, fresh green beans tantalized with bits of bacon, and a basket of those wonderful biscuits beckoned.

"Need anything else?" Brent asked.

We shook our heads, eyes wide. Oliver offered one of his shortest prayers ever and, honestly, we dug in like we hadn't eaten for days.

Brent came back to ask if everything tasted all right and then plunged into telling us where the six (*six? In this small town?*) churches were: two different kinds of Baptist, a Church of Christ, Methodist, Assemblies of God and one unaffiliated. Three had no cemeteries associated with them, and the independent congregation was only twenty-some years old, so Brent doubted it would be any help to us. Somewhere in all that explaining, Brent pulled out a chair and joined us at the table. Uncle Ollie gave me the briefest glance; even if he hadn't, I understood by the slight stiffening of his spine that he wasn't entirely pleased.

As for me? I have to admit that the attention of a man that good looking was terribly flattering. And a check in the plus column for the town of Collinsville. It was looking considerably more interesting, in my opinion.

"The oldest cemetery in this county is a ways outta town," Brent said, pointing in its direction, I assumed.

"Any chance there's a church there too?"

"No, sorry. Burned down decades ago—and all the church records with it. Still interested in checking out the cemetery?"

I hesitated, wondering how overgrown it might prove to be. "Might be worth a look."

"It's out Possum Ridge. Can be tricky to find, though, so I'd be glad to take you."

Oliver wiped his mouth with a napkin—the only thing that saved me, his having the good manners to do that—for he was surely about to decline the offer when I jumped in. "That would be incredibly helpful. Are you sure you have time?" The possibility of mosquitos, spiders, and even snakes were quickly dismissed at the idea of Brent's company.

Uncle Oliver stared at me with surprise. "I thought you weren't any too anxious to explore cemeteries. And besides, I imagine Brent is much too busy with his responsibilities here at the restaurant."

"Oh, it's no problem, really. E.A. can cover for me, and Kate's s'posed to work the next couple days too."

"Kate? Is she your sister?" *Did my controlled rise in inflection sound indifferent enough?*

"Oh no, no relation. We hired her a couple months ago since business picked up. Mama will—and speakin' of her, here she comes now."

A slightly plump, pretty woman came out of the kitchen, wiping her hands on her starched white apron and calling greetings to others as she worked her way towards our table. Uncle Ollie remembered his good manners and stood as she approached.

"Oh, please sit, sit! I just come to welcome you all to Collinsville. I hear you're new to town, and I always make an effort to meet first-time visitors." Smiling broadly, she put her hand in Oliver's outstretched one and then reached for mine. "We hear tell ever so often people come to Collinsville just to eat at Byrd in the Hand. Sounds like you all have other business to be tendin' to, but I hope y'all will come visit us again." Her hair had obviously once been black, but it was salt and pepper now, and both sons had inherited her sparkling, jet black eyes. "I'm hopin' y'all found everthin' to suit you?"

"Mrs. Byrd—"

"Call me Mama Byrd. Everone does. And y'all are?"

"Oliver. And this is my niece, Julia. I must say, Mrs.—er, Mama Byrd," Oliver corrected, granting her one of his widest smiles, "that was one of the finest meals I have *ever* had the pleasure to consume. In my entire life."

"Oh, land." She was smiling and blushing like a young girl. "Pleasures *me* to make people happy."

"We will most definitely be back. Isn't that right, Julia?"

"Absolutely. It was delicious, Mama Byrd."

Flustered still, she was a flurry of movement, checking the tie of her apron, patting her hair which was pulled up in a neat bun. "Well, I must be gettin' back to my kitchen. E.A. tends to enjoy addin' spices to whatever's simmerin' if I don't keep a close eye on him."

"Thank you again," Oliver said, and Mama Byrd bowed her head just slightly before making her way back to the kitchen.

"Mama always has a time keepin' an eye out for E.A., I'm sorry to say. But that's neither here nor there. So tell me. Where you from? You midwesterners, I'm guessing?" Brent asked. "More coffee, sir?" Glancing towards me, he stared intently into my eyes. "Can I fetch you another co-cola?"

I shook my head *no*, but Uncle Ollie motioned for a refill. "Yes, please, and the midwest it is, not far from Chicago," he offered.

I was about to say more when Oliver nudged me under the table with his shoe, right on the shin. He had on expensive walking shoes too, the kind with dense, lethal rubber soles. I started in surprise—fortunately Brent missed the entire interaction as he'd been concentrating on re-filling Uncle Ollie's cup—and I gave him a *What on earth was that about?* look. He responded with wide eyes and the slightest shake of his head.

Somehow the two men settled onto the subject of fishing, where the best fishing was around here and the proper types of bait to catch whatever. I wasn't the slightest bit interested, so I sent out a quick call to Guy.

-You there?

-A bit busy myself at the moment.

-I have a confession, Guy.

I took a breath. It was never easy to plunge into subjects we strongly disagreed on. Guy was like a spare conscience, my second self through which I viewed so much of life. Whenever we were divided over an issue, I felt a near-strangling inner turmoil. He was most definitely going to be upset with me.

-I decided to do it, Guy. I'm looking for my roots. Searching for *me*.

-You what? Where are you, Jules?

-In Tennessee. In Collinsville, where it all began. Well, as much as I know at this point.

Silence. I knew he'd be angry. But I instantly felt sick to my stomach with worry—worry he'd shut me out in protest, he was so irate. I didn't think I could bear that. Not now.

-Aren't you going to say anything? I really need you to help me through this, please. Guy?

"Brent! *Brent!*" Suddenly present as if by magic, E.A. must've sprinted back to our table. And Brent wasn't actively responding to E.A.'s voice, he was staring so intently at me.

"Mama needs you in the kitchen," E.A. stated emphatically, in a tone that had the familiar ring of a bossy big brother attempting to browbeat the younger. I noted a silent exchange of hostile glares between the brothers, and then, abruptly, *both* turned to look at *me*. I glanced from one to the other, feeling puzzled and yet flattered by their attention. Brent's pupils were dilated, his lips slightly parted, head tilting towards me with unfeigned interest. An interest that I most likely telegraphed right back.

E.A., however, continued to stare openly at me with narrowed pupils, pushed down brows and a distinct downturn at the corners of his mouth. Clearly, he wasn't pleased with Brent and his overflowing displeasure spilled over onto me as his eyes took in (and found wanting?) every inch of me. I had little patience with someone whose undisciplined feelings splash and burn like coffee from a too-full cup in a moving car. *So be it*, I thought to myself. I set my jaw, narrowed my eyes, and stared right back. Gauntlet thrown. Two could play this game.

A sideways glance at Uncle Ollie showed he'd been oblivious to the entire exchange between the three of us. Give my uncle an honest-to-goodness homemade meal and his attention was fully held captive: he was totally absorbed in buttering and devouring yet another biscuit.

Men, I thought to myself. *The whole lot of them: unbelievable.*

Finally, Brent broke the stalemate. "I will defer to my younger brother, though it pains me to do so. Julia, unfortunately I have business to attend to tomorrow. Does Wednesday work to explore the church property?"

I nodded, finding it hard to speak under the continued glare from E.A. Oliver, however, was shaking his head, apparently ready to decline Brent's invitation when I suddenly found my voice. "We could just take a quick look, I suppose. No harm in that, right Uncle Ollie?"

He gave me yet another furrowed-eyebrows look but merely shrugged his shoulders, his mouth still stuffed with biscuit.

"Just come on over to the restaurant when you're ready, okay? Sometime late morning?"

"Sounds good."

Brent gave E.A. one more dramatic look—pasting on a smile that clearly was for my benefit alone—and strode towards the kitchen. I watched him go, noting the strength in the stride of his legs. *Bet he's a runner*, I thought to myself.

E.A. cleared his throat, asking, "Anything else I can get for you? Pecan pie? Red velvet cake? Mama's desserts are every bit as good as her entrees."

His voice sounded thin, and he caught Uncle Ollie's eyes, barely glancing in my direction. *What on earth? This man has the emotional maturity of a middle schooler!* I silently seethed.

"I believe you, son, but I'll have to pass. I'm way too full for another bite. How about you, Julia?"

Suddenly, I couldn't wait to get out of there. "No, thank you. Next time, maybe. Shall we split the bill, Uncle?"

Oliver scoffed. "Nonsense, darlin' girl. Want this gentleman to think we northerners don't know how to treat a lady?" He winked at E.A. "The bill, please?"

E.A. waved him off, however, emphatically stating, "No, no. This one's on the house. Just our small way of welcoming you all to Collinsville." Oliver argued, but E.A. was insistent. "Just come back again—that's the best way to thank us. That an' let others know about us. We'll let you pay the next time, I promise you." Crossing arms over his chest, E.A. suddenly fixed his penetrating stare on me again. Reflexively, I moved my chair back away from him. "About this proposed trip to the church grounds. You do understand it's overgrown and untamed. There will be all sorts of…shall we say, extremely *nasty* creatures out there? Everything from mosquitos and ticks to copperheads and rattlers?"

I met his stare, connecting for only a moment before we looked away, both of us sensing the threat of an embarrassing social *faux pas* of some sort.

Searching out the window for anything to scrutinize rather than meet E.A.'s gaze again, I asked, "Are you trying to scare me, E.A.? Because I would think—I would hope—that your brother wouldn't think of putting my uncle or me in any real danger."

E.A. hesitated and Uncle Ollie took the opportunity to step into the awkward silence. "No one's risking life and limb for an ancestry search. *No one.* And now that's settled, great to meet you, E.A." Uncle Ollie gave him a firm handshake and offered, "Good night to you, and our most sincere thanks to you, your brother and your delightful mother. We will most definitely be back."

Uncle Oliver took my elbow, steering me towards the door and out into the still, close night. In my opinion, it was up for debate whether it was stickier outside—or in. "Whew. Not a hint of a breeze out here. You suppose it's like this all summer?" I asked.

"No, of course not," he deadpanned. "It gets worse."

I chuckled and casually slipped my arm through his. We'd only walked a few steps in companionable silence when I noted a rhythmic chorus chirping in the background. "What's that sound serenading us?"

"Tree frogs. Their singing will either lull you to sleep or keep you awake. It depends on your frame of mind."

We settled into a leisurely stroll back to the motel—probably mostly because we were both so full—but that phrase jogged my memory. "Speaking of frame of mind. Why did you kick me under the table?"

"Oh, sorry. Was I a little overzealous in my efforts?"

"You think?"

"Our agreed-upon story, remember?" He pulled me in closer. "Notice I didn't give our last name?"

"Uncle Ollie, this is silly. Those people were wonderfully kind and have volunteered to help us. How could you possibly suspect them of anything even remotely sinister?" I motioned to the buildings around us. "Take a look, will you? Talk about small town America. I can't believe that wonderful family—well, besides the obvious competition between the two brothers, and the fact that Brent exceeds E.A. in every way so that E.A.'s absolutely green with envy—"

"Looked to me like he was simply demanding equal time."

"What? You mean—"

"They were competing for your attention. Trust me; it's what brothers do, Julia. Compete."

"Brent? Forget that theory—he's way beyond my strata. Can't believe he wants to take me anywhere. And as for E.A. Well, I don't think I want his attention."

"Whatever. Let's see what we can find out tomorrow and go from there. In relation to you driving around with Brent on Wednesday, that is. Not sure I like that idea at all."

"Not sure you get to weigh in on that decision." The lights of the motel's parking lot cast Uncle Ollie's face into shadows. I squinted up at him, attempting to discover his mood. "Are you going all protective on me again? Like I can't watch out for myself with a *guy*? Honestly, Uncle Ollie. Wouldn't be my first rodeo, you know."

"Got your key?" He waited patiently as I fumbled around in my purse, finally remembering to sheepishly fish the key out of my jeans pocket. As Oliver opened the door for me, he said, "Julia, I came along for two reasons: To keep my pledge to your father"—I felt a twinge of pain at the mention of him—"and to watch over you on this trip because I'm your first line of defense and back up. Should those be needed." He stuck his head in, giving my room a quick perusal. "This may not be your first rodeo, darlin' girl. But it happens to be *my* cowgirl this particular fella's after. And I, for one, am not allowing him to rope you into anything even slightly suspect."

I laughed out loud as I planted a kiss on his cheek. "You are too much, Uncle Ollie."

After taking Moppit out to accomplish her business, he instructed, "Make sure your door's locked and chained. You need anything, anything at all—don't you dare set foot out of this room—you just give me a call or knock on our shared door, okay?"

"I promise you, I'm heading right to bed, I'm so worn out. You've got to be absolutely exhausted too."

"I am at that. Good night, Julia. Let me know once you're up in the morning, will you?"

"Depending on how early I wake, I might go for a quick run. Care to join me?" I challenged, knowing this was one time he wouldn't offer to come along.

"No, I think not. Wouldn't want to make you look bad."

I laughed again, stretching up onto my toes so that I could plant another kiss on his cheek. "Good night, Uncle Ollie." And then I shut the door and used the chain lock, as instructed.

Guy was there in a heartbeat.

-What do you think you're doing?

The fury in his voice was unmistakable. I plopped onto the bed in bewilderment, my feeble and subconscious attempt to diffuse his anger?

-Guy, I had to come here. I have to *know*. Please understand. You said you did, remember?

-Jules, I said I'd sanction your search right up until you put yourself in danger. And I sense it—danger's all around you. You should never have taken the risk.

-Oh please, such drama. Guy, I'm simply not that important to anyone. This is ludicrous! Both you and Uncle Ollie are over-reacting. And that reminds me. Uncle Ollie's here with me, okay? And believe me, he is bound and determined to keep me safe. He's like a veritable guard dog or something. Teeth bared, straining at his leash, protecting his territory. There's this really intriguing guy—Brent's his name—and he—

-Frankly, I don't want to hear it.

So what's the attitude about? I wondered. I mean, we're like brother and sister that way, having good laughs about the worst date ever. Or serious discussions about what traits we're looking for in a future spouse. The cynicism could be off the charts sometimes. So why this, now?

-Okay, Guy. So now's not the time. I'm way too tired to argue. And though I have no idea what time zone you're in, you're obviously worn out too. Cranky, irritable—*I was revving up with an attitude of my own at this point*—need-a-good-night's-sleep tired. How 'bout tomorrow we try to discuss this as adults, agreed?

He took a breath. I knew he was tense, could picture him rubbing the base of his neck.

-Jules, I lose it a bit when I'm worried about you, and I'm sorry for coming across—

-Like a total jerk?

-I was trying to apologize, k? Please, just promise me this: You'll be cautious with everyone there. And I mean *everyone*. Promise?

-Promise. Won't trust the sweet, engaging guy working the front desk, the one who needs to stand on a stool so he can see over the counter. Not Mama Byrd either—she's the adorable and sweet chef at the wonderful A Byrd in the Hand restaurant, the one everyone calls *Mama*. Won't trust her for a millisecond, she appears so threatening. And definitely not her two sons. Not the one who's a friendly, personable dreamboat and certainly not the other. Can't figure out what's up with him. But he appears to be a green with envy, wanna-be on the same level as my sibling kind of guy.

-How could you possibly know all that from one meal there?

Of all the gripes or questions I could've predicted he'd come up with, I never saw that one coming. I shook my head in frustration.

-Guy, we're arguing in circles. I'm going to bed. I love you, but you're not even remotely rational tonight. Or nice. So good night.

-Jules, I'm not done yet.

-Oh yes, you are.

And just like hitting the button on a remote for the television, I clicked him off. Picture, sound, vanished. I'd hear about it the next time we talked, but hey. We were getting nowhere with that discussion.

There was one more conversation I needed to have that night. I didn't want to, and I put it off until I lay my head on the pillow. Even then I considered waiting until morning. Took a deep breath, closed my eyes, and plunged in.

Okay, God. So I'm here. In Tennessee. I made a leap of faith to come here, rather unlike me, to be sure. But unfortunately, that courage didn't make my other feelings evaporate. I'm still scared. Tense. Anxious. And insecure—very much so. It's shadowing me, Lord, hovering over everything. With Mom and now Dad both gone, Melissa across the country, and as for Uncle Ollie...he's so dear. But he can't be everything to me, or everywhere. How do I be sensibly cautious—and at the same time, be ready and willing to take the next leap of faith? How do those fit together in a life as messy as mine is?

About what Uncle Ollie says too—that Dad didn't leave a space for me to mourn Mom? Of course I mourned Mom! Growing up, Dad's emotions could dominate at any time. They'd burst over us, drawing us into a vortex. We didn't live on level ground, but that was our routine. It was what I knew. So when Mom's death brought more of the same, why would I expect otherwise? I found my space. We did okay. It's just the way we functioned.

God, I think Uncle Ollie wants me to have some sort of grandiose illuminating experience. Or a purging of repressed emotions. Like there's this bundle of stuff inside me that...that I'm not fully recognizing? If there is some truth to what Uncle Ollie says...well then God, I need your help to see that. What I need is...you.

I took a deep breath, pausing a moment to understand what I specifically needed—right now—from my God. *No matter what happens, Lord, most of all, I need to feel you beside me. Because I'm afraid—afraid to find out who and what I really am. You know everything, so you already know. Nothing's a surprise to you.* I feel my throat tighten, and I swallow back the threatening emotions. *I'm so scared of what's out there. What I'll find. Lord, help me. Please.*

I watched Moppit do her usual three circles before she settled down for the night and then I mimicked her: I flopped around before settling onto a somewhat comfortable spot. Amazingly, sleep came quickly, but not terribly deep because I heard those annoying mice again. My apartment is an older building, so mice find their way in. They scratch around in the ceiling above my bedroom, making their nests up there. I sigh, disgusted by the thought, telling myself to remember to call the exterminator. I chuckle at my cleverness, that I remembered to put it in the positive! And then I bolted up-right.

I'm not in my apartment, I suddenly realize, scanning the room, taking in the unfamiliar shadowed outlines of television, dresser, the digital clock on the nightstand next to me. 2:14 a.m. *Did I dream the scratching sound? Or is it real?*

I listened intently until—there it was again. The noise I heard in my dream is *real*. Definitely not mice, but instead, I can hear the door handle being jiggled back and forth. Someone attempting to get in?

"Who's there?" I shout, not thinking before my impulsive outburst. "You're at the wrong room!" I'm fully awake now. And put out. *How dare some drunken idiot wake me in the middle of the night like this?*

I reached for the lamp on the nightstand, fumbling until I find the knob. The light is a rude jolt to my eyes and I shield them a moment, blinking, before I hunt for my robe at the bottom of the bed. And now whatever drunk is out there stops twisting the handle—and begins pounding on my door instead. *The nerve!*

"Just a minute!" I yell. "Honestly, this is—"

"Julia! It's Uncle Ollie. Are you all right? Please open the door, Julia."

I peeked through the tiny hole—just to be sure, though I'd know that voice anywhere—undid the lock and chain to find Uncle Ollie. In his pajamas, bare-footed, hair tousled, glasses askew on his nose, reaching out to pull me into a crushing hug.

THE GRAVESTONES' SECRETS

3 of June, 1588

My Descendants,

Every day brings new dangers upon us, and new occasions to fear for our very lives. Were it not for Chief Manteo, we would surely give in to our despair!

Because of Catherine's and my mind talking, I have heard the rumors of the Spanish Armada's plans to attack England. No one here would believe this to be true, so I must hide my growing worries for Governor White's return to us even as Mistress Eleanor speaks of her father's Promise to come back to us with victuals and supplies, such as needed to sustain us here. All members of our colony believe in her Hope save me, Mauro, and I must always conceal my aggrievement from all.

It is thus immeasurable irony that our mind talking brings me such worry and yet such joy at the very same. For my Beloved's voice brings me a wealth of Hope! My own father Manuel taught me the Path of Hope as he lived a life of joy despite the untold hardships of being separated from his Mother at birth. There are those who would call him cursed for his sixth finger on the one hand, inherited from his Mother, AB. Yet, undaunted, he not only overcame such as would make most men cower, but my father persevered, and even prospered. I lay claim to his Courage and Boldness rather than any curse that some would say passed by blood to me, his son Mauro. I have not the sixth finger, but do possess his Faith in God Alone and our God's Mighty Power!

And I have my Catherine, the one who is the delight of my life. No curse could ever exist in the Joy we alone know in one another!

With Hope,
Mauro

CHAPTER FIVE

Considering how much shorter I am than Uncle Ollie, and how a hug from him, therefore, means my face gets mashed against his torso—well, it's not the most dignified position to be in. This hug was also unusually extended, demonstrating his near panic, to my amazement. He kept me captive until finally he pushed me away, though he still held my shoulders in a grip much like a vice.

"Julia. I can't tell you how—well enough of that. Did you get a good look at him?"

I frowned. Absentmindedly tightened the belt on my robe. "Who?"

"*Who*? The man you were yelling at. You should've been able to see him through the peep hole."

"Oh. I didn't get there in time to see, but I assumed he was just some harmless drunk. He obviously thought—"

"Julia, darling. Let's discuss this from *inside* your locked door." He glanced around the parking lot, and putting a hand at my back, gently guided me back into my room. "Tell me *exactly* what happened."

"I was dreaming about mice—there's mice in the attic above my apartment that make these scratching noises in the night. And then I came awake enough to realize I wasn't home, so it couldn't have been mice!" I looked up at the ceiling and shadowy corners of the room, fighting the sudden urge to jump onto a piece of furniture. "You don't think?"

"No. Don't get distracted, darling girl. What happened next?"

"Well, I *thought* I heard someone fumbling with the lock." Suddenly I felt rather foolish. And irrational. "Explaining this out loud makes me think maybe…maybe the conspiracy theories have affected me more than I realized? Maybe there never was anyone at my door? 'Cause when I looked out the peep hole, there was no one there. Well, except *you*. Maybe I wasn't yet fully awake?"

Uncle Ollie sighed. "Good theory, but false. I heard something out here, and it sounded suspiciously like someone finagling with a lock. Namely, the lock on *your* door."

"But don't you think it likely he was—"

"A drunk mistaking this for his room? That's the theory we're going with."

"Well, certainly, nothing else makes sense."

He took a deep breath and shook his head. "I suppose you're right. The fact remains, I don't like it—sober or drunk, *no one* should be attempting to get into your room. So we're keeping our in-room doors open at night. I want to hear if you so much as squeak." He gifted me with one of his infectious grins, adding, "Or a mouse does. Sorry, couldn't resist that. He opened the outside door again and instructed, "Bolt and put the chain on this door behind me, immediately. Then I'm going around to open my adjoining door to your room."

Not until he'd checked the locks on my door and windows, harangued Moppit ("Why didn't you bark? What kind of watchdog are you, anyway?") *and* me ("I assure you, we'll report this to the manager in the morning"), and tucked me into bed did Uncle Ollie return to his room. Even after all the excitement, however, I slept soundly until a sliver of sun slipping through the curtains woke me. Lying still, I waited for my companion: The sad weight of Dad's death, marking a new day. I sluggishly rolled over and squinted at the clock. The blurry numbers appeared to be eight, three and two.

Pushing myself up into a half-sitting position, I leaned forward to view Moppit's empty bed. "Moppit, where are you?"

"She's over here with me," came the disembodied voice from the next room. "I fed her, took her out. Now she's sitting here staring at me with those pleading eyes, insistent I give her a treat, evidently. Where've you put the dog biscuits, Julia?"

"What is it with you men? They're in her satchel, same place you found her food."

"Now see, there's the problem. You hid them."

By the time I'd climbed out of bed and put on my robe, Moppit was happily crunching away while Oliver appeared absorbed in the *Clairborne Chronicle*. I pulled the pages down so I could peer into his face. "Sorry I slept so late. I imagine it's way too hot by now to consider a run. Mind if I climb in the shower before we get some breakfast?"

"Go right ahead. But make it quick. The coffee provided in the room leaves much to be desired." He snapped the paper back into place. "Moppit's biscuits are looking better with each passing minute, too. I'm sorely tempted to dunk one into this pathetic coffee."

"Testy this morning, are we?"

"Lousy night's sleep will do it every time." He peered around the paper at me, frowning. "That. And *worry*."

"Your choice to do that number." I hummed "Don't Worry, Be Happy," but wasn't rewarded with another scowl for my efforts. *Maybe Uncle Ollie doesn't know that one?*

-Doesn't know what?

-Guy, honestly. You're eavesdropping.

-Have to. Probably the only way I'm going to figure out what all you're up to today. Which is what, by the way?
-Not telling. And I need to get into the shower.
-So go ahead.

I put my hands on my hips and stared into the mirror, frowning at my reflection but directing all my thoughts towards Guy.
-You know I can't do that. It's like you're with me. Go *away*.
-You know very well I can't see you.
-Guy!
-Okay. But I'm going to be back soon. Finding out where you're going and what—
-You do that, Sherlock.

Since A Byrd in the Hand wasn't open for breakfast, we drove around town a while, finally settling on a small restaurant that looked like it had possibilities: Its parking lot was bustling, and that seemed a positive sign. If the locals went there, it had to be good, we reasoned.

Once again people were friendly and helpful, and we exited about an hour later with full stomachs, a cup of steaming coffee to go for Uncle Ollie and directions to the hardware store. Uncle Ollie was being cryptic about "a couple things he needed" and the server who waited on us was insistent we visit there—whether or not we needed to actually purchase something.

"Mark my words. You'll not forget havin' been to the Collinsville Hardware Store," she quipped, head bobbing, a conspiratorial grin on her lips.

I was quizzing Uncle Ollie about what he was searching for when we walked in and stopped, staring. Just inside the door sat a rather large woman, her feet in a cardboard box (*Tennessee Tom's Tender Chicken* stamped on the outside), a heat lamp positioned so it was directly over her feet. She had a brightly colored quilt wrapped around her head and shoulders and yet, what was especially ironic? She stared at Oliver and me as though *we* were the strange ones. Her piercing gaze through bright blue eyes—though obviously well advanced in age, she had no sign of cataracts and appeared to see quite well—shifted from Uncle Ollie to me and back to Oliver again.

"I don't know y'all."

Uncle Ollie didn't miss a beat. "No, you wouldn't. My name's Oliver."

"I don't know no Oliver."

"Well, see, we're from a ways north of here."

She nodded, and narrowed her eyes. "Northerners. You aim to be civil? Or you like them that're in such a all-fired hurry they ain't got time to be civil?"

Oliver eased himself onto the chair next to her, granting her one of those famous smiles of his. We watched her weathered, heavily lined face morph in a heartbeat. All those wrinkles settled themselves into one engaging expression: A wide, partially toothless smile, molded and yet crinkly and soft at the same time. She was one of those carved granny apple faces come to life.

"I'm Miz Odell. Pleased to meet you, Oliver. And your daughter's name is?"

"This is my niece Julia."

She patted the empty chair on her other side and held out a wrinkled hand, surprisingly small and petite in comparison to the rest of her. I shook it, noting while I did so that her feet were also tiny. Tiny and *bare* under the light of the heat lamp. I'd tried not to be obvious in my curiosity, but my glance downward didn't go unnoticed.

"Circulation," she pretty much shouted, and I jumped. "Ain't what it used to be. This here lamp helps." She shifted a bit in her chair, pulling the quilt tighter around her shoulders. "Now, what is it you come for? My son'll be tickled to fetch it for you." Over her shoulder she yelled, "John Amos, where you got yourself off to? We got us some customers here."

From somewhere in back we heard, "Be there in a minute, Mama. Had us a delivery to unload."

"What's that?"

"He said he'd be with us in a minute, Mrs. Odell. Evidently a delivery truck dropped off some things out back," Uncle Ollie offered in explanation.

She reached out to pat Oliver on the arm. "Gives us some time then, don't it? Everbody what comes to Collinsville searchin' for somethin'. What is it you lookin' to find, and how can I hep you?"

"Well, I need a couple things from you, Mrs. Odell. First, I need ammunition for a Smith and Weston semi-automatic nine millimeter."

My mouth dropped open. Mrs. Odell, on the other hand, took it in stride, merely nodding her head. Clearly this was not an infrequent request.

"Work gloves—for both Julia and me. And lastly, I need some information."

"First two're easy enough. John Amos'll get them for you soon's he's finished. But I'm thinkin' information be in *my* depart-ment." Smiling broadly, she'd lovingly stretched out every vowel and lingered over each syllable. "What is it y'all's needin' to know?"

"Julia and I are doing ancestry research, Mrs. Odell. Where do you advise we look for that kind of information?"

She shook her head and frowned. "You'd think the courthouse. But it ain't goin' to be much hep, I'm sorry to say. Go 'head and ask them what might've made it through fire 'n flood, but it ain't much, I'm thinkin'."

Nodding in agreement, Oliver mused, "We read as much. Sounds like our research is going to be a bit of a challenge."

"You got that right."

"We were wondering if any local churches might provide some help, maybe have some records. And their cemeteries? Wondering if they might give us more of a *personal* connection to those roots too."

"The old Crotin Springs Church had it a cemetery. Church's long gone many a year now. But the ole cemetery's still there, though the undergrowth's bound to be a bother." She leaned closer to Oliver and offered, "Best get you a scythe. You'll have a dickens of a time findin' much in them weeds. But I s'pose it's worth a good look."

I didn't like the sound of heavy undergrowth, but made the mental decision to put off worrying about that until we actually saw the grounds. *Besides*, I told myself, *how reliable can someone be who sits with her feet in a box in the hardware store?* I had to bite my lip to keep from grinning.

"Crotin Springs sounds familiar," Uncle Ollie said. "Where is that?"

"Out Possum Ridge. John Amos can tell y'all how to get there. Might could save you a trip, though. What family is it you're wantin' to know 'bout?"

My first thought was Mrs. Odell appeared sharp enough to spot a lie a mile off. And though I didn't sense one smidgen of danger from this friendly, outspoken matriarch, I had no intention of making an enemy of her, either. We needed all the friends we could get in this town. I uttered one quick, silent prayer, and took a deep breath. "My aunt's family. Blevins is the name. Did you know any of them?" Mrs. Odell physically flinched. My eyes darted over to Oliver, wondering if he'd noticed, but he gave no indication that he had.

"Mrs. Odell, are you all right?" Oliver gently probed.

She sat up straighter, pulling the slipping quilt tight again. "Course I am. Just ain't thought on them poor folks in a while, that's all. Lucille was the last of 'em. When her and Jimmy was killed in the awfulest car crash Collinsville's ever—"

"Car crash? They were in an accident?" I attempted to keep my voice level and even, but doubt that I succeeded.

"Terrible thing it was. Happened only four year ago, nineteen and ninety-three, it was. The last day o' March, 'bout three o'clock in the afternoon. I recollect that day like yesterday. Car caught alight afore anyone could hep 'em out." She shook her head, sighing. "We all prayed Lucille and Jimmy was gone long afore…you know."

I'd been sitting forward in my chair, straining towards Mrs. Odell and whatever she could tell us. But now I sat back. *They're gone, and I only missed them by four years. I'm not going to meet them after all.* And then, *Am I sad? Or relieved?*

Uncle Ollie broke into the silence. "Any other Blevins here? Their parents? Aunts or uncles? Lucille's maiden name was Gibbons—that's the other ancestors we're tracking. Any Gibbons you know of?"

"Oh, I'm sure they's distant kin scattered round the county, Blevins 'specially. But funny thing 'bout both them two: Lucille and Jimmy was the onliest children from their families. Doesn't happen often round these parts, that's for sure, what with the big families we usually birth. That's one thing we Collinsville folks generally does good—have babies!" She chuckled before suddenly growing somber again. "Don't know as much about Jimmy's family, but I knew Lucille's well. Her sweet mama had the awfulest time birthin' babies. One after another was stillborn. Others weren't right, you know?" She shook her head. "I tried to help them young'uns. But they wasn't with us long, neither."

"How was that, Mrs. Odell?" Oliver asked. "Were you a midwife?"

The wrinkled face relaxed in her remembering, and she sighed with pleasure. "I was at that. Some said I was best in the county too. But Reba, poor soul. Wasn't nothin' any of us could do for her. Nor all them sweet babies." Mrs. Odell turned to look me in the eye. "All of 'em—Lucille and Jimmy, all their babies too—they's all buried in the cemetery here in town. It's next to the Baptist church, if you's interested." She looked away again, reminiscing, it appeared. Her voice changed back to a sing-song cadence again, "But that Reba, she had her a sunny sort o' disposition, in spite it all. Always grateful God give her and Israel the one and onliest—their Lucille. Some said them Gibbons was twice cursed. They's talk 'bout how many generations of Gibbons had 'em so few babies what survived. And then there was the other matter."

"Other matter?" I asked. Silently I cursed myself for blurting out the question before thinking, realizing I wasn't sure I wanted to know the answer.

"Hey, folks. Sorry to be so slow to help y'all." John Amos moved into our formerly intimate circle, wiping his hands on a rag and reaching out to take Oliver's in a firm handshake. When he turned to me, I could see the fine lines beginning to form in his face, fanning out from his mouth, framing his own twinkling bright blue eyes. In a few years, he would be the male version of the Odell carved apple. "What can I help you all with today?"

Uncle Oliver went off with him to find what he needed, but I stayed with Mrs. Odell. Partly because of my own remaining curiosity. But also because Mrs. Odell reached out to hold onto my arm, her grip surprisingly strong.

"Appears you's gettin' a two-fer-one today: Since Lucille was the onliest child, she inherited the Gibbons' homesite. It's just catty-wampus from the Crotin Springs Church and cemetery. If you find the one, you're likely to find the t'other. Might still be a few outbuildings around—all tumbling down, as you'd expect. But enough still there as you might want to take a look see. Recollect, though: You 'n your uncle mustn't wander too close to them woods, you hear?" She held up one finger to emphasize her warning. "That there's backcountry. And you daren't be messin' as folks get mighty pro-tec-tive. We hear tell of stills out that way. You understandin' what I'm tellin' you?"

I nodded. "Yes, mam. I do. Mrs. Odell, about Lucille and Jimmy Blevins. You talked about babies they lost. But did any of their children survive?"

She cleared her throat. "I wasn't midwifin' no longer by then, but Lucille had the very difficulties as her mama. The curse, you know. Sorry to tell you this, child, as I hate to dishearten your search." She patted my hand. "But Jimmy and Lucille didn't have no young'uns when they passed. That's what made it sad and bittersweet at the very same. They didn't leave nobody behind, no poor little orphans. But they didn't leave no legacy neither. One of the worst things can happen to a family, I'm thinking. No one to carry on your name? A sorry thing, that. Sure did set tongues to waggin' 'bout the curse again."

A couple moments passed before I realized my mouth was hanging open again. My thoughts went a bit fuzzy when I heard Mrs. Odell say Jimmy and Lucille didn't have any surviving children—and then *the curse*. She was looking at me like she was waiting for an answer, and I had no idea what she'd asked.

"Then again," she drawled, her eyes wide open, "They was *rumors*."

"Rumors? About what?"

"One of them babies what was said to be born lifeless, *wasn't*."

"Wasn't—?"

"Wasn't lifeless. But was spirited away. For *safety*."

We stared into each other's eyes for a few moments, and I got the eerie feeling we were both trying to read each other's minds. *If she only knew*, I thought to myself.

"But why wouldn't their baby be safe here?" I asked, breaking the silence.

Mrs. Odell shrugged her shoulders but then leaned in closer to me, whispering, "Melungeon blood. Blevins *and* Gibbons. Mystery always part 'n parcel with them Melungeons. Stories told 'bout them round here, plenty far-fetched ones too." She nodded her head, soberly. "You familiar with them Melungeons?"

Fortunately, I was saved by Oliver and John Amos' reappearance. Mrs. Odell fixed one puzzled stare on me and then evidently her Southern manners clicked in: She let my inability to respond go as John Amos graciously gave Oliver directions to the Crotin Springs Church cemetery. But Mrs. Odell wasn't quite done.

"They's one more thing I needs be tellin' you. Concerns Miz Esther."

"Miz Esther?"

"You never know what Esther Abel's goin' to say." Conspiratorially, she offered, "She's in the home, you know."

"The home?" Mrs. Odell just kept nodding at me like I'd catch on eventually. Which I didn't.

"Home's over to the Methodist church, run by them people. Don't much like to visit, but I do. Now 'n then."

John Amos and Oliver had finished talking, so I looked up at John for an explanation. "Is it a home for—"

"Them that's not quite right. If you get my meanin'," Mrs. Odell responded, nodding her head and folding hands in her lap.

"Oh, okay. And this Mrs. Abel's there. Is she senile?"

Mrs. Odell chuckled under her breath. "I s'pect you could say so. Been that way *many* a year, though." She shook her head, as if dispelling an unpleasant memory. "Some would say's due to her havin' the Sight."

"The Sight?"

"The gift of *seein'* things. Miz Esther used to live out that way by the Gibbons. Knew 'em right well. You might want to see iffen she recollects anything helpful."

Evidently Uncle Ollie and I were both immediately struck dumb, because rather than commenting on *that* fascinating bit of news, we merely thanked John Amos and Mrs. Odell profusely for their help, moving rather eagerly, I must admit, towards the door. We assured them we'd be back soon to visit and let them know how our search was progressing. When I glanced back to wave what I hoped would be perceived as a friendly goodbye, I saw Mrs. Odell staring after us with a look of—what was it? Concern? Worry? Or was there even a touch of fear and alarm written across that unforgettable face?

"Quite the character, eh?" Oliver asked, chuckling under his breath. "Was she helpful? Good. You can update me over lunch. And now's not the time to go into much detail, but let me just ask: How are you feeling in relation to the news about your biological parents? I can't imagine what you're feeling, Julia."

"Actually, I can't quite imagine it, either. Tragic how they died, but honestly, I think I'm somewhat relieved." I glanced up at him, feeling embarrassed. "Is that normal?"

"I don't think there's a 'normal' reaction to any of this, darling girl. Any highly unusual situation produces who-knows-what kinds of reactions. That's what I think!"

"You're the best at making excuses for me, Uncle Ollie. Hey, there's the library. How about if we stop in? Might be worth a look." My gaze roamed from the large sickle in Oliver's grasp to what I knew his sack contained. "Don't you think all that's a bit of overkill? Whatever, I think a quick trip to the car first is a must, don't you?"

"Oh. You're right. I would imagine these are somewhat discouraged in the library."

"You think? Looks like we've stepped right out of a teenage slasher movie. And by the way, you failed to mention you were *packing*. So did you bring Dad's gun? Or yours?"

"I packed underwear, but I didn't tell you about that either."

"Very funny. So what other things did you bring along that you failed to mention?"

"You really want the entire list? Let's see now…toothpaste, floss, razors, socks—"

The library looked to be a renovated double-wide, certainly not impressive by the standards of the Wisconsin libraries I frequented. But one glance showed it was often used (perfectly neat, rarely visited libraries were anathema to me; what good was that, I ask you?), lovingly cared for (even though it was literally stuffed with shelved books, I spied a cozy nook with two well-worn chairs and decent lighting for readers) and filled with one of my very favorite scents: old books. I assumed the collection wouldn't include rare or expensive copies, but that didn't matter. What I loved, pure and simple, were the stories within those covers.

Though we couldn't see anyone at the front desk, we could hear her, reshuffling noises coming from behind it. On the counter were several stacks of books, a mug of steaming coffee (Uncle Ollie, eyes closed, leaned in like an addict to smell the dark roast aroma) and a collection of bookmarks, announcements from local schools, and scattered pens, pencils and scraps of paper, obviously for jotting notes. I thought it looked *perfect*.

"Hello? Could you help us, please, mam?" Oliver asked, in the general direction of the source of the noise. "We're doing some ancestral research. I'd also like to know where you found this heavenly smelling coffee." He smiled knowingly at me and winked as we waited to meet our imagined librarian—the older, matronly, stern-faced one who was also most efficient.

"There's no *mam* here to help you," the still disembodied but decidedly male voice responded cynically. "But I can. If you'd like."

To our stunned looks, E.A. stood up to face us. He sported bed-head hair, an unshaved morning shadow and already, an attitude. So much for the place being *perfect*. The two of us locked stares, which Oliver either totally missed or chose to ignore.

"E.A. What a pleasure, again." The two men shook hands and I saw E.A. relax into Uncle Ollie's genuine friendliness. "Now I know why the coffee smells familiar. Is the restaurant open yet? I must have a cup of that."

E.A. leaned against the counter and began picking up books, glancing at titles, sorting them into piles. "Not till eleven, I'm afraid. But tell you what: If you knock on the back door, Mama'd never turn down anyone who asked for a cup."

Oliver shook his head. "Wouldn't think of pestering her. I'll stop by later, after opening. So you're the librarian, eh? I do like a man who appreciates books."

E.A. smiled, and I noted again how relaxed he was in his skin. If you ignored the uncombed hair and lack of a shave, he still looked athletic and good looking in a casual sort of way in his crisply ironed shirt and nice-fitting jeans. And then I realized what I was doing: Looking E.A. over from head to toe, even leaning forward to take in the fit of those jeans. *Why am I reduced to acting like an adolescent every time I'm around one of the Byrd brothers?* Fortunately, he and Oliver were so busy chatting that they both missed my inspection.

Uncle Ollie was explaining our interest in any local histories or journals, and that Mrs. Odell had told us where to locate the Crotin Springs church and cemetery. "Any chance you have a book on Collinsville's history and its inhabitants?"

"As a matter of fact, I do. Oliver, you grab this stack, and Julia, is it? You take this one, please. Follow me." He led us down a row of bookshelves to a cart nearly overflowing with other books waiting to be re-shelved. "I used to work here part-time, but since I've taken on keeping the books for the restaurant, I fill in only for emergencies. Miz Wells was feelin' bad this morning, so she called and asked if I'd come in for the day." He sighed, shaking his head at the overloaded cart. "Thought if I could get some of this done for her, it would...well, I'll be honest. Miz Wells has cancer, and that's the sad truth of it."

Oliver and I both offered our sympathies, and I queried, "Her prognosis?"

"Not good. We'll be lookin' to hire a new librarian too soon." He glanced around at the rows of books, love and appreciation evident in his gaze. "Miz Wells has been a major mentor in my life." He cleared his throat. Abruptly dropped his stack of books onto the cart, motioned for me to drop mine there too and then turned around. "*The History of Collinsville*. Right over here, if I'm not mistaken. Yup, here you go." He reached up to pull a small, battered paperback from the shelf. "Not much up-to-date. But I'm thinkin' you're not needing that, right? Ancestral history, you say?"

I pretended to be absorbed as I flipped through the pages, finding illustrations and photographs scattered throughout, many with the familiar Melungeon look.

"Yes, it's a hobby of mine," Oliver answered nonchalantly. "Trying to fill in some blanks from way back on my late wife's family tree."

We heard the door open and an older man's voice call out, "Miz Wells? You here?"

"If you'll excuse me, I need to see to Mr. Arnold." As E.A. walked towards the front desk, he threw over his shoulder, "Feel free to browse a while. You'll find we have a pretty decent collection for a small town."

I waited until E.A. and Mr. Arnold were chatting away so we wouldn't be overheard. "So how many people are there in this town?"

Oliver shrugged his shoulders. "No idea, but I'd venture a guess at no more than ten thousand or so."

"And out of those ten thousand people, it just had to be *that* guy who works here? Seriously?"

"Ah, there's a restroom. Keep out of trouble for a moment, will you, Julia? I'll be right back."

"I resent that—" But he merely waved me off with a smile in response. I flounced onto one of the comfortable old chairs and was skimming down the chapter titles when E.A. settled into the other chair. Stubbornly, I refused to look up and acknowledge his presence.

"You still goin' with my brother tomorrow?"

I turned a page. And then another, taking my sweet time. My own silent protest of his butting into what I considered none of his business. "Far as I know."

"My brother's not…how should I put this?"

I peered up at him, my mouth set in a firm, unrelentingly grim line.

"My brother's not known for being reliable. Sometimes he says he'll do something and then, well, he doesn't follow through. Or bother to show up."

"Funny. Brent pointed out that your mother has to keep an eye on *you*."

E.A. scoffed and protested, "That's ridiculous. But it is common knowledge around Collinsville that you can't rely on my brother."

"And your point is?"

"It'd be better if you'd wait a day or two and go out to Crotin Springs with me instead."

"Better for whom?" I bristled. "Certainly not for me considering how wonderfully *pleasant*"—I dramatically emphasized the word—"you are every time you're around me. So why would you want to?"

His body visibly stiffened, and the pupils of those flashing dark eyes dilated to pinprick-sized dots. "Actually, I didn't say I wanted to. I merely said I *would*."

I stood up in a huff, glancing towards the restroom door, impatient for Oliver. Unfortunately, he wasn't to be found yet, but I decided I was done with this conversation. "Well, then. There's certainly no reason to put yourself out on my account." My anger drove me to get out of there as fast as I could, so I turned and hurried towards the exit. I was pushing open the door when E.A. caught up with me, putting his hand over top mine. Snatching it away like I'd been seared by a hot iron, I stepped back so I could glare up at him. I shot him my very finest teacher's "*You Are in So Much Trouble*" look.

"Please. I'm sorry. I didn't mean any of that." He ran a hand through his hair, making it stand on end even more—if that were possible. "I'm not usually so, so perverse. Really. Why is it you seem to bring out the worst in me?"

I pulled myself up to emphasize every inch of my five-foot-two height. "Oh, so *I'm* to blame for your bad behavior? If that was an attempt at an apology, it was about the sorriest I've ever heard. Now, if you'll kindly get out of my way, I'd like to leave. Now."

"I swear you could start an argument in an empty house," E.A. just managed to spit out before he turned to see Oliver standing next to him.

"I take it things still aren't going so well between you two?" Oliver asked E.A.

Leave it to my uncle to point out the obvious.

—

I opted for a fast-food lunch since I knew Brent wouldn't be at their restaurant today. I also wasn't about to risk running into E.A. again, just in case the library was closed over lunchtime. We were nearly done eating before I was ready to talk about what happened. "I don't get him at all, Uncle Ollie."

"Who?"

"Like you don't know who I'm talking about. That boorish, egotistical, obnoxious—"

"Whoa. That's a bit harsh, isn't it?"

"So. You do admit to knowing I'm describing none other than E.A. And no, it's not too harsh at all. I swear he took a dislike to me the minute I walked into his restaurant." I distractedly played with the straw in my drink. "I bet he's prejudiced against all Northerners. That's his issue, bet you anything it is."

"Julia. Not likely, my dear. Could be you remind him of somebody. More likely—maybe he reminds you of someone. Someone *you* don't like? Could be that's why you provoke him."

I stared at him in disbelief. "I don't believe this. You never—you're taking *his* side."

"Darling, girl, if there are sides to be choosing, I am always and forever on your side. I'm just pointing out that he seems overly sensitive to your…what's the word I want?"

"Presence."

"No, no, not at all. If anything, like I pointed out once before…I would guess he's actually attracted to you, just like his brother Brent."

I choked on my pop. Or whatever it is they call it here. I coughed for a couple minutes while Oliver patted me on the back and continued to wax eloquent. He had a captive audience, so to speak.

"Julia, you can be clueless about your charms. How they affect men and their responses to them. You tend to miss clear warning signs too. Both of which appear to be tied up in your interactions with those brothers." Oliver drained the last of his coffee and then made a face, grumbling, "Horrendous coffee.

We're going to Byrd in the Hand tonight, so you'd best figure out a way to make peace with that situation."

"You'd sacrifice my peace of mind that easily. For a better cup of coffee. Or is it the biscuits?"

"Either, or both. In a heartbeat. You'll figure it out—figure *them* out. So what other information did you get from Mrs. Odell? You don't meet someone like that every day, eh?"

"Think you can change the subject that easily?"

"Absolutely. What else did she say?"

I shook my head, sighing, conceding defeat again. "That Jimmy and Lucille—honestly, I can't begin to get my mind around their being my biological parents, let alone say that out loud—she said they didn't have any surviving children. *None.*"

"Mrs. Odell actually said that."

"Sure did. No namesake left behind. No one to carry on their legacy. *Unless*…she said there were rumors that one child—just the one that survived—was *spirited away.* For the child's *safety.* That's exactly how she put it, Uncle Ollie." I stopped, feeling disoriented. Like falling asleep in a strange place and not recognizing where you are when you wake up.

Uncle Ollie said softly, "I imagine that had to feel a bit strange."

I studied my cuticles. Sighed and shook my head as if that simple action could clear away the mess of emotions that were clogging my thinking. "She also said they're buried here in town, in a cemetery next to the Baptist church. Along with all the other babies Lucille had who died." Oliver didn't say a word, waiting for a reaction of some sort from me, I suppose. The words hung in the air over us but I didn't have the courage to give them form: *My brothers. My sisters.* "I suppose we should go visit them at some point, but I'm not ready for that yet, Uncle Ollie."

He reached out to pat my hand. "Absolutely understandable, Julia. Whenever you're ready. Or not."

I concentrated a moment, pondering what I'd felt when Mrs. Odell told me about them. Sad, maybe? Or was it more like being empty? Certainly, I was confused and felt disconnected, something like an out-of-body experience.

-Jules? Jules, are you okay, love?

-I don't know. I feel so strange, Guy. Like I'm watching a movie, only the movie is about *me*. And I don't want to see it, not really, but it keeps drawing me in emotionally, whether I want it to or not.

"Julia, where are you, darling girl?" I jerked a bit, startled, and Uncle Ollie reached out to take my hand. "Do we need to go back to the motel? Let you rest?" He suddenly looked terribly determined. "Be truthful, Julia. Should we leave right now and head back home?"

"Oh, heavens, no," I said emphatically, attempting to fully shake off the odd experience of both Guy and Oliver asking me if I was okay at the same time. Once again, my multi-tasking at this should be far beyond what normal people would ever know. The only thing close to it might be television personalities, newscasters possibly, who wore headsets requiring them to speak and listen to a conversation via the headset at the same time. But I could hardly seek out someone like that to empathize with my ambidextrous listening, now could I? I'd likely be the very next one interviewed, and just as quickly transported to the nearest institution for *"them that's not quite right,"* as Mrs. Odell said so eloquently. Still, I would welcome the occasional admiration of someone who appreciated my dexterity in these unique situations.

-I'm with Uncle Ollie, Guy. I'll get back to you as soon as I can, okay? But yes, I'm doing fine. Honest.

-Please be careful. Chat later?

-Absolutely.

See what I mean? How easily I move from one conversation to the other? "As a matter of fact, I'm feeling re-energized," I announced to Uncle Ollie. "How about an adventure this afternoon?"

-An adventure? What adventure? Jules, you can't—where are you going?

-Now you're eavesdropping again. But we're going to explore a church, that's all. What could be less dangerous than *that*, I ask you?

-You can't. Don't go—

"I'll go where I want to!"

Oliver's bushy eyebrows shot up dramatically. "O-kay. But did I miss something here, Julia? Sounds like we've been wrestling when I don't recall the match. I mean, I did suggest going home, but—"

"I'm sorry, Uncle Ollie." I closed my eyes and shook my head. That's what I get for being overly confident; never fails that I'll mess up. "Guess I am feeling a bit defensive."

"Apology accepted." He leaned towards me and his eyes lit up. "You can make it up to me this way: How about we go church hunting this afternoon? Just scout out where it was… get the lay of the land, so to speak. And the cemetery's evidently right there too…waiting for us to explore."

I frowned. "You're like a kid with a new toy. You just want to try out your new sickle."

—

When Oliver insisted on driving, I didn't argue. We weren't far out of town, however, when he pulled over to the side of the road.

"What's up?" I asked Oliver as he turned off the car and climbed out. He didn't say a word in response as I watched him open the trunk, remove a small object and then lean over the trunk as he handled something. Whatever he was up to, his movements were quick and efficient; he wasn't wasting any time or energy as he completed his task. Finally, he slammed the trunk closed and then stashed a small bundle under the driver's seat before I could get a good look at it. "Uncle Ollie. What are you up to?"

He glanced behind us before pulling back out onto the road. "Up to? Why, I'm only planning ahead. Being pro-active concerning a small matter of safety."

I gasped, realizing what he'd just done. "You didn't load the gun, did you? Did you really just put a loaded gun under your seat?"

"Need I remind you of my background? I'm quite capable of handling this. Quite." He pivoted his head and shot me a look I don't think I'd ever seen before. I imagine it was the same determined visage he presented on the battlefield all those years ago, just before he set his sights on a mark. Though I reminded myself he was the same tender-hearted Uncle Ollie I knew and loved, I'd never witnessed this side of him. It was instantly intimidating. "It is loaded, Julia, and locked too, of course. Until I assess the situation—what this place we're going to explore is like—well, I intend to keep it close by. Must I remind you of my promise to your dad? And you?"

"I know, I know. But isn't this a bit of overkill?"

"John Odell also warned me to be extra cautious. I guess there are old stills out this way and, believe it or not, the kind of people who wouldn't hesitate to shoot should we be perceived as a threat to their livelihood. I guess they're always on the lookout for *the Law*, as they say."

"Mrs. Odell said the same thing. I assumed she was being overly dramatic."

"I don't think that's the case, unfortunately. And then we have the other factions we need to be on the lookout for. Whatever, we'll be sticking close to the ruins of the church and the old cemetery, that's for sure."

We were quiet for a while, and I stared out the window, an attempt to gather my thoughts. More so, trying to still a racing pulse. I knew Guy would be outraged were he to hear of this line of reasoning, so I focused on blocking him out again, completely. Studying Oliver's profile, I asked, "You're taking this very seriously, aren't you?"

"I always take you and your protection very seriously, darling girl."

Our conversation, by necessity, switched to the mechanics of safely negotiating the sharp curves, narrow bridges and various animals on the road, including two cows, a good-sized turtle and one mangy looking dog. That, and trying to understand John Amos' directions.

"He said to make a left by the Smith's big red barn."

"Uncle Ollie, there must be a zillion big red barns out here."

"But the Smith's barn sits right next to Crotin Springs Creek."

"Interesting. Mrs. Odell said the church we're looking for—what's left of it, that is—that it was originally named Crotin Springs Church, obviously named after the creek that's flowing along here. Why does that sound familiar somehow? Does it to you, Uncle Ollie?"

"No. But neither do any of the vague directions we received."

"This creek winds all over the place! Oh, there, just up ahead. That's Holler Road, the sign says. Did John Odell mention that one?"

"Holler Road was the second right after turning left by the Smith's barn."

"This is impossible."

"I remember he said to look for an abandoned home in disrepair. It's not the Gibbons' family's original home—that's farther back, a good distance down a small, winding road.

What's left of it, that is. But first we need to find the newer home that will lead us there. That it, you suppose? Looks like it might be." He pointed, slowing down enough that we could confirm the location.

-Jules, where are you now? Are you okay?

He sounded frantic. Had he figured out what we're doing?

-Of course I'm okay. Uncle Ollie and I are only looking to locate my family's homesite. And a church. No harm in that, is there?

"Would you look there—betcha it's the overgrown gravel road. By golly, we've found it, Julia!"

-No harm? No harm when someone tried to and nearly succeeded in—? Jules, I want you to go back to your motel. Get out of there, *now*.

-Guy, you can't be serious. Not when we've just found it! We'll discuss this, *later*.

I'd pay for that bit of temper, but after the confrontation with E.A, I was in no mood to deal with yet another bossy male. Honestly, I hadn't been near Brent since yesterday, but he was looking better with each passing moment in comparison to the men I was rubbing shoulders with lately. Including my uncle and his equally overly protective instincts. Talk about mass hysteria and paranoia.

Ironically, my fears of tackling exactly what Uncle Ollie and I were about to do—battling through dense undergrowth to locate buildings or gravestones—were being shoved aside in my pique at all the men trying to control me! Apparently, my stubbornness had at least one beneficial side effect: I was primed to take another leap of faith. Right into humidity, heat, bugs, and weeds hiding all manner of unknown critters, including snakes.

Oliver turned onto the road—such as it was—and gingerly drove onto what was left of the gravel drive. He turned off the ignition and we both opened our doors. Immediately I felt struck by the oppressive heat; compared to the air conditioning in the car, the humidity was nearly suffocating in its density.

I closed my eyes a moment, took a deep breath. And before stepping out into that unknown, I uttered a quick prayer. *God, help me, please! May my obstinacy continue to fuel my will!*

There was a constant barrage of bug sounds—a pulsating hum, and a cricket-like chorus of accented beats. The humid air itself seemed to work like a speaker, extending, magnifying the orchestra of insects. The ever-present vines (the South's famous kudzu?) flourished everywhere, covering everything. It was just plain creepy to me—literally *and* figuratively. I got the eerie feeling that if I stood in one place too long, I could be swallowed up by the voracious plant too.

But all of my attention was pulled toward the remains of the house that stood before us: Disintegrating outside walls, a gaping hole where the door had been, filthy, spider-web covered windows. Peeking inside, I spot mangled, uneven floorboards and the chimney—where a single vine grew up from the floor and snaked up the side. I stared at the rotting ruins, holding my breath, trying to imagine it with a family inside. My family. Jimmy and Lucille with a newborn—me. I could almost hear a baby crying when Uncle Ollie put his arm around my shoulders.

"You okay?" he asked, softly.

"Yeah, it's just…a lot to take in."

Uncle Ollie tentatively pushed a foot against the floorboard just over the threshold, and the board instantly caved in. "Best we don't even try to go inside. Don't want to risk a sprained ankle for either one of us."

I looked around the room—seeing the now bare walls, while outlines of lighter spaces gave evidence that pictures—of family? *my* family?—once hung here and there. The kitchen was just barely visible from our view at the front door, and pretty much cleaned out. At least, I was guessing it was the kitchen from the two rickety shelves barely clinging to the walls, a filthy sink and what looked to be the rusted edge of a stove. I guessed a bedroom or two went off to the left and back. And there wasn't much more left to even look at, sadly. Clearly, lives had been uprooted and moved on—anything left taken after the horrendous tragedy of the owners' deaths. I took a deep breath and purposefully turned away, pivoting towards the gravel road. "Let's see what we can find up ahead." I looked up into Oliver's eyes. He nodded, once, and smiled.

"Lead us on, darling girl."

For a few yards, the undergrowth was mostly ground cover with small trees and bushes sprouting here and there. That was going to be tough enough to work through as we looked for signs of buildings and later, gravestones. But several yards back the growth steadily grew taller and denser until it looked nearly impassable, with thick woods just beyond. The sickle was definitely going to get a workout today, as were Oliver's muscles. Add that to the list of what I owed the dear man. Any frustration I felt at his over-protective instincts evaporated in the guilt for what my issues were putting him through.

Standing in the knee-high weeds, I complained, "How're we ever going to find anything in this?" I shook my head, already battling discouragement. A bee buzzed my ear and I dodged, batting it away.

"First things first. Let's get into our hiking boots. And wait till you see me swing this amazing tool. I'm about to show you that a burly mountain man resides in this body." He put one foot out, sunk in some mud and then groaned. "A solitary mud puddle had to be positioned exactly right here? So much for my newly polished shoes."

I laughed at him. "So much for the burly mountain man!"

We leaned against the back bumper to remove shoes and tug on boots, and the little energy that chore required caused sweat to already bead up on my forehead. I'd pulled up my hair into a ponytail and put on my Sundhamn Stars ball cap (a co-ed softball team I played on every spring). I removed it now to mop my forehead before yanking it back on.

"We haven't started yet and I'm already covered in sweat." I swatted at a small cloud of tiny bugs doing a frenetic dance in front of my eyes. "And what's with these bugs? Hand me the spray, will you?" I was busy spritzing a good amount on both of us when I suddenly stopped, the can held in mid-air. My gaze dropped to the ground as I frantically searched all around us.

"What?" Oliver looked at me like I'd lost my mind. "Did you lose something?"

"Snakes."

"You lost a snake? I don't recall you bringing one with you, but—"

"Hilarious. The place has got to be literally crawling with snakes."

Oliver perused the area and removed his cap, scratching the top of his head. "Won't try to convince you otherwise, Julia. But you do have sturdy boots on, and they're great protection."

"Actually, I had intended to use them for hiking. As in up beautiful mountain paths with breathtaking views. I didn't plan for an overgrown jungle. With snakes."

"Here. Take this." He handed me another cap he'd brought along, one with *John Deere* on the front. "Switch out yours with this one and any guys seeing you will be impressed. Could be the snakes will see how macho you are and stay away also."

"I beg your pardon. My ballcap is plenty macho. Remember our record last year?"

"No, but I'm sure you're about to enlighten me."

"Twelve and three, I'll have you know."

"Isn't that klutzy bottled blond from the bank one of your teammates?"

I rolled my eyes and removed the beloved Stars cap, tossing it into the trunk. Jamming the ugly John Deere onto my head, I admitted, "She's our best home run hitter's girlfriend."

"Case closed."

Already I felt hot, sticky, smelly, ugly, and wary. But I wasn't going to be a whiner; I squared my shoulders, vowed to consider this a grand adventure and give it my best shot. Slipping on my backpack, I asked, "So. Are we ready to do this thing?"

"Just about." Oliver pulled the gun out from under the seat and tucked it into the waistband of his jeans. I shook my head at him, knowing it was pointless to argue. We both pulled on our newly purchased work gloves and Uncle Ollie picked up the sickle, taking a couple practice swipes on some tall weeds next to the car. "Sweet. This baby works great. I feel like—what's the guy's name? The crocodile one?"

"Use it to cut the heads off any snakes we see and I'll call you whatever you want. I'll even broadcast to everyone in Collinsville what a burly mountain man you are. Especially Mama Byrd."

"Ah, the admiration of one's niece is a gift to be treasured. And quite frankly, I wouldn't mind if Mama Byrd took notice too." He winked at me. "No, indeed. Not at all."

Oliver set out at a steady pace, his stride evenly matching the rhythmic swing of his tool. I willed myself to move, following in his footsteps, proceeding boldly until everything seemed to wind down into slow motion. Through a panic-inducing kind of tunnel vision, I could just make out Oliver a few steps ahead. He'd continued on his way, oblivious to my distress, assuming I was moving right along with him. But my view of him continued to diminish, like an old-fashioned television screen winking closed.

And then I stopped, frozen in place.

My heart felt like it could explode from my chest, the pulsating "*th-thump! th-thump!*" nearly deafening in my ears. The world took a quick spin—vertigo, my brain registered and enlightened me—but no rational explanation could keep me from leaning over, placing my hands on my knees to breathe easier and beg the earth to *hold still*. I wanted to attribute every bit of these physical symptoms to my concern for snakes, but instinctively, I knew it was more than that. Way more.

"You doing okay back there?" Oliver called out over his shoulder.

Determined to get myself under control, to hide this reaction from him, I pushed constricted air out of my lungs. Breathed in and swallowed. Standing up straight, eyes closed, I offered, "Doing great. Just great." To myself, I whispered, *God, help me. I'm frightened—and too cowardly at this time to probe what's really the issue here. Help me to just walk forward, for now, feeling you right beside me. Trusting you*. My prayer from last night came to mind, and I reminded myself, *It's like a tiny leap, just this one step. Decide to trust, Julia*. Gathering every bit of courage I could find within, every ounce of faith I could grab onto, I determinedly moved forward—only a small step, but a step, nonetheless. And then I took another. My heart slowly settled back into a more normal rhythm, my breathing calmed, and the world stopped spinning as I focused on and eventually caught up to Uncle Ollie's broad back.

Lord, we have work to do, you and I. But thanks for helping me now. I breathed a sigh of relief before saying *Thank you, God,* once more.

The gloves were a huge help as we worked our way farther down the overgrown road. Oliver used the sickle to cut the larger undergrowth and vines (quite the scourge, that kudzu) that impeded our continuing in the general direction which the road took us. My job was to help him gather up the detritus and toss it out of our way. We made pretty good progress until any sign of the gravel and stones disappeared completely; at that point, we simply stood there, hands on hips, as we had no idea which direction or how much farther we had to go to find the original homesite.

Oliver recounted how John Odell had said the Gibbons' home's foundation was "out there a ways." He'd also described the church (with the graveyard right next to it) as being northwest of that same home—that was about as specific as he could get with his directions and distances—but said he doubted that we'd locate the church itself. Evidently most of its foundation stones had been carted off to start another church elsewhere. Since the gravestones were likely toppled over and covered with dense vegetation—or even disintegrated altogether if originally made of wood—the only way to locate the cemetery was to begin at square one: the original home. That had to be our starting point to find anything else, John advised. Needless to say, no matter where we looked, it was like searching for the proverbial needle in a haystack. Except the haystack was also hidden. In a jungle of ubiquitous kudzu.

"How about if we work our way outward, in kind of an expanding three-quarters circle? No sense backtracking, obviously, and this way we'll hopefully pick up the gravel road again. Or hit on something else," Oliver suggested.

I nodded my approval of his plan, once more wiping the sweat from my face with my hat. The annoying whirling mass of tiny bugs was back, choosing to hover in front of my face again. I swatted at them, but they immediately returned, claiming it their place of residence, it appeared.

I watched in amazement as Oliver, ever the gentleman, pulled out a clean white handkerchief to mop his brow.

"Your manners are absolutely genteel. I swear you should've been born in the nineteenth century."

"Darling girl, I almost was."

I chuckled at him as he put a hand to his back and made a face. "By any chance, is there a Jacuzzi at our motel?"

Irritated, I swatted at the bugs again, useless as it was to do so. "I think I saw one out by the pool. Could be we'll both be checking it out tonight, huh? What is with these bugs, by the way? Do you have a small cloud in your face too, or are they just keen on me?" I felt a tickle on my arm and smacked there, assuming it was a bug chowing down. Sure enough, there was a small black smear on my arm. "Yuck. Honestly, there must be a zillion insects out here."

"That's why I suggested long sleeves, my dear. And no, I don't have my own personal cloud of bug fans. Did you make the mistake of putting on lotion with a fragrance?" I glowered at him and he continued, "Sorry. Should've warned you about that. But at least crawling creatures aren't attracted to scents like airborne ones."

"Thanks for that."

-Jules, please tell me you're okay.

-Of course, I am. Don't be paranoid.

-I can't stand not knowing. If you're going to insist on being this reckless, you've got to check in with me. Say, every five minutes or so.

-Guy, that's ludicrous! I'm not in a position to watch the time like that. For one thing, Uncle Ollie and I are just a tad busy out here. We're cutting and tossing nasty weeds. Swatting pesky insects and on the lookout for snakes at the same time. What on earth would I tell Uncle Oliver when he noticed me checking my watch?

-I don't know. You'll think of something.

-No, I won't. Because I'm not going to do that. *I'm fine.*

"Let's take a water break, darlin' girl. Good idea?"

"Excellent idea, Uncle Ollie. Your timing is impeccable."

We pulled out water bottles that dripped with condensation, but I'd packed them full of ice, so they were still delightfully cold. When we both immediately put the bottles against our foreheads, we chuckled at our mutual, instinctive reaction.

"I have one suggestion for our future explorations."

"What's that?"

"Next time—if there is a next time—let's come first thing in the morning. When it's hopefully a bit cooler."

"What do you mean, *if?* Of course, we're coming back! But that is a very wise and logical idea. I second the motion." I swatted the evidently ever-present cloud of bugs again. "Hopefully less bugs first thing in the morning, too, eh?"

"How about we work about another hour and then call it a day? I think we're both reaching 'well done' cook temp."

"Sounds good. I mean—to leave in an hour or so, not that we're *well done*."

"Amen to that."

-Guy? Just checking in. We're only going to stay about another hour, k? The heat's just brutal this afternoon out here.

-You could just head home, you know. And I mean *home* as in *Wisconsin*.

-*Seriously?* Guy, I've come all this way. I'm not quitting before I find any answers.

-What answers? What do you expect to find out in the middle of nowhere?

-Something more about my biological parents. And my grandparents and *their* parents—focusing on the Gibbons for sure. Mrs. Odell even hinted about curses. I don't know what I'm looking for, to tell you the truth. But I know there's more to learn and it's *here*, Guy. Somewhere, *something* is here. My biological parents are dead, I learned that already. Killed in a fiery car crash, according to Mrs. Odell. She sits in the hardware store with her feet in a box, by the way.

-I'm sorry about your parents, Jules. I don't know what to say.

-Not much to say. They died in the crash, and according to Mrs. Odell, Jimmy and Lucille Gibbons had no surviving children. *None.* She tells me this while I'm sitting there looking at her. Ironic, right?

-Here's what's ironic, Jules. Listen to what you're saying: They were killed in a car crash. Don't you find that just a bit coincidental? What if the crash was caused by the very same people who forced you into the ditch? And your father, Jules? You've got to consider the real possibility these people could be there right now, love. You could be in grave danger!

-Guy, the police are convinced there was no conspiracy. It was all just a horrible coincidence—my little fender-bender. Dad's heart attack and then his accident.

-I thought the police determined it was inconclusive? Whether the heart attack caused the crash—or the other way around?

-Yes, that's what they said. But Guy, honestly. There's simply no logical reason anyone would want to hurt my dad. Or me.

We'd worked steadily while Guy and I chatted—or rather, argued—when Oliver swung the sickle and hit something hard enough to make the sickle vibrate in his hands.

-Hang on, Guy. Oliver's found something.

"Goodness. Thank heaven for these leather gloves, or the sickle would've jerked right out of my grip. But just look here what we've found." He reached down to pull aside the vines and undergrowth. "I do believe we've stumbled onto a stone step of some sort. This is most likely your grandparents' home."

"Amazing. I can't quite get my mind around that."

"Let's work a rectangular shape, shall we? Be interesting to find the outlines of the building, discover how big it is, agreed?"

"Sure."

-We've found the homesite, Guy! I need to concentrate better. Work with Uncle Ollie in tandem here for a while. I'll catch you up later on what we find, okay?

-Jules, don't—

-I'll tell you later, I promise. Gotta go.

I shut him off, but I could sense he was there still. Hovering.

And why did I have this nagging sense he was getting closer all the time? Had he left wherever he lived and was now on his way to Tennessee, determined to find me and stop me? I didn't have the wherewithal to think about that right now, so I concentrated on shutting him out. Sometimes stopping communication between us was like putting up a concrete barrier; I could easily keep him separate and away from my innermost musings. Other times I have to admit that barrier was no thicker than a mesh veil, and I struggled to keep our thoughts and feelings from intermingling, intertwining.

Today that separation was the filmy veil. Oh, I needed him. I wanted Guy to help me sort through life and death and grieving and finding who Julia Anne Johnson—Gibbons/Blevins?—is. But at the same time, I was terrified. Guy would call me to absolute honesty; there'd be no denying of feelings I wasn't yet ready to identify, let alone begin to sort through and deal with. I'd have to concentrate and fight hard to keep Guy on the other side of that veil—the other side of intimacy from me.

Then the thought struck me, *Am I doing the same thing with God? Keeping him on the other side of a wall—the other side of vulnerable intimacy with me too?* For now, I pushed it all aside: Answering that question. Figuring out just where I was with God. Dealing with Guy.

Oliver and I had been bent over for some time now, both of us searching for any signs of the outlined building. Our discoveries came in fits and starts as we slowly located foundation stones. Finally, we both stood up in jubilant acknowledgement: We'd definitely found the outlines of a building. Smiling, I straightened and stretched, putting a hand to my back and rubbing at the ache there. I heard a car back-firing in the distance—which startled me, causing me to jump backwards—and in nearly the same instant a loud insect made a *zing!* sound as it whizzed by between Uncle Ollie and me.

"Good grief. Was that ever one huge bug—" I attempted to get out but then, to my utter amazement, Uncle Ollie literally tackled me. And by that, I mean a full body take down.

I can't imagine the sight we presented. I'm on the ground, my face smashed into a pile of weeds we'd just cut. And Oliver? He's lying diagonally on top of me, his chest continuing to press my face into that pile of nasty smelling weeds. Finally, he lets me raise my head high enough so I can spit out, "Uncle Ollie, what on *earth*?"

Through heavy breaths he replied, "That was no giant bug, Julia. That was a bullet." I turned my head, and in my peripheral vision I caught the distinct outline of Oliver's gun. "Cover your ears." His voice was crystal clear now, steady, surprisingly cool.

I placed shaking hands over my ears, and then I could feel his body jerk from the recoil as he fired three quick shots into the woods.

THE GRAVESTONES' SECRETS

11 of June, 1588

My Descendants,
Even though we have been separated by years and an ocean of water, my yearning for Catherine does not wane, but only grows with each passing day. I long for her to join me here as I long for the sunrise each daybreak, dispelling our nighttime fears. And then our good Chief Manteo attempts still to bridge the chasm between us by his discourse with those Savages who pose continued challenges to us all.
Those who dwelt here before us—alas!—left a damaging legacy: Captain Ralph Lane put to death their Chief Wingina, because of a stolen cup. (One can only wonder, could it have been merely missing?) Thus, we surmise all fifteen Souls of that Colony holding the fort before us were in turn murdered by the avenging Savages of Wingina's tribe. Can we wholly blame them for their attempts at justice, save for the cost of so many Souls, assuming some innocent among them? Would we not do the very same, should one of their Savages put to death a Soul from our group for stealing parcels—and from what they hold to be their land? The land given them by their gods?

And such it is that we fear for our very lives also. Many are making plans, and are desirous to move on from here, seeking Safer Territory elsewhere. If such travels become necessary for me also, I shall tell my Catherine of them.

Thus, as my heart and soul long to beg my Beloved to join me here, I shall refrain from doing so. Her life is much too precious to me. Far too precious indeed.

Ever, Mauro

CHAPTER SIX

At first, utter silence. Everything around us—even the zillion annoying insects, evidently—stopped to listen and wonder after the shocking sound of that reverberating *bang! bang! bang!* I know I was holding my breath, so I assumed whoever was out there in the woods was doing the same. Limbs temporarily frozen also, just like mine. Although my dilemma was partly due to the fact that a six-foot-two, one-hundred-and-ninety-pound man still lay on top of me. Not that I'm complaining, considering that same dear man most likely saved my life. Besides thankfulness, the only other coherent thought going through my mind was that I desperately needed to block all of this from Guy. He'd be frantic and insistent, culminating in a demand that I explain everything. *Now.*

The next thing we hear are the sounds of loud footfalls breaking through underbrush and tree branches in the woods beyond. Fortunately, however, the sounds are growing dimmer, hopefully signaling that the shooter is running away from us.

And then—honestly, what on earth prompted *him* to show up? Of all the people in this entire world I had no desire to interact with at that moment, it had to be E.A. who flops onto the ground next to us? Who invited him—with a gun in his hands too? *Uncle Ollie, even though you've just saved my life,* I promise myself, *if you've invited E.A. without telling me, there will be consequences.*

"E.A." I hissed, absolutely furious that he was inserting himself into my life like this. "What are you—"

"*Shut up*, will you? Let your uncle and me listen to determine if the shooter's gone or not."

He spoke in one of those "guy whisper voices" which was no whisper at all. And he's griping *at me?*

"Oliver, you go around to the right; I'll circle left. And Jul… Julia, you *stay put*. Don't move one single inch from this spot, you hear?"

"Uncle Ollie, are you going to let him—?"

"Yes. I am," strongly accentuated, to my disgust. "Same plan I would've suggested. Stay here, Julia."

I watched as both Oliver and E.A. eased into crouching positions and proceeded to stealthily advance into the woods—E.A., surprisingly, nearly as light-footed as my uncle. I knew Oliver had training from his years in the service. But E.A.? He didn't fit the type.

But then, he clearly owns a gun, I noted as I sat up, brushing sticks, leaves and all sorts of smashed vegetation from my torso, arms and legs. I glanced around, envisioning creepy-crawly critters of every sort nearby and nearly stood up before remembering Oliver's stern instructions. I sighed, and then, resigned, decided I'd have to keep watch for Oliver and E.A.'s return in this prone position. But I wasn't happy about it.

Fortunately, it wasn't long before I heard voices, the two of them "whispering" again. I couldn't hear what they were saying, but I caught how serious their voices sounded.

"Did you find anything?" I asked, standing to greet them, relieved to finally be back on my feet.

"Nothing," Uncle Ollie answered.

"That's it? That's all you have to say?"

From E.A. this time: "Nothing more to offer."

I glared at both of them, alternating between venting my anger at Oliver and then E.A. "Uncle Ollie?"

He sighed, shaking his head. "Didn't find a thing, Julia. Shooter's long gone. Left behind some broken branches and crushed undergrowth where he might've been, next to some nasty barbed wire."

"Any sign of a still?"

"Nothing," E.A. said, removing his ballcap (I noted *First Baptist* was printed in bright blue on a background of stained white) and wiping his brow with it. "But I'm thinkin' it's not too far off. They obviously don't want anyone setting foot in *their* woods. And they were pointin' out that barbed wire fence clearly announces *keep out*." He nodded towards the trees. "Oliver, your returning shots put whoever at notice. And just in case either of you is wondering, there's no cause to call the sheriff. He'd just laugh and then advise us to keep plenty clear of that barbed wire fence. *That's* our clear boundary."

"Pretty much what I assumed," Oliver began. "But are we agreed—?" He and E.A. stared into each other's eyes, silently communicating, nodding. Excluding me from their nonverbal discussion.

"What's going on, you two? If you're making decisions about something, then just hold on a doggone second." I put hands on hips and stood up straighter, throwing back my shoulders—anything to appear taller. "I get a say in this too, gentlemen. We just found the homestead. I won't be chased off by some drunk who's protecting his illegal swill!"

"Okay, you've had your say. Now, Oliver, what do *we* say?"

His audacity was almost more than I could bear and my already ratcheted up emotions erupted like a volcano. "Excuse *me*. Just who do you think you are? Deciding for me? How dare you! I will make my own decisions, and you have no business deciding anything concerning me, let alone if I'll continue searching for evidence of my family…and…and, oh durn. *Shut up*, Julia."

Uncle Ollie closed his eyes and shook his head. "Are you quite finished?"

I slumped, surrendering every bit of the "height" I had supposedly gained. "It would appear so." Now I was angry at E.A. *and* myself.

"Did you really think I bought that line about looking for your aunt's relatives?" E.A. asked.

I clenched my fists and wished I could swear a blue streak at him. All those words were surely right on the tip of my tongue!

"Brent and I knew right off that was only a ruse for the real reason you're here."

"Now, how would you possibly know that? Believe me, you don't have the faintest idea about anything." I almost added *smarty pants* but stopped myself just in time. Goodness, I'd been around third graders far too long.

E.A. raised his eyebrows, glancing from me to Oliver and then back again. "You two are about as transparent as young sardines."

I glared at him. "What on earth does *that* mean?"

"He means—" Uncle Ollie began, but I cut him off.

"*I know what he meant*. But that's probably the stupidest simile I've ever heard in my life." I knew I was back to mimicking third graders again, but it appeared I was simply going to run my mouth, regardless.

"I beg your pardon," E.A. offered, sounding so reasonable and mature that this time I clenched my teeth to keep silent. "It's a direct quote from a classic, I'll have you know. It's from—"

"I DON'T CARE WHERE IT'S FROM," Uncle Ollie declared. I jumped and E.A. looked decidedly uncomfortable; clearly the two of us had pushed our bickering beyond my normally patient uncle's limits. "Now. Let's start over, shall we? First, we need to make a decision about whether we stay here or not. And if we're going to stay a while, then we're certainly not going to waste time arguing over *perfectly ridiculous topics*. Honestly, I do believe you act like brother and sister. Ten-year-olds, at best. Are you two related somehow?"

"Absolutely not!" E.A. and I both spit out. In perfect unison.

It was so well timed and unexpected that all three of us were silent for just a split second—before erupting in laughter. I suppose we needed the tension breaker, as we carried on long enough that we needed to plop down onto a good-sized log in near exhaustion. I'd pulled out water bottles and was passing those around when E.A. glanced at me and then reached out to touch my cheek. I jerked away, in what? Embarrassment? Disgust? Was I still that angry with him?

"Hold still a sec, will you? You've got a smudge there and I'm just trying to—" he worked at the area a bit, roughly rubbing my cheek with his index finger "—to get off this bit of dirt."

My stomach did this weird somersault and then I could feel that familiar muscle contracting in my throat: A major hiccup was on its way, and it was promising to be embarrassingly loud unless I could get his finger away from my face, immediately. I swatted his hand, insisting, "That's good enough. We're going back to work any minute now (I emphasized those last words with direct glares at each man), so I'm only gonna get more dirt on me." I took a big swig of water and stood up. "Speaking of that, let's get busy, shall we? E.A., I assume you have work to get back to? What about the library you were supposed to be manning today?"

"Closed. Staff's prerogative."

I sneered at Oliver. "And how did he find out we were out here, anyway? Did *someone* just happen to mention that possibility to him?"

To his credit, Oliver at least had the decency to look sheepish.

Now it was E.A.'s turn to receive my ire. "You drove all the way out here—with a gun in tow, I might add—just because Oliver mentioned we might be looking for the Gibbons' homesite?"

"Actually, I was on my way to the Clairborne Gun Club for target practice and thought I'd swing by to check on you two. I know there are stills out this way, and the sort who guard them. Pretty rough characters." He glanced at me and shrugged his shoulders. "I'd say it was good luck for you I was here—and armed."

"I'll second that," Oliver added. Though he opened his mouth to say more, he immediately closed it when he turned to look at me.

I made a *pmpbh!* sound. "You boys always stick together, don't you? One invents a story and the other swears by it."

"Where did you leave off, anyway? Have we found anything yet?" E.A. asked.

"We? There is no *we* here, E.A. You're heading back to town."

"No, the way I see it is *you* are."

"I am not—Uncle Ollie, tell him, will you?"

"Julia. I would feel ever so much better if you at least went back to the car. E.A. and I can take care of ourselves, but you—"

"Will stay." I ignored E.A. entirely, as there was simply no way I'd concede he had any right to weigh in on this. Inwardly, I was hesitant, to be truthful. But my need to overrule E.A. was strong enough that it cancelled out any fears. *And wisdom?* an inner voice whispered. Even then, my obstinacy reigned again: I crossed my arms and stared intently at Oliver. When he started rolling his eyes, I knew I'd won.

"E.A. and I are convinced the shooter is, first of all, long gone. And secondly, we both agree that shot was meant as a warning—never intended to hit one of us or he would have." Oliver turned to directly face me, giving me a fatherly look. "However, *if* you are going to remain here, then we will not turn down E.A.'s generous offer of protection and help, especially in light of the challenging conditions we face." He turned and plowed through the weeds to stand by one of the cornerstones we'd discovered. "This must be the northeast corner. John Odell said the cemetery was directly northeast of the house. Therefore, I suggest the three of us fan out a bit from here."

E.A. had tagged along behind Oliver, moving to follow his suggestions. But I merely stood, arms crossed over my chest, debating, scowling. Until Oliver called over his shoulder, "Planning to stand there until the cloud of bugs finds you?"

I sighed, admitting defeat even as I tugged on my gloves and set to work.

Oliver continued to use the sickle as needed while E.A. and I pulled and tossed underbrush, searching for any hint of a headstone. It wasn't long, however, before E.A. offered, "Oliver, I can't imagine you're used to heftin' a sickle back n' forth all day. How 'bout you let me take a turn?"

"I can't imagine working at the restaurant or shelving books in a library means you're using one much either, E.A."

"Oh, good heavens," I pronounced, dramatically. "Two macho men and one tool. Do I need to take over?"

Both shot me disgusted looks. But Oliver handed the sickle to E.A.

Feeling gratified, I smirked. E.A. shot an exaggerated sneer right back and then turned away to begin swinging in wide arcs, covering a good deal of ground quickly. I stole glances at him, noting the almost graceful and even rhythm of his movements. Clearly E.A. *did* have experience at hard labor, though he'd never catch me admitting that to him. I also took in the set of his jaw when I caught the line of his profile, and the slight twitch of muscle there as he concentrated. My eyes traveled downward to where earlier he'd rolled up the sleeves of his shirt, so that now the muscles in his upper arms and forearms stood out, distinctly outlined. I watched them flex and ripple with each movement until I finally caught myself.

What on earth is wrong with you? You see a few muscles and go all weak in the knees? Get yourself together, Julia. You can't stand this man, remember?

-Can't stand who?

-Whom.

-Whatever. Who is it you can't stand? Notice my correct pronoun usage with that one, Grammar Sheriff. Still looking for the homesite? Are you taking care of yourself, Jules?

Good. He obviously didn't pick up on the gunshots at all. I'm surprised I was able to keep him in the dark, though. He must've been preoccupied.

-Jules?

-I'm fine. Still here. We'll certainly find the cemetery any minute now, I'm sure of it. Isn't that exciting?

-I'm over-joyed.

-Guy, you've made the point several times that you're not in favor of me being here. But you can rejoice with me for progress, agreed?

I could hear him sigh. Resigning himself as I smiled in victory. My soulmate never could deny me for very long.

-I do, and I will, Jules. I understand how much this means to you. But back to your anger and frustration with someone; that came through loud and clear. Just who is your wrath directed at, anyway?

-Whom.

-Jules!

-Oh, it's that same insufferable brother I told you about before. The one from the restaurant. He may be the most frustrating man on the planet, Guy. Every single thing he does drives me insane.

-Everything? Isn't that a bit of an over-statement? You can't find one redeeming quality?

-Not yet. The man's like a giant human splinter. Totally irritating.

-Really?

-For one thing, there's his obnoxious opinions. He has the audacity to believe he's right one hundred percent of the time.

-I doubt that.

-You doubt what?

-That he thinks he's right *all* the time.

-I don't believe this. You're as bad as Uncle Oliver. You're taking his side when you don't even know the man!

-I'm just feeling for the poor guy, that's all. Trying to get you to be more...I don't know. Rational? Fair?

-I know *exactly* what you're doing. It's the 'good ole boy' network at work here. Again! You're all in this silly men's club and you stick together, no matter what. But wait, Guy, I think I found...

"Hey! Look at this! It's a gravestone, I'm sure of it."

Oliver and E.A. hurried over so that all three of us crouched over the stone, tugging and pushing roots out of the way so we could free what lay beneath. Finally, we brushed aside the remaining dirt to view the entire stone and the carving written there. Out loud, I read, "Baby Boy Gibbons. 1915." I sat back on my heels, emotions suddenly coursing through me. "I guess I wasn't thinking much beyond simply finding these gravestones. Nothing about the reality of actual people buried here. And babies—babies who died so young they weren't even named." My throat constricted, and I swallowed down a surge of sadness. Barely above a whisper, I reflected, "This is a sacred place, isn't it?"

Oliver put a hand on my shoulder, giving me a gentle squeeze. "It is indeed, Julia. And we shall treat it as such."

"What's this at the bottom?" I worked at the vine and mud sticking to the stone until I finally could make out the letters. "It's just *CRO*. Did they start carving a word and then just stopped, not finishing it?" Both Oliver and E.A. shrugged their shoulders, obviously as puzzled as I was.

"Did you bring along paper and pencil?" E.A. asked.

"You mean for etchings, don't you? Good idea, but no, I didn't think of that."

"I have both in my truck. I'll run back and fetch them for you."

I nodded. "Thanks. That would be helpful."

He carefully picked his way back out of the area around the stone and then sprinted out of sight towards our parked vehicles.

"You really should cut him some slack, you know."

I chose to ignore that remark and instead began searching for other hidden stones. I was quickly rewarded for my diligence: I found one almost immediately, though the inscription was still covered by the tenacious vine. "Uncle Oliver, look here. How did we miss it? And I think there's another one to the left."

"I guess you get so used to staring at kudzu you miss what's right before your eyes." He leaned down for a closer look. "I wonder what this one says."

The roots were even more firmly attached this time, so E.A. returned just as we'd uncovered enough to try an etching. Placing paper on the stone and rubbing the pencil back and forth several times, we read together, haltingly, as we watched the words being revealed: "'Baby Boy Gibbons. 1912.' And look—down here, there it is again: *CRO*."

"Oh. Oh, my." I sat back on my heels and looked up into E.A.'s face. His eyes met mine, and to my surprise, I saw genuine compassion residing there. For just a moment, I felt the beginnings of a connection. And then, just as quickly, I sliced it like cutting a length of ribbon, clearing my throat and looking away—anywhere but in E.A.'s direction.

Oliver had moved on to the next one. "The pattern continues. *CRO*'s at the bottom. And this one says 'Baby Girl Gibbons, 1913.' I can't imagine—how hard life was for them."

I felt tears pooling in my eyes and knew that if I didn't get myself under control, I'd be outright crying. Determinedly, I willed the tears away. For one thing, I wasn't about to appear the weak and emotional little woman in front of E.A. But mostly, I wondered how I could be so moved by a family I'd never met—and who lived nearly a century ago? I bit my lip, instantly tasting blood.

"You all right, Jul—sorry, Julia?" He appeared emotionally wrought too, for whatever reason. "I keep stammering over your name. Sorry."

"Yeah, well, it's a tough one to pronounce." The taste of sarcasm felt good in my mouth, and it helped divert my emotions to a place that felt safer.

E.A. turned awkwardly, jerking his body so that his back was to me as he continued to search the rough ground for more stones. Mere seconds had passed when he said, "Found another. Are you sure you're ready for this, *Julia?*"

His pointed jab earned a glare. I wiped my face on my sleeve and stood up, not caring that the sweat, grit, and tears would all leave ugly, telltale smears. "Of course I want to know what it says," I spit out. "That's why I'm here, after all."

"'Martha Sarah Gibbons, born April, 1919. Died June, 1919,'" he read out loud. "And then there's more on this one. It says, 'No longer in our arms, but ever in our hearts,' followed by the *CRO*."

I knelt down to caress the words, as if I could connect with these people by doing so. As If I could actually touch *them*.

"Here's another with a sentiment," Uncle Oliver offered. "'Mary Sarah Gibbons, born January 1916. Died July 1916. Our little angel.'"

Even though I tried to deny away these emotions, they pushed right back at me, demanding to be recognized. Felt. The thought suddenly hit home: These truly are *my relatives*. It's *my family* that's buried right here in this soil. "The gravestones. The people...the *people* who were here," I stumbled to find words that put form to emotions threatening to split me wide open. "It's like they're...like they're communicating. Reaching out. To *me*." I glanced up into Uncle Ollie's eyes; feeling utterly overwhelmed and embarrassed, I grabbed paper and pencil to avoid a meltdown. Frantically working at the etchings, I blinked away tears blurring my eyesight so that I could see the stone, hold the pencil at the correct angle. Eventually I was doing a fairly decent job—at the very least, you could make out enough words to figure out the name, dates, the gist of the sentiment. And on every single one the cryptic letters *CRO*.

Oliver and E.A. had continued working and must've been successful in finding more stones, but they were keeping their voices low. I caught on to their attempt to give me some time to myself before I had to process more heart-wrenching deaths; no matter their underlying motivations, the sensitivity was appreciated. Something was nagging at me too, but I couldn't place what it was. I sat back on my heels and turned by face towards the sun. *Something...something feels familiar*, I thought to myself. *Like a déjà vu.*

"Julia? We've located the parents' graves, off to the side a bit here," Oliver said.

I slowly unwrapped my stiff limbs and stood, and while my curiosity was piqued, I was hesitant. *God, what a sick mess of denial I am*, I confessed. *How on earth did I think I could handle all this death so easily? And that I could so easily dismiss their connection to me?* "'Fannie May Gibbons, 1896 – 1937, Loving Wife, Devoted Mama.' How endearing that it says *Mama* instead of mother. And of course, it has *CRO* engraved at the bottom." Doing my best to sound simply observant, I offered, "She's the one who lost all these little ones, isn't she?"

Oliver nodded. I could feel his questioning look, wondering if I was okay. Or not.

"I thought they'd just be old gravestones. Old and ugly and meaningless, I suppose. I never thought that…that they'd *speak* to me. Emotionally." I swallowed, fighting back an eruption of tears. Looking up to meet Uncle Ollie's gaze, I added, "I never imagined I'd feel any sort of connection to them."

"They're your *people*, Julia. I'm honestly rather proud of you to feel this way. This gravestone here? It's the father: 'Elijah Manuel Gibbons, 1895 – 1945; Having Six and Sight,' and that's all we can make out, unfortunately. Figured out a word here and there, like *Lord,* and this part appears to be something about *his Maker.* But it's just too worn away, I'm afraid. Even the *CRO*, assuming it was once there, is gone."

"So Fannie May was only forty-two. I would imagine burying all those children…no wonder she died so young. And Manuel lived to be just fifty."

"Life expectancy was much shorter back then," E.A. offered. "And life was particularly hard in these hills. Still is for a good percentage of people here."

We were all quiet for a bit, taking that in. Respecting those who'd gone before, and the many who still suffered under Appalachia's shadow.

I sat back on my heels and took a deep breath. "I wonder if that's what the *six* refers to—the six children buried here? I do hope they didn't lose more than what we've found." I looked up at Uncle Oliver, trying to imagine the devastation of losing that many.

"It's late. We need to get you back to the motel, and after we're sufficiently cleaned up, I'm taking you to Byrd in the Hand for a decent meal."

Readily conceding, I gathered up the etched sheets and my backpack and silently trudged back to the car. Suddenly, my boots felt like they contained lead; every step was an effort. I could feel the straps of my backpack eating into my shoulders, and the air had become even more oppressively thick with humidity. Sweat made every article of clothing sticky, and wisps of escaped hair clung to my forehead, cheeks and neck. That stubborn, all-too-familiar cloud of bugs had taken up residence around my face again, but when I swatted them away I noted the sweet smell of honeysuckle. *Was that here before?* I wondered. *How could I have missed it?* The scent was as heavy and dense as the humidity. *God, what else am I missing?*

Guy's voice came fast and urgent.

-You found the cemetery, didn't you? You found what you went looking for. But I'm worried about you, Jules. Get some rest tomorrow?

-I can't, Guy. Too much to do. And I'm thinking I should do something with my uncle—something fun. Something to make up for today's misery.

-What did you have in mind?

-He expressed an interest in exploring a place called the Gap. It's supposed to be beautiful, and nearby.

-Just you and your uncle, right? No one else? Because it would be better if it was just the two of you.

I paused a moment, feeling instantly resentful.

-Why would you assume that—or, actually, why would you not want, say...Brent, probably...to go with us? I like him, Guy. If you met him, I think you would too!

I felt his hesitancy move in like a fog extending its tentacles across a valley. Was it wariness? Distrust? Or was it simply insecurity?

Guy had never reacted negatively towards men I'd been interested in before. Not that any of those had actual potential, developing into a full-fledged relationship. But whatever this was, I felt the beginnings of a wall grow between us, a frightening distancing that I don't think I'd ever experienced with Guy before.

-Guy? What's going on? Why are you—?

-Nothing. Just worried about you, Jules, that's all. Catch you later.

  I figured we could work on fleshing this out once Uncle Ollie and I were in the car and on our way. But after E.A. helped us pile everything back into the car and we'd pulled out onto the road, things got awfully hazy as I leaned my head against the passenger headrest. And promptly fell sound asleep. I didn't wake until the car stopped and I felt a hand lightly touch my arm.

  "Julia, darling. We're back at the motel. I remember the days when your dad or I would carry you into the house, but I'm afraid those times are long past."

  I yawned and stretched, turning to him with a contented smile. "Oh, Uncle Oliver. That nap was just what I needed—well, that plus a long shower. Clean clothes too, of course."

  "And a good meal. How quickly can you be ready? I'm not up to a late night. It's definitely early to bed for me."

  I glanced at my watch. "How about we meet at six-thirty? That good? And it will be early to bed for me too, I promise. If I don't get in an early morning run, I'll be so out of shape I'll embarrass myself at my next race."

  "Perfect. Now, let's just make sure all is well here—" Oliver opened the door cautiously to peer into my room. Moppit let out a high-pitched *yip!* and immediately bounded over to greet us, wiggling like crazy. Oliver reached down to pick her up, instantly rewarded with several licks on his chin. "I'll take her out. Bet she's starving too. Do you still have the dog biscuits hidden?"

I grinned up at him. "Of course, in the same place. And thank you, Uncle Oliver. I know I don't say that nearly enough." I scratched behind Moppit's ears to buy myself some time and composure. My emotions were far too close to the surface recently. "I couldn't have done this without you."

He squeezed my shoulder, softly saying, "I wouldn't be anywhere else, darling girl. I'll see to Moppit first. And six-thirty it is."

I cranked up the air conditioning and stood in the shower for a terribly self-indulgent amount of time. Standing there, breathing deeply, allowing the water to wash away every bit of sweat, grime, smashed bugs, insect spray and weariness. One thing I couldn't wash down the drain, though: regret.

God, here I am again. I feel so strange, so dis-connected. Missing Dad even as I sort through a myriad of feelings about him and Mom. What was our family life like, really? Was it the healthy, happy one I've always assumed? Or have I changed feelings and facts in my memories to make my past what I wanted *it to be?*

I sorted through the vivid memories of my last conversation with Mom before she died. Initially, we were laughing so hard about something—I can't recall exactly what now. Our relationship had grown so close and easy and open, but I wanted her to accept and understand what I had with Guy. In the spur of the moment, I decided to plunge right in and brought up "the voice" that I heard, hoping this time maybe she would believe me? But the look of shock and then disappointment on her face made me instantly sick at heart, and I swallowed back my words. Ran from the kitchen to my room. Where I threw myself on the bed and sobbed into my pillow.

It was only a few hours later when Mom fell to the floor. A brain aneurism taking her from Dad and me, instantly. I had no chance to say good bye. No opportunity to fix the chasm I'd put between us. No time to redeem myself in her eyes. And that last look of alarm and utter disbelief on her face? I'll carry that with me always, a burden of regret that feels heavy on my soul. Accompanied by the bitter truth of rejection.

So, God, how do I begin to process my feelings about this other family—my actual relatives, my ancestors? Today's adventure provided the proof: They truly existed. They were real. I felt...them. Amazingly, I knew their pain deep in my body, Lord. Which has added yet another layer of rejection in my soul. Why didn't they want me? My adoptive parents couldn't accept my mind talking with Guy. But what could a newborn do to warrant not being wanted? To not meriting love?

I grabbed the side of the shower as the world began to spin, shaking my head at the irony: Pretty much everything in my life is out of kilter. Why wouldn't I feel dizzy? I moved under the spray again, allowing it to splash on my face.

Lord, are you pushing me to take another leap of faith? I want to believe there's something important I'm supposed to discover, right here in this little town. And I want to believe I'll find unconditional love here, not more rejection. I shook my head at myself when I realized: *I can be courageous when men are protecting stills—by shooting at me. I can brave kudzu. Bugs. Even the possibility of snakes. But discovering all my past holds means I have to uncover the truth about all the people in my life—those already gone, and those still alive. Once again, I'm that odd, frightened little girl. Once strange, always strange, Julia.*

I attempt to identify the feelings that lay hidden beneath, but it all feels like a riddle within a puzzle, and the answers either elude me—or I subconsciously avoid them. But then I squeeze my eyes shut, focusing this time on my all-powerful God.

Please, God. Help me unravel this. I do sense that I must start here: Besides Uncle Ollie, I can't begin to trust people—and figure out who I can trust here in Collinsville—until I first learn to completely trust you.

I rested my head against the cool wall of the shower a moment, appreciating the solid feel of it in my turmoil. *I'm just like the Roman soldier. Lord, I believe. Please help me overcome my unbelief.*

Knowing I was way too emotional to talk with Guy, I blocked him out for the second time that day. *How much could he sense?* I asked myself. *By intentionally keeping him away, am I actually inviting him to be more distrustful?* It was risky, I was sure of it. But I just needed some time...to myself.

About to throw on an older t-shirt and jeans, I stopped, reconsidering. Instead, I reached for a new camisole—a lacy one, in pale yellow that seemed to compliment the color of my skin. A white linen skirt and gold sandals seemed to further boost my self-confidence, so that when I checked the results in the mirror, I realized I needed to complete the look. I'd done nothing besides pull my hair into a ponytail and skipped applying anything but the barest essentials of make-up since we'd arrived in Collinsville. Tonight, however, I decided to blow dry my hair and try out the newly purchased mascara that promised to "make your eyes get noticed!"

And exactly who did I want to notice me? I mused, grinning at my image.

Certainly, it was Brent. I mean, after all, he definitely was the better looking of the two brothers. No contest there. But more so: He appeared more congenial, more considerate (although, admittedly, that wouldn't take much on Brent's part; E.A. was that frustrating, in my opinion), and then there was the fact that he didn't provoke me every other minute.

Which made me realize maybe I *did* want E.A. to take note tonight also, just so I could rub in my total disinterest. Kind of a "look at what you're missing" message.

When Oliver saw me, he let out a low whistle. "My goodness, girl. You didn't tell me it was dress-up night. I should've put on my sport coat."

I smiled my thanks. His response had provided the self-assurance boost I needed. If Oliver noticed, I had to believe certain others would too. "That shower did wonders, Uncle Ollie. Do you feel as rejuvenated as I do?"

He sighed, a long, drawn-out breath that sounded as though he was resigned to something. A bit surprised, I stared up at his profile. "At your age, dear girl, a shower or a good night's sleep or some decent protein can alleviate the aches and pains, sore muscles, even weary bones. But at my age, Julia, well, let's just say all those nasty aches seem to hunker down in, staking out their territory. It's rather like the relative who's supposed to stay only a couple days—but ends up eating your favorite snacks, drinks all your best wine and monopolizes your favorite television-watching chair for a week."

I laughed at him and took his proffered arm. "Does that mean you're going to be sore for a week from swinging that sickle? I'm going to feel awfully guilty if that's the case, Uncle Ollie."

He patted my hand and then winked at me. "All for a good cause, my darling girl. If Mama Byrd notices my bulging muscles, then it will be worth every ache and pain."

We were both still chuckling as Oliver pulled open the door to A Byrd in the Hand, and though I'd noted the parking lot seemed pretty full, we were both surprised to see just how busy the place was.

"Goodness," Oliver said, "I never thought we'd need a reservation. I don't see one open table, do you?"

But Brent caught our attention, waving us over and pointing towards a small table tucked away in a corner. Once we were closer, his eyes noticeably widened as his gaze traveled from my head to my toes. I hid a self-satisfied smile of victory while Uncle Ollie gave me an overly exaggerated wink.

"Julia. Wow. You look stunning tonight." He held my chair and turned to give me his full attention. The smile he flashed had to be in the one-thousand-watt range with those perfect white teeth. I also took in the square jaw, masculine lines framing a sensual mouth, that unruly lock of hair again. I caught a whiff of cologne too—not the cheap stuff, which I hated. And not too much, either, which I also detested. "We still on for tomorrow?"

"Well, I—"

"You're not backin' out on me, are you?" Brent asked. Oliver looked at me with surprise too.

"No, not at all. Just considering a slight change of plans."

"I'm up for anything. Just you name it."

"Actually, I was thinking a day of rest and relaxation sounded pretty good. I'm sure you must know of some fun hikes around here, Brent. Possibly the Gap? What do you think?"

"Oh, I'm thinkin' a hike sounds near perfect." He handed both of us menus as his eyes quickly scanned the room. "Hey, I need to check on some other tables, but I'll be right back for your orders. And we'll find us a few minutes to chat, I promise. The place I'd like to take you tomorrow isn't far, and you'll love it. The Pocket, it's called. We'll hike out there. Take a picnic lunch. Swim."

"Really? We can swim there too?" The thought of getting into a cool spring after a hike sounded wonderful.

"Absolutely. And it won't be crowded tomorrow neither. We might could even have the place all to ourselves." Brent pointed to the insert that listed tonight's specials. "I'm recommendin' the largemouth bass. Mama fixes it with breading that's out of this world good. What can I get y'all to drink?"

"You'll come with us, won't you, Uncle Ollie? On the hike, I mean? We could see The Gap another time."

He was preoccupied with studying the menu but still managed to mumble, "Going to be sore again tomorrow, I'm thinking. I'll pass on the hike, if that's okay with you, darlin' girl."

I'd just opened my mouth to respond when a pretty twenty-something woman arrived at our table with tall glasses of iced tea and a basket of rolls. "Good evening. My name's Kate, and I'll be servin' y'all tonight." Her voice was lilting, smooth—overflowing with that Southern charm thing.

Oliver smiled broadly, shaking his head. "Switched servers on us last night too. Can't complain, though, as I'd say you're a ton prettier than the one who showed us to our table."

She chuckled, revealing a deep dimple in her left cheek. As dark as I am, Kate was my opposite just like Melissa: She had long blond, wavy hair (no bleached job either; hers was clearly the real deal); fair, slightly freckled skin; big, beautiful light blue eyes ringed with long lashes; and model thin. Taken all together, she looked the part of the fair princess while I would be typecast as the wicked witch.

"What can I get y'all? Did Brent tell you 'bout tonight's specials?" She went on to explain the varied offerings, but Oliver and I stuck with Brent's recommendation. We ordered the bass with sautéed fresh local vegetables and wild rice.

Oliver immediately pounced on the rolls, but I searched the room, impatiently seeking something that would settle my restlessness. What that something was, though, I had no idea. Brent, possibly?

As Uncle Ollie spread butter on the still steaming dinner roll, he held it out in front of me, demonstrating how the butter melted immediately. "Oh, my goodness. Is there anything much better than hot, fresh bread with butter?" Oliver took a bite, and I had to chuckle as he closed his eyes and sat back in his chair. "Ahhhh. I wouldn't have thought anything could top those biscuits. But this roll? It's a contender."

"You know how Dad loved to eat." My voice cracked just a bit as I thought of our last meal together at the Italian restaurant. "But you take eating to a whole different level, Uncle Ollie. Watching you, I sure do get the old adage that the best way to a man's heart—"

"Is through his tummy!" Myra Byrd stood before us again, hands on hips, the same wide, beautiful smile gracing us that we'd seen earlier from Brent. "Good evenin', y'all. No, stay settin'," she demanded as Oliver attempted to stand. "Had me a minute to slip out, so's when Brent told me y'all were here, I thought I'd come say hey."

"A pleasure to see you again, Missus—"

"Please. Call me Myra."

So, last night it was Mama Byrd, but tonight it's Myra? Better watch out, Uncle Ollie, I thought to myself. I was thoroughly enjoying the sweet scene being acted out before me.

Oliver gallantly tilted his head towards her. "Myra it is. I can't tell you how much I'm delighting in these dinner rolls. They are absolutely delicious."

"Why, thank you. Oliver." She fidgeted a good bit, and I could feel her hesitation. It was clear she wanted to say something but was shy and nervous about doing so. Finally, she started talking, and once she began, it all came out in one long breath. "Brent says him and your niece here is goin' to the Pocket tomorrow so I was wondering—since Byrd in the Hand is closed on Wednesdays—that is, it has been ever since my dear William passed years ago, God rest his soul, so's I was wondering, Oliver, if you'd like to go on up to see the Gap as it's right pretty up there and I was thinkin' as y'all be visitin' here for the first time you might really like that." She stopped suddenly and took a deep breath. "I'm meanin', I could take you. If you'd like that."

Oliver's eyes twinkled and that grin of his took over, revealing his boyish charm to the max. Mama Byrd appeared to be smitten with Oliver already, but if there was any hesitation on her part, she didn't stand a chance once confronted with that smile. "I would be honored, Myra. Honestly, I can't think of a better way to spend my day—since Julia's going to be well taken care of, that is, in the company of your son."

Totally flustered now, poor Mama Byrd couldn't decide where to look, so her gaze flitted all over the room. "Oh my, well then. So that's all settled. Shall I pick you up at the mo-tel at eight? Or is that a might too early?"

"Eight is perfect."

"I'll pack us a lunch to tote along too."

"But I hate for you to go to all that trouble—"

She shook her head and looked Oliver square in the eyes. When it came to the topic of cooking and the kitchen, there wasn't a hint of shyness about her. Obviously, that was Mama Byrd's domain, and she ruled it well. "Tain't no trouble atall. I'll just put us in a few things. Some leftovers and the like."

"Well, then. I won't turn that down—more of your wonderful cooking."

"Oh, tis nothin'." She waved one hand in the air, indicating how insignificant that task would be. "Now, I'd best be gettin' back to work." She smiled at me and then nodded in Oliver's direction, evidently too shy to look him in the eyes again. Her sweet girlishness was touching; I gave her a warm smile and a quick wave before she hurried back to the kitchen.

As dramatically as I could, I turned my body around to face Oliver square on. I gave him another of my practiced looks, eyebrows raised. "So. What an interesting development. And my, how the aches and pains have disappeared completely! Must've been that scrumptious, healing roll."

Before I could grill him anymore, though, Kate arrived with our food. We'd taken only a few bites—the bass was delicious, and the vegetables grilled to perfection—before Brent was back to confirm the time for our departure the next day.

"What if I pick you up at ten?"

"Sounds good. That will give me time for a quick run in the morning," I replied, wiping my mouth with the napkin. "What should I bring?"

"Well, as for lunch, Mama's always got somethin' round I can put together to make us a meal. You'll need to bring along a swimsuit and towel."

"Can't I contribute something?"

"Just yourself."

"I'm so looking forward to it, Brent."

Suddenly E.A. was next to his brother, frowning. Actually, he was scowling again, pretty much his favorite facial expression, it appeared. "Looking forward to what?" He proceeded to give me the once-over, starting with my hair, skimming downward over my camisole, and even trying to see my skirt, though it was mostly hidden under the tablecloth. I could feel myself squirming a bit under his scrutiny and was frustrated with myself for doing so.

When the black look persisted, however, I got huffy. All that work to put him in his place and this was the reaction I got? Inwardly I was seething, defensive, but I worked hard to make my voice as cool and nonchalant as possible. "I don't think it's any of your business, E.A."

Brent poked him in the ribs and E.A. momentarily turned his bad humor away from me towards his brother. But he wasn't about to let it go; he turned to glare at me again. "Anything that involves my brother and you *is* my business."

"*Excuse me?*" What did it take the man? Less than one minute to totally provoke me again?

"And aren't you a bit cold in here, baring your shoulders and back like that? Every sensible girl in the South knows to bring a sweater for the AC."

I swear to you my mouth dropped open. The *audacity*. And what *century* was he born in?

"Brent, Mama needs you in the kitchen. And how 'bout you fetch one of her sweaters while you're in there. For Julia. Before she freezes over."

Brent turned to me—all seriousness, I assumed, until he crossed his eyes and made me nearly laugh out loud—calmly saying, "Summoned once again to the dungeons. But never fear, fair damsel, for I shall return. To protect you from the ire of the fire-breathing dragon!"

As Brent turned on his heel to run the errand, a loud laugh did escape before I could stop it; as expected, I received yet another glare from E.A. "Yeah, he's hilarious, all right. What's he got planned for the two of you anyway?"

I crossed my arms over my chest and stared right back at him. "As I stated already, I don't believe that's any of your business." Glancing over at Oliver, I noted he was gleefully shoveling down his meal, not missing a beat (or bite) because of my on-going conflict with E.A. He gave me a slight smile before stuffing the last of another roll into his mouth. "Don't stop eating on my account, Uncle Oliver."

He shook his head *no*, mumbling, "Mmph mphn't." I assumed that translated to *I won't*.

E.A. leaned forward, and in a measured, soft voice, he pretty much hissed, "Julia, please listen to me. I tried to warn you last night but evidently you weren't hearing me. Brent is…he's… the truth of it is, you can't trust him, Julia."

I was appalled. "What an awful thing to say about your own brother."

"Look, he's going to be back any second now. I *will* find out what you're up to, so you might as well tell me now."

"If you *have* to know…we're going on a hike to…oh good grief, what was it called? The backpack? The fanny pack?"

Oliver choked and E.A. looked dumbfounded.

"Well, sorry," I shrugged my shoulders, as an involuntary, pronounced shiver passed across them too. *Blasted timing*, I thought to myself. *Did E.A. notice that? I hated that my body was doing something he'd take as proof he was right.* "Obviously I can't remember what it's called," I said, acting as though nothing happened, picking up my fork and waving it at him before I took another bite of the bass. "You'll just have to ask Brent, I guess. And please tell your mom how delicious this is, will you?" With that, I dismissed him with another wave of my fork.

Fortunately, he got the hint and huffed his way back to the kitchen.

"That was masterfully done, my dear," Oliver said, chuckling and still choking a bit at the same time.

"What was?"

"The not remembering bit."

"Uncle Ollie, I wasn't lying. Honestly, I really can't recall the name. Are you saying you do?"

"Me? I'm not saying a thing, darling girl. If there are any pluses to be gained from growing old, it's a bit of wisdom in dealing with women. Generally, I have learned when to keep my mouth shut." He reached into the breadbasket, pulling out yet another dinner roll. "And right now is one of those times. Definitely." I watched him carefully split it and spread on a pat of butter. "Not counting eating this, however."

Raising one eyebrow, I asked, "So is that the last roll?"

"It is, and all buttered and ready for you too."

As he placed the roll in my open palm, I gave him a huge smile.

—

I'd set my alarm for six-thirty, hoping to hit the road right after the sun was up. I knew Uncle Ollie would pitch a fit about my going out while it was still dark—no sense trying to sneak out either, as he would definitely hear the slightest creak of my door—so just after sunrise would have to do.

I rubbed my eyes, blinked them several times, rubbed them once more. Resigned myself to the fact that there was no way my eyes were up to contacts at this hour. Since my glasses would only slip down my nose in this humidity, I elected to go without, figuring anything I needed to see, squinting had to be good enough.

Moppit popped up her head, but I put a finger to my lips. "Shhh. Be patient. I'll be back before you know it." I petted her, gently easing her back onto her bed. She snuggled down in, rolling only her eyes up to watch me. "If you play your cards right, girl, I bet you can con Uncle Ollie into extra treats later too."

Quickly changing into a tank top, leggings, and my Nikes, I peeked out my door. Discovered it was the perfect time for a run: The sky was a shade of blushing pink, humidity was doable, and male birds were busy making their case (to impress the girls, of course) with a variety of melodious calls. I stretched, made note of the time, and set off down one of the now familiar roads.

Since I'd missed several days, I was a bit concerned how I would feel. But once I fell into my regular rhythm, it felt good. Surprisingly good. Legs relaxed, swinging my arms, breathing easy. It was shaping up to be a good workout for me.

-Jules? You out for a run?

-Yup. Been too long, but it feels good.

Glancing to my right, I saw a runner a couple blocks away. *That looks like Brent*, I thought to myself, my heart skipping a beat. Squinting, I gave him another look. *It is Brent; I'm sure of it! I knew he was a runner. Maybe he'll join me?* Anticipation made my breathing a bit erratic again, and I had to smile at myself. *You're not much better than Mama Byrd around Uncle Oliver, Julia. Calm down*, I lectured.

-Guy, I think we're going to be interrupted. Another runner's about to join me. Let's pick this up later, okay?
-Sure. Enjoy your company.
-I think I will, Guy. I really do.

I heard his steps behind me, and so with a huge, eager, positively silly grin on my face, I turned around to greet…E.A. The disappointment was like a punch to my gut.

"Oh, it's you." So much for enjoying the company. Or my run. *I wonder if he can exasperate me in less than a minute again,* I mused.

He fell into stride alongside me, and in spite of myself, I did notice his legs. They were long, very well defined in muscular tone, shaped just like a dedicated runner's legs should be. And for whatever reason—probably mostly because they weren't Brent's legs—they irritated me beyond belief.

"Thanks for the warm greeting." E.A. glanced over at me, and I could tell that he'd been running for some time already this morning. His cheeks were flushed and he was dripping with sweat, but his breathing was still noticeably even and deep. All the signs of someone who runs regularly. But there was something else there too, that, despite resistance on my part, softened my heart towards him: For just a fleeting moment, his face clearly registered hurt.

"You were out early," I said, making an effort to keep my tone light-hearted and friendly.

"Yeah, I like to get at it right when the sun's comin' up." He motioned towards the right with his head. "Turn down this way. Road's got a nice, wide berm. Heads out of town, winding beneath some trees. Believe me, the shade'll start to feel good."

"You're asking me to trust you? I got the impression the Byrd brothers were never to be trusted."

E.A. was quiet a moment before responding, "When you were a kid, did you have do-overs when you played ball?"

I smirked. "Yeah. Mostly in kickball. Why?"

"I need a do-over with you. Jul...durn it, *Julia*, I'm asking for a do-over. Because I've acted like a mule's backside and I'm genuinely sorry. Could we pretend we've just met? Start over?" He glanced over at me, eyes clearly searching, asking for mercy. For just a moment, I saw a glimpse of the little boy who'd batted a ball through a window, shattering it in a million pieces. Having to own up to what he'd done, but desperately wanting forgiveness. A do-over.

Still, though his eyes sucked me right in, I couldn't let him off too easy. "Just a mule's backside? Nothing worse than that?"

He shook his head and grinned, shyly. I hadn't thought there was a shy molecule in him. "You wouldn't be askin' a good Southern boy to curse, would you now?"

"Not if it got him in trouble with his mama."

"Oh, if she heard, it would do that, for sure."

We both laughed, just as we turned down a lane that was nearly breath-taking in its beauty. The morning sun rose to our left, and the oak trees lining the creek (and following the road) were giants, so the shadows cast by their trunks provided welcome relief, just like E.A. had promised.

"Stupid new laces. I need to stop a minute, Julia. Shoe's untied."

E.A. moved to the berm as he squatted down to re-tie his shoe. I sensed more than heard a car coming—much faster than it should've been, and especially on this winding road. When I turned around to confirm my suspicions, I saw a black SUV—why on earth did it happen to be black? And an SUV too?—barreling towards us. I guess all the insecurities and utter terror of that night came rushing back, because of all my options, I did the absolute worst thing: I froze. I also failed to alert E.A., didn't shout, didn't get farther off the road, didn't duck down between the perfect barriers—those red oak trees. Instead, I stood there, staring at that SUV like a deer in headlights. Until

E.A. grabbed me just in the nick of time, sending both of us sprawling into the ditch. For a few moments, we were a tangled mess of flailing limbs, sweat and the detritus that's always found in a ditch by a busy road.

I sat up, trying to regain my equilibrium when E.A. demanded more than asked, "Tell me you're all right? That was way too close!"

"Actually, I—"

But he didn't even give me a chance to reply, for once he'd given me a quick perusal—*Why did he suddenly appear so angry again?*—he jumped up, staring after the car that was already out of sight. "I didn't catch the plates—the fool. How I'd love to get my hands around his neck." He reached out to me, grabbing my hands to pull me up. "You got a good look at the front, didn't you? Any kind of special plate there?"

I was pulling bits of leaves and sticks out of my hair, checking to make sure all of my limbs were in one piece. "What? Special plates?"

"Tennessee doesn't require a front license plate. So was there anything on the front? You know—a plate with a car dealership or a school team or mascot. Something on that order."

I shrugged my shoulders. "No idea. I don't have my contacts in."

And then I got the scowl treatment again. *So soon, we're back to that?* I thought to myself, sighing. *What did we have? Five minutes, max, of peace between us?*

"Let me get this straight: You can't see a blessed thing. But you're out running. In a strange place. And just yesterday you were shot at, for cryin' out loud."

"What's that got to do with anything?" He tried to help me dust grass and dirt off my legs, but I angrily swatted his hands away. *Hadn't we done this same routine just yesterday?* "That was back-country boys protecting their still. This was some idiot speeding on a country road. He's probably late for work."

E.A. stared into the distance, frowning, the muscle in his jaw twitching like mad. "Tennesseans don't generally speed, Julia. We go slow. We're not ones for hurryin' anywhere." He turned to look at me, hands on hips, anger pulsating off him like sparks of electricity. "Part 'n parcel of our nature. And that fool was headin' *away* from town, not towards it. Any other half-brained ideas?"

"Yeah, just one," I threw back at him. "Your do-over's over."

I gave him one last scathing look before feeling the rush of adrenaline that comes with budding anger. I turned on my heels, running back up the road, towards town. Away from what I considered the most maddening man on this earth.

THE GRAVESTONES' SECRETS

15 of June, 1588

My Descendants,

How is it that I long more for Catherine with each passing day? How is it too that I feel closer to her with each daybreak? I see Catherine's eyes in the colors of the Sea. I glimpse her lips in the pastels of the Sunset. And I touch her hair in the hues of the blooms of this glorious Land. Catherine is not here with me. And yet, she is.

I clutch this B in my hand and picture it hanging about Catherine's graceful neck. It signifies Beloved to me, and me alone, as I rub it between my fingers.

It once belonged to my father's Mother, so wrongfully accused and condemned to Death! One Soul here caught glimpse of it hanging about my neck and inquired as to its meaning. Stammering, as though a lovesick fool, I allowed as though it once belonged to my Betrothed. Am I not clever in your eyes?

How I long to talk with my Catherine this night! Have I mentioned that she is the delight of my life?

*Your devoted,
Mauro*

CHAPTER SEVEN

I hadn't run far when Guy started pounding on my door. Well, obviously, not literally. But that's pretty much what it feels like when he gets like this. Demanding. Insistent. *Let me in!*
-Jules? I'm getting a clear sense that it didn't go well? I thought you were happy someone else was going to join you?
-Wasn't who I thought it was. Or *wished* it was.
-Oh. You seem...irritated. Did *he* cause that?
-Did. Does. Like no other. It's the same man I told you about before. He's simply *maddening*, Guy.
-What did he do now? Are you certain you're not misjudging him?
-Stop defending the slug again! He's overbearing and obnoxious and presumes way too much. Like just a couple minutes ago when he over-reacted again.

Too late: Now I'd waded into it big time. How am I going to dodge the issue of the black SUV? Stupid, Julia, really stupid.

-What happened?
-Nothing.
-You just admitted he over-reacted to whatever *it* is. Was. So something *did* happen.
-Well, sorta.
-Jules!

I elected to try the blasé approach. It rarely worked with Guy—he could see through my shenanigans far too easily—but I didn't have many alternatives. In the past, evading only tended to ramp up his pursuit of the truth. He could be like a bloodhound on the trail of a raccoon.

-So he'd stopped to tie his shoe, and there was this car that drove by. It was a little close to us. No big deal.

-How close exactly?

-Not much, really, but he tackled me, for cryin' out loud—which was absolutely unnecessary. I'll be picking gravel and grit out of my hair and ears for days.

-What make and color was the car?

-Guy, I know where you're going with this...

-I'm not *going anywhere* with this but to look for the facts. It was black, wasn't it? And an SUV? Jules, you've got to go to the police.

-Oh, now that's ridiculous.

-Three incidences now, Jules. Count 'em. How many warnings do you need before you do something about it?

-Calm down, Guy. In the first place, the sludge—

-Are you referring to this same guy again? Slug, slime, sludge. Settle on one name for the poor fellow, will you?

I stopped running then, leaned over to place hands on my knees and catch my breath. In the short time I'd been out running, the humidity had grown intense and was zapping my strength—either that, or I'd gotten out of shape way faster than I'd realized. This Southern food was simply too tempting. As I stared down at the blacktop, a feeling of déjà vu came over me with such force I shook my head in surprise. Was this particular part of town reminiscent of somewhere back home? Or could it merely be Guy's repetitive concern about the coincidence of my dad's and my accidents? He'd always been protective of me, in a big brother kind of way. But this felt almost eerie somehow.

-Okay. I give up. Once Uncle Ollie hears about this—and there's no sense my trying to keep it from him as E.A. will spill it for sure—he'd make me report it anyway. The police will look at me like I'm crazy. Make me fill out a stupid form, most likely. But then you and Uncle Ollie and E.A. will all be happy, right?

-Good for Uncle Ollie. You've stopped running, haven't you? Are you close to the motel?

-No, I just stopped to rest a minute. The humidity is—

-I know. It's awful.

-How would you know that? *Unless you live in the South too?* I probed.

- Everyone knows it's humid in Tennessee. Good try, Jules, but you know that's off limits.

-Let me get this straight: You know where I am. But I still don't get to know where *you* are. What's fair about that?

-Stop over-thinking it, Jules; just listen to your heart for a change, will you? And get to the police station, this morning. Gotta go.

-Hey—don't dismiss me when you've dropped a bomb like... oh. You're getting into the shower, aren't you? Okay, I'm gone.

-Don't you know it's my love for you that drives me at times like this?

-So you say. But both you and Uncle Ollie are determined to smother me with your overly protective love sometimes. And especially since...since...

-Jules, I'm so sorry. I wish there was some way I could better comfort you.

-How about you be less obsessed with my safety?

-May I humbly suggest that E.A. might also be driven by—

-Don't even attempt to go there, Guy. Honestly, that's *ludicrous*.

-Oh Jules.

And with that, he was gone.

I ran back to the hotel, slowing my pace as I entered the motel's parking lot. Putting hands on hips and walking slowly around the perimeter of the lot, I attempted to calm my breathing and frenetic thoughts.

God, what was that about? Could it have been coincidental that—AGAIN—the SUV was black? And driving that fast—when E.A. insists people in this part of the South don't do that? What's true, God? What should I believe?

I know one thing. I'm starting to feel afraid. Whether that's warranted or not—true or not—my feelings don't hinge on fact.

And my greatest fear? I'm terrified of losing someone else that I love—that you'll take someone else from me! That's why I don't want to fully submit to your will, Lord, giving you full control. I say that I want to, but it's only that—lip service. Because underneath, I want to be in control. I'm never going to find the courage to jump out in faith if I can't trust you. With my future. With those I love. With all the secrets Mom and Dad hid from me. And with what I need to discover here about me and who I am.

Oh, God. I know—I'm not handling this well. And the thought of a true jump of trust? Oh, no. Definitely not ready to do that.

That's only a figure of speech, right?

I laughed at myself and shook my head.

—

Moppit greeted me with a wagging tail and kisses. Uncle Oliver appeared to be no less enthusiastic, although he thankfully limited his kisses to only two, one on each cheek. Clearly, he was looking forward to his date with Myra Byrd today. He was in such a jolly mood I hated to ruin it with my sobering news, but I knew he wouldn't be pleased if he found out later—and especially from another source like that rat E.A. So I took a deep breath and spit out the entire scenario in one rushed, succinct exhalation. Oliver plopped back down in a chair, giving me a wide-eyed look.

"Oh my. I'll call Myra to cancel and we'll go straightaway to the police station."

"Uncle Ollie, don't be silly. There's no need for you to do that." I yanked off one shoe and a dank, smelly sock. "I'll go. I'm capable of doing this myself, you know."

"It's not your capabilities I doubt, dear girl. It's your follow through."

I gave him a sharp look as I worked on removing my other shoe and sock.

"And don't give me that look. You know very well what I'm talking about."

"I do?"

"Now you're giving me a dumb look, which is not acceptable either. You know very well there are far too many coincidences here. Two accidents back home. The shot yesterday."

"First of all, need I remind you that the police totally dismissed any connection between Dad's accident and my hit 'n run? As for yesterday, Mrs. Odell warned us about the protective people out there and their stills, so we have to assume those boys were warning *both* of us, Uncle Ollie. It's all perfectly explainable."

"Until you put them all together."

I shivered and then wrapped my arms around myself. The shift from rigorous exercise and nearly suffocating humidity to being inside the air-conditioned room was giving my inner thermostat fits. Oliver offered me a sweater but I shook it off. "I'm fine. In need of a shower. Uncle Oliver, please don't cancel your picnic with Myra. I'll be fine—I promise. Look, here's what I'll do: I'll ask Brent to take me to the police station. That way I won't have to go alone. And I promise I'll tell them everything. That work for you?"

He hesitated, narrowing his eyes in concentration, but finally granting a begrudgingly offered, "Well, okay. Just know I'll want a full report of what they said. And what they want you to do."

"I will do that. Promise."

"What about Moppit?" Moppit jumped up at the mention of her name, cocking her head, ears forward. "Want me to take her with us? I bet Myra would like that, and I know Moppit would enjoy a short hike."

"Sure. That would be great."

"Hop in the shower before you catch your death of cold." He glanced at his watch. "Myra will be here in about thirty minutes, so Moppit and I will most likely be gone by the time you're dressed. Now, when you're at the police headquarters, don't forget—"

"You should say, *remember* to—, right? It appears we need to work on remembering to state things in the positive!"

"Clever girl."

I reached up to put a hand on his chest. "I *will* remember, I promise. I'll go. I'll be fine. Have a wonderful time with Myra. You've earned it, putting up with me and Moppit these last few weeks. Go. And enjoy."

He leaned down, planting another kiss on my cheek. "Darling girl, there's no such thing as 'putting up with you.' You're my favorite niece, after all."

I laughed, raising up on tiptoes to give him a kiss back. "Flatterer, considering I'm also your *only* niece."

I watched that boyish smile appear again and wondered how often Aunt Susan was able to resist him when presented with one of those heart stealers. "That right? Well, I guess you're doubly my favorite then."

He earned another chuckle for that one.

After a refreshing shower, I pulled on my gear—pants that I could easily roll up to my knees if I wanted instant shorts, a t-shirt underneath a long-sleeved blouse, and my much-used hiking boots. Into my backpack I tucked a swimsuit and towel, a comb and sunscreen, and at the last minute, I threw in a notebook and pen. I was planning to pick Brent's brain about the area and its history, so I might want to take notes.

I started getting anxious when nine o'clock came and went. It was nearly nine thirty—I was peeved by then, I'll admit—when I finally heard a knock on my door.

"Julia, I'm so sorry I'm late. At the last minute, Mama needed me to run a couple errands, and they took longer than I'd planned. Forgive me?"

I looked into those heavily lashed eyes and realized there was nothing to forgive. Not when he was here before me, flashing that mega-watt smile. "Nothing to forgive, Brent."

"Ah, you're sweet." Before I realized what was happening, he leaned down and brushed a soft kiss on my lips. "Sweet indeed," he whispered, staring into my eyes.

A thrill coursed through me—*When was the last time I'd felt like this? I couldn't even remember*—and I smiled up at him.

"Ready to go then?"

"Am I ever."

He took my backpack and held the door as I climbed into his little sports car. That sort of chivalry—holding the door for a girl—was becoming rare back home, but evidently Southern boys still practiced being gentlemen. My guess was their mothers saw to it, and I could picture Mama Byrd enforcing those rules.

"I do have one favor to ask of you first, though." I would never stoop to using womanly wiles (first I'd have to figure out what on earth they were), but I gave him my best *I need your help* type of look.

"Anything. Just name it."

"Mind if we swing by the police station first?" I noticed he flinched but quickly recovered, turning to me slowly with a quizzical look on his face.

"You rob a bank last night or somethin'? Turning yourself in?"

I grinned. "No, but I will confess to considering murder this morning."

"Murder, eh? Who you aimin' to kill off?"

"Your brother, actually."

"No crime for the thought. If there was, I'd been sent off to prison some twenty years ago."

Grinning at him, I added, "He seems to rub a lot of people the wrong way."

"Tell me about it. He can act meaner than two cats in a flour sack. But back to this police station thing. You serious?"

I smiled at his expression but then sighed, realizing how convoluted the whole situation was. I needed to make a quick decision: I could be evasive with the facts (which would probably only make Brent ask more questions); make up a story (which I was not skilled at; Oliver said my "tell" was terribly obvious, though he wouldn't explain what it was); or decide to trust Brent and simply give him a brief outline of the truth. I chose the last option.

"Well, it's complicated, but before I left home, I was sideswiped and run off the road by a car. A hit 'n run, actually."

"Whoa. You get a good look at the driver?" He kept his gaze forward looking, diligently watching the road.

"No, didn't see a thing, as a matter of fact. Not the driver or the license plate. The police back home were taken with my lack of observational skills."

"So why the need to report that now? And here in Collinsville, of all places?"

Taking a deep breath, I explained, "Well, there's more to the story, unfortunately." I went on to tell him about my dad's accident—which of course led to the side-bar explanation about his death. Brent was quick to offer condolences and even reached over to squeeze my hand when my voice caught. He merely shrugged when I shared about what happened at the homesite—evidently that was pretty much expected down here when you ventured too far out in the country and wandered near someone's property. But when I told him about this morning's SUV incident, he reacted with alarm.

"SUV again, huh? What color?"

"Black. Know anyone with one of those?"

He shook his head. "Most people round here drive a pick-up." Brent patted the seat between us and grinned. "Or old clunkers like mine. But hey, this here's Claiborne county's only police station. Let me give you a quick lesson in pronunciation: It's pronounced *sher-f*. You gotta mostly jump right over the *i*. Give it a try?"

"Sher-f," I promptly repeated.

"Excellent. You're a quick study."

I laughed. "Thanks for the tutorial, Brent. And for…your understanding."

"Understanding for what?"

"Well, for humoring my uncle by bringing me to the station. If it were up to me, we'd skip this meaningless visit. Thanks for helping to put me at ease about it too. I just want to get this over with."

"Then let's do it."

He gave my hand one more squeeze before we filed in and faced two intimidating deputies. Granted, they appeared to do everything in their power to be accommodating, and each asked questions for clarification. But their frequent puzzled and skeptical looks showed they were in agreement with me rather than Guy, E.A. and Uncle Ollie: They were convinced these random accidents were merely coincidental (especially in light of the fact that the police back in Sundhamn had decided that too), and so they reassured me I had nothing to worry about. However, one deputy promised to keep an eye out for a black SUV, and even went so far as to assure me that "If I locate 'im, I'll give 'im a stern warnin' about speedin' in my county. Most likely someone from outta town—no disrespect meant to you, Miss." I quickly told him none taken, and he continued, "But Collinsville folks don't tend to be in such a hurry anyways."

I almost told him that's pretty much what E.A. had said, but I assumed Brent wouldn't appreciate my mentioning his brother. So I just smiled and told them thanks for their advice and help.

They asked why I was here (a vague response about searching for family roots went over okay, it seemed), where I was staying and for how long (I answered truthfully that I didn't know), and promised me that one of them would also take a ride out to the Collins' homesite. "Ain't no call for someone to be shootin' like that, even if they are protecting private property." Deputy Jenkins hitched up his pants and placed his hat firmly on his head. "I'll see to it this mornin'. But you let us know, Miss, if you have you any more of them unusual co-incidences."

I smiled to myself, noting how Southerners appeared to savor the feel and sound of vowels on their tongues.

"Once Sheriff Buttram hears about this, he might suggest you hire on one of them bodyguards for you, Miss." He turned to the other deputy, asking, "You think Ronnie Gibson might be interested?"

Both deputies and Brent chuckled at their inside joke, and I gave Brent a questioning look.

"Um, Ronnie's a big guy," Brent explained, matter-of-factly. He glanced over towards the deputies, "You guess he's what? Six foot seven and over three hundred and fifty pounds?"

"Let's just say Ronnie's so big it's easier to go over top him rather than around."

We all laughed and I thanked the deputies, offering, tongue-in-cheek, "I'll certainly take your suggestion about Ronnie into consideration. As for right now, we're on our way to—where is it again, Brent?" As usual—trying to remember the name of the park—I rubbed the scar next to my little finger. Also, as usual, it didn't do one bit of good to spark my memory.

I looked up at Brent and noticed, for the briefest moment, how he clamped his mouth shut in a grim line. Was that irritation shadowing his features? Just as quickly, however, his face relaxed and he answered quickly, "The Pocket."

Sensing I'd displeased Brent somehow—but clueless in what way—I purposefully took the conversation towards a light-hearted conclusion. "So anyway, that's where we're headed to hike and picnic this afternoon. Should we see Ronnie out there, I'll take that as a sign I'm supposed to hire him. On the spot."

"I 'spect you'll be talkin' to his knees, since I reckon that's 'bout as high as you'd come to Ronnie—the little bit you are!"

All three men enjoyed another chuckle at my expense before I thanked them again and Brent and I filed out, followed by Deputy Jenkins. He tipped his hat at us as he climbed into his squad car, reassuring us the Collins' homesite would be safe enough the next time Oliver and I ventured out there.

When I casually mentioned that I needed to tell Uncle Oliver everything the police had said, I noticed that Brent was sporting quite the smirk on his face.

"What?"

"I can't tell you how excited Mama was about her *date* with a certain gentleman."

I smiled, picturing the two together. "My uncle too. And he's certainly earned a day off. Cutting weeds and digging for gravestones yesterday. In heat and humidity. Poor man."

"When you thinkin' you'll go out that way again?" Brent asked. "I'd like to tag along with you. Oh, one word of warning:

Best discourage my brother 'bout going along. Going *anywhere* with you, actually. Kate has her a temper, and she was mighty steamed E.A. was with you yesterday."

"Kate was angry with me? Why?"

"You met Kate," he stated, matter-of-factly. I nodded at him, but my image of the sweet woman we met last night didn't fit with her having a temper. I also couldn't picture E.A. and Kate as a couple, but that could've been due to my not being able to picture *anyone* having that kind of relationship with E.A. "Didn't you know her and E.A. was a couple? They're pretty serious. Not that she has a ring or anything. But she just told me it won't be too much longer before she's sportin' some sparkle."

"Oh. Don't know how I missed that." I felt a little strange all of a sudden. *Am I feeling that much sympathy for Kate? Must be, poor thing.*

"Problem is, Kate's got her a nasty jealous streak. My advice is to steer clear of E.A. Just a heads-up." He turned to look at me, giving me a quick smile that vanished as fast as it had appeared. He shrugged, nonchalantly dismissing the subject, and asked, "So when you goin' back out that way?"

The quick change of topic forced me to put aside my strange and, quite frankly, irrational feelings about E.A. and Kate. I tucked some stray strands of hair behind my ears and cleared my throat, giving myself a moment to re-focus on Brent. "Hmmm. Maybe tomorrow? You available?"

"I will be, one way or another."

"I don't want to take you from the restaurant. If your mom needs you, I mean."

"Actually, I'm supposed to show some homes tomorrow, but I can schedule around that, no problem."

"Show homes? You a real estate agent too?"

"I am. But before we go there, I'd like to know more about Julia Johnson." With that, he turned to look at me, eyebrows raised.

"Not so much to tell, really." I pivoted and leaned against the passenger door so I could better view his profile. I noted the line of his forehead, the distinguished nose. Traveled down his full lips (which I knew already were incredibly soft to the touch) to that square jaw. It was unnerving how good looking he was, but it was also the perfect time to take it all in, familiarizing myself with each curve—while he was concentrating on driving. Totally legitimate to stare back at him while answering his question, right?

I told him what it's like to be a third-grade teacher. How the students' minds are just starting to expand conceptually and that makes it an age that's more fun—and more challenging. As I explained it to him, I realized how much I enjoy teaching, how much I looked forward to getting back at it in the fall.

"You really like little kids? I mean, that's quite something. Wanting to spend all day with 'em, day after day after day. For months. Years, even!"

"When you put it that way, I guess it sounds rather monotonous. But honestly, it's not. You just never know what their curious little minds are going to come up with. Every day is unique in that respect. Keeps me on my toes, that's for sure."

"It would keep me on *edge*." He turned to smile at me and we both smiled at his little joke. "Interests?"

"Triathlons. I do as many as I can during the season up our way—which isn't very long, as you would guess. Averages out to about three a year."

"Impressive. You must really be into swimming too, eh?"

"When I'm not running, I'm on my road bike—or doing spinning classes in the winter when I can't bike outside. And yes, I swim laps at least twice a week."

"Never done a triathlon, but I run 'bout four times a week. Leave E.A. in my dust, by the way." (With great self-discipline, I managed to keep myself from looking down at his legs. He had on shorts, and I was most curious to see if his legs were even more muscled than E.A.'s.) "I enjoy Nascar races and I like country music. Bet that comes as a big surprise, eh?" He winked at me, nodding his head. "Let's see, what else? I hear the Houston Oilers are gonna move to Tennessee, season starting this fall—excited about that. Hmmm, what am I leaving out?"

"Any college?" I queried.

"Took several business courses at a community college, but didn't stay at it. That's when I got my real estate license. When I'm not helpin' out Mama, I'm hustling round the county, showin' homes. Keeps me busy and brings in some pocket change."

"Only pocket change? I would think you'd do quite well."

"Well, now you've caught me bein' modest, I suppose. Considerin' I was top seller in the county last three years running. But who's countin'?"

We pulled into an empty gravel parking area. "We're the only ones here? How wonderful if we have the park all to ourselves!"

Brent gave me a serious, searching look that took me by surprise. And then I realized the possible ramifications of what I'd just said, flushed in embarrassment, and stumbled all over myself as I tried to explain. "I mean, it'll be nicer if it's not busy. With crowds of people. On the trail, and in the water?" Finally told myself to just shut up, I'd done enough damage. Shook my head and closed my eyes—another immature reaction on my part, a childish one. Did I think closing my eyes would make my blunder disappear?

And then I felt Brent put a hand under my chin and pull my face up to his. Giving me another feather-light kiss. When I finally opened my eyes, I saw he was grinning at me, a smile that reached up to put a twinkle in his eyes. "I love that about you."

"What? That I say dumb things?"

"You're uncensored sometimes. It's endearing."

"Actually, it's embarrassing. Totally humiliating at times."

He dropped his hand—my skin still felt all tingly where he'd touched me—and nodded his head towards the parking lot. "If it was the weekend, this place would be packed. Could be there's some what hiked in. Those college kids from up the Gap can be a nuisance. But I'm thinkin' we're about to have us a private walk and swimmin' hole to boot."

When Brent popped open the trunk I saw he'd come well prepared: Backpack, a quilt to sit on while we ate, and a cooler I assumed was full of delights from Mama Byrd. "I just need to put this food in my backpack and we'll be ready to go. Hand me those things, will you?"

My stomach grumbled in anticipation as we loaded thick sandwiches made with crusty bread (which I had no doubt was baked this morning by Myra); homemade potato chips (they smelled heavenly); containers of sliced fruit; and lastly, brownies bursting with nuts and chocolate chips. Myra had also sent along a good-sized container of iced tea, of course. Brent was going to be weighed down until we consumed this feast.

"We can put some of this in my backpack, Brent. I don't mind, honestly."

"Nah, I'm good. Fortunately, we won't be hiking very far." He looked over my clothes. "You did bring a swimsuit, right? Can you roll up those pants? Gonna get hot mighty quick. Bug spray?"

I nodded. "Already taken care of. And yes—give me just a sec with these pants."

By the time we set off, the sun was pretty high in its arc. We were both breathing heavily and in need of drinks from water bottles by the time we reached what Brent termed the "pinch of the Pocket." While winking at me—and taking a good swig of water—he explained that "It starts to pinch your muscles a bit when you have to climb over these boulders. You agree?"

"Considering you're hoisting all the weight, I agree you're getting pinched, all right. Can't I take something? How about the quilt?"

"Nope, I'm fine. I figure we've got 'bout a half hour till we get to the best spot for lunch. It's close to noon and I'm already 'bout to die for wantin' to dig into the feast Mama's made."

We climbed over dozens of good-sized boulders, waded through stretches of the stream (only getting our shoes and shins wet up to this point), and trekked over well-worn dirt trails shaded by overhanging tree branches as we followed the winding course of the stream. The water was amazingly clear. No matter the depth, I could see treasures lying at the bottom: Smooth stones, other rocks with a sparkly glint highlighted by the sun, sticks and branches of all sizes, the shells of snails, and always, an assortment of tiny darting, frenetic fish and bugs. Several times I saw a dragon fly hover over the water, its iridescent colors reflected in the pool. In calmer sections, a spider had set up shop, its web stretched over the water below like a hammock. Beware the bug that was lured to that resting spot! Sometimes the stream was a narrow rush of water spilling out between boulders; other times it would widen out to form a shallow pond, perfect for wading. The entire time, however, it gurgled and bubbled playfully, delightfully. I couldn't wait to wiggle bare toes in its cool, sparkling water.

Eventually I spied a welcoming green bank—grass and moss forming a bit of a shelf over a good-sized pool of water—and instantly knew this was our destination. Brent stripped off his backpack and I eagerly followed suit. After only a moment's thought, I tugged off boots and socks too. I carefully stepped down into the water and, after a quick intake of breath—it felt strikingly cold compared to the hot confines of my boots—I exclaimed, "Oh, my goodness, does that ever feel good!"

Brent shook out the patchwork quilt and placed it on the ground. "Wait till you swim in it." He nodded up stream. "There's a perfect swimmin' hole up a ways further. I'm thinkin' the odds are good we'll have it all to ourselves based on us not seein' anyone else on the path. Ready for a sandwich?"

"Yes, please. Brent, those sandwiches look divine."

He stretched out on the quilt, leisurely reclining as he took a large bite of his. "Help yourself to the fruit and chips. Be warned, though; Mama's chips are certifiably addictive."

I made myself comfortable—feet still dangling in the water—and turned my face up to the bright sunlight. "No doubt. I think all your mama's cooking is addictive. It's a wonder all three of you don't weigh over three hundred pounds."

"Like Ronnie, eh?"

I chuckled. "I don't dare mention that to my uncle. He'd take the suggestion seriously. We'd be interviewing Ronnie as my personal bodyguard in a heartbeat."

Brent put down his sandwich and placed his hands behind his head as a pillow, elbows out. He closed his eyes, and I took the opportunity to stealthily examine his legs. (My conclusion: They were muscular all right, and wonderfully defined. But no more so than E.A.'s—which made me frown a bit, as I was rooting for Brent to beat his brother in every department.) Swatting a bug from his face, he asked, "Tell me more about your dad. And yourself." He raised up on one elbow so he could study me, it appeared. "Why're you really here, Julia? There's more to the story, isn't there?" He reached for his sandwich and took another bite, but his eyes never left mine.

Under Brent's scrutiny, I wavered for only a moment before I decided to come clean. *You've got to trust somebody here*, I told myself. *Better Brent than E.A., that's for sure. God, help me to know what all I should say.* I chewed slowly and held up a finger, stalling for time because I could sense Guy pestering me, and obviously, I wasn't about to ask his permission to share. Sure as anything, Guy would warn me to keep quiet. Well, I wanted to do this my way—without asking his advice first. Or Uncle Ollie's. About time I started doing that anyway.

Pulling my feet up out of the water, I pivoted to face Brent directly. "Actually, the reason I'm here is pretty complicated. And then in another way, it's really not. Sorry I'm being ambiguous—I haven't told anyone this before, quite this way. So it's difficult." My voice caught, and tears pooled in my eyes. "You see, just before my dad died, he told me I was adopted." Saying the words out loud was more emotional for me than I'd expected.

"You had no idea before then?"

"No. Needless to say, it was pretty traumatic to hear."

"I would imagine." There was no discernible empathy in his voice, no strong reaction. I thought he might move closer to me. Take my hand. Even kiss me again. But I reasoned he was probably just being patient, attempting to give me the space I needed to get the story out. "You must have connections to Collinsville somehow."

"My biological parents were Lucille and Jimmy Blevins."

He nodded, encouragingly. *He's trying to help me stay calm,* I thought. *That's what he's doing—granting me a calmly listening, reassuring presence. Soothing. Composed. How discerning and sensitive of him to know that's exactly what I'd need.*

"I was only about five years old when they died. But I remember that day. I 'spect most everyone round here does, their dyin' like they did."

I reached for my backpack, searching for the paper tablet and pen I'd brought along. "I'd like to take notes on anything helpful you can tell me," I said. "I take it the accident was pretty horrific? You know Mrs. Odell? At the hardware store?" He nodded and rolled his eyes, and we both grinned, conspiratorially. "She told me about it. Said the fire was pretty bad, huh?"

"Folks talked 'bout it for a long time. So why you searchin' out by the cemetery of the old church? You know Lucille and Jimmy's graves are in the cemetery in town next to the Baptist church, right?"

"Yes, Mrs. Odell told me. Out at the old cemetery we're hoping to find—oh, I don't know. Something. Anything. Clues on gravestones about relatives. Maybe locate an old building of some sort, anything left behind. When I was at the library I picked up a book on the history of Collinsville."

"Don't believe I've read that. Am I missin' out?"

"I can't say, really; I've only skimmed it at this point. But I did read a little last night about springhouses and how people used to store all kinds of things there. I guess I was hoping… well, you know how it is when you're really curious about something. You get your hopes up. That's why I want to go out to the homesite and graveyard one more time. I just have this sense there's *something* worth finding out there."

"What is it you're hopin' to find?"

Guy was doing the equivalent of yelling at me by this point. I ignored him, which means you could say I pretty much slammed the door in his face. In "mind talking" language, that is.

"Oh, I don't know. You know how a woman's intuition can be. Uncle Ollie's not thrilled about going back, but even he can't argue with a woman's intuition." I winked at him.

Brent rolled his eyes and groaned, but I refused to take the bait. Instead, before I lost my courage, I made a quick decision to trust Brent, completely. Uncle Ollie probably wouldn't be pleased, and I knew Guy would have a fit. But there was no earthly reason why I *shouldn't*. No rational reason at all. "Ever heard the word *Melungeon*?"

He shrugged his shoulders. "Yeah, a few times. Many here have Melungeon blood, I've heard."

"So the Blevins scribbled that word—among some other cryptic references—on a letter Uncle Ollie and I found with my adoption forms. Unfortunately, that sheet had gotten wet somehow, so most of it was illegible except for a few phrases and that one word: *Melungeon.*" I reached for a drink of iced tea, noting Brent followed my every move, never taking his eyes off me. He was obviously fascinated by my story, and I knew I'd found another advocate to help me figure out my illusive past. "Anyway, my uncle and I googled *Melungeon,* and we learned a good deal. Did you know the Melungeons' origins are considered *mysterious?*"

"Interesting."

"So evidently, *I'm* Melungeon. For whatever reason, that was cause for anxiety on the Blevins' part."

Brent's eyebrows shot up and he let one loud "Whoa!" escape. "Were they anxious for *you*? Or anybody associating *with* you?" He leaned away from me, exaggerating his posture. "Wonderin' now if I shoulda brought my twenty-two with me today."

I laughed, though a bit nervously. "Well, by all indications it made my dad anxious for me. At least, that's the impression I got from my last conversation with him, and that Uncle Ollie and I got from the cryptic letter." I shrugged my shoulders and shook my head like I was clearing cobwebs. I pointed a chip at him. "See, it was right before that I was run off the road by the black SUV. Like I just told the deputies—though it's mere speculation, since the police said there was no conclusive evidence—maybe my dad was run off the road by the same car. And when we were shot at the other day…" I left my sentence hanging.

"That was nothin' but back country boys protectin' their property sure as I'm Brent Byrd. But can you think of anything else 'bout your adoption what could shed some light on those incidents?" He searched my face with a look that felt like a caress and then reached over to put his hand on mine, giving it a gentle squeeze. No longer teasing, he nodded at me, pulling me into the depths of those eyes once again.

"It's the strangest thing. I've got it with me—actually, I've kept it with me ever since we first discovered it. Probably superstitious about it by now, I guess."

"What's that?" His voice was soft, but I could tell he was eager to share this intimacy with me.

I put aside the tablet and pen and unzipped a pocket in my blouse, pulling out the gold *B*. I held it out for him to see, cradling it in my palm. "This. This ugly little piece of jewelry."

For several seconds, Brent said nothing. He didn't even make a sound, apparently holding his breath as he stared at the misshapen, jagged *B*, seemingly mesmerized. When he spoke, however, instead of any sort of expected guess as to its value, he stated matter-of-factly, "Unsightly thing, that's for sure."

"Yes, definitely. I can't imagine why the Blevins kept it for me. Must've been sentimental to them, I guess. Think it was originally a pendant?"

"Nah." His tone broached no argument. "No loop or hook that I can see."

"Agreed. Only a tiny bit of bump at the top. But there are sharp places on the bottom." I pointed those out to him. "See here? Makes you think it once had hooks of some sort there."

Brent took the *B* and held it up to my throat, flipping it upside down. "Maybe it hung like this?"

My skin tingled at his touch, and an awkward laugh evidenced my discomfort. "Brilliant. You should be a detective," I managed to get out.

"Or a jewelry designer?"

We both stared at the pendant as Brent held it up before us, small and pathetic looking in contrast to his big hand. I sighed. "Pitiful inheritance, huh? But that's it—at least, from my biological parents. Besides all the mystery, I mean. I inherited a boatload of that."

"So there wasn't anything else in the safe to help you figure things out? Other documents? No diaries or journals—nothing like that?"

"No. Nothing except that one piece of paper. The letter."

"So what else did it say? You mentioned phrases you couldn't quite make out?"

"Nothing that made any sense."

Brent narrowed his eyes at me. "You're holdin' out on me, I can tell. How'm I gonna play detective if you don't share all your information?"

I could feel a hiccup threatening, but I swallowed it back down like an over-sized pill that was uncomfortably stuck in my throat. I was determined not to hiccup, giggle or mention anything about six fingers. And there was no way in the world I'd *ever* bring up the subject of mind talking. Sharing confidences with Brent could only go so far, after all. "Nope. Nothing worth mentioning, I assure you."

We both stared at the *B* as Brent tilted it back and forth so that it picked up and reflected the bright sunlight. If you discounted all the dents and broken parts, it did look somewhat better, glistening like it was now. "I'm guessin' this belonged to your mama, given to her by your daddy. She would've considered it somethin' special, even though it certainly can't be worth much. Still, I understand it's special to you, Julia, just the same. You want me to keep it for you? We've got us a safe at the restaurant for keepin' important papers. I know Mama'd be happy to store it there for you."

"Oh, thanks. Like you said, there's no value here to make it worth putting in a safe ever again. And I know this is just silly, but I feel better having it with me. All the time." I took it from him and put it back into my zippered pocket. When I looked up, I saw that Brent had moved even closer to me. Quite close. "I, um…I've just become used to having it where I can touch it anytime I feel the need, and—"

When he kissed me this time, I noted right away that this one was entirely different from the others. This was no soft peck. On the contrary, it was long and leisurely, the kind of kiss where his lips explored mine, making me forget everything else, including the fact that I still had my pen in my hand. Which then went limp so that I dropped it right into the water. The sudden "*plink!*" sound startled us both, and we pulled apart, laughing. "Sorry. I dropped my pen." We both looked down and I pointed to the bright blue. "There it is," and I hopped down to get it.

"I would've offered to be the gentleman and fetch it for you, but you didn't give me a chance."

"Course not. I just wanted an excuse to get in the water again."

I waded around while I finished off my sandwich, sticking my big toe under sticks and rocks to see what wonders might be hidden beneath. Brent stretched out again as he watched me. He'd already finished his sandwich and evidently polished off all the fruit and chips he wanted because then he was digging into the brownies, pulling out a treat that I could see was going to be almost like one just out of the oven. Its chocolate chips were gooey, softened by the heat, and it looked delicious. He took a big bite, and when he looked back up at me I had to laugh out loud at him. Smeared chocolate covered his lips, and as he held out a hand towards me, I saw his fingers were smeared a dark brown too.

"Ready for another kiss?" he teased.

"I think I'll pass! What do you say we get all this cleaned up and head for the pool you told me about?" I climbed up onto the bank and dried my feet on the quilt, sat down to pull on my shoes and socks. "I'm thinking there's only one way you're going to get all that chocolate off you: with a thorough dunking!"

We hiked for another fifteen minutes before the stream opened up to form a picturesque scene. I had to stop to take it all in. You would think someone had planned and built this swimming area—it was that perfect. Grass grew around much of the edges, but there was also an inviting little sandy beach, bigger stones perfectly arranged to function as stools, and even a weeping willow growing right next to the pool. Its branches hung gracefully out over the water, arranging themselves artistically as the finishing touch for the artist's painting.

"Look up there," Brent instructed, and I followed his pointed finger.

"That can't be a natural vine. No way."

He just grinned at me in response.

"Really?"

"Last one in—and I mean swingin' out into the water by the vine—is a monkey's uncle. I'm headed to the men's area; girls' changin' room is that way."

"Changing room?" Puzzled, I turned the direction he'd nodded. There was definitely a path to follow, and at its end, boulders surrounded by dense foliage. *Girls changing room indeed*, I mumbled to myself. Feeling a good deal self-conscious, I stripped down and pulled on my swimsuit in record time. As I was stashing clothes into my backpack, I heard a *whoop* followed by a loud splash. I couldn't help the smile that spread over my face when I spied Brent, hair plastered to his head, a goofy grin highlighting his features, and arms flailing as he treaded water.

He let his gaze follow the outlines of my suit and produced a loud wolf whistle before yelling, "Come on in, beautiful. It feels great!"

Gingerly I climbed up to the launching pad, so to speak, to reach for the vine. It was a good thickness; I wrapped my hands around it and gave it a good yank. Knowing it had already held Brent's weight was little reassurance. *He could've pulled it just enough so it would promptly break for me*, I thought. I checked it several times and looked up at it from all different angles until Brent—now sitting at the sandy beach area—called out, "What're you waitin' for? You figurin' it's a butler's bell pull? If you think someone's gonna bring you one of Mama's brownies, you'd best think again!" He stared up at me, squinting slightly, grinning wickedly. "Maybe you'd rather have some melted chocolate? You could let go that vine a lot quicker if you had some on your hands."

"I don't think the letting go will be a problem."

"Then you haven't seen many cowards on a swingin' vine!"

I laughed. "You got me there. But you won't be seeing one today, Mr. Brent Byrd."

Some enterprising soul had actually managed to tie a knot on the end of the vine, so after climbing even higher—up onto another boulder—the trick was to jump up onto the vine, hands clutching it high enough so that you could position your feet on top of the knot. That way you'd get a wide swing out over the pond and an even better thrill when you let go, dropping several feet. My heart throbbed like it had jumped up to my throat, and my stomach rolled like it does when a roller coaster begins to crest that first steep hill. *Don't let Brent see how scared you are*, I told myself. *You can do this!* I closed my eyes, whispered a quick prayer, took a good breath and jumped—my feet landing right on the knot so I got the maximum swing. I could hear Brent hooting loudly as I let go.

Nothing could have prepared me for that plunge, however, as the water was ice cold. Bursting up through the surface, I gasped, "Why didn't you warn me it was freezing?"

"Does that mean you don't want to go again?"

"Are you kidding? I loved it!"

We must've climbed up the boulders, launched out over the pond and generally acted like two boisterous kids for about an hour. It was thirst that finally compelled us to take a break. Sipping the still cold iced tea (Brent had the foresight to stow the two big jars in the water at the edge of the frigid pool), we stretched out in the sun. After so much steady exercise, the cold water didn't provoke a shock, but it was still noticeably chilly every time I made that plunge. The sun, therefore, felt almost luxurious on my arms and legs. I closed my eyes and let out a contented sigh.

"Bored?" Brent asked, teasingly.

"Goodness, no! Actually, I was thinking how—only six months ago—I never would've pictured myself in Tennessee. Jumping off a vine into a freezing cold pond." I peeked open my eyes to gauge Brent's response. I wasn't expecting to discover he'd closed his eyes also, but what was most surprising was that his face looked totally blank: There was simply no emotion registered there. *Did he doze off to sleep that quickly?* I wondered.

-Jules, what are you doing? Are you okay? Why are you—

-Whoa, Guy. Calm down; I'm fine. No, actually, I'm more than fine. We're having a ball here, Brent and I, and—

-Please, Jules, listen to me. You have to get out of there. Now.

-Guy, you're being totally unreasonable. Honestly, there's no reason—

"Earth to Julia." I started at the sound of Brent's voice. "Looked like you'd checked out for a minute there." Brent was getting up, stretching. I'd been so tuned into my conversation with Guy I hadn't even heard him shift positions. "Not sleeping, were you? Are you positive I'm not boring you?"

"No, not sleeping. And I am *definitely* not bored. I was just, um, meditating. Musing about how much I'm enjoying the day." Brent took my hand and pulled me up so that I stood, imitating him now, hands on hips too. "Specifically, I'm enjoying my far superior form for the newly created Olympic sport of *vining*."

The last few plunges, we'd begun scoring each other's jumps. Though I'd given Brent an *eight* on one of his, he'd not granted me anything above a *six*. Needless to say, a good deal of bantering had accompanied those subjective scores.

"Is that a challenge?" he asked.

"You betcha it is," and I gave him one quick, hard push to the mid-section. Since I caught him completely by surprise, Brent barely even got out a yell of protest before he went sprawling into the water. *That was one great dunk*, I congratulated myself, giggling like a school girl.

I scurried up the boulders to the vine, where I taunted him below as he glared back, slowly treading water. "Have a good fall, Brent?"

"Revenge is a dish best served cold. You are about to experience very sudden cold, my dear Julia."

He grinned, a challenging sort of smile that sent a chill down my back. I hiccupped before I grabbed the vine—*What on earth? Why now?* I wondered—and swung out over the water, most definitely the best swing I'd pulled off the entire afternoon. When I let go, I noted Brent was only a few feet away from me; I knew he could cover the distance in a heartbeat. I surfaced long enough to take only one quick breath before he was on me, pushing my shoulders down. I struggled—trying not to laugh as much as I was attempting to get free from Brent's firm grasp—when utter pandemonium broke out.

I first sensed more than actually felt or saw other bodies in the water with us. Hair—plenty of incredibly dense hair was pushing up against me and I fleetingly wondered, *Who on earth has this much hair?* Suddenly it dawned on me: A *dog* was swimming beside me now. A rather large dog, as a matter of fact, pumping powerful legs and for whatever inexplicable reason, grabbing my arm in a firm grip—not biting or breaking the skin, amazingly. But firmly pulling me towards the bank.

Surfacing, choking and gasping for air, I struggled to get a decent breath and wipe the water from my eyes. When I could finally see well enough to make out what was going on, I first noticed the huge black snout of a yellow Labrador retriever (he'd finally let go of my arm, at least, after his irresponsible owner called him off), not two inches from my face. The dog was snorting like crazy as he swam, so I frog-kicked away to avoid the delightful "spray" coming from that enormous nose. When I did, I pivoted to move right into the face of E.A., in the water! I glanced up to the bank, and just as I suspected, there stood Kate too. Glaring at me with nothing short of contempt.

I was livid with E.A., and I was going to let him know it. "What are...what on earth are *you* doing here? Did you jump in with all your clothes on? Are you completely out of your mind?" E.A. turned his back to me and swam towards the bank. "And is this your dog?" I sputtered in between gasps for air. "Did you know he had my arm in a vice grip?" E.A. pulled himself up onto the bank, also choking and coughing up water, though I had no idea why. I noted he was indeed fully clothed, except that he was in his stocking feet; his boots were nowhere to be seen. He pretty much flopped onto the ground, taking in big gulps of air.

And if Kate was still sending daggers at me, that was nothing compared to the looks the two brothers shot at each other.

"What..." Brent panted, spitting out only a word or two in between wracking coughs, "what was...that...about? You nearly drowned me—you and that...that mangy dog of yours! I swear, E.A., you have pushed too far this time."

I pulled myself out of the water and discovered my legs were shaking so badly I could barely walk to retrieve my towel. Once I'd wrapped it around me, my teeth decided to join the frenetic dance; they began chattering, uncontrollably. I tried moving my legs while hugging my arms and the towel around me as best I could, but nothing seemed to be helping. Having competed in as many triathlons as I have, I'm familiar with the early signs of hyperthermia. I've diagnosed it in others and helped treat it. But it's another thing entirely to recognize it in yourself—and admit to that.

E.A. jumped up and rushed towards me with a determined look in his eye, but I stubbornly held out an arm, palm up and out, insisting, "I'm fine. Just let me—"

But obviously he was having none of it, and my resistance was short-lived: My arm fell limply to my side as E.A. wrapped his surprisingly strong and muscular arms around me, hugging me to him, roughly massaging my whole body back to warmth.

The Lab, its distinct wet dog aroma permeating my senses, plopped down on my cold feet, rolling its big dark eyes up to meet mine.

"*Stay*, Clancy," E.A. commanded. "And you," he quietly whispered into my ear so that only I could hear him, "you stay put too. Listen for once in your life, will you? Brent was…Jul… *Julia*, durn it! *Brent was trying to drown you!*"

THE GRAVESTONES' SECRETS

20 of June, 1588

My Descendants,
  Alas, treachery! The Savages press our lives to the brink of Death by their threatening and hostile actions towards us. We are forced to abandon our fort here at Roanoke Colony, and must soon take leave of this place, once we can gather victuals and supplies such as we can carry upon our persons.
  And more treachery! We brave adventurers must part ways, separating into two groups, which I shall soon explain. I know not which direction my soon-to-be former companions travel, but they have carved CROATOAN upon a post—some ascribed message they determined to leave for our own Captain Fernandes before he set sail. Since I was not present at the meeting when the message was agreed upon, its meaning is unknown to me. Therefore, since I will be setting off on a separate journey, I have determined to carve my own mark, with its own message, for my Catherine. Though I know she shall never see this with her own eyes, I have told her of my carving in our mind talking. This sign shall be

CRO

signifying Catherine (C) rejoices in (R) Mauro (O), forever—a witness that Catherine delights me, Mauro, and as such we are forever as one in Holy Matrimony. My heart rejoices that this sign, a testimony of our love, shall be here in this glorious new Land, Roanoke Colony.

This sign shall also be a witness that I Mauro am alive and have escaped, traveling westward in this New World to seek a Home where I can live peaceably among whatever new Savage Tribes I might find.

And now the reason why I must venture forth to discover a separate path from my companions: One among our colony who sighted my B hanging about my neck has conspired among others, and these contentious men have guessed at its origins. Alas, I should have heeded my dear Father's warnings and kept the B hidden away. Therefore, I must set out apart from the main group, with few companions, and only those I deign to trust. They are worthy men, and God-fearing. We pray for God's blessing as we leave within two daybreaks.

I will miss our dear little Mistress Virginia. Shall she survive in this New World with all its dangers? I dare to hope and pray that Our Lord would allow.

As I also dare to hope that God will grant me mercy and grace—to survive, and to bequeath to you, my Children, my Descendants, my Royal Heritage.

Mauro

CHAPTER EIGHT

Reflexively—or was it intentional?—I jabbed an elbow into E.A.'s stomach just below his ribs. E.A. sucked in a deep breath and jumped back. I turned around to catch him rubbing the tender area, a look of surprise on his face.

"What was—?"

"You know very well. Don't play dumb on top of being despicable." My anger truly had warmed my blood as any evidences of hypothermia suddenly vanished. Concerned about Brent, I noted that he was still stretched out on his back, one arm draped over his face and his stomach heaving as he continued to recover from whatever contrary thing E.A. had done to him. And Kate? So much for her love and loyalty to E.A. She was down on her knees, bending over Brent, stroking his arm! I spit out in E.A.'s general direction, "I'm going to get dressed now, so I'd appreciate some privacy while I'm in the 'women's changing area.'"

Brent jerked upright, completely ignoring Kate. "Julia, are you okay? I've warned E.A. to keep that dog away from people. It attacked me first and then went after—"

"That's *enough,* Brent." E.A.'s voice was steely cold, razor sharp in its hostility. I watched the two brothers glare at each other, their faces bright red, chests heaving, lips slightly parted (honestly, were they about to bare their teeth?). It felt like Kate and I were nearly singed by the heat of their exchange as we watched, riveted. I wondered if Brent would escalate the conflict, throwing out an angry retort—or worse yet, a punch.

"Go ahead and get changed, Julia. I promise no one will bother you." Brent nodded his head at me. "We'll leave the swimmin' hole to Kate, E.A., and his attack dog."

"Brent—" Kate began, but Brent silenced her with a raised palm.

"Remember what we talked about the other night?" he asked, clearly insinuating that she should remember the discussion—and keep quiet.

Kate looked up to meet E.A.'s eyes at that point, who immediately shrugged his shoulders, muttering something inaudible under his breath.

I had no idea if E.A. and Kate were having a lovers' spat, but I'd had enough of both of them. Turning abruptly, I tripped over the Lab; though no longer lying on top my feet, he'd obeyed his master and was still lying right next to me. I nearly took a nasty tumble when E.A. reached out to grab my arm just in time, steadying me. I could sense he was searching my face, trying to make eye contact. But I stubbornly avoided his gaze, turning my back to him and walking off in a huff.

Our good-byes were awkward and stilted, to say the least. Brent and I were mostly quiet as we hiked back to his car, and my thoughts were a jumble of open-ended questions. How could I possibly make sense of this mess? Brent accused E.A. of being unbalanced; E.A. insisted Brent was not to be trusted. And a potential *murderer? Of me?* That sounded delusional, none of it was rational, and I could find no logic to the brothers' wild accusations. If anything could be explained in this convoluted story of sibling rivalry, it appeared that E.A. was emotionally unbalanced. For whatever inexplicable reason, that made me incredibly sad.

We were pulling out of the parking lot when I finally gathered the courage to ask Brent, "What was that really all about? What's up with you two?"

Brent shook his head. "You don't know my brother, Julia." He turned to look at me, concern heavy on his features. "I spoke to Kate about helpin' E.A. talk through his *quirks*, shall we say? He can be paranoid. Delusional even."

"Tell me about it. He nearly caused us all to drown!"

"Yeah, because of his out-of-control dog! I can't tell you how much I *hate* that dog."

I shrugged my shoulders, noncommittally.

"What did E.A. say to you, anyway?" Brent queried. "I imagine it was something totally crazy about me?"

I laughed. "Yeah, it was crazy, all right. He said you were trying to drown me!"

Brent jerked his head to stare at me for a few seconds, and then glanced back at the road before also checking the rearview mirror. Pulling off onto the berm, he turned off the car and reached out for me, pulling me into his arms. One arm cradled the back of my head, and he whispered into my hair, "Julia. I think I'm falling in love with you. I could never hurt you, Sweet. *Never.*" Pulling away from me so he could look into my eyes, he asked, "You don't believe E.A., do you? God, I can't imagine you thinking that of me. Please tell me—"

I lightly touched my fingers to his lips. "Shhhh." I rested my hand behind his neck, applying just the slightest pressure to indicate I was ready to be kissed again. This time, Brent pressed his mouth to mine in an urgency that left me feeling slightly bruised once we finally pulled apart.

Still, even after I'd signaled my desire to be kissed—a clear non-verbal message of trust, as far as I was concerned—Brent wasn't ready to let it go. "Say it. Tell me you trust me and you don't believe E.A."

I took both his hands in mine. "Of course, I do. And I don't for a second believe what E.A. said."

Brent nodded, solemnly, before starting up the car and driving back onto the road. We kept our discussion light, focusing on the fun we'd shared at the Pocket—before E.A. and his dog crashed our party. But when he dropped me off, he barely brushed his lips to mine before promising, "I'll call later. About tomorrow." He looked thoughtful, and surprisingly, suddenly downcast. I was just about to ask him what was the matter when he offered, "Actually, I just remembered some commitments I have tomorrow."

"I thought you could schedule your showings around our time at the homesite."

He ran a hand through his hair. "It's this guy who…well, let's just say he's high maintenance. Filthy rich."

When Brent reached out to put a finger under my chin again, I felt the familiar thrill from his touch, but I noted some ambivalence mixed in. *Is it only disappointment about his backing out of tomorrow?*

"He's a guy I gotta make happy, Julia. Pays t' keep clients like him on your good side, you know?" He dipped his head lower, easing closer to me. "Am I forgiven?"

I smiled. "Nothing to forgive. Make him happy, Brent. Find the perfect house and then we'll celebrate. How's that?"

He kissed me lightly once more. "You're amazing, Jules."

I jerked back away from him, drawing in a rush of air. Eyes wide, I stared into his, searching.

"What? What's wrong?"

"It's just that nobody ever calls me Jules. No one except this one friend."

"A *male* friend?"

I nodded.

"A *close* male friend?"

"Yeah, well, no. Not really. Close."

He narrowed his eyes at me. "Does he live near you?"

"No. No, actually he lives very far away."

"Oh. Good," Brent said. "I'm glad."

Suddenly klutzy and fumbling, I reached for the door. "I need to go. Talk about paranoid people. Uncle Oliver will be worried about me."

"I'll call you later, okay?"

I waved good bye as, all thumbs still, I vainly searched the multitude of pockets in my backpack for the key to my room. *He called me Jules. Obviously just a quirk of fate. But goodness… what a shock. Great job acting nonchalant when he did,* I chided myself. *And earlier, why couldn't I simply say, 'I trust you, Brent'?* I sighed, finally locating the errant key, realizing the most important question I needed to ask myself: *Did either of those things convey something significant—or not?*

—

"You did what?" I stared at Uncle Ollie, mouth open, body frozen with one hand raised and poised to comb through my freshly shampooed hair.

"Julia, darling, I thought you'd be pleased."

"You knew E.A. and I haven't been getting along. And that doesn't even take into account the stunt he pulled this afternoon." I turned to the mirror, grimacing at my reflection as I combed through a knot in my hair. Since A Byrd in the Hand was closed on Wednesdays, we were planning to eat at the local diner. Myra—it was *Myra* all the time now from Oliver—had told Uncle Ollie their meat loaf was worth the trip.

"What stunt was that?"

I let out a deep breath I wasn't aware I'd been holding. "Brent and I were having a perfectly wonderful afternoon. The natural swimming pool there was perfect, Uncle Ollie, and it had a vine you could climb on to swing out over the water. I can't tell you how much fun that was."

He grinned, nodding. "Did that once when I was a kid. I'll never forget how hard we laughed, your dad and I."

Turning to look at him, I asked, "My dad did it too?"

"Sure did. It was at a church camp. Long gone now, I'm afraid." He smiled and I waited, hoping he'd share more. "Problem was, there was decaying roots leaching into the water. Dark bits of itchy stuff always ended up in your trunks. Made for some itchy patches, if you get my drift."

Grinning, I offered, "Now that just sounds nasty! Fortunately, there was no hitchhiking residue in this swimming hole. The water was crystal clear. But oh, was it cold! So anyway, as I was saying, Brent and I were having a wonderful time when suddenly E.A. and Kate show up."

"Kate?"

"You remember her. Kate was our server last night. The tall blond? Turns out she and E.A. are soon to be engaged."

Oliver frowned. "Somehow that doesn't work for me."

"Oh. Why's that?"

"'Cause I get the distinct impression E.A.'s interested in *you*."

I spun around to face him. "Now that's *totally* laughable. The way he treats me? And now we've circled back to the reason for this discussion in the first place: E.A. has this dog, a Labrador retriever. And I swear he purposely sent the dog into the water after me. It grabbed my arm, Uncle Ollie." I held out my right hand and turned my arm over several times, surprised to discover no bruises from the dog's teeth. "Honestly, it's a wonder I wasn't left with a bloody stump."

Oliver stifled a laugh by covering his mouth with his hand. When I glared at him, he immediately sobered and cleared his throat. "A-hem." He raised his right index finger. "I'd just like to point out that Labs have very soft mouths. If the dog wanted to bite you, he would've done so. Evidently he was only intent on pulling you out of the water since I don't see one mark on your arm."

It was time for another "teacher look" from my arsenal: This time I gave Uncle Ollie the "I Won't Even Dignify That with a Response" reaction. He cleared his throat again and the finger went down. "As I was saying," I continued, "E.A. had the audacity to accuse Brent of trying to *drown* me. Can you believe he'd even think to accuse his brother of doing that? That's an atrocious accusation. It's baseless and just plain horrible considering it's his brother, Uncle Ollie. Needless to say, I'm not going anywhere with E.A. Not tomorrow. Not ever."

"But I'm afraid it's too late, Julia. Brent's busy, so I was pleased when E.A. volunteered to go with us in his stead. By the way, did you know Brent's a real estate agent?"

"I did." Frustrated, I tried one last tactic. "I could go alone."

Oliver merely laughed. And proceeded to get ready to go to the diner.

Peeved, I called after him, "You're not even going to comment on my idea?"

"I did already," he yelled back. "That wasn't an idea. It was a fantasy." I could hear him slipping on a jacket, gathering keys. "Ready to go? I'm starving again. Don't quite know what it is with this Southern air, but I can't remember when I've been this hungry."

I grimaced, patting my stomach. "Hope I'm not gaining weight. I can't remember the last time I put away this much comfort food—mashed potatoes, biscuits, gravy, rolls."

"Hush! You're only making it worse. You suppose the diner offers mashed potatoes with their meat loaf?"

"Uncle Ollie. This is the *South*. You could probably order mashed potatoes with your mashed potatoes."

"That's not a bad idea!"

Later that evening when Brent called, I tried to break the news gently to him about E.A.'s accompanying me tomorrow. "There was no way I could change my uncle's mind, Brent. I tried convincing him otherwise, all through dinner."

"I still don't understand what you expect to find. Except bugs and snakes."

An involuntary shiver ran down my back. "Don't say that. I hate snakes."

"Well, I'm just warning you again about E.A." The disgust in his voice was apparent. "You know he has the mean streak of a starvin' river rat. And his bite's 'bout as bad as his dog's."

I took in a deep breath and let it out, resigned. "Well hopefully, this trip to the homesite will be considerably less dramatic!"

―

Once I was settled into my room for the night, I called Melissa, eager to tell her about Brent and E.A. But all I could get was a busy signal, so that finally, I put the handset down for good. *Maybe she's talking with this new guy?* I wondered. *If so, I'm thrilled for her. Could be he's the one that turns out to be the keeper!* I smiled to myself, imagining what a Melissa wedding would look like. *Hmmm. Possibly at a vineyard? Or maybe a beach?* I knew Melissa would never let me down for creativity and originality.

I'd put off Guy for far too long, and my guilt meter was running high. Further procrastinating would only make a twitchy situation even worse. It was time to reach out, the moment my head touched the pillow.

-Guy, can you talk now? I've missed you.

-Sure you have time?

His rawness was palpable. I knew our conversations had been much less frequent since I'd been here, but explanations would only come across as lame excuses. And I so wanted to heal his hurt.

-I haven't been as available, have I? I'm so sorry, Guy. Forgive me?

-Ah Jules, please forgive me. You're busy, and I'm being a self-absorbed putz. I know you need to get a lot done there while you can. I've just missed you, missed hearing your heart. Your laughter and even the teasing. Told myself to hide my disappointment from you, but neither of us is much good at that, are we?

-Not in relation to each other, no.

I thought to myself—but hid from Guy—that I'm so grateful for how completely real we can be with each other. Because our intimacy is something I cherish. The way Guy understands me and all I am and still accepts me. Loves me. That's an amazing gift, and I'm convinced it's the closest imitation of God's love by another person. Whenever I imagined what my future husband would be like, I wondered how we would ever duplicate what Guy and I share.

-Jules?

-Hmmm?

-Do you trust me?

His question felt like a sucker-punch to my gut, the bare need and vulnerability singeing like my heart like I'd splashed boiling water over my hand. Guy's honest question proved he was equally sensitive, and since I respond to any tenderness from him like a reflex—empathetically feeling it myself—I could feel it as much as the pillow beneath my head. There've been countless times I've wanted Guy to be a real, live person standing before me because I've so needed a real, physical hug. But never before had my heart and body yearned to embrace him as much as they did right now.

The uncanny coincidence of the conversation I'd had with Brent just a few hours earlier caused me to instinctively pull my knees up to my chest, a fetal-like position in response to the stress. Brent had asked almost the exact same question, hadn't he? Once again my mind was caught in the quandary that there's little grey area when it comes to trust.

I felt a tangle of emotions. But there was no hesitation in my answer.

-Of course, I trust you, Guy. *Always.*

I could say it to Guy. No hedging. Believing it with my whole heart.

-I needed to hear you say that.

-I've always trusted you. From my earliest memories, right up to this very moment. Into the future for as long as we have together.

He was quiet for a few moments, and I wondered what he was thinking, what he was hiding from me. Instinctively, I knew it wasn't the time to probe. But I wished he'd tell me.

We talked for nearly an hour, getting caught up on what was happening here. I told him all about Brent and E.A., how sweet Brent was. How E.A. never ceased to hit all my buttons, infuriating me. And I filled him in on all Uncle Ollie and I had learned, what we hoped to glean before we left for home, and what our plans were for the next few days.

Guy was quieter than usual, but I assumed other issues in his life were pressing in on him—problems he didn't want to share with me, no matter how much I pestered him to. He said he wasn't about to dump more on my plate, insisting I already had too much. Honestly, though, I did long to hear more about him; everything was just way too much about me right now. But when I yawned, he said it was late, that we both should get some sleep.

-Guy, I need to say something to you before you go.

He paused again, and I sensed it was insecurity, coated with fear. Somehow, I had to do something…say something to get us past this tenuousness between us.

-What's that?

-The reason I trust you? Well, actually, it's a host of things—because of what you mean to me, the kind of person you are. You're my best buddy; you always will be, Guy. You're the first one I can't wait to tell good news, the first one I go to for a shoulder to cry on—though too often that turns into my whining. You're wise and kind and loving and compassionate and trustworthy. Trustworthy in every single way. I need you. And I love you as my very best friend.

I waited for the expected sense of relief from him, the physical relieved exhale of breath that's been held in. But it didn't happen. If anything, he seemed even more withdrawn.

-Jules, how I wish—no, never mind that. But I do need to say this: I'm not what you think I am. You have this grand vision of me. I can't live up to all of that, never will. Someday you're gonna be...you're gonna be so...

-Guy, stop. That's just not possible. When we finally get to meet each other for real—and I sure hope that will happen someday—I know you'll be all I thought you were, and more! Know what? We're both tired. Let's get some sleep and we'll talk tomorrow, okay? Since I'll be working with E.A., I'll definitely need to de-brief. And believe me, there'll be plenty I'll want to share with you since I have no intention of talking much to *him*.

He was quiet for a few moments, and I swear—What's the book title? Men Are from Mars and Women Are from Venus? They truly are from a totally different planet than women—he was smirking. Or snickering? Whatever, I was way too tired to even attempt figuring that one out.

-Night, Guy.

-Good night, love. Sweet dreams.

—

I ran in the morning, intentionally taking a different route. If I had to spend a good part of the day with E.A., I wasn't about to add one more minute of time to that torture.

Uncle Ollie and I were waiting for E.A. to pick us up when he started in again, pleading E.A.'s case.

"I do think you've misjudged him, Julia. Look how he's volunteered to spend time with you, helping like this."

I scoffed. "Yeah, and I bet his future fiancé is thrilled about it too."

"Why don't you ask him about that?"

I gaped at Oliver, shaking my head in amazement. "You've got to be kidding. Tell me you're not serious."

"I'm perfectly serious. Maybe you mis-heard what Brent said. Or meant."

There was a knock at the door, so I quickly shot back, "I didn't misunderstand, and don't you dare breathe a word of this to E.A. Knowing him, he'd take it that I was jealous of Kate or something equally ridiculous!" Opening the door, I proceeded to give E.A. one of my best fake smiles. I barely got out a greeting before Moppit ran to him, jumping up to put front paws on his knees. When he looked down at her, she barked, demanding attention. E.A. scratched behind her ears, grinning and commenting, "Cute dog. You're a mite smaller than mine."

"Her name's Moppit. She also happens to be much *friendlier* than that dog of yours," I said, coating my words with sarcasm.

E.A. gave me a perplexed look and reached down to pick her up. Traitor that she is, Moppit snuggled into his collarbone as he continued to make over her. I gave her a dirty look in return, but the shameless hussy has no discretion. As long as Moppit's getting attention, she'll be anybody's best friend.

"There's this woman I know," E.A. offered, suddenly switching to a more serious tone. "I think she might be of help. She's not...well, she's somewhat senile, though she was never quite right to begin with, if you get my meaning. But sometimes she's brilliant, and she can recollect things from the past better than anyone else in the whole county."

"Esther Abel?" Oliver asked.

E.A. put Moppit down and met Oliver's gaze. "Yeah, that's her. How did you—"

"Mrs. Odell told us about her," I interjected. "She recommended we visit Mrs. Abel too."

"What if the three of us go see her now?" Oliver was nodding his head already. I frowned. "It's best to see her in the morning 'cause she's the sharpest then. And about a half hour, maybe forty-five minutes at most is all she can handle. Last time I stayed longer she dropped her chin to her chest and started in to snorin'. Right in the middle of somethin' she was telling me."

Oliver chuckled while E.A. shook his head and grinned. I noticed how the skin around his eyes crinkled when he smiled; combined with his jetblack eyes and those thick, long lashes, the effect was an openness that invited and drew you in. *So why did it seem like everything he did pushed* me *away?* I wondered. *What was it about his personality that gritted on me so?*

"Seems like the perfect time to visit her." Staring into my face, eyebrows raised, E.A. waited.

"You're suggesting the three of us visit Mrs. Abel right this minute? Don't we need to call first? Give her a day's notice?"

E.A. shook his head emphatically. "Not necessary. She loves company, always."

I stalled for time, tapping a foot, thinking through options. Escape routes, to be truthful. But I knew it was a forgone conclusion. "Sure, okay. Whatever." I glanced down at my boots and jeans (the same pair I was wearing from our last trip out to the homesite; needless to say, they were mud and grass stained, and they didn't smell especially pleasant either). "Shouldn't I change clothes first?"

E.A. grinned. "Trust me. Miz Esther'll love the whole look."

"Even the boots?"

"'Specially the boots."

Walking out to the parking lot, I scanned the assortment of vehicles there: Three compacts, a couple older sedans (both looked to be held together with duct tape and luck) and a pick-up. My dad's Lexus was missing. Alarmed, I turned to Oliver, but he was offering an explanation before I could voice my concern.

"Oh, Julia, I'm so sorry. Completely slipped my mind. Myra stopped by this morning and asked if I could take her on an errand. I was hesitant to leave while you were out running, so I said she could just take your car. I do hope it wasn't too presumptuous of me?"

"Oh, of course not. Happy to let her use it." But the repercussions of that immediately hit me as E.A. strolled towards the pick-up. He opened the passenger door and motioned for Oliver and me to climb in.

It was fairly new, clean, and probably on the smaller size for a pick-up in this part of the country. And in the back? The Labrador retriever welcomed us by putting his front feet on the wheel cover. He was panting, ears up and tail wagging excitedly.

"You're not serious. You really brought your dog along?"

Matter-of-factly and with a quick shrug of his shoulders: "Me n' Clancy go just about everywhere together."

"Uninvited. Right into ponds too," I mumbled under my breath.

"What was that?"

"Oh, nothing." And then I looked into the cab. No backseat area, of course. Only one fairly short front seat. Someone had to voice the obvious. "You don't expect all three of us to sit here, do you?"

E.A. laughed. "Well, I didn't think to offer the alternative, but you're welcome to ride in back with Clancy. Hey, boy! Want some company?" Oliver started to laugh too but immediately sobered when I turned to frown at him. "Otherwise," he bowed now, dramatically and insufferably, "your coach awaits, my lady."

The self-congratulatory smug look he wore required more self-restraint than I could muster: I made sure my elbow connected with the same spot under his ribs I'd targeted yesterday. E.A.'s quick intake of breath informed me I'd found the tender bulls-eye again, and I smiled up at him sweetly. To his credit, however, he didn't utter a sound. *Guess I gotta grant him one point*, I thought to myself. *I do admire a guy who honors quid pro quo.*

There was an awkward moment when Oliver signaled for me to climb in first. I shook my head *no*, but he was adamant. Evidently the official rule book for "Guys in Trucks" dictates that men don't sit next to each other; if there's a female present, she's granted the "privilege" of being in the middle. Not bothering to disguise my disgust, I climbed up the running board and plopped into the cab, leaving a good six inches between E.A. and me.

Then Uncle Ollie tried to shut the door.

"Julia, darling. I need a tad more room here."

I scooted over another inch.

Both men, in perfect unison, said, "*Really?*"

Which of course made us all laugh out loud, relieving my built-up tension. So in the general spirit of making the best of it, I elected to let E.A.'s past discretions go, at least for now. Magnanimously grant him one more do-over. First, however, we needed to get past the fumbling with our seatbelts and the "Whose belt is this? Mine? Does it fit—no, this one's not mine" fiasco, which led to awkward and embarrassing touches all around. But I was still absolutely intent on keeping our thighs from touching when the very first turn E.A. made slammed my hip right up against him again. I instantly flinched because I felt a shock. It wasn't a negative kind of touch with a high "ick factor," but instead, a current. Like the buzz of a slight electrical charge.

"Sorry," I mumbled.

E.A. looked over at me, eyes seeking mine. The worry lines were back between his brows. "No need to apologize, Julia." He shifted his gaze, turning to stare out the windshield at the road ahead. "Actually, I kind of like you being here." Glancing over at Oliver, E.A. started to blush, quickly adding, "I meant *both* of you. Glad to take you both to visit Miz Esther."

I realized then that every time I was around E.A., I came away more baffled by this enigmatic man. *Was he trying to say he's glad I'm sitting next to him? If so, what a two-timer he is. Poor Kate! And if he didn't mean that at all—and he blushed because he was embarrassed that I might've taken that wrong—why act nervous about saying something totally innocuous in the first place?* Once again, the man made absolutely no sense to me.

Nonchalantly, I stole peeks at the profile of this Byrd male, comparing him to Brent, noting as I did earlier that E.A. came up wanting: The lines aren't quite as sharp, the lips not as full, the jaw not as square or defined. At the same time, there was a softness that was appealing. *Then he goes and breaks the spell by talking*, I said to myself, almost laughing out loud at the observation.

"I'd best give you a heads-up about Miz Esther," E.A. offered.

Oliver leaned forward so he could see him. "Are you going to warn us about a shotgun under her bed?"

E.A. chuckled. "I wouldn't think the home would allow it, but you never know with Miz Esther." He turned a corner again, sending my body shifting towards him once more. "Let's just say I can't guarantee she doesn't have one hidden somewhere."

"We're in for quite the experience, eh?" Oliver asked, a note of excitement in his voice.

"Oh yes, most likely. I've heard plenty of stories about her over the years, mostly 'cause Mama says Miz Esther's related to us somehow, way back."

"Related, hmm? That's interesting." I gave him a knowing look, like that didn't seem odd to me. "What kind of stories, if you don't mind my asking?"

"Well, there's the main thing. She's got the Sight, people say."

"Mrs. Odell said the same thing. What exactly does that mean?"

"Mama puts it this way: Miz Esther *knows* things, much more'n people give her credit for."

I tried to inch away from E.A.—the place where our thighs were touching seemed to burn like fire—but Oliver had me boxed in like the proverbial sardines in a can. I was stuck right where I was, like it or not. "What kinds of things?"

"She's warned people about calamity comin'. I've heard stories about her telling people when a family member was 'bout to pass or a storm was comin' or predicting a terrible accident."

"Car accidents?"

"I s'pose. Years ago, Collinsville had a real bad one. People still talk about it now 'n then, what a horrific crash it was. Folks say the little truck didn't have a chance when the eighteen-wheeler ran a stop sign. Pick-up instantly burst into flames, two inside—husband and wife. No one could do a thing to help them." E.A. was silent for a couple moments, like he was giving respect to the dead. "Heard Miz Esther saw it comin.'"

I stiffened, realized I had to ask. "What were the victims' names?"

"Jimmy and Lucille Blevins. Mama still won't talk about it, as she was real partial to Lucille."

I tried to keep my breathing steady as I took that in. *So Myra was friends with Lucille. How do I find out more about the Blevins, without giving away who I am? Or should I just go ahead and confess all to Myra, trusting her too? One thing for sure, I wasn't about to reveal anything to E.A. as there was no question that I wouldn't—couldn't—trust him. Heaven only knows what he'd do with my secrets.*

When E.A. said we were there to visit with Mrs. Abel, the nurse who'd cheerfully greeted us immediately sobered, informing us "This isn't one of Miz Esther's better days." She looked from Oliver to me, asking, "Y'all from out of town? Hate to turn y'all away, so I s'pose you can visit for a little while. Just recollect she tires mighty quick on days like today, so you'll likely have less 'n a half hour afore she's noddin' off. Or chasin' y'all off!"

We responded with appreciation and a promise that we wouldn't stay long. "We'll take our cues from her," E.A. added. "I know when Miz Esther's chin starts droppin' it's time to say our good-bye's."

"You know where the sunroom is, E.A.? She was wantin' to look out yonder at the park across the street, watch the young'uns play. I reckon she might be takin' a bit of a snooze right about now. Won't hurt to wake her if she is." E.A. started down the hall with Oliver and me in tow when the nurse called after us, "Oh, one more thing. Whatever you do, don't mention no sales people—especially them real estate people. Sends her into a tizzy. And don't mention no government neither. Them people *really* get her fired up."

Under his breath, Oliver murmured, "Them people get plenty of us fired up."

I chuckled and E.A. added, "A-men to that."

We walked into a bright, pleasant room with a large bay window. Several elderly people sat on chairs about the room, most in wheelchairs, throws on their laps, and a few with walkers parked beside them. Only about a third of the group appeared to be awake, and every one of those turned to gawk at us as we walked in. Oliver and I noticed Esther before E.A. pointed her out: Her head was thrown back over her wheelchair, mouth wide open, snoring louder than anyone else in the room.

E.A. leaned down next to her and lightly touched her shoulder. Slowly raising her head, she squinted at E.A., and we watched the spirit of the woman slowly come alive as her eyes ignited with a slightly wicked spark, the corners of her mouth turned up and a touch of pink spread across her nose to her cheeks. "Here's my E.A. 'Bout time you come t' see this ole woman agin."

"You're right: It's been far too long since I visited this *young* woman. Forgive me?"

Bless her heart, she giggled like a young girl at E.A.'s flattery. Her eyes—sparkling and crackling now with the intensity of a bonfire—shifted over to me. "Since you brung your sweetheart to meet me, all's forgiven."

Horrified, I opened my mouth to protest when E.A. twisted around so that momentarily his back was to Esther. He mouthed the words, *Let it go!*

I was about to set the record straight anyway—*Let it go? Over my dead body!*—when E.A. trumped my move.

"Don't miss a thing, do you, Miz Esther? This here's Julia. Julia Johnson." E.A. reached back and firmly took my hand, yanking me forward (I wasn't about to make it easy for him) until Mrs. Abel had a good view, and then he kissed the top of it. Which sent about a zillion volts of electrical sparks right up my arm to my shoulder—nearly causing another hiccup, which I thankfully swallowed back just in time. I'd need to put aside pondering that bizarre reaction for later, but now, all I could do was tug my hand away, feigning embarrassment in front of Mrs. Abel. I could feel the heat from my bright red face, so faking that was pretty easy. I could also hear Uncle Ollie muffling laughter behind his hand again. I didn't know who I'd light into first later—E.A. or Uncle Ollie. But they'd both earned a sharp retort the moment we walked out of here.

Mrs. Abel's eyebrows shot up and her eyes opened wide. "Oh, now I's knowin' you, chile! You two call me Miz Esther, hear?" She peered at my face, apparently taking in all my features.

"You's so pretty, but then, E.A.'d knowed that! He talkin' with you? Special, ain't it?"

I could only nod, since talking with E.A. had been anything but special. Unless she meant special as in *infuriating*. Admittedly, few had that particular effect on me, so in a way, talking with E.A. was indeed "special."

"Me an' my beau, my intended, we loved talking too. Oh, I can call up them days like they was yesterday. Didn't matter atall how far apart we was. We was always talkin'." She sighed and closed her eyes, remembering, I assumed. Suddenly she sat forward, squinting up at Oliver, asking, "Who might this other gentleman be? You ain't one of them—"

"No ma'am, he's not," E.A. interrupted, anticipating speculations that might send her off on a tangent; we were quickly eating into our allotted time. "This is Mr. Oliver Johnson, Julia's uncle."

Esther held out her hand to Oliver. I noticed her fingers were still long and lovely, the skin—though wrinkled—was relatively unmarked, and there wasn't a trace of a tremor. "Well, Mr. Oliver Johnson. This here gal's right lovely. E.A. deserves the best, and I recollect he be gettin' just that."

"Oh, our Julia's the best, all right. Won't get any argument from me on that matter."

Esther shifted her attention towards me then, reaching out, motioning for me to move closer to her. When I did so, she cupped my chin in her hand, and her eyes roamed over my face. I'd expected her hand to be cool and rougher to the touch, but it was surprisingly warm, and soft as the finest silk. "Oh, chile. You's totin' a weight in your heart. It be way too heavy for one young as you is."

The tenderness in her face and voice pulled me in like a magnet. I don't think I could've looked away if I tried, and the kind words of empathy produced instant tears.

Esther softly stroked my cheek, and I leaned into her hand with a sudden yearning like a child longing for the security of her mother's lap. "Melungeon blood in you is strong, gal." I nearly jerked backwards, I was so startled, but she held my chin firmly and her eyes widened in alarm as she sucked in her breath. "I see they's comin'. Tain't no curse"—she shook her head, emphatically—"like some what has Melungeon blood. No curse in you, praise God. But sweet gal, they's comin'."

Her breathing suddenly pronounced, Esther jerked back her hand, positioning it over her heart. Out of my peripheral vision, I saw Oliver leave the room. But I was so mesmerized that I continued kneeling before her, silent and waiting. Spellbound by whatever she had to tell me.

"E.A.," she rasped, groping now for him, grabbing his arm in a death grip. "She's in danger, ain't you knowin' it? They's comin'. The air, that's what's they's after. Lucille and Jimmy, I knowed they spirited her away." My mouth dropped open and I could feel myself breathing in tandem with Esther now, our chests rising and falling in a weirdly synchronized duet. "I see how you're lovin' her, E.A., see it in your eyes plain as day. But *be doin' somethin', son!* 'Cause they ain't no hidin' her here, no place what's safe in the Cumberland!"

As Esther's voice rose in intensity, the men and women around the room were becoming agitated too—like she was the conductor leading an orchestra towards a crescendo. Some groaned while others merely fidgeted, but several were crying out and calling for what I assumed were lost loves, spouses who were no more. It was all frightening to me: Esther's near hysteria, though most of what she'd said made no sense; the eerie and sad sounds of others echoing around the room; but more than anything, the truths she knew about my life and had revealed to E.A. But I had no place else to look for help—no one other than E.A. When I sought his eyes, I discovered once again a look on his face I couldn't make sense of. Because in that moment, he *did* look like he cared about me. Deeply.

E.A. put his hands on Esther's shoulders, his attempt to calm her. She would have none of it, however, and shook him off.

Her voice was shrill as she tried in vain to push up out of the wheelchair. "You must be protectin' her, E.A. They's comin'. Get her out. Get her out, I tell you!"

Esther's strength was spent, and she sunk back into her wheelchair. Eerily silent now, she stared ahead through seemingly sightless eyes. E.A. and I had stood, motioning each other to push her towards the nurses' station when two aides arrived with Oliver. One nurse immediately checked her pulse while the other softly asked, "Miz Esther? Y'all right, honey? Got yourself a little worked up. Come on now, Miz Esther. Answer me."

I expected a scolding from one or both nurses, but they only attempted to reassure us. "Don't be frettin'," one of them offered, patting my hand. "Miz Esther just gets herself over excited now 'n then. No call to blame yourselves, since we hear she's been prone to these spells ever since she was a young'un. She'll be right as rain after a good nap, won't you, Miz Esther?"

Esther's eyes focused and she looked up at the nurse. "Need me a shot o' whiskey. Pa always said twas the onliest medicine a body ever needed." She held up two fingers, positioning them a couple inches apart. "'Bout that much is all. Just a little shot'll do it."

The nurses were pushing her towards the door when one of them turned around, giving us a pronounced wink, saying, "Yes, ma'am. Comin' right up, Miz Esther. We'll be pouring that whiskey soon's we get you settled in your room." As they proceeded down the hall, she called over her shoulder, "Y'all don't be afraid to come back now. Miz Esther be needin' your company. And the exercise—ain't that right, Miz Esther?"

I didn't utter one word as we left the building, but I could vaguely hear E.A. rehashing to Oliver, in a hushed whisper, all that Esther had said—or tried to say, since he also noted that most of it was disjointed and made no sense. Clancy barked once at us in greeting as we approached, but E.A. silenced him with a rub behind the ears. I had no idea what E.A. and Oliver were feeling, but I knew I felt mostly numb. And I had no idea where to begin discussing all that had happened, all Esther had said. I firmly decided, however, to completely ignore her comments about me being E.A.'s sweetheart. *Nothing* good would come from bringing up that. *But what was that nonsense about the air? Maybe she meant the sky, that someone was coming on a plane?* I wondered. *And just who was coming? And why on earth was she insisting I should hide?*

E.A. echoed my thoughts, musing, " *'They's comin'.'* Who could Miz Esther have been referring to? Either of you have any ideas?" E.A. looked at Oliver and then me, searching our faces for answers.

"Don't look at me. I'm as clueless as you are."

Oliver took one of my hands into both of his, clenching it tightly, rubbing it with his thumb. "Whoever they are, Esther made one thing clear: They're dangerous. And they intend to hurt Julia." He looked past me, over to E.A., who nodded his head as though the two of them had telegraphed a message and plan and were now agreeing to carry it out.

"Now wait a minute here," I said, shaking my head. "How much of this are we going to believe is credible? I mean…really?"

E.A. started up the truck, but we merely sat there as he stared straight ahead. I watched him clench his jaw, that muscle twitching again. "I suppose that depends how much is based on truth." He turned to look at me, his gaze intense. "Are Lucille and Jimmy your biological parents?"

Time seemed to stop for a few moments. At first, I heard only the low, uneven rumble of the truck's engine, but then I caught the sound of children's laughter. Chirping of birds. The buzzing drone of a low-flying plane. Above all, I heard the pronounced beating of my heart. *Lord, do I dare trust this Byrd brother? Seems to me I shouldn't, but what choice do I have now, after Esther pretty much spilled all my secrets—heaven knows how she knew all she did! I feel like I've been backed into a corner—a dangerous one.* I felt Oliver squeeze my hand, and I took a deep breath. "Yes, they are." I waited for E.A.'s response, expecting a lecture, a dozen more questions or a demand that I immediately go back to Wisconsin. Instead, his compassion nearly did me in.

E.A. sighed and then pointed to our left. "Their graves are right across the square," he said softly. "Would you like to visit them?"

I nodded, too emotional to speak, but Oliver added, "I think that's exactly where we should go, E.A. This is perfect timing."

This cemetery wasn't at all like the one out in the country, for it showed signs of constant, loving care. The grass had been recently cut and neat flower beds were everywhere—colorful varieties of plants dotted the grounds along with bouquets in canning jars next to stones—so that the sweet smells of vibrant life were in juxtaposition to a place dedicated to the dead. We parked under the shade of a huge oak, E.A. commanded Clancy to *stay*, and then E.A. led us to the plot where my ancestors lay.

"There's the stone where your mama and daddy are." He nodded his head towards the right. "Your daddy's family's just up the hill."

The stone was quite large in comparison to those that we'd discovered out at the family cemetery. The name BLEVINS was in bold at the top, with Lucille's and Jimmy's birth and death dates underneath, and then a bible verse was quoted at the bottom. I noted that, surprisingly, the letters *CRO* weren't on my parent's gravestone.

"Do you come here often?" I asked.

"Mama's brought flowers for 'em plenty of times; there's something about—well, I just like to come with her. But to tell you the truth, I imagine anyone who has relatives in this cemetery has put flowers on Lucille and Jimmy's graves at one time or another." He removed his hat, a gesture I took as a sign of respect. "They were well loved, Julia. Their deaths touched us all."

Just as he'd said, their shared stone was surrounded by a variety of planted and cut flowers—some so fresh they must've been put there this morning. I inched closer, my hands so nervous and twitchy that I stuffed them into my pockets. In light of my parents' poverty, I wondered who paid for the stone when E.A., apparently anticipating my question, offered, "The town took up a collection. And Mama told me they found that verse written inside the cover of Jimmy's bible: 'The Lord shall fight for you, and ye shall hold your peace. Exodus 14:14.'"

"Why do you suppose—?"

"It's when God parted the Red Sea for the Israelites," E.A. explained. "I looked it up when I was just a kid, after I'd been here and wondered that very thing. Read the whole passage through like I was readin' it for the first time. Later I read a different version, one that translates it this way: 'The Lord will fight for you, you need only to be still.'" He knelt down, absentmindedly plucking the dead blooms and tossing them aside. "That's the message of Lucille and Jimmy's deaths—at least, always has been for me. Whenever things look 'specially bad, it's a reminder God's still in control. He will fight for us. Our part's to trust him with whatever happens."

Oliver's voice was soft too. "Julia and I recently talked about when you have nowhere else to turn, you must find the courage and faith to just jump. Might feel like you're pitching out into nothingness. But it's really about jumping into God's arms."

E.A. solemnly nodded, and Oliver bowed his head as though in prayer.

As for me, I stared at the words on the stone through a film of tears, and the lump in my throat felt huge as I struggled to swallow. *You don't have a clue, E.A., how your words are like a barb piercing my heart. Is it really as simple as that? Or so easy? God, how on earth do I trust you that deeply—when every part of my life is in such a mess?*

"Would you like to keep one of these roses? As a remembrance?" When I hesitated, E.A. added, "You know, it sounded like Miz Esther believed Lucille and Jimmy sent you away secretly—for your protection. Considering how they died, well, you have to wonder, you know?"

He looked up at Oliver—who nodded—and then at me. *Did he expect me to agree that my "spiriting away" and secret adoption were somehow to protect me? From what—or whom?* It all seemed so far-fetched. *What on earth would make me a target for anyone? There was nothing special about me, nothing at all. And it was then that it suddenly hit me: The déjà vu I'd experienced? Now I knew why the letters* CRO *seemed familiar.*

-Guy, are you there? Here's something really strange that I just remembered. Yesterday, on the gravestones? On every single one that we were able to make out what they said, there were three letters down at the bottom: *CRO*. I couldn't put together where I'd seen or heard that before until just now when E.A. mentioned my adoption. Guy, in the water-stained letter that was so difficult to read, one of the things that *did* stand out was exactly that. Those same three letters. No idea what that means in the letter—or on the gravestones. But ironically, maybe surprisingly, there's no *CRO* here, on my parents' stone. None of this makes sense. And I have *no clue* what it means.

-E.A. brought up your adoption because—?

-Esther said something about me being 'spirited away' by my biological parents. So, obviously it's not a secret any longer about my adoption, and that the Blevins are my biological parents. Now E.A.'s intimating there's something special about me that would warrant some sort of special adoption, and the need to get me away from here because of the danger. Isn't that ludicrous?

-But you are special, Jules.

-Oh Guy. That's only because you love me. Your bias doesn't exactly make you a fair judge.

-I don't want to be a fair judge. I want to always be in your corner, to be with you wherever you are.

My heart skipped a beat.

-Are you coming to me?

-Maybe soon, Jules. I hope so. But that depends...

-Depends on what? Guy? *But there was no answer to my question. At least not yet, for he was gone.*

"Don't you think it odd that Jimmy's middle name is also Gibbons?" I watched Oliver follow the etching of *Jimmy Gibbons Blevins* with his finger. "In some cultures, sons take their mother's maiden name as a middle name. But using Gibbons is puzzling. Were Jimmy and Lucille somehow related?"

E.A. nodded. "I've been told they were—very distant cousins. One of those cases where it's so far back, it'd be hard to trace." He continued to work around the flowers, pulling a couple weeds near the profusion of yellow, orange and red marigolds. "It's through the same branch where Mama says we're related. To Miz Esther. And Jimmy."

I jerked as if I'd been slapped. "What? You're related to Jimmy?" I stammered as I tried to sort through the ramifications. "My...*my father?*"

"Only tellin' you what Mama says she's been told." He shrugged his shoulders. "And like I said, way back...so distant there's no record. And no proof."

"Then let's go find it," Oliver said.

I looked up at him. "What're you suggesting?"

"That we go to the courthouse. It's on our list of things we wanted to do."

E.A. stood, rubbed dirty hands on his jeans, and glanced down at his watch. "It's nine-forty-five now. What if we go out to the homesite for a couple hours first—that is, if we agree it's safe. Oliver, did you speak with Deputy Jenkins?"

"Had a good conversation with the deputy," Oliver said. "We're cleared to go—if you're still intent on putting in more time out there, Julia." To my answering nod, he added, "Well, then I also vote we go now when it's cooler. Then we could make a trip to the courthouse after lunch. Where I assume it's air conditioned?"

E.A. smiled. "Just so happens that the mayor's office is also in the courthouse. Your assumption, therefore, would be correct."

"Julia?"

"I agree: Let's head out to the homesite now. And if the courthouse still seems like the best place to go this afternoon, then so be it."

I saw E.A. hesitate a moment and hang back as Oliver and I started walking towards the truck. When he caught up with us just a few moments later, I was touched by what he'd done. "You might want to double-check, but I think I got all the thorns." In my open palm he placed one perfect rose from the wild bush that grew beside the Blevins' monument.

I held it up to my nose to breathe in the sweet scent, but when I glanced over at him, I noticed his thumb was bleeding. "Looks like one of the thorns got you, though."

He shook it off. "Oh, it's nothing. I thought you should have something *from them*."

Before we climbed into the truck, I reached down into the pocket of my jeans and pulled out the *B*. "Actually, I do have something from them. This was with my adoption papers." I placed the *B* in his hand and watched for his reaction, interested how it would compare to Brent's.

He appeared puzzled by the *B* and brought it closer to his eyes, peering at it from all different angles. Rubbing it along the bottom, he commented, "Feels like it used to have hooks along the bottom here." I nodded in agreement. "Strange there's no evidence of a loop along the top, though. Had to be Lucille's pendant, don't you s'pose? Oliver, what do you think?" he asked, as he handed it back to me.

E.A. started up the truck and we pulled out onto the highway. Funny how the close confines of the cab now felt almost cozy instead of uncomfortable—once E.A. cranked up the air, that is. I realized that implied I was feeling more relaxed around E.A. and wondered why. *Was it because of how considerate he was about the cemetery?* I asked myself. *And because he gave me the rose?*

"Very old gold pieces can be more than eighteen karats—possibly twenty-four," Uncle Ollie was saying. "Makes them soft and pliable, so they're prone to getting dinged and bent up. If your *B* is actually really old, Julia, that could explain why it looks so bad."

I studied the *B* with new eyes. "Interesting theory. You could be right, Uncle Ollie. Don't know why I never really considered that before, but I guess I didn't entertain the idea that Lucille and Jimmy would own something that valuable." I rubbed it between my fingers, appreciating the ability to touch something my mother once held in her own hands. "Sounds terribly prejudiced of me, doesn't it? My assumption that they wouldn't own anything of worth?"

We pulled onto the gravel path of the homesite and E.A. shut down the truck. As he climbed out of the cab, he threw over his shoulder, "Maybe you ought to re-think some of your assumptions about Southerners."

"What does that mean?" I asked, immediately on the defensive. All three of us got busy applying sunscreen and bug spray, putting water bottles into our backpacks, pulling on gloves. Still peeved about E.A.'s comment—Oliver would define it as itching for a fight—I pulled on mine like they were boxing gloves. Which reminded me of another bone I had to pick with him. "By the way, why did you encourage Esther's assumption about us? Haven't you taken Kate to meet her?"

Oliver happily trudged on ahead with Clancy trotting at his heels. But E.A. stopped in his tracks and spun around to face me. "What on earth are you talking about?"

The look on his face was pure bewilderment with a measure of anger mixed in. *We're back to that, are we? Looks like we're in for another scrimmage.* "You and Kate, that's what I'm talking about. Brent told me—"

"What? What did Brent say now, pray tell?"

"I would think you'd *want* him to tell me. Tell everyone. That you and Kate are soon to be engaged."

E.A.'s face morphed from anger to surprise to hilarity. "If his lips're movin', he's lyin', Julia! Don't you know an outright fabrication when you hear one? I'm no more engaged to Kate than...than I am to *you*," said with a look like he'd just stepped on a gooey wad of gum.

Then he had the gall to turn his back to me and walk away. I didn't particularly care to look at his back just then because, by golly, he owed me an explanation, not sarcastic ridicule.

And he'd managed to insult me yet again! "How was I to know Brent was lying? And actually, how do I know who to believe right now? Maybe *you're* the one who's not telling me the truth," I shouted at him. The harder I tried to catch up to him, the faster he went, and the longer I looked at his retreating back, the *madder* I got. "Will you kindly stop for just one stinking second?" At that moment, the slime—*how was I to know E.A. would take me literally?*—stopped so abruptly I ran right smack into him, tripping over his feet and stumbling.

Before I knew what was happening, he'd whirled around quickly enough to catch me, steadying me in his arms so that my head was flooded with the male scent of him—musk and sweat and dog and detergent and just the slightest hint of roses. Just as quickly, he pushed me out and away, his eyes boring into mine. *Was it anger reflected there? Hurt? Or a combination of both?*

"You've got a decision to make, Jul…*Julia*. Are you gonna trust Brent? Or me? Because one of us is a lyin' traitor."

THE GRAVESTONES' SECRETS

23 of June, 1588

My Descendants,

Gone! All that remains behind of me, Mauro, at the Colony of Roanoke, the City of Raleigh, is my carving on a tree, a testimony of our love: CRO. My companions mock me, but not with ill intent, for we journey together now, and they are agreeable and courageous and adventurous at heart. Though we face new challenges at every turn, we press on, trusting the Almighty God for our future here.

As a boy, my Tutor tirelessly taught me from the Holy Bible—translated in our native tongue, and thus ever guarded for its priceless worth to us. Sadly, though most eager to learn, I was not the best of students. And yet, sometimes, My Teacher's lessons reached a place in me that stirred my Soul, and such was the story of Esther. Her Courage and Faith were lessons in themselves, and I have ever wished that I could prove as brave should I be tested. These past years have been such a test, and thus my Testimony must be as Esther's: If I Perish, I Perish. Knowing my God, my death will not be in vain!

My beloved Catherine and I talk often of this Faith that we share— in God and His Only Son. That Faith in His Power and Him alone is what sustains me, and I know that Catherine pleads with Him for my safe journey as well.

We have met with more adventures than I can pen, but as for now, I am safe, even while knowing danger as our constant, enduring companion. We are weary, but we press ever Westward in this New World.

Always,
Mauro

CHAPTER NINE

I stood there stupidly, staring up into his eyes. When I started to stammer, E.A. merely let go and turned back down the path we'd followed two days before, walking determinedly away from me.

"E.A., hang on a minute!" My mind was a jumble of questions, but E.A. was right. *Which brother* was *I going to trust? Which one did I ultimately feel safer with—E.A.? Or Brent?*

"What now?" he pretty much shouted over his shoulder, clearly still furious with me.

Clancy raced back towards his master, nuzzling E.A.'s hand and then happily bounding off towards Uncle Ollie again. *At least Clancy's enjoying himself,* I fumed. "You've put me in a precarious situation here. I don't know *who* to believe."

"*I* put you in this situation? Seems to me you got there all on your own," he threw back at me.

"Well, I didn't ask for any of this—my dad's passing and finding out I'm adopted and every bit of this mess I'm in." I was feeling royally sorry for myself, and especially since I wasn't getting what I truly wanted from E.A—a bit of empathy. Was that too much to ask? As scatterbrained as my thoughts were, my worries went right back to Esther's warning. "What Esther said about someone coming. What do you think she meant?"

"Why're you asking me? No idea, Julia." He added, sarcastically, "Why don't you ask Brent? Apparently, you think he has all the answers."

I chose to ignore that. "But should I listen to her?"

"Wise people tend to at least give Miz Esther's Sight some careful consideration."

I stopped a moment, taking that in. "But what—?"

"Hey, you two. I've found something! Come on over here." Oliver was motioning to us with one hand and clutching Clancy's collar with the other.

E.A. beat me there, so I rudely elbowed my way in between Oliver and Clancy. All three of us leaned over, hands on knees, where—through the thick undergrowth and down about a foot—we could glimpse a small area covered with trimmed boards. Eagerly, we kneeled down, pulling them away when Oliver offered, "I'm guessing it's a well. Be careful, E.A. Plenty of nails sticking out everywhere, nasty enough to pierce right through gloves. That's why I grabbed Clancy. I was afraid he'd step on one."

"Clancy can be right curious, determined to get his nose in whatever. And I'm with you about it being a well," E.A. added, grunting as he tugged on a particularly stubborn board. When it finally gave way, we saw it had been nailed to several others. "This was a make-do cover. Help me lift it, Oliver." Clancy inched forward and E.A. sternly ordered, "Clancy, *sit*. If it is a well, we surely don't want you fallin' down the blamed thing. We'd need a crane to haul you outta there."

All three of us leaned over the dark hole, curious, excited to find something from another generation. *How many years has it been since this well's been uncovered?* I wondered. Lifting the last boards unleashed a smell that assaulted us with a potent slap: Dank, musty, earthy, the mingled odors of mold and mildew and decay. If a scent could ever be considered tangible, this was it. Oliver sneezed once, violently, and sat back on his heels.

"I'd forgotten. You're allergic to mold, aren't you, Uncle Ollie?"

He sneezed violently again and pulled out his handkerchief. I smiled at him, my uncle the gentleman. I was astounded whenever he produced a white, freshly ironed linen handkerchief, and pulling out one in this environment seemed nearly miraculous. When he blew his nose, making that familiar honking sound, I urged him to move away. "There's no need for you to expose yourself to this. Why don't you look for other buildings? There's got to be more right in this vicinity."

Oliver didn't argue but instead stood, sneezed again (another honking nose blow too) and asked, "Mind if I take Clancy with me? This dog is incredibly smart, E.A. I have to give him the credit for finding the well. I was merely the trusty side-kick."

"Absolutely. Like I said, Clancy's naturally curious, so he'll be nosin' around everywhere." E.A. lifted a rope out of his backpack, adding, "Did you find any rocks around here, Oliver? About the size to fit in your hand? I'd like to test the depth of the well."

He was still untying the rope when Oliver delivered several stones. "Here you go. One of those do? Good. I'd like to stay and listen for the splash but—*a-choo!*—I think I'll mosey over this way with Clancy. Come on, boy. Let's go hunt for other interesting finds, shall we?" Clancy looked up at Oliver, ears alert and head cocked—tail wagging the entire time—and the happy companions wandered away from us.

"You suppose anything else is down there? I mean, besides water, of course." I peered into the hole, trying to imagine a storage area down there somewhere. "Didn't people sometimes store things in a well?"

"I think you've confused a well with a springhouse—that's a building above ground, built on the side of a creek. They kept butter and milk, other perishables there." He glanced over at me, grinning wickedly. "But if you don't *believe* me and want t' climb down, check it out for yourself…"

"Very funny. I'll pass."

"Oh, so you wanted *me* to go down and explore?"

I didn't bother answering, but made sure he saw my look of disgust.

E.A. picked up one of the stones, transferring it from one hand to the other before dropping it down the well. Counting out loud, he said, "One, and—" We heard a splash, followed by waves of scent that filled our nostrils again with the acrid odors of earth and minerals. "Water doesn't smell foul, so I'm guessin' it's from a natural spring that's a tributary of the creek. The regular flow keeps it from gettin' brackish." He sat back on his heals a minute, concentrating. "Okay, if I remember correctly, you square the time, multiply it by thirty-two and divide that in half. Stone fell about a second an' a half…" E.A. closed his eyes in concentration before stating, "I figure 'bout thirty-six feet deep. Down to the water, I mean. No idea how deep the water is but I doubt it's more 'n a couple feet."

"You're kidding, right?"

"What?"

"The formula you used." I shook my head, and I'm sure my skepticism came across loud and clear. "Can you really measure how deep something is that way?"

E.A. looked away from me and shook his head. His voice thick with bitterness, he spit out, "You really don't trust a single thing I say, do you?"

Something inside me gave way then, like a pop. Rising to the surface like a bubble boiling in a pan, I shot right back at him, "Brent tells me not to trust you. You warn me not to trust him. Brent informs me you and Kate are engaged. You insist that no, you're not engaged. Brent and I have a wonderful time all day yesterday, laughing, getting to know one another. We're teasing, dunking each other in pure fun when *you* show up. Uninvited, belligerent, and accusatory. Accusing Brent with attempting to *drown* me—really? How on earth could you possibly believe that of your own brother? Attempted *murder*, E.A.? When Brent had been nothing but the perfect gentleman all day: kind, affectionate, caring, and quite frankly—though it's really none of your business—a very good kisser." I'd thrown in that last bit out of pure contrariness, but he'd asked for it.

E.A. froze like he'd been turned to stone. He opened his mouth to say something. Stopped, pressed his lips together as if choosing his words carefully, and began again. "God as my witness, I don't know who Miz Esther was talking about when she insisted 'they's comin'," he responded, his voice no more than a hoarse whisper. "But I take her warning about you being in danger seriously, Jul...*Julia*. *Very* seriously."

He glared at me with fire flashing in his eyes. Part of me was still furious. But another part was ambivalently pulled towards him in a way I had no explanation for. "Then give me one reason why Brent would want to harm me. You have no rational answer to that, E.A.!"

"Miz Esther's warning wasn't rational either, was it? You heard her—same's Oliver and I did. She told *me* to protect you—not your uncle, surprisingly. And *not Brent*. By God, I will do just that, even if you fight me every step of the way. *Brent's* the danger, Julia. Not me. Until you get that into your head, you're more vulnerable than you could imagine." He broke away from my gaze to peer back down the dark hole. "Feels like the rope reached the water. Since it's forty feet long"—he glanced over at me again, sneering, a mocking tone to his voice now—"I guess that means my figurin' isn't so unbelievable after all."

I bit back one nasty response, but my tongue wouldn't be totally tamed. "I'm really sorry Esther put you out by making you promise to protect me."

"Seems we all have our crosses to bear."

That one hurt, but I wasn't about to let him see that. "You are insufferable, E.A."

"Well, I've been called far worse, that's for sure." He finished re-coiling the rope and stuffed it into his backpack. "Shall we go help your uncle? Or are there any more compliments you'd like to toss my way? My hands're plenty dirty from messin' with this well. I don't have my hair cut in the latest style, my cowlick was at its best this morning and I haven't shown you a good time yet today."

I bristled at his petty speech, clenching my fists in indignation.

Rubbing his chin, he continued, "I didn't shave this morning, so I've got a stubble like number four sandpaper. Know what I ought to do, though? I ought to kiss you, that's what. Give you yet one more thing to be comparin' to my brother." He leaned toward me, so close I could feel his breath on my face. My heart pounded and my breathing accelerated as though I were out on a training run. I was just about to close my eyes—anticipating his leaning in to put his lips on mine—when he said with that now all-too-familiar flinty edge of his, "But I won't grant you the privilege. Wouldn't want to show up Brent, clearly demonstrating his inferior skills and messin' up your tallying board."

Humiliated—*Did he guess that, for a moment there, I was stupidly expecting that promised kiss?*—and insulted, I opened my mouth to throw back a biting reply when Oliver's voice interrupted us.

"Hey!" he yelled. "Come here—I've found something else!"

E.A. got up immediately to go to Oliver, but I sat there on my heels, reeling in my confusion and anger.

-Guy? I need you. Are you there?

-Not now, Jules.

I knew it was totally unreasonable to expect him to be at my beck and call, and I couldn't do that for him. *But I sure would've appreciated any reassurance you could've sent my way, Guy.*

Uncle Ollie and E.A. were pulling at some boards nailed over the door of a small shed by the time I arrived. The problem was that tugging too hard could make the entire structure fall apart, fragile and rickety as it appeared. Clancy was busy sniffing around it like a bloodhound, and he soon scared up the reason why: A mouse darted out from under the door—right over my boots. Which caused me to screech and jump back, scaring both Oliver and E.A. so that they jumped too. "Sorry. It was a mouse."

"Goodness, Julia," Uncle Ollie complained. "Sure wish you could give out a warning before you do that." E.A. rolled his eyes at me.

"This may come as a surprise to you two, but I didn't *plan* to do that. Mice apparently don't give warnings either."

As they cautiously opened the door, all three of us peered inside, our curiosity causing us to nearly bump heads. There were tumbledown shelves lining the walls, but otherwise, the only other items appeared to be plants growing everywhere, cobwebs, the expected assortment of creepy-crawlers and shadows—shadows highlighted by dust-filled arcs of sun slicing through gaps of warped boards.

To speak with anything other than a hushed voice seemed intrusive. Softly, I asked, "What do you suppose this was? A storage area?"

E.A. nodded. "I s'pose so." He and Oliver looked over the shelves, checking for anything left behind.

"Hey, here's an old watering can," Oliver exclaimed, holding it out to me.

I reached to take it with a touch of awe, wondering whose hands had last held it. *Had a relative of mine watered a garden? Was it for the utility of vegetables, or a flower garden for the heart?*

I rubbed my hand along the curve of the handle and looked up to find E.A. watching me, studying me intently. "What?"

He shook his head. "Nothing."

I knew it wasn't *nothing*, but there was no sense trying to pull it out of E.A. The man was pure stubbornness, wrapped up in prickles.

I turned away from E.A. to concentrate. And to get a bit of privacy on the pretext of a need for fresh air. "It's stifling in here," I fussed, taking off my cap to mop my forehead and push back the escaped wisps. "If there's nothing else for me to see? Okay, I'm outta here." I walked the short distance to the creek where Clancy was standing in water up to his belly, helping himself to a drink. "Taste good, boy?" I asked. He looked up at me—I swear it looked like he was grinning with delight—with water dripping from his jowls. I pulled off boots and socks and gingerly stepped in with him, exclaiming, "Oh, that feels heavenly, Clancy. No wonder you're standing in your drinking bowl."

-What's heavenly?

-The creek, Guy. It's sweltering, and the water's delightful. Clancy and I are just taking a bit of a break. I needed some time away from E.A.

-Clancy? You got *another* man hanging around?

I chuckled.

-Not quite. Clancy's a yellow Lab. Oh, he's brought me a stick to throw, Guy. And now he's after it, splashing water everywhere—including me! So why are you always defending E.A. anyway?

I threw the stick for Clancy again, laughing at him. Not minding at all that he was getting me soaked in the process. I had no idea what Uncle Ollie and E.A. were up to, but as long as they were busy for a while, that was fine with me. E.A. and I needed some space.

-Maybe it's more about....a different perspective. He might be hurting too, you know.

-Why on earth would he be hurting?
-I can't speculate on that, Jules. But always attributing the negative to him might not be an accurate picture of what he's really experiencing. You act defensive when you're hurting.
-Do not.
-Jules.

"Julia, darling. Are you ready to go? What on earth?" Oliver chuckled at Clancy and me as we climbed out of the creek—well, Clancy took it in one easy leap while I gingerly watched my footing. Naturally, Clancy shook himself at that very moment, soaking me one last time and gifting Uncle Ollie with a light spray too. In between chuckles, he added, "You're nearly as drenched as that dog, darling girl."

I sat down on a rock to pull on socks and boots. "Didn't mind that at all. It was fun—and very refreshing, actually!"

"Hey, boy! Have a good time?" E.A. reached out to pat Clancy's head, obviously not minding the wet kisses and fur. "Thanks for playing with him. Chasing sticks in water is probably his favorite game."

I started to respond sarcastically but bit it back. Since we had a moment of peace between us—and E.A. had even thanked me—I decided to be gracious. For the time being. Glancing from E.A. to Uncle Ollie, I asked, "Did you find anything else? Buildings? More gravestones?"

Oliver nodded. "A few more gravestones, but they were all so old—too worn and stained to read. Found some boards here and there. The nails were a hazard, so we decided to call it a day."

I picked up the watering can and asked, "Any reason why I can't take this with me?"

Both Oliver and E.A. shook their heads. "Used to be your family's property," E.A. offered. "Nice to have somethin' as a keepsake."

He sounded wistful all of a sudden, and I wondered what that was about. But I was quickly distracted by a new concern. "You know, that brings up a good question. Who owns this land now?"

E.A. shrugged his shoulders. "No idea. We could ask at the courthouse."

"Gotta tell you," Oliver said, "I'm concerned about that well. It's far too dangerous with only boards loosely covering it."

"I agree," E.A. said, and motioned with his head. "Let's get back to the truck. We'll need to grab some lunch before we visit the courthouse. Oliver, how 'bout you and I drop by the sheriff's office? Let 'em know that well needs fillin' in. Heaven knows why anybody would be out this way, but I'd feel responsible if someone got hurt now that I know about it." I watched E.A. squint his eyes a bit, contemplating a solution, I assumed. "You know, I imagine they'd appreciate me volunteerin' to head up that project."

"You'd need some fill. And a backhoe."

"Yeah, a backhoe or bobcat would do the job."

I looked from one to the other and smirked.

"What?" both asked, in nearly perfect unison again.

"Macho men and your tools. You'll be pounding your chests and grunting next."

I was even more conscious of our thighs touching in E.A.'s truck, noting the electrical charge had amped up even higher. But I consoled myself with the knowledge that once we got back to town, we wouldn't need the truck any longer. *I'm definitely driving my dad's car to the courthouse*, I promised myself. *I'll be in the driver's seat and an arm's length from anyone who chooses to ride along. As a matter of fact, there's no need for E.A. to go to the courthouse with Oliver and me. Certainly, he's got work to do? What business is it of his concerning my ancestors?*

We grabbed a quick lunch in the kitchen of A Byrd in the Hand. Knowing the owners certainly had its perks: We were encouraged to sample pretty much anything Myra was cooking and baking that morning—which meant Oliver enjoyed at least one bite of everything. We sat on tall wooden stools around the huge island, taking turns telling Mama Byrd about the well and the visit to Esther too. Of course, that meant spilling my supposedly secret story again, but I figured since her sons knew, we might as well fill her in, also. And honestly, as I looked into her face and saw the compassion and empathy registered there, I realized I probably trusted her more than any other member of the Byrd family anyway. We agreed to get together soon so she could tell me about Lucille, and how beloved she was.

When Oliver talked about my dad's death, Mama Byrd touched my hair. I turned towards her, and she gathered me into her arms, pressing me to her, food-coated apron and all. This was no quick release type of hug—or the kind when the other person stiffens, signaling boundaries that shouldn't be breached. Instead, she pulled me into the contours of her body and held me there, gently patting my back. It had been too many years since I'd been consoled by my mom, and Mama Byrd was a perfect stand-in.

We were all eating blackberry pie—still warm, with ice cream—when Mama Byrd asked, "So where y'all off to this afternoon?"

I had a mouthful, and was attempting to swallow so I could answer when E.A. said, "The courthouse. Julia wants to search the archives, see what we can find about her ancestry. And you know what, Mama? I thought it would be a good time to check ours, too. See if I can uncover that connection to Miz Esther you've mentioned."

Mama Byrd's back was to me, so I could conveniently frown at E.A. without her seeing. "Oh, E.A., honestly," I fairly cooed,

"Uncle Ollie and I have kept you from your work far too long already. I'm sure your mom needs you right here."

She turned around to look at us, wiping hands on her apron since they were covered in a layer of flour from mixing dough for tonight's rolls. "No, actually y'all, I'm way ahead o' my schedule. Did me some prep work last night, knowin' I needed to run them errands this mornin'. Since you and Oliver so kindly lent me that nice car, I got all the supplies I was after. I can spare E.A., no problem." She chuckled, and her bright eyes lit up. "Course, maybe E.A.'s worn out his welcome and y'all's ready to ship 'im back to me!"

Oliver jumped into the fray immediately, vehemently denying that any Byrd was ever anything less than wonderful company. "Isn't that right, Julia?"

"Mama Byrd, you're an amazingly gracious and generous host. Brent's ever the gentleman and so fun to be with," I answered, carefully crafting my response. "And there just aren't words to describe E.A." I swiveled in my chair to look over at E.A., smiling sweetly.

"Well, then. It's settled. You'll be meetin' Opal Mullins over to the courthouse. She's in charge of records. I'll warn y'all: For one thing, Opal's organizin' can be a bit haphazard. And then she's also a tad, um…how shall I put it?" She pushed her glasses up higher on her nose, leaving flour smudges on her face and glasses. "Protective? Yes, that would be it. She hovers over all them important papers in her care. But no matter. I'm sure y'all be locatin' ever thing you're wantin' to find."

After helping to clean up our dishes, we profusely thanked Mama Byrd for the delicious lunch. We were gathering our things to head out when E.A. put an arm around his mom, giving her a hug. Oblivious to the flour that had made its way onto his shirt, he reached for a towel, gently wiping flour from Mama Byrd's face and glasses. *Was this an act, put on for my benefit?* I wondered. I was so busy speculating about E.A.'s intentions that I turned too quickly and clumsily tripped over Clancy again. In a heartbeat, E.A. was right there.

"Whoa, you okay?" he asked, grabbing my arm, steadying me. "Clancy tends to find ways to be constantly underfoot."

The familiar electric current shot right up my arm once more, and I yanked it back out of his grasp in exasperation with myself: For my clumsiness and also the mortifying and baffling response that happened pretty much every time E.A. touched me. I shook my head in disgust at my reaction and then glanced up at E.A.

For a split second, I could've sworn I saw hurt register on his face again. That impression disappeared in a heartbeat, however, when he cynically quipped, "Good going, Grace." Then he nonchalantly added, "Might as well all ride in my truck again."

"I think not," I stated emphatically. "I'm walking back to the motel to take care of Moppit. Then I'll drive myself to the courthouse." I glanced over at Oliver. "Uncle Ollie, you coming with me?"

Oliver hesitated and then surprised me by electing to go with E.A. "I think I'll hitch a ride with E.A. We could drop by the sheriff's office. Give them a heads-up about the well?"

"Great idea," E.A. said. "After that we'll head over to the courthouse. Since Mama warned we'd be walkin' into a disorganized mess, the sooner we get at it, the better." E.A. petted Clancy while Oliver climbed into the truck. "Want a ride to the motel?" he asked me. "Clancy'd let you ride in the back with him, wouldn't you, boy?"

I scoffed. "Does your magnanimity know no bounds?"

"Clancy and I will take that as a *no*. Oh, and don't feel like you need to hurry. Your uncle and I will undoubtedly enjoy the peace and quiet of the document room."

I crossed my arms over my chest and glared at him. "Insinuating it'll be peaceful without *me*?"

"Never said that. Your inference."

I narrowed my eyes again. "Have I told you lately how rude you are?"

"Not in the last five minutes, as I recall. But you just remedied that, eh?" He was chuckling as he climbed into the cab. And as I huffed and puffed my way across the parking lot—not from exertion, but instead, my racing temper—E.A. drove by, giving his horn a couple well-timed blasts. Of course, I jumped, and I could hear E.A. laughing as he leaned out his window, yelling, "Sorry 'bout that. Only watchin' out for your safety. Sworn to protect you, you know."

"Yeah, about like a rabbit protected by a rattlesnake!" I shouted back.

Moppit was thrilled to see me, covering my hands with sloppy kisses, like usual. I spent some time letting her soothe my ego, soaking up her unconditional love, returning it with lots of ear scratching and several of her favorite treats. Since I reeked of the unique wild scent of a Tennessee creek—and only a good cleansing would take care of that "cologne"—I opted for a quick shower and then donned a fresh blouse and denim skirt.

-Guy? You got a minute?

I'd hoped to tell him about my ambivalent feelings, the total confusion swirling within concerning Brent and E.A. I'd also remembered something about the creek that Clancy and I were in, Crotin Springs Creek. Was it just a coincidence that Crotin—assuming it's spelled with a C—begins with the letters *CRO*? Could it be somehow important that the church was named Crotin Springs too? I closed my eyes, trying to concentrate on that odd, smeared letter, and exactly what it said. I was wishing I'd brought a copy with me when I suddenly saw it, like it was right in my hands: *CRO* was written there. Whether it was only a part of the word *Crotin* or if it was written to stand alone, I didn't know. But *CRO* was in all caps. And *that* was significant.

–Guy? Please, are you there?

I would've loved to get Guy's take on all of my musings, but he must've been exceptionally busy. I knew he'd never just ignore me. *Would he?* The mere thought stung, and I quickly dismissed it.

By the time I opened the door to the courthouse and asked the receptionist where I should go, Uncle Ollie and E.A. had spent about an hour without me. Which made me more than a little nervous.

"You joinin' them two fine lookin' men?" the receptionist asked.

I debated for a moment before deciding how to answer. Nodding my head, I calmly replied, "Yes, I am. And *my uncle* is a very handsome man indeed."

She opened her mouth to comment. Evidently thought better of it. "Well, then. Head down the hallway to a door what says 'Records.' Miss Opal'll be pleased to assist you."

"Thank you." She followed me warily with her eyes—I glanced back a couple times to find her still staring after me—since I admittedly hadn't been very forthcoming with friendly conversation. But I knew all about gossip in small towns. There was no way I was giving anyone the ammo that a visitor from up North said that E.A. Byrd was handsome. *Not on your life.*

I opened the door labeled Records cautiously, since it looked like there was someone or something leaning against it on the other side. That was my first clue Mama Byrd hadn't exaggerated one bit: That *thing* leaning against the door was a precarious stack of boxes looking to topple at any moment. I gingerly stepped around them and hurried to the relative safety of the only desk situated like an island in the small but stuffed office. I'd never seen such a small space filled with so many boxes, stacks of papers, old books, official and unofficial looking papers, old newspapers, photographs—all apparently totally unorganized. I was hoping my initial perception was wrong.

A tiny, elderly woman came from a back room. She had bright red hair (*Did she actually think that looked natural?*), glasses resting on the end of her nose (*She peered at me over the top of them*), was wearing a dark suit with white animal hair all over it (*For whatever reason, I was convinced it was cat hair*), and wielding a cane. I surmised immediately that the cane served several purposes, and not all positive. "Can I help you, young lady?"

"Um, yes, please. I'm Julia Johnson." When her face remained blank, I leaned back to peer out the doorway, attempting to see down the hall behind her. "Aren't there two men here? Didn't they mention I'd be joining them?"

"Did. But I don't *presume* anything, young lady."

She looked me over, head to toe, making it clear I did not pass inspection. *Goodness, what would she have done if I hadn't showered and changed clothes?* I wondered.

"I'm Miz Opal Mullins. Follow me, but don't be touchin' nothin'. Valuable information stored here." She used the cane to point out objects as we passed them: "Framed document from former Mayor Henry Robertson right there. Passed in his sleep two year ago come August, bless his soul. Irreplaceable words, right there. See that?" I nodded, soberly. "That's a proc-lo-mation"—another Southerner enjoying every vowel—"from our sister city in *Japan*, I'll have you know." Opening another door, holding it with her cane—I knew it had multiple uses—Miss Mullins escorted me down a set of stairs. We traipsed through a dingy hallway in desperate need of new linoleum and a coat of paint until we came to another door labeled "Historical Documents."

Miss Mullins motioned to me by putting a finger to her lips and slowly opening the door only a few inches to peek in.

"We're doing just fine, Miz Mullins," the slightly muffled voice of E.A. responded. "Only researching what you told us we could, I promise you."

She pushed the door open wider with her cane, and immediately I noted the unmistakable musty scent of old books and papers, that unique smell of books stored in a basement for decades.

"I told these young men the rules," Miss Mullins stated. I caught Oliver's eye and we both stifled grins. "See to it y'all abide by 'em, 'specially the one 'bout not touchin' this here cabinet. Otherwise, if y'all have any questions, I'll be up in my office." With that final word and narrowed eyes, she turned and left us.

I walked farther into the room and stood there, baffled. Lost in a maze of stacks, separated out by narrow passageways through the multitude of piles and shelves—shelves stuffed full and overflowing with boxes and books and loose papers. *How on earth will we ever find anything in here?* I asked myself. Out loud I mumbled, "I can't even find you two—let alone be able to locate a register for a specific date. Talk about a needle—"

"We're over here," Uncle Ollie interrupted. He promptly sneezed to further help me locate two grown men nearly swallowed in the mass of...*stuff.*

"Mama Byrd wasn't exaggerating, was she?" I found them in a corner, sitting, several opened books around them. "You didn't actually locate something useful, did you?"

Oliver blew his nose with yet another clean handkerchief. "Uncle Oliver, isn't this going to be too much for your allergies?" He waved off my question, blowing his nose and answering, "Not missing this. Besides, I anticipated the need; took an allergy pill right before lunch. Hadn't sneezed once until you walked into the room."

"Well, I promise you, I don't have mold growing on me." I looked around, taking in the disorder again and added,

"Yet." Shifting my focus to E.A., I asked, "That true? About his sneezing?"

"So now you don't trust your uncle either?" E.A. mumbled, but his attention turned quickly back to the big book on his lap as he pointed excitedly. "Look here. I found it: 'Elijah Manuel Gibbons, born 1895 to Zechariah Manuel Gibbons and Naomi Smith Stanley.' Julia, you'll want to see this."

I crouched down onto the clammy floor, wedging in between Oliver and E.A. Felt like we were right back in the truck again, packed in, thighs touching. This time there was no avoiding our arms being up against each other too, so I was intensely aware of every inch of electrified skin rubbing up against E.A.'s. I put my finger to the names, wanting to make the physical connection. "I remember that name—Manuel." I looked up, seeking E.A.'s eyes. "Didn't Lucille's father *and* her grandfather both have Manuel as a middle name?"

"Yeah, they did. Not so unusual around here to be repeatin' names, carryin' on tradition in the family. But it's rare to repeat one so many times. Makes you wonder if there was a specific reason to replicate it that often. Skipping some generations, but always returning to the name."

Uncle Ollie added cryptically, "That's the dominating question. *Why?*" E.A. and I turned to him, nodding in agreement. "Stands to reason a name repeated for hundreds of years—if that is the case—was handed down because there was something special about the original. The Manuel who started it all."

"What's the oldest register here we can find?"

"Wait a minute. Miss Mullins' rules, gentlemen," I reminded them. "Did she say anything else was off-limits in here? Besides the one cabinet?" I glanced up at the door, wondering if she'd regularly check on us—and kick us out if we dared to break a rule.

Oliver was shaking his head *no*. "We have permission to look at anything else that's here and available. But we must put it back *exactly* where we found it."

One "*Ha!*" escaped before I added, "Like there's any rhyme or reason to this…this…"

"Place looks like parts of Sundhamn did in nineteen seventy-three. Right after the tornado ravaged everything in its path." E.A. and I both turned our attention to Oliver, eyebrows raised. "Except maybe those areas actually looked better than this?"

"Excuse me?" I could hear Miss Mullins, but couldn't see her. All three of us popped up high enough to see her diminutive form standing behind a row of filing cabinets. "Just checkin' on y'all. Need help findin' anything?"

E.A. looked at Oliver and me and shrugged his shoulders, eyes twinkling. "Never look a race horse…" he whispered, and stood to approach Miss Mullins.

"What's that, young man? Speak up."

"I said you have perfect timing, ma'am. We really need to see the oldest register you have. One documenting the town's origins. Have anything like that?"

She leaned against her cane, but I knew it wasn't due to weakness—and I assumed E.A. realized that too, since he made no move to steady her. If we were going to get helpful information from her, we needed to treat Miss Mullins like gold. I caught Oliver's eye and we both nodded—unspoken communication that we were on the same page.

"Oh, I recollect where that might be," she advised, pointing with her cane. "Have a look in that there cabinet."

"You said that was off-limits, Miz Mullins," E.A. obediently offered. I smiled inwardly at his shrewd diplomacy and did my best to keep from snickering.

"Since I'm here to be supervisin', y'all can open it." She reached down into the pocket of her suit jacket, pulling out a ring holding at least a couple dozen keys. Sorting through them one by one, she took her sweet time. I was beginning to wonder if this would take all afternoon when she finally announced, "This here's the very key. Open it carefully, mind you."

Oliver and I moved to stand right behind E.A. as he turned the lock and slowly opened the doors. An even more pungent scent wafted from those stacks, and it was immediately apparent why: These books were so old they were disintegrating. Softly, E.A. moved his fingertip over the dates printed in gold on the spines.

"The oldest would be seventeen fifty-three. That's the year Collinsville was founded."

In a solemn voice, E.A. asked, "Ma'am, do I have your permission to remove that book?"

Miss Mullins held up her pointing finger, dramatically, and moved to a desk where she carefully pushed everything aside—evidently making room for the treasured registry. Then she nodded, slowly; once E.A. had placed the book on the desk, she put a hand into her pocket, pulling out a pair of white cotton gloves. Theatrically—we followed Miss Mullins' every move; my goodness, she was enjoying this!—she tugged on the gloves before finally reaching out to open the fragile cover.

"Unfortunately, this here *or-ig-inal* register's in such pitiful shape 'cause it was exposed to the elements over the years—that bein' two fires and a number o' floods. We're most fortunate it survived atall." She smoothed the pages, touching them with the tenderness of a lover. "When I took this here position many a year ago, my first responsibility was to faithfully copy everything in this here book. Didn't have no copy machine here in Collinsville back when, so I took it to Knoxville. Was scared silly I'd lose it or have a accident or some such, but we both made it home safe."

"And you've been in charge of keeping it safe ever since?" Oliver asked.

"Yes, indeed. Whenever they's predictin' a possible flood, we come to fetch the cabinet. Tote it upstairs to keep all these books safe. I've come down here many a time in spring, just to check on these here books."

I wanted to ask why it wasn't kept in a special vault, and especially on a main floor or second story, out of flood-prone areas. But I had a feeling it would be something to the effect of *"Because we've always done it this way."* My intuition also sensed it wasn't wise to question Miss Mullins' way of doing things.

"I'm givin' y'all this special privilege 'cause you say Miss Johnson here is a di-rect relation to the Gibbons family." She cleared her throat and turned another page, smoothing it before moving her finger down to the first line. "Y'all can see here our foundin' father was one Benjamin Manuel Gibbons. This here's his signature. And the date is July four, seventeen and fifty-three."

All four of us stared at that signature and the accompanying date with a bit of awe. In the background, I could hear a fly buzzing, beating itself against the small window above the door. Otherwise, it appeared we all were holding our breath, it was so silent in that room—a sacred room holding testimony to the last breaths of hundreds of people.

"Do you know anything more about him?" E.A. asked.

"Well, course I do. My job to know them things."

When Miss Mullins began turning pages and pointing out all kinds of information, this much was clear: She had a captive audience. She wasn't about to be rushed. And she was going to make the most of it.

"We know Benjamin was grandson to one of the first white men to set foot on Claiborne County soil. Historians think he might've known Daniel Boone. Imagine that!"

"What was his grandfather's name? Do you know?" Oliver asked.

"The grandfather's name is long lost, and such a shame too. There's record here—" She ran her finger down the page. "See *Jacob Manuel*, right there? Benjamin talks 'bout his father Jacob. Mentions his grandfather too, but never spells out his name."

"Why is that, do you think?"

"Well, now there's the rub. You heard tell of the Melungeons?"

I took in a quick breath and Uncle Ollie reached for my hand, squeezing it.

"We have," E.A. answered.

"Then you're knowin' they's mystery 'bout them people." Miss Mullins lifted her eyes to connect with each of us in turn. "Historians don't know where the race come from—if they're part Indian, white, slave or a mix of all them who migrated here. No one knows for sure, and some say that's 'cause they didn't *want* people knowin' where they's from."

I blurted out the question before I realized how unwise it might be. "Why would the Melungeons want their origins kept secret?"

Miss Mullins shifted her gaze towards me, and her penetrating stare made me uncomfortable. Leaning in even closer, she hoarsely whispered, "'Rumor has it bein' dangerous to know, child." Looking down at the book again, she turned the page. "Plenty stories 'bout them Melungeons. It's said too that there's a diary what's never been found."

"A diary?" Oliver said, rubbing his chin. "That would prove immensely helpful."

Miss Mullins eyes were wide in alarm. "Not if the danger outweighs the findin', I'm thinkin'. But if you want to know more 'bout that, you must be visitin' Miz Esther Gibson." She peered at us over her glasses. "She's over at the home, you know."

"We saw her just this morning, as a matter of fact," E.A. offered.

"Best go see her again if y'all has more questions like that," Miss Mullins offered, smugly.

"What else can you tell us about the Gibbons line?" I queried, hoping to pull as much information out of her as I could. "Like the name *Manuel*. Seems like nearly every son was given it as a middle name. Why would they do that?"

Slowly, deliberately, she closed the book. "Fetch me 'nother book in the cabinet. The one what looks most like this one."

E.A. motioned for me to get it, his gaze intense as we met each other's eyes. *Was he intentionally giving me the opportunity to hold one of these precious books?* As I picked it up, running my hand over its time-worn cover, I did feel a sense of living history in the palm of my hand—but was it really *my* history? Part of me wanted to feel a connection, so when I looked up to see E.A. and Oliver both watching me, I tried to respond positively. But the emotions were all locked up inside in some strange way.

Miss Mullins opened this one with equal care, and as she ran her finger down the list of names, she read out loud: "Benjamin Manuel Gibbons, 1708 – 1762; Jeremiah Manuel Gibbons, 1744 – 1826; Joseph Manuel Gibbons, 1792 – 1828. That 'nough? Or are you wantin' me to keep goin'?"

"Now, let me see if I'm understanding this correctly," Oliver surmised, rubbing his chin.

"Bet you're gonna ask just what I was wonderin'," E.A. said under his breath.

"Does mean each generation had only one surviving child—who was always a son? And each son had the middle name of Manuel?"

Miss Mullins cleared her throat. "This here book be the *o-ffi-cial* record. Certainly, there was daughters what survived too. But the ancestors obviously weren't carin' to make note of them. They were notin' the *males* what survived. Could be they wrote down only the *firstborn* males' names too."

We were all quiet for a few moments. Taking in the ramifications, I presume—and what that could portend.

"Don't you find that odd? Why wouldn't they record the female births, like most registries like this do? Or other males?" E.A. asked. "Unless it had something to do with inheritance and—"

"Primogeniture," Oliver added, finishing E.A.'s logic. "*Fascinating.*"

We listened, spellbound, to Miss Mullin's explanation.

"Indeed. We were a *pa-ter-nal-istic* culture for generations. The oldest male was the inheritor. If we can trust what folks recorded in these here books—and *we've no reason not to*—these men were the ones who inherited and passed on the family name. There's no reason for 'em to lie 'bout what mattered to 'em and what was worth writin' down. And there's no difference in this list from generation to generation and on."

She paused, and I swear we all leaned in closer, hanging on her every word.

"'Till Reba and Jake Gibbons. They's the first exception. 'Cause I know for a fact they had 'em only one survivin' child. But she was a *girl*. Named Lucille. And then the most terrible tragedy ever happened."

E.A. finished the history. "Lucille and her husband Jimmy Blevins died. In a car crash."

"Childless. No survivin' heir, endin' the *di-rect* line," Miss Mullins stated emphatically. She turned to stare at me over her glasses. "Which is why I made the exception of lettin' you see these here books, Miss Johnson. To prove you was lyin'."

Of all times. Unfortunately, my mouth was already hanging wide open in utter bewilderment. There was simply no stopping the hiccup.

—

Later, after dinner at A Byrd in the Hand, Oliver slipped into the kitchen to have a cup of coffee with Mama Byrd. It took a good bit of convincing on my part to get him to do so, and especially since all I wanted to do was go back to our motel and head straight to bed. My back ached, my head hurt, and my heart was just plain weary. But no matter how much I argued, Oliver was adamant about me not walking back to the motel by myself; he insisted E.A. accompany me. Under considerable protest, I reluctantly agreed. Getting back to my room and into pajamas was so appealing I'd put up with E.A. to accomplish that goal.

-Guy?

In my weariness, I needed to hear something from him. *Anything.* But once again there was no response. Without thinking, I sighed, despondently, and E.A. turned to look at me. "You okay?" he asked.

"Sure. Just tired."

We walked side by side, and as I snuck glances at him now and then I was struck again by my first impression of E.A.—before he'd begun to aggravate me at every turn. He walked in a way that seemed to announce how completely comfortable he was in his own skin. Hands stuffed into the pockets of his broken-in, casual jeans; a good, confident stride; straight posture but not so you'd think he practiced balancing a book on his head; and a habit of leaning slightly towards whomever he was speaking to, much like Oliver did. He made you feel like you were important to him. Worth listening to, certainly.

I enjoyed the companionable silence—which was very refreshing, for a change—until I heard E.A. take a deep breath. I wondered what was coming now. "Julia, can I ask you something?"

"Can't stop you from asking. But I can't promise I'll answer." I did look up at him, though, offering a slight smile of encouragement.

"I was just wondering if we could agree to be friends." He kicked a stone, watched where it rolled and kicked it again. When it landed near my feet, I took a turn. "I know we've rubbed each other the wrong way a time or two."

I made a sound in my throat, but though tempted, didn't comment.

"You think more than a couple?" He grinned, and I really did like the way his smile pulled in his eyes. "I'm asking your forgiveness for the times I've offended you. I can't explain why it's happened. I just—"

"Want another do-over?"

He chuckled. "That didn't go so well the first time. Let's just say I'm truly sorry. I know we'll never be more than friends"—he paused, apparently due to a catch in his voice—"but I would really like that. For us to be friends, I mean."

"Does this mean you're giving me permission to date Brent?"

"Julia, that's not—"

"I was teasing, honest I was. But E.A., I really don't understand this…this *thing* between you and your brother."

"There's no *thing*, Julia. Someday maybe I can explain, help you to understand. Never mind that, but please. Don't go off somewhere alone again with him, okay?"

I wasn't about to promise any such thing, so I changed the subject. "Fascinating what Miss Mullins told us about your ancestor too, wasn't it? Miriam Gibbons, half-sister to Moses Manuel, born in eighteen fifty. Miss Mullins didn't seem to think a half-sister counted, did she?"

"Obviously not. Only the direct line is of merit in her estimation. Well, if you weren't lying, that is," E.A. grinned and then winked at me. "So how many cousins removed you think that makes us?"

"No idea. I never could figure out the second or third cousin stuff."

"Um, since you've agreed we can be friends. I have a confession to make."

I looked at him, warily. "What now?"

"Oliver and I talked about a lot of things today—things weighin' him down with responsibility. I think that's why he told me."

The wary look on my face changed to alarm. "Told you what exactly?"

E.A. kicked the stone again, avoided meeting my eyes now. "About the two incidents, Julia. The black SUV that caused your accident. And your dad's." I picked up the pace to walk away from him, but he reached out to grab my arm. The blasted current shocked again, but no matter how much I tugged and jerked, he wouldn't let go of my arm. "Don't, Julia. Stop just a minute, will you?" Resigned, frustrated, I looked up into eyes that looked into mine with utter transparency. "I care about you, blast it. Can't you see that?" He let go and backed away from me, pacing back and forth, running a hand through his hair. "You put those together with the black SUV that nearly hit you when we were running. How many times does your life have to be threatened before you'll pay attention? How many people have to tell you you're in danger before you'll listen?"

"Besides a crazy woman in a home—"

"Not true. A perfectly sane official record keeper also warned there was danger for Melungeons. And the letter your father referred to just before he died. Oliver told me about the cryptic warnings there too, Julia."

"He had no business telling you that. And Miss Mullins' warning would include all Melungeons—you included, E.A. Not just me."

"All those generations of Gibbons noted for evidently having a surviving male child until Lucille. And then Lucille and Jimmy are killed in a freak accident after you'd been secretly spirited away. Don't all the coincidences prove anything to you?"

We were at my motel door and I searched my purse for the key.

"Julia?"

"It proves one thing. You're meddling in something that's none of your business, E.A."

"You're not going to blame your uncle for telling me, are you?"

"No. I'm not mad at *him*," I stated, letting the implication speak for itself.

I opened the door and though I tried to block his way, E.A. leaned in to make a quick inspection of the room. "At least promise me you won't let anyone in. Besides Oliver, of course."

I rolled my eyes. "There's no one in this sweet, sleepy little town who's going to bother me. Honestly, you and Miss Mullins have quite a gift for the dramatic."

"And you have quite the gift for being obtuse."

"You can't be civil to me for anything, can you?" I tried to shut the door, to put the barrier between us, but he extended a hand, holding it open. "What now?" I asked. When he met my eyes again I was torn by mixed emotions, for I could swear his face was wide open with blatant vulnerability. And was that *hurt* that I saw again? How could he change so quickly from being angry to resembling a wounded animal caught in a trap?

"Can I take you to see Miz Esther once more tomorrow? And then I promise you, I'll never bother you again." He locked eyes with me, his black ones soft, liquid, wanting. It felt like he was filling himself up with me. "You have my word, Julia."

I felt so torn, and yet: How could I turn him down? "Sure. What time is good for you?"

"Well, I think we'd best go with what's best for Miz Esther. Mornings are—"

"When she's the most lucid. I remember. Eight 'clock okay?"

E.A. nodded. "Perfect." Now transforming into a shy middle-schooler, he jerked his hand back to his side and ran the other through his hair again, setting the cowlick on end. "I'll, um, see you tomorrow morning then. Good night."

I shut the door and peered through the peep hole, but his back was to me. Once again, I felt clueless and mystified by Brent and E.A.

-Guy?
I so needed to just hear his voice.
-Guy, please? Are you there? I really need to talk to you.

Nothing. Instantly my headache worsened, the throbbing behind my eyes intense. *I felt sick at heart and worried. Beginning to feel panic. Was he hurt? Unconscious, possibly? Rarely had we gone this long without talking, and I missed him desperately. I couldn't imagine living without him. Couldn't entertain the idea of even attempting that.*

-Guy, I'm worried about you. Just let me know you're okay, please?

I paced the motel room for a while and finally decided to call Melissa. As I dialed her phone number, I murmured, "Please be there, Melissa. *Just be there.*"

"Julia! How are you? What's the latest? I've got five minutes before I need to run, so pack it in, girl."

I smiled, amazed at how much of her personality Melissa could reveal in a short greeting. "Oh, Melissa. I—" And immediately I started sniveling. So little time to get caught up with her and I waste it like this?

"Julia, are you all right? Do I need to fly out there? I could come, you know. What airport do I fly into?"

"Mel, no. Honestly, I'm fine. Just let me"—I dabbed at my eyes and blew my nose with one of Uncle Ollie's borrowed handkerchiefs—"let me get myself together. I can't figure out either of these two men I've met, Mel. And they're my distant cousins, if you can believe that! There's E.A., who drives me insane. And then his brother Brent, who's just...well, he's simply amazing."

"Oh my. This sounds encouraging, cousin or no! Are you in love with this Brent?"

"Melissa! I am not—"

"Then you're in love with E.A. That makes more sense, maybe, since it's always the guy who drives you crazy that ends up—"

I had to interrupt her. "Mel, stop! *Seriously?*"

"You know how intuitive I am."

"Yeah, like you told me this last guy—the one before the administrator, remember him? You said that *he* was a keeper, right?"

"Oh, that story's not over yet."

I was silent a moment, taking it in. "But you were *so* angry at him, and you told me you'd moved on—you said you showed him the door! And what happened to the dreamboat administrator?"

She sighed, and I knew exactly what look she had on her face in that moment: It's a sheepish look with a cheeky grin. "Bit of a rebound here, Julia. And anger and love are not mutually exclusive. They work in tandem. Frequently."

Suddenly the room spun crazily around me. I'd been standing, but I immediately flopped onto the bed, slinging a pillow over my face. *Every once in a while, Mel's insight could make me speechless.*

"Julia? Are you there?"

"Yeah, I just—"

"Hey, gotta run. Call me tomorrow, okay? Late afternoon. We'll have all the time you want to talk. We can even pull an all-nighter if we need to."

"No date then?"

She was smiling again; I'd bet on it. "That's *Saturday* night. Love you, Julia. Ciao."

I reached for Moppit, pulling her close so we could snuggle, stroking her soft fur. "I guess I needed to hold somebody," I murmured. "Shall we go outside once more before bed?" Her ears perked up, the definitive sign a trip was needed.

I sat up slowly, testing my vertigo, and then made sure I had my key before we headed outside for the nearest patch of green. Moppit was smelling every blade of grass, tree trunk and light pole, so I leaned back my head to look up at the stars. They were incredible here—bright, abundant, glorious.

-Guy? *Please* be there.

His silence was disheartening, but the blatant wonder above called me to seek my God.

Lord. It's me again. This sky…this world…beneath all this wonder I feel incredibly small and powerless. I've learned life can change in a heartbeat—leaving me…wanting. My mom, and then Dad. Please don't take Uncle Ollie for a long, long time. And not… not Guy, please, God?

I choked back a sob, and groping my way like a blind person, I plopped down onto a bench.

How ironic that Melungeon *can mean "I am what I am," when I still don't have the faintest idea anymore who I am. I read about ancestors and surviving sons and I touch their names on their gravestones, but I still feel adrift. I came here for answers. But I only feel more lost and confused.*

And if I were to lose Guy—Where is he? Why doesn't he answer me, God?—it would be like losing another chunk of me. Every rejection, every loss, every painful experience I've suffered has cut away at my heart, leaving me with…less. At what point is there so little remaining that I lose the ability to connect with what has worth in this world?

I know you are the bond that holds me together….and me, to others. But I also know that I've pushed you away. Because it feels like you've rejected me, too. I'm so afraid of more hurt…more rejection…more…you.

I swallow. And the words erupt from the innermost parts of my soul.

I'm afraid of you.

I lean over, putting my face in my hands, and let the flood of tears come.

I want a soulmate to feel safe with. Someone with *me, someone touchable. Guy's not....can't be. It's time I gave up that childish expectation that Guy and I will meet in person one day. That's not going to happen, is it? Finding that soulmate who is safe feels like too much to ask.*

I choked on my tears and then laughed out loud. *What does* safe *really mean anyway?*

The word mocked me for its illusiveness, and I felt more tears push at my eyes. *Is that the point? That nothing's safe? You aren't, God. From the rejection over my mind talking to learning I'm adopted—it's a testimony of an entire life that was never safe. The few times I did feel protected and secure? Were those merely an illusion?*

An illusion.

I felt a knife to my heart, and gasped for breath. *Is Guy only an illusion? I've never* once *doubted, in all these years. But have the doctors been right? Am I just now finally waking up from my life-long sick attempt to manufacture safety through someone I've created in my mind?*

I grabbed the edges of the bench to steady myself. Because suddenly, nothing felt remotely secure—not the bench I was sitting on, not the pavement beneath my feet, not the sounds of the town around me.

I think I know what you want me to do. I've circled right back to that leap of trust again, haven't I? But God, the truth is you've stripped away pretty much everything I've ever loved. And even if I were to gather enough courage to make that leap—what then? Would you just strip away more?

Then all my fears swirled to an epicenter like a tornado reaching down to touch the earth. *I'm supposed to jump into your arms, in trust.* I stood up, slowly walked towards my door.

But how do I know you'll catch me, Lord?
The truth is, I don't.

I'd just walked inside and closed the door, Moppit in my arms, when I heard the gunning of an engine.

Peeking through the blinds, I spot a car's headlights coming towards my room—a big, dark car. *Is it an SUV?* I wondered, panic just beginning to stir. The jarring shift back to the reality of physical danger was like a slap to the face; I hurriedly swiped away tears and determinedly closed the blinds. Leaning against the wall and closing my eyes, I willed myself to calm down, take slower, deeper breaths. Finally, I forced myself to turn around and spy through the blinds once more. Where I watch a black SUV drive ever so slowly by my room.

THE GRAVESTONES' SECRETS

27 of September, 1588

My Future, My Children, My Descendants,
Catherine's silence speaks louder to me than ever did the sweetness of her voice in my Mind. How can I bear this? So intent upon my safety was I that I did not, could not, foresee the fever that would take her from me, my very heart. The emptiness I feel is almost unendurable, and if not for my Lord's presence in my life, the ache for her voice would surely drive me to Death's Door also. Still, I ask myself, can I find the will to continue living without my Beloved?

This shall be my last testament, which though broken by Death, remains in the eternal Home of Love, our reward to come and where Catherine awaits me, in Heaven.

Since by God's direction I must remain in this temporal World—at least, for the immediate present—and I have secured a home in a Gap of the New Land, one far from the Sea. Far from the City of Raleigh. Far from all that would painfully remind me of my Beloved. We journeyed far to this land of lush vegetation and hills and Savages who accept us into their midst with open arms. Only we two have survived to settle here: I, Mauro, and one companion, John. We have agreed to build our homes here, to join our minds and hearts to this Land. It is rich in its own ways, and we shall seek contentment, if not happiness on my part.

I clutch the letter B to my heart, where my sweet Catherine forever shall reside. My pen now goes silent in grief. To anyone who shall find this poor Writer's word, know these truths:

I, Mauro, am a Child of God. I shall worship Him forever!

I am the only son of Manuel, son of the true Queen of England, Anne Boleyn. I and all my children and future heirs must keep this truth secret. Revelation, alas, brings only death!

I was devoted to my beloved cousin, Catherine, with whom I shared the joy of Mind Talking as long as God allowed.

I Mauro solemnly swear that my greatest legacies are my Grandmother Anne Boleyn's pendant, the letter B, testimony to my journeys, and my future descendants as the Rightful Heirs to the Throne of England.

On this day of Fifteen hundred and eighty-eight I pen these Truths, upon my word,

Mauro

CHAPTER TEN

I'm in the dark, foul hole once again, and my terror at finding myself here brings despair to my heart. My feet begin to slip and the familiar panic begins. I know that if I fall farther down this black abyss, no one will ever find me. No one will even think to search for me because—the truth is—*there's no one left to notice that I'm gone.* No parents. Not Uncle Ollie. Not Brent. And not E.A. or Guy. I am totally alone. Assaulted with the reality of my situation, understanding now dawns. *No one cares. Not even God.*

The sadness presses down on me, and I struggle to draw breath. I'm slowly suffocating in the blackness of my mud-filled coffin. The lid slowly closing.

I jolt upright in bed, breathless, gasping for air. *The nightmare,* I realize. *Still.* I swipe at my face, discovering it's wet with my tears.

Oh God, I pray. *Why does this nightmare continue to torment me? What must I do to make it stop?*

I look down and note the covers testify to my restless night: They're wrapped around me so tightly that I need to untangle them before I can pull my feet out. I sit up, vaguely cognizant of a new weight on me…*something else I was worrying about?* And then I remember. *Guy.*

-Guy? Please answer. Are you awake? Let me know you're okay, *please?*

Silence.

He's just not awake yet, I tell myself. *He does exist—of course he does! I was just tired and not thinking rationally last night.* Which makes me laugh out loud, because honestly. The irony isn't lost on me: How could I possibly be sane? To think a mind-talking friend actually exists?

There's nothing to be anxious about, I reassure myself. Guy's real, of course he is. And he's fine. He's still sleeping, that's all.

God, I would know if something's wrong with Guy, wouldn't I? You wouldn't…you wouldn't take him too, would you? Please, God, please, was all my mind could form into a prayer this morning.

I climbed out of bed and stretched while Moppit watched me, eyes following my every move. "Stay put; I'll be back soon." She put her head back down and sighed, and I consoled her with a scratch behind her ears.

Pulling on running clothes and shoes, I checked on Uncle Oliver. He was sawing logs, big time. I posted a note that said: *Off to run at six, will be back around seven. And yes, I promise to be careful and I have my cell.*

I peeked out the blinds again. No black SUV's in sight, but I still opened the door with caution.

I wasn't prepared for the blast of moist heat that envelops me. It was easily ten degrees hotter than yesterday—or felt like it because of the higher humidity. *The sooner I get this over with, the better,* I told myself. *It's only going to get nastier as the morning goes on.* I took a good drink of water and set off at a decent pace.

Avoiding the streets where E.A. and I had crossed paths, I ventured into parts of town where I hadn't been before, staying where there was the safety of early-morning traffic—in cars and on foot. The mourning doves began their cooing first, followed by dogs barking their morning greetings. Lights flickered on in homey kitchens, businesses' back doors were open with delivery men carting in supplies, and the smell of bacon wafted from eateries offering breakfast.

I let my mind roam to the verse we'd seen on Lucille's and Jimmy's graves. *My parents' graves*, I corrected, whispering it into the morning. I shook my head, the truth of that still a foreign concept. *But why Exodus 14:14 on their gravestone?* I wondered. I liked the version E.A. quoted better—"The Lord will fight for you; you need only to be still"—and I repeated it over and over, in rhythm with my pace. *Was it a verse they clung to as they lost child after child, a testimony to those left behind? Or did they know I'd come back one day in search of them, and this was what they wanted to say to me?*

No answers settled into my heart, only more questions. And though I called out to Guy several times—usually I prayed when I ran, but sometimes I talked with Guy—his continued silence was almost more than I could bear, making an hour's run feel twice as long.

When I came within sight of the motel, I could see someone sitting on the curb outside my room. My heart gave a bit of a jump until I realized it was either Brent or E.A. Squinting, I attempted to figure out which one was sitting with arms crossed over his knees, head low, staring down at the pavement. He looked dejected, if I was reading his body language correctly. *It's definitely E.A. That's his truck—and Clancy in the back. But why is he here so early?*

He jerked his head up, evidently startled when I ran next to him, and quickly stood.

"Daydreaming?" I asked, panting, bent over with hands on my knees. "Or were you sleeping?"

"Actually, neither. Mostly lost in thought."

He shuffled his feet and gave me only brief glances as he continually shifted his eyes away. If I didn't know better, I could've sworn he was acting shy. *What's up with this?* I wondered. *One moment he's all cocky and sure of himself. And the next he's like a ten-year-old boy talking to a girl for the first time?*

"I brought something for you." I raised my eyebrows in curiosity as I watched him reach into the front seat of his truck. "You forgot the watering can, and I know you wanted to keep it." It was filled with beautiful pink roses. "You left the rose from your parents' graves on my dashboard. Unfortunately, it was pretty wilted by the time I found it. So I went back this morning. Cut a few more."

"More than a *few*, I'd say." I lifted the flowers to my face to inhale the rich scent. "They're beautiful, E.A. Thank you. Looks like you scoured the can too?"

He shuffled some more, avoiding my eyes altogether now. Staring off into the distance, he shrugged his shoulders. "Wasn't a big deal."

"And you really did get these roses from the cemetery? The bushes next to Lucille and Jimmy's grave?"

E.A.'s eyes narrowed a little bit—offended by my question, I assumed? But he only nodded. The door opened and we both turned to find Uncle Ollie smiling at us.

"Well, good morning! Julia, I can see you've had a successful run. E.A., delighted to see you, as always." He beckoned to us. "Come on into the AC, you two. Way too hot to be outside if you don't need to be, eh?"

"Actually, um, I'm way early," E.A. stammered, jingling his truck keys in his hand. "I just wanted to drop off those flowers, get 'em out of the sun. I'll be back in 'bout an hour if that's okay?"

I nodded. Before Oliver could even start to argue—it was clear he would've enjoyed E.A.'s company—E.A. climbed into his truck and was waving goodbye.

Oliver turned to me and shrugged his shoulders. "Looks like you're stuck with just me."

I kissed him on the cheek. "I'll gladly be *stuck* with you anytime," I teased. "But I'm sure you'd prefer I clean up first. I promise to make it quick."

Oliver and I had just ordered breakfast when he quickly scanned the room and then scooted his chair over closer to me. "Interesting news to share with you."

"Oh, what's that?" His cloak and dagger approach was either pure drama—or he did indeed have something important to tell me. Either way, he had my attention.

"As E.A. said, Myra was very close to your biological mother, Lucille. Julia, she had always known about you. She knew that Lucille and Jimmy had secretly sent you away."

Now *I* glanced around the room to see who was there. "*Really*. When I talked with Brent yesterday, he acted clueless about everything. Does that mean she never told Brent or E.A.?"

"Myra said she's explained as they've asked questions over the years. Not wanting to lie to them, but not giving any more information than was necessary. But she was quite adamant that she also swore both boys to secrecy.

"It was an interesting conversation, Julia. We were both stepping around it cautiously." He stopped talking and stared out the window, suddenly lost in his thoughts. "I think she was still protecting Lucille—trying to keep that confidence, I mean. Protecting E.A. It goes without saying that I was protecting *you* also."

"Why on earth would she need to protect E.A.?" I asked, baffled by Oliver's conjecture.

"Haven't quite figured that out yet. But this was interesting: She said Brent's been asking more questions about you lately. Seemed to be in relation to some of his real estate clients."

"He just mentioned a client to me—a 'filthy rich' one that he needed to keep happy. How could that possibly be connected to me?"

Oliver sighed. "No idea, darling girl. But more people knowing about you makes me that much more nervous."

"And protective!" I added, patting his hand.

When we returned to the motel, E.A. was sitting in his truck, waiting for me again. I'd just volunteered to drive my car—E.A. was insisting on driving his truck and so we were primed for another argument—when Oliver heard the phone ring in his room. After he'd stretched the telephone cord so that he could stand in the doorway to chat, E.A. and I listened to the one-sided conversation. "Well, good morning to you too. What's that? Oh no. Uh-huh. Yes, I agree. Absolutely. Wait just a moment, Myra." Oliver turned to us, giving E. A. and me the abbreviated reason for Myra's call: "Turns out Myra's had a minor catastrophe in the kitchen. A leaky pipe has made a bit of a mess, and she's asked me to come help."

E.A. immediately responded, stating, "No, no, *I'll* go, Oliver. There's absolutely no reason to bother you—"

"Actually, she told me why she didn't ask for you. Insists you need to accompany Julia, because she knows Miz Esther probably wouldn't talk to just Julia and me. That's why I need to rescue your mother. And *you* need to help Julia." He pulled the phone closer to his ear again. "What's that, Myra?" Oliver's smile stretched across his face, and I didn't have to let my imagination roam far to figure out the gist of what Myra was saying now. Oliver sobered a bit and cleared his throat before adding, "It's decided then. Mind if I take the car, Julia, darling? I might need to run some errands, pick up whatever's needed to get Myra's kitchen back in working condition." Concluding his conversation with Myra, he added, "I'll be there in a few minutes. Yes. Yes, of course. Bye now."

"You sure you won't be needin' my help too?" E.A. asked. He looked distressed, but Oliver waved him off.

"I assure you I can handle this. And besides," Oliver leaned towards E.A. and winked, "certainly you must understand by now how much I enjoy your mother's company?"

For a moment I expected E.A. to blush, he acted so embarrassed. But he recovered quickly, putting a hand on Oliver's shoulder. "The feeling's mutual, Oliver, as you well know. And I couldn't leave Mama in better hands." E.A. turned to me, asking, "Ready to go? Weatherman's warning about a bad thunderstorm today, and I know Miz Esther views storms as omens. Once the thunder and lightnin' kick up, she'll be so preoccupied we won't get much helpful information."

I kissed Uncle Ollie goodbye. "This could be interesting."

We were silent as E.A. drove to the home, suddenly awkward with each other. I could sense tension rising in him as clearly as the increasing barometric pressure. His movements were jerky, his speech—when he did talk—was stammering, and he still pretty much avoided meeting my eyes. Resigning myself to the silence between us, I called out to Guy again, though I was afraid to even try at this point. The unknown felt safer than—well, I refused to give conscious thought to alarming speculations.

-Guy? What's wrong? Are you okay? Please just answer me, Guy. *Please.*

Stillness in the cab of the truck, and silence in my mind. An uncomfortable lump formed in my throat and tears threatened. I stared out the passenger window, willing myself to get my emotions under control when I felt E.A.'s hand squeezing mine. I hurriedly blinked away the tears and looked up at him, questioning.

"I, um, I know you've had a lot to process these last several weeks. Facing Miz Esther again can't be easy."

So that's what he thinks I'm being emotional about, I realized. *Esther. What she might say about my past.* He continued to stare straight ahead as he drove, and I allowed my silence to be affirmation.

"I promise I'll do my best to make this helpful for you. And not hurtful in any way, if I can help it."

"Thanks, E.A."

The same nurse greeted us as before, and this morning she was very positive about Esther's state of mind. "She's right talkative today." She nodded at us, smiling. "Good day for a visit, I'm thinkin'. At least, till that storm starts a movin' in."

Esther was sitting by the bay window again, but her wheelchair was positioned so she could see us as soon as we walked in. Her face lit up when she recognized E.A. "Well, hey!" she called, holding out both hands towards him.

E.A. took them in his, holding them briefly in his own. It was yet another thoughtful gesture that caught me by surprise, but obviously not Esther.

"And you brung your sweetheart again," she drawled, reaching her hands towards my face. I leaned down, eager for her touch, and she pulled me close to place a soft kiss on my cheek.

E.A. and I hadn't argued this morning—not yet, anyway—so maybe that's why her assumption didn't rankle as much as yesterday?

"I'm right glad y'all come back. Been thinkin' more 'bout Melungeon blood what's in you, chile. I knowed you's talkin', an' I'm thinkin' you has six fingers, too." I was emphatically shaking my head *no* when she took both my hands in hers—with a surprisingly strong grip. She examined one and then the other until she discovered the tiny scar next to the pinkie finger of my left hand. Her face lit up and she exclaimed, "I *knowed* it! They was a finger right here. You don't recollect it?" she asked, noting my obvious unease.

"I don't...I've never—"

"Course you ain't recollectin', what's the matter with me? Lucille and Jimmy woulda had 'em take it off when you was but a babe. Telltale sign of Melungeon blood, and your mama and daddy was protectin' you, any way they could."

I looked up at E.A., seeking, what? Empathy? Or answers? He met my eyes, and for just a brief moment, seemed to reach all the way to my soul. Connecting to me there in a way that felt uncomfortably intimate. Even though the conversation with Esther had made me feel uneasy, I quickly switched my gaze back to her rather than look into E.A.'s eyes a moment longer.

"Won't find nothin' 'bout mind talkin' and six fingers in that Collinsville book."

"*The History of Collinsville*, you mean?" I queried. "I've been reading that."

Esther chuckled. "Onliest ones knowin' less 'bout the *real* history o' this here town be the mayors." She retained her strong grip on my left hand and reached for E.A.'s right one. "E.A., recollect what I tole you? They's comin' after the air and you needs get ready. The diary, now that's where you be findin' truth-tellin' history, 'bout Mauro and his daddy Manuel. His mama—God rest her soul—done had Manuel, the heir, spirited away, just like Lucille and Jimmy done you, chile. But them renegade royalty, they ain't havin' no *threat* to 'em. E.A., are you hearin' what I'm tellin' you?"

E.A. nodded, but then turned towards me and ever so slightly shook his head. "I'm tryin' to follow, Miz Esther. But can you tell me, exactly, who is it that's coming? I don't quite—"

She quickly scanned the room—eying the few around her with a frown—and then tugged his hand towards her, pulling E.A. in closer, whispering, "They's some here what knows. *Outsiders*—supposed realtors, they said—been snoopin', askin' questions." Suddenly Esther seemed agitated, and she anxiously glanced over her shoulder again, evidently worried that someone was eavesdropping. "Some's too close to you, E.A. You best be right careful." E.A.'s gaze shifted over to me again, worry lines deepening, highlighted, as his face noticeably paled. "You best find that diary, is all I'm sayin'. It's right there. *Find it,* you hear?"

Tense and demanding, Esther waited expectantly for answers from both of us. "I'll do my best, Miz Esther," E.A. said. "I promise you that." When she turned to me, I nodded my head.

"Tis at the homesite, somewheres. Lucille and Jimmy, they hid it good. And I'm here to tell you, trouble's brewin' same as this here storm what's comin'." Esther's hands started shaking—so badly that her fierce grip on E.A.'s and mine caused our arms to shake in a subtle paroxysm of mounting hysteria right along with her. I tried to pull free from her grasp, but she clung to me even more tightly.

"Storm's comin'. It's a omen—warnin' 'bout evil comin' too." Esther raised her voice now, and other residents nearby began fidgeting, reacting to the storm brewing right there in the room. "Y'all familiar with my namesake, *Esther,* in the Bible. Says she offered up her very *life* to save her people, and that Esther declares, '*Iffen I perish, then I perish!*'"

She was still clinging so forcefully to E.A. and me that I could feel the beat of her pulse in my hand. And her eyes! They were lit up with the intensity of a raging fire.

"Ever one's gotta make that leap o' faith one day, knowin' it's what our lovin' God asks of us. And it don't matter iffen I perish, *'cause I know where I'm fallin'!*" She pivoted then to look straight at E.A. "You needs be ready, E.A.—*watch out for her!*"

I saw the nurse hurrying towards us, worry written on her features. But Esther wasn't done yet, and waved her off, fussing, "*Don't*—I ain't done yet, gal!"

"Oh yes, you are, Miz Esther. Time for your medicine and a nap. Now, let go 'em, Miz Esther." She pried Esther's fingers from our hands and looked at us imploringly, whispering, "Might be best if y'all didn't come tomorrow."

Still, Esther was determined to have the last word, so even as she was being pushed from the room she shouted over her shoulder, "Listen to me, E.A. Watch the storm, 'cause it's bringin' evil with it in the wind. You hearin' me? *They's evil in the wind!*"

I watched, frozen in place, until the two of them were completely out of sight. Involuntarily, I shivered. Wrapping arms around my chest, I glanced over at E.A., discovered he was staring at me, unblinkingly. The worry lines were still there, prominent between his brows and on either side of his mouth. "*What?*" I threw at him, too many questions implied and bound up in that one-word query.

"Gotta get you back to the motel. Where you need to stay put—for the remainder of the day." He roughly took my arm, propelling me down the hallway towards the door. But his gruff manner and authoritative attitude brought out the stubbornness in me yet again: I would *not* be bullied. And especially not by E.A.!

I attempted to jerk my arm free—as always, the annoying fizz of electricity present at his touch—but his grasp was much stronger than Esther's. "I beg your pardon. Since when do you tell me what to do?"

"Lower your voice, you're makin' a scene," E.A. hissed at me. "Stop acting like a child, Julia. Didn't you hear a word Miz Esther said? *Your life's in danger!*"

"Of course, I heard her. But you can't honestly believe—" E.A. pushed the door open to the outside, and the drastic change in the weather caused both of us to momentarily pause in shock. The humidity was nearly overpowering, the air so dense it felt like you could grab a handful and hold it in your fist. Reflected color painted over everything—like a wash over an antique piece of furniture—pulled our eyes upward where we noted a sickly yellow sky, the harbinger of a nasty storm. Now perfectly still, the air felt hushed, like all nature was waiting, holding its breath before she released her fury. I was still frozen, facing towards the west where one patch of sky was a threatening dark greenish brown when E.A. tugged me forward again.

"Hey. Take it easy, will you?"

"Jul..Julia, I'm sorry." He was back to stammering again, but this time the obnoxious, demanding dictator still accompanied it. "I just…I'm so worried about you that—we've got to get you back to the motel." As he raced there I gingerly rubbed my arm where he'd grabbed me; when E.A. noticed, he apologized profusely. Still, his tone hadn't changed, and if anything, it grew in intensity. "You'll need you to secure your door—lock, bolt, chain. Whatever's there, do it all. I'll head to the restaurant and then send Oliver back immediately to watch over you. But don't you *dare* open that door to anyone other than Oliver, you hear?"

"I've been through storms before, E.A. Honestly, isn't this a bit of an over-reaction?" When his only response was to increase his speed and check the rearview mirror several times, I noted, "You're taking this very seriously."

Now he looked at me like *I'd* lost my mind. "You just now figurin' that out?" We pulled up to the motel, parked next to my car. But before I opened the door, E.A. leaned over and put his arm across me, pinning me in place while he scanned the parking lot. "No black cars in sight, at least. Nothing that wasn't here earlier."

"You remember what cars were parked here when we left?"

"I made note of them earlier, so yes, I do." He walked me to the door, opening it for me and taking a quick look inside. His eyes constantly shifted in every direction until he barked instructions at me again: "Remember, do not even *think* about opening this door before you look to see who's out here. Oliver should be back in about five minutes. You have my number, right? I'll be at the restaurant and I can get here in minutes if you'd need me also." All his instructions had come out in a rush, but he stopped suddenly and looked deeply into my eyes again—that same searching look that had flustered me earlier when he seemed to have the ability to peer into my soul. "You and Oliver should go home. Right after the storm passes." Still staring into my eyes, he stammered out, "I, um, I think you'll be safer there."

The abrupt change of subject was puzzling, and I struggled to track onto what he was thinking. "Go home? Have you forgotten about the diary? I want to go look for it since Miss Esther said—"

"It's not to be found, Julia. We tried. Forget about it—forget all of this! You and Oliver need to go home." His voice broke, and he licked his lips. Took a deep breath before slowly reaching up to put a hand to my cheek. The electric response caused me to jerk away and I saw hurt descend on his features as clear as if I'd slapped him.

"E.A., I didn't—"

But he was belligerent again, commanding as he pulled the door shut between us, "Remember what I said. *Don't open this door,*" he shouted.

I stood there, listening to the sounds of his truck driving away until, surprisingly, I heard him come right back. *Wonder what he forgot?* I asked myself, curious. *Probably has one more order to bark at me.* Moppit had just jumped up on my leg to get my attention, so I picked her up before opening the door.

I sucked in a breath of surprise when I saw it wasn't E.A. after all. It was Brent who leisurely leaned against the door frame and tilted his head towards me, grinning confidently. "Hey, Julia. How 'bout we go for a ride?"

Parked behind him was a black SUV.

—

I held onto Moppit like she was a lifeline, the only thing keeping my head above water. She squirmed, uncomfortable in my tight grasp, but I wasn't about to put her down.

"Brent. I wasn't expecting you." Glancing up at the sky, I noted the storm was closer. The wind had picked up and the ominous dark clouds were stealthily advancing. "You know, that storm looks a bit ominous, and I'm pretty busy right now so—"

He leaned farther into the doorway, effectively blocking my ability to close the door. Still, he appeared at ease, not anxious about anything. Including the approaching storm, evidently.

"Oh, now Julia. What's there to do right now besides go for a ride with me, eh?" He motioned flippantly towards the scene behind him. "Nothin' much happenin' out here, really. Nice time for a drive in the country, don't you think?"

"It's about to storm, Brent. Probably not the best time to be out."

I glanced nervously towards the SUV, trying to make out who was sitting behind the wheel. Evidently, I didn't nuance my curiosity very well since Brent volunteered, "That's Kate. She'll be drivin' her uncle's car back to his house now. Nice of him to let us borrow it now 'n then, don't you agree? So we'll be needin' to take your car, Julia. Get your keys, will you?" He patted his jacket pocket, where I could see the clear bulge of a rigid object. My heart started racing and Moppit, sensing my rising panic, squirmed in my arms again. "You don't want me to pull this outta my pocket, Julia." He reached over to pet Moppit. "Cute dog. Wouldn't want to hurt her."

I froze, the threatening tone alerting me to the danger I was in. *E.A. was right*, I thought frantically to myself. *He was telling me the truth all along and I didn't believe him.* "I'll just put Moppit in her bed," I suggested, backing up slowly, knowing the motel phone was nearby. But Brent was having none of that.

"Just put the dog down and come with me, Julia. And no, you won't be needin' your purse neither. My treat tonight," and he chuckled at his creative attempt at humor.

I waited while Brent stopped to give Kate a kiss, cooing to her, "Almost done, darlin'. Once I finish here we'll be on our way to London before you know it." Kate threw me a contemptuous, victorious look and drove off, gunning the big car, making the tires squeal. "That girl o' mine. Has her a bad tendency to get a bit loose with her drivin'. Runs cars off the road sometimes, can you imagine? Been known to nearly plow right over careless runners too."

I stared at him in shock, my fears gathering and building like the storm clouds above us. Insecurities I'd worked to push aside pressed at me until I felt dizzy, and I reached out to hold onto the side of my car.

"Oh, come on, Julia. The helpless female act? Like I'm gonna buy that? Miss triathlete suddenly becomes the fair damsel in distress?" He chuckled, calmly informed me I'd be driving, and began barking out directions where I should turn. It was pretty clear we were headed to the homesite, and I felt my stomach knot in fear. *God, help me*, I pleaded. *How do I get out of this mess?*

It wasn't until then that I even thought of calling out to Guy, but then I told myself there was no reason to, it would only worry him, he was hundreds of miles away, for all I knew. *Besides*, I thought, *he hasn't answered me all day, and not since yesterday afternoon*, which caused another shot of pain. *But if E.A. was right and Brent truly is intent on killing me, I want to at least try to reach Guy. If he's...if he's still alive. If he's truly real! Just one last time, to say goodbye.*

-Guy? I'm kind of in a mess here, and I don't even know if *you're* still alive. Please, Guy, are you there? If I'm in the kind of danger I think I am, and I'm going to die, I need to talk to you one last time. I love you and—

-Jules? What do you mean you're in danger?

The panic in his voice was undeniable, even though—for the moment, at least—I could only feel joy that he was real and alive and answering me.

-I was so worried about you, Guy, when I didn't hear from you. Were you ill? I even wondered—but are you okay?

-Jules, none of that matters. Where are you? Tell me why you're in danger.

-It's Brent. He's—

"Excuse me? Earth to Julia, I asked if you knew the way to your ancestors' dump from here." He eyed me warily, glowering in disapproval. "I've heard all the wild tales 'bout you Melungeons. You can't really do that stuff, can you?"

"I don't have the faintest idea what you're talking about."

"You're lyin', Julia Johnson. You know exactly what I'm talkin' 'bout." Brent studied me for a minute, and I could feel myself start to fidget under his scrutiny.

-Jules? Tell me where you are!

"Let's just keep talkin' here, keep that little mind of yours busy. I never believed all the fanciful stories 'bout mind talkin' and six fingers and all that. But I don't think we'll take the risk. So what shall we talk about? I know: Let's start with how much I enjoyed kissin' you." He reached over to caress my arm and I flinched. I knew only fear at Brent's touch now—and pure revulsion. "Ah, come on, Julia. You liked that plenty fine before. Such a pretty thing too." He made a *tsk, tsk* sound, mocking me, curling up his lips in an eerie imitation of a smile. "Really a shame there's only one way to end this story."

Leaning closer towards me, Brent moved his hand to the back of my neck. I cringed. "Thought the story'd end in Wisconsin. Supposed to. We drive all the way up to your dumb state in Kate's uncle's big ole SUV. Followed your little blue Toyota Camry. Guess what I come to find out?"

I shook my head and scooted farther towards my door, attempting to move out of Brent's reach, telling myself to stay calm and think clearly.

"Now, Julia. You needs be answerin' me with words, you hear? Julia?"

"Yes. I hear you."

"Good. Just makin' right sure there's none of this mind talkin' going on. So anyway, when we crashed into that little blue car and sent it flyin', imagine my dismay when I discovered it wasn't you after all."

"You killed my dad. No, you *murdered* my dad." I spit out the words like I couldn't stand the taste of them.

"Didn't neither. Heard he had a heart attack and—"

"Because of the shock of being run off the road by you!"

"Not my fault, girl. If you'd been in your own car like you were supposed to be, none o' that would've happened."

I glared at him, throwing back, "What do you mean? When you realized I wasn't in that car, you came after me next. Tried to force *this* car off the road."

Brent was quiet for a moment, clearly confused by what I'd said and mulling over this information. "Don't know what you're talkin' about." He stared out the windshield, momentarily lost in his own thoughts, and I took my opportunity.

-Guy, he's making me drive to the homesite. I know you have no idea where that is, but it's helpful to me...just to tell you...

I could just barely make out Brent's voice in the background, droning on, "Anyway...I knew you existed 'cause Mama told me some time ago. Didn't know what all that meant—you being the last survivin' Gibbons and all. Some folks from England filled me in on your...*ancestors*, let's say."

I focused on Guy, on hearing only him.

-Keep him talking, Jules. Every bully loves to talk about himself more than anything else. Ask him questions. Anything you can think of. Lead him on.

"Julia!" He smacked me on the arm and I jumped, jerking the steering wheel to the right, nearly crashing the car into the ditch. Pulling the gun out of his pocket, he rested it on his lap, barrel pointed towards me. "Just a little reminder in case you think mind talkin'—or tryin' to get us into an accident—would get you outta this. Do we understand each other?"

A huge crack of thunder reverberated, and despite Brent's warning, my startled reaction caused the car to skid on the gravel road once more. He picked up the gun and aimed it at me. "Did you think I was kiddin' you, Julia?"

I shook my head *no* and instantly thought better of it, adding, "No, Brent. The thunder startled me, that's all. I'll be more careful, I promise."

The storm was moving towards us with a vengeance now, and just as Esther had predicted, it brought evil with it. The whole sky was an ugly shade of greenish black, and though it was still the middle of the day, it was getting darker by the moment. Lightning streaked across the sky and only a few seconds later, thunder boomed. I tried to steel myself every time I saw a flash, clutching the steering wheel so hard my hands ached.

The first splats of raindrops pelted the windshield, and I flipped on the wipers, was reaching for the lights when Brent ordered, "Leave the lights be. Careful now. That's it—park the car right here."

We sat there a moment, my hands shaking so badly I tucked them under my thighs, hoping Brent wouldn't notice my fear. I remembered Guy's advice to keep him talking, so I took a deep breath, and asked, "Can I ask you a question?" I granted him my full attention, flattering him, hoping only sincere curiosity registered on my face.

"You can ask. Won't promise an answer. Would help your cause to ask *nicely*, though."

He rubbed my neck again, and I fought the urge to wrench away. "The first time Uncle Ollie and I were out here?"

Brent grinned, lifting his chin, proud of his accomplishment. "Yeah, had me a little target practice that day."

I shook my head at my naivete. "It never was men protecting their stills. It was *you*."

"Your stupid uncle ruined my plan that time. The old bugger nearly shot me too."

Under my breath I whispered, "Wish he had."

"Oh, now Julia. That's not nice. 'Specially considering how kind I was to you the day we went to the Pocket. You almost blew the whole point of the day when you blabbed to the sheriff where we were goin'." He scoffed, making a *hmph!* sound. "Like those bozos could figure out anything anyway, but you did make it a challenge. 'Till you initiated a game of dunkin'." Brent shook his head, frowning. "Woulda worked perfect if that brother of mine and his blasted dog hadn't shown up."

"Was it you who tried to break into my motel room Monday night?"

He smirked. "I'd had a tad too much to drink. Wasn't one of my better plans."

"I still don't understand. What is it you want from me, anyway?" I held up my hands, palms out as in surrender. "Why can't I just give you what you want so you can let me go?"

Brent laughed out loud and a beat later a lightning display split the sky with a concurrent roar of thunder. We both jumped, but Brent had suddenly turned furious, and I pressed my back against the door, retreating as far from his fury as I could.

"You fool. You still don't really know, do you? I already explained it. It's *you*—you're the only one in the way, don't you see? I have to kill you to get what I want; then I can make a claim. The only way you can give 'it' to me is to die, you fool!"

I still stared at him, completely dumbfounded. "Give you *what?*"

"The throne of England. You're the rightful heir of King Henry and Anne Boleyn."

My mouth fell open and I slowly shook my head. "That's preposterous. Brent, killing me isn't going to—" But he was no longer listening and I'd timed out with the stall tactic. He climbed out of the car and came around to my side, yanking the door open and roughly grabbing my arm. Pushing me ahead of him, he walked right on my heels, the gun pointed at my back. I stumbled frequently, and every time I tripped he touched the cold end of the barrel to the back of my neck. A stark reminder that it was useless to run. And how utterly powerless I was.

Suddenly the rain came down in a pounding deluge. It was so loud that Brent had to lean forward and shout into my ear to be heard. "We're headed to the well I heard you discovered, Julia. I'm sure you know the way." He pushed the gun into the bones of my neck and I shuddered. "No sense fightin' it. Sides, the well's a fittin' grave for a Gibbons, isn't that so?" I could hear him chuckling, and the thought struck me that he was truly mad—insane with greed, denying the reality of my humble ancestry, even if it was a bit quirky as a Melungeon.

I spotted the cover of the well and froze in fear. The thought of falling into those depths—even if I was already dead—was almost more than I could bear, and my knees started shaking badly. "This is it, right?" Brent asked. He motioned with the gun. "Take the cover off." I tugged at the heavy boards, ripping a gash in my hand from an exposed nail.

"Brent, please don't do this. It's nonsense—I'm no *heir*." Unbidden, the memory came rushing into my consciousness. *Esther.* She'd warned us about people coming after me, saying they were after the *air*—which of course, made no sense at all. I'd attributed it to the ravings of an old woman with dementia. But Esther knew exactly what she was talking about. It was still an absurd idea. But we'd totally misunderstood: she'd meant *heir*.

"Where is it?" Brent demanded. "The *B*. I know you have it; you keep it on you all the time, you said. It was hers, you know. Anne Boleyn's own *B*. Look at pictures of her and you'll see it on her neck. I need it for proof and then I'll have the throne for sure. Plus all the riches with it." I inched away from him, but he motioned me back towards the well. "Back that way, Julia. Stand right there. Give me the *B*, blast it. *Now!*"

Glancing back over my shoulder, I saw the dark well looming like an evil open mouth. It was my nightmare, about to come true! All the horror of that dream pulsed through me, and a sickening stab of fear split down through my body. I reached into my pocket and pulled out the *B*, clutching it in my palm one last time.

"Hold it out now. Carefully. Hand it over so—" Lightning struck nearby in a spectacular fireworks display, momentarily distracting both of us as we turned to gawk at it. And then a crack of thunder shook the ground beneath us so violently the vibration traveled up into our bodies.

But both of us were caught even more unawares when Clancy—appearing out of nowhere, it seemed—created a domino effect: Lunging towards us, he nearly knocked Brent to the ground, who reached out to grab me at the last moment. Brent was still quick enough to seize me by my hair, evidently fully intent on forcing me to fall headfirst into the gaping hole.

-Jump, Jules!

Guy's shout exploded into my mind.

-Don't let him push you down headfirst! Trust me, love. More so, *trust God! Jump!*

I didn't have time to argue—not one instant for my fears to over-ride Guy's command. But what did flash through my mind was how astounding it was—to hear Guy repeat exactly what he and Uncle Ollie had told me I needed to do. And the very thing I argued about with God that I did not want to do!

With Clancy's help, I wrenched myself from Brent's hold just enough to twist around—every miniscule effort feeling as if we were moving in slow motion—and see Brent reach out in one last effort to grab me again.

But I jumped.

Falling until I was swallowed whole by the hungry well.

I screamed as I plummeted. But even in my terror I had the presence of mind to grab at the sides of the well as I descended, eventually toppling onto a small ledge, my bruised and bloody hands grasping at exposed slippery roots. I simply crouched there for a moment, trying to calm myself enough to slow my panicked gasps for air, deciding to first take stock of what was injured. Leaning against the wall—slimy, cold and filling my nostrils with that overpowering smell of dank mold and mildew—I willed myself to let go of one root with my right hand so I could feel ankles, knees, shoulders. Cautiously switching hands, I checked both arms, discovering I was bruised, scraped and gouged. Several cuts were oozing blood, my hand from the nail scrape, especially. But miraculously, I had no serious injuries. Yet.

Shouts from above pulled my attention upward, and when lightning flashed I caught a glimpse of two figures locked in battle. For the next few minutes, my view of the scene above was like an old-time movie, constantly flickering white to dark, produced by the lightning storm directly overhead. I'd never seen or heard such repetitive and violent lightning and thunder, and the packed earth of the well answered the duet: It reverberated every time thunder rocked the ground. My position was precarious at best, and as rumblings constantly shifted my prison, it became even more so.

Momentarily, I closed my eyes, trying to shut out the hopelessness of my situation. And the rejection I'd carried with me down this hole. Never would I have imagined that my nightmare would come true. That I'd end up in this well. Completely alone. My heart pounded so hard I was afraid it would knock me off the ledge. My legs, already tiring, tensed from the strain, shaking—*just how long could I stay on this precarious shelf? I'm going to fall farther down if it loses much more dirt....God, please. Don't abandon me. Not again. Not here.*

Have you abandoned me—am I alone? If you're here, I need you to reach out to me in some way—please don't let me suffer rejection yet again. All I've wanted my entire life is to be fully loved. To be fully accepted as I am. Mom and Dad—they tried, I know they did. But they couldn't, not completely. They were either ashamed of me or embarrassed by me. And then I learn I'm adopted—rejected by yet another set of parents.

If they didn't love me enough, then how can you? Why would you care about me—once strange, always strange Julia?

I even jumped down here, my attempt to trust you. Is that what a leap of trust brings? Feeling alone? Abandoned? The silence of yet another rejection?

And then the verse flowed into my mind—the one engraved on Lucille and Jimmy's gravestone, in the translation E.A. had quoted. "*The Lord will fight for you; you need only to be still.*" I felt something inside me start to give way, like a knot slowly untying. The thought that all those years ago that message was carved onto my parent's gravestone. *God, did you plan for those very words to meet me here, in this well, at this specific time?*

A few tears slipped from my eyes; I could barely feel them as they ran down my muddy, rain-soaked cheeks. *I know I've fought you. And blamed you—for my mom's death. Then Dad's. And for being adopted—finding out like that.*

But did I have it all wrong? Those times when I thought I was all alone, you were with me, weren't you? It was an opportunity for me to anchor my faith and trust in you alone—not an extension of my mom's faith. Nor my dad's. And not my biological parents' faith either. Is the right perspective that you granted me a time of true intimacy? The chance to feel just you....and me?

Instead, I blamed you and pushed you away. I kept out the only one who could truly heal me. The only one who'd love me, no matter what. I know I've reached for all the wrong things to feel secure, but I want to grasp what is truly secure, Lord. In this well...on this precarious ledge...help me grasp you alone. Once more I jump into your arms, God. No matter what happens—whether I fall to the bottom of this well or I climb up to see the light of day again—I choose to trust you.

One reverberating shot rang out, and startled, I jerked back hard against the cold wall. More dirt and rocks fell from my precarious ledge, and when I heard them splash into the water below, I shuddered. Finally finding the courage to move my head and peer upwards again, I begged God to keep E.A. safe, if he was indeed the courageous one fighting Brent.

-Guy! I think E.A.'s here—at least, I know Clancy is. So maybe I have a chance? Are you there? I need you so desperately, my love, and I'm so afraid. I know God's with me, but I need to hear your voice. Just this one last time. *Please* talk to me, my love.

I squinted up into the flickering light where I could just make out Clancy's form, looking down at me and barking, alerting whoever had survived—E.A.? *I'm begging you again, God, because I'm so indebted to E.A. I know I've hurt him. Please, may it be him and not Brent!*

-Guy? Are you there—?

"Jules? Jules, I'm here!"

Struck dumb for a moment, I couldn't make sense of the voice and where it came from. Was it audible? Or was it only in my mind?

"Oh God, please—Jules, answer me!"

-Guy?

-Yes, Jules, I'm here! Answer me, love. Look up!

I gaped up into the darkness just as lightning illuminated the opening of the well. There I saw E.A. staring down at me, his face a picture of utter terror—and something else? Desire? Love?

-Guy? I don't—?

-Yes, it's me, Jules! Do you have any broken bones? Can you grab a rope?

-Yes, I mean no, no bones broken. My fingers are nearly frozen, and pretty cut up and muddy. But I think I can grab a rope. You have one?

His face disappeared and I instantly panicked.

-It's all right, Jules. I'm right here—*I would never leave you!* Just getting the rope from my backpack. Here, I'm tossing it down. Can you see it?

The rope dangled next to me and I cautiously let go of a root. As I reached for it, however, the shifting of my weight caused the weakening ledge to crumble a bit more.

Immediately, I breathed a prayer of thanks to God that Guy was helping too, that he and E.A. were somehow miraculously working in tandem to get me out. *Lord, once again you're showing me that you're with me! I'm* not *alone—never have been, even though it might've felt that way.*

-I'm on a ledge, Guy. It's breaking away. I'm going to fall further down—

-*No*, you won't, I won't let you. Grab the rope, Jules. It's looped on the end. Put it over your head and pull it down under your arms. Hurry, love. We can do this. *I've got you, and I'm never letting you go!*

Once again the lightning flashed as I glanced down to check my foothold, and I caught the bright gold glimmer of my B next to my foot. But there was something else too: A space carved into the side of the well, just opposite me, lined with—what was that? Bricks?

-Guy, the gold *B* is at my feet. And there's a small storage area across from me, in the side of the well. I can see something in there, Guy, something small, something wrapped in leather, I think. It could be a book—*the diary!* I'm going to try—

But as I gently shifted my weight to reach towards the storage area, more earth gave way—perilously close to the B now. *You can't get them both,* I told myself. *Choose.*

I felt a sizeable chunk fall and my left foot go slack; more clods of dirt splashed into the water below.

-Jules! What happened? Are you all right? Do you have the rope?

-I'm fine, Guy. Another portion of the ledge gave way. Yes, I have the rope. But my hands—they're so cold and stiff I can barely grip it. And I want my gold *B*, Guy! It's all I have from them.

-Jules, forget about the *B*. Forget the diary. I want *you*, love. It's *you* I need. Is the rope around you? Can I pull you up now?

I wanted to sob in desperation when the rope kept slipping through my frozen fingers. But I swallowed it down, telling myself I needed every ounce of concentration and strength to get the rope in position. I switched hands, finally fitting it under both arms just as the ledge gave way completely. Screaming again, I felt myself drop a couple feet—and then catch safely on the rope that encircled me.

-I've got you, Jules! Hold onto the knot above you. Bring your legs up at a ninety-degree angle and walk up the wall as I pull. *You can do this.* One slow step at a time. *Come to me, my love.*

Slowly, foot by foot, slipping backwards frequently on the slime and mold of the well, I made steady progress until I was near the top.

And then suddenly I realized how utterly confused I was. As I broke free of my prison, rising up high enough to see out, I spotted E.A. at the top of the well. But Guy had been talking to me at the same time. Had I mixed up the two? Was I losing my mind?

-Guy? E.A.?

"Yes, love, it's *me*." E.A.'s voice broke with emotion as he lifted me up with his strong arms, clutching me to him, crushing me against his chest. When one of his hands moved to the back of my head, gently tilting my face him up to his, I realized—finally putting it all together—that I stared into the eyes of my beloved. "Oh, Jules," he whispered, and I could feel his breath on my lips. "I've waited a lifetime for this." His lips, tenderly and tentatively searching at first, took my breath away as he claimed me with a demand both sensuous and pure—because this was E.A. and Guy at the same time, vulnerable and baring all to me. No guard, no holding back, no miles or barriers between us.

Separating so we could draw breath, he pulled me tightly against his chest once more. I felt the strong, steady beat of my love's heart against my own. And the knot I'd known inside me completely untied, stretched out, and then re-tied, tethering me forever. To him.

For once in my life, I didn't hiccup. Instead, I sobbed.

The tears erupted now—gushing out, overflowing, mingling with the steady rain that still pelted both of us. I cried for the death of my dad, how I missed him every single day, and for the terrors stalking me ever since. For being adopted, feeling abandoned and alone and so vulnerable. I cried for the terror that Brent had brought to both of us, fear mixed with disappointment and pain.

But most of all, I cried because I was *found*. From the top of a terror-filled, abandoned well, God saw me jump. And caught me in his arms. I was a different Julia now, but I knew better who that person was, and I also understood that I had *never* been alone. I might have thought so when I tumbled into that well. But I knew without doubt that two had gone in together—God with me—and two had climbed out, to be pulled into my love's arms.

"Jules, love, talk to me. Why are you crying? Are you hurt?" Frantically, E.A. held me away from him so he could check me over, his feverish gaze running from the top of my head to my feet. "You're bleeding. Oh God, Jules, I thought…I thought…"

Through my choking sobs I managed to say, "I'm okay. Just scraped and bruised." I pulled myself back into the safety of his embrace again, adding, "I'm crying because…because of everything. I know now how much God loves me. That he was with me. Always."

E.A. whistled for Clancy and the big dog was suddenly there—sniffing me, licking my cheeks and hands for the salt of my tears. "Come on, boy. Jules, we have to get you out of this downpour. You're shaking—too much. If I don't get you warm, and quickly, I'm afraid—"

He stood, picking me up, carrying me in his arms to the shed we'd found only yesterday. Kicking open the door, E.A. hurried inside, where we discovered the dusty old storage shed was now a sweet haven. For though it wasn't completely dry—the gaps between the boards meant rain was leaking in—it was dry enough for us to huddle together, staying out of the storm until its fury passed by. E.A. gently set me down and then tugged off his backpack. He pulled out a small tarp and a blanket: The tarp he put on the ground and then sitting down, he pulled me into his embrace, wrapping us both in the blanket. Clancy lay down next to us, adding his warmth like an offering.

I looked up at E.A., taking him in, really *seeing* him for the first time. Because now I gazed at him through the lens of my love for Guy. I touched his hair—waves dripping wet and subdued, but cowlick still stubbornly resistant to any taming—and then traced the line of his jaw, up his cheek, down the bridge of his nose to his lips, exploring the lines and contours like a blind person feeling the face of another for the first time. I smiled and said through chattering teeth, "Why didn't I know it was you? How could I have been so thoroughly stupid?"

His voice husky with emotion, E.A. responded, "I thought…I thought you hated me." The wounded look covered his features again, but he didn't look away this time. Now it all fit together: The suffering in his eyes, the pain I'd caused him. I felt his hurt, too, and I reached up to offer what healing I could, putting my lips to his again.

"I never hated you. I think subconsciously I was fighting a battle with myself and—"

"But you jerked away from me in revulsion. Every time I touched you."

I rested my hand against his cheek, imitating Esther's tender gesture. Only now understanding physical responses that made no sense just hours ago, I willed him to believe me, explaining, "Never revulsion. *Never*. Know what it really was? You sent a charge of electricity into my body every time we made contact, E.A. *Guy*." I smiled, suddenly feeling shy. "My physical body recognized you—even if my mind and heart didn't. Or maybe my heart did too, and I just wasn't listening. Oh E.A., why didn't you tell me sooner? I hate it that I've hurt you so."

He swallowed, opened his eyes wide, letting me glimpse into his soul. "I was afraid you'd reject me. And then, I had to wait on your timing. God's timing too? I wanted you to come to me, to recognize me, to want *me*—E.A. Guy. Each of us. Both of us, as one.

"But I've hurt you too, Jules. I didn't answer you last night or this morning because I was steelin' myself to let you go. Preparing to send you back to Wisconsin. I can't tell you what that did to me—the thought of never holding you, kissing you, havin' you *with* me, physically with me. To have you here, this close, but never be able to—?" He shook his head, eyes closed. "So I pulled back, pulled away. I was tryin' to protect myself, even though it cut right to my heart every time I ignored your call. Can you understand and forgive me?"

"There's nothing to forgive. I love who you are—inside. Your courage, your wisdom, the godly man you are. I love every inch of you outside too, each God-designed part. Eventually, I want to know *every* part of you." I grinned, intentionally roguishly. "Someday, I will."

E.A. chuckled. "Once we're married, we'll make sure of that."

"How stupid of me to once think we were more like brother and sister." Mischievously, I added, "We are distant cousins, remember. When we have kids, one could have a wonky eye."

He chuckled. "Guess we'll just have to take our chances." And then instantly turning more serious, he looked me over. "Your color's better, and your lips aren't blue any more. Soon as we can, we need to get out of here. Still feeling chilled?"

I cuddled closer to him and tucked my head under his chin, feeling like I could never get close enough. "I'm doing much better. But E.A.—what happened to Brent? Did I hear a gun shot?"

"Yes, unfortunately. When we struggled, his gun went off, but I think the bullet merely grazed his arm. How do I even begin to explain to Mama—?" He let the question go unanswered, and I reached for his hand, squeezing it in mine.

"We'll find a way, together," I reassured him. "And my uncle? He'll help." Smiling up at him again, I offered, "You know, he really has grown to love her in just this short time. That's pretty obvious."

E.A. nodded, smiling back at me, and I snuggled even closer, feeling a deep sense of belonging and fitting, like I'd never known before. "You know, we have another problem. How do we explain this complete transformation of our relationship? E.A., we've gone from angry and bickering to not being able to keep our hands off each other."

"Easy. I just tell 'em one trip down the well knocked some sense into you—ouch! No fair pinching. But Mama knows pretty much everything, Jules. I told her about our mind talking as soon as I was old enough to explain."

I was tempted to pinch him again, out of pure envy. "And she *believed* you? Why?"

"'Cause she's Melungeon too, Jules! She's never had the gift herself, but she knows others who do. Like Miz Esther."

I shivered then—whether from this news or a chill, I had no idea. But E.A. re-situated the blanket, pulling it tighter around us.

"Why did you keep all this secret from me, E.A.? My adoption especially?"

"Wasn't my place to tell you that you were adopted."

"Agreed. But once I knew—?"

"Because Mama made me swear not to tell a soul. And I think she would've done 'bout *anything* to keep her friend Lucille's daughter—*you*—safe. Keeping from spilling information was a challenge, though. Nearly tripped up so many times too when I knew things I shouldn't. Like calling you *Jules*. Do you know how many times I almost called you *Jules* instead of *Julia*? Had to pretend I stammered like a dithering fool to cover it up. And the worst part? The mere *thought* of Brent touching you sent me into a rage when I knew…oh, Jules, you were in such danger. How many times did he try—?"

"It was Brent who shot at me, not men protecting a still. And he admitted he tried to drown me—railed about Clancy's rescue." I reached over to pet the big dog and received a lick on the hand in thanks. E.A. let out a low whistle and gave me a *told you so* look before pulling me tighter against his chest. "He caused my dad's death. How do I forgive him for that? And what on earth are we going to tell Uncle Ollie? And especially your mom?"

"The truth. That Brent got it into his head you were a threat to him, for whatever reason. Mama is...well, she's gonna be pretty upset and deeply hurt, and they'll be repercussions for Brent for sure. Legal ones, too." He sighed, shaking his head. "I still can't figure out what it was that sent him over the deep end."

I bolted up right. Felt my heart beating faster again. "Brent told me why, E.A. He's convinced I'm Anne Boleyn's heir."

"*What?*"

"Remember what Esther said? Something about royalty feeling threatened? And about me being in danger because 'they were after the heir'? I thought she meant *air*—like the air we breathe. Which didn't make any sense, but I'd never have figured out what she was actually referring to."

I watched understanding dawn in E.A.'s eyes. "*Heir*—as in *inheritor*. Coming down through all the oldest male Gibbons—to *you*. Through all those generations, Jules. That's...incredible."

"Does your Mama know about this too?"

E.A. shook his head. "Honestly, I don't know. Anytime I quizzed her about why you were taken away, she'd give vague answers. But how on earth could Brent think the line goes back to Anne Boleyn?"

"No idea, but this"—I reached into my pocket and pulled out the *B*, earning a familiar frown from E.A. as I did so—"Brent said this was hers, Anne Boleyn's. The *B* stands for Boleyn, and E.A., I've seen paintings of her wearing a pendent exactly like this—with three pearls attached to the bottom of the *B*, right where the jagged prongs are. Can you *imagine*? I just realized too: I had it all wrong. *This* is the letter Dad was talking about. It has to be!" I stared at it, fascinated.

Frowning once again, E.A. lectured, "Jules, I swear you are dog-determined to do the opposite of everything I ask. I told you not to…if you'd—"

I put my fingers to his lips. "But I didn't fall. I'm here because you saved me. And oh goodness, I nearly forgot, so is whatever"—I tugged at the waistband of my jeans, reaching for the package I'd retrieved from the well. "Oh *no*."

"What?"

"I got the package too, E.A., and tucked it into my waistband just before you pulled me up. But it must've fallen out."

"If that's the case, and it fell in the water…"

"I know. It's gone for good, and we'll never know the answers to so many questions."

"Like why Brent tried to kill you. Does he think he'll inherit money or something?"

"That and something else. The *throne*."

E.A. scoffed. "That's totally ridiculous. So like Brent with his aspirations at grandeur. I wonder how he came across his information. Bet you anything he snooped in a home his realty company was showing. Remember Miz Esther complained about some realtors."

"Know what? That reminds me. Remember her saying something about 'you two talking'—"

E.A.'s eyes lit up. "Oh my—you're right! *She* knew. Miz Esther knew all along about us mind talking!"

I looked down at my pinky finger, rubbing the small knot there. "She was insistent this was a sixth finger, E.A. If it was—." My mouth dropped open and I drew in a huge breath of air. "I just remembered something I read years ago. Went through a stage when I was fascinated with Henry VIII. E.A., I read some historians who said there were rumors that Anne Boleyn had a sixth finger. Probably had it removed when she was a baby, just like I did. Because any deformity back then was considered—"

"A sign of sin. Or the devil."

"I know we can only speculate. But what if Anne Boleyn did have a baby who survived, a baby with a sixth finger? If they thought that was a sign of the devil, then—"

"They'd sneak the baby out. Send it to another country, probably."

I shook my head in amazement. "It's all just too much. But there is this one other thing." I fidgeted, not wanting to put words to my fears, giving them validity. "Brent said he didn't cause my accident. He admitted to my dad's, but not mine." I closed my eyes, remembering the multitude of emotions I'd felt that tragic night. "There was no reason for him to lie at that point. So, was my accident just a freak thing? A coincidence?"

E.A. was silent for a moment. And that scared me as much as any positive answer could. "Jules, I can't imagine anyone else giving Brent's apparent delusions even a measure of credence."

I nestled against his chest again, feeling safe in the circle of his arms, and needing his strength to flow into me. "There's more. I forgot to tell you the most important thing I found in the well. But I'm anxious about what else I need to tell you."

"Oh, Jules. As much as we've shared over the years? How could you hesitate to tell me anything?"

I took in a big breath and let it out before beginning. "It's about how I felt about God. I guess Dad's death and my adoption was the last straw. I stopped trusting him. And then I realized I was afraid of God too." I could feel E.A.'s heart beating against my cheek, and his arms tightened around me momentarily, a reassuring hug. "Finally, I realized I'd pushed away the one and only One who could heal me—the One who never stopped loving me, even when I pulled away from him." A sob formed in my throat, so that I could barely choke out, "Isn't his love amazing,

E.A.? Suddenly I see his grace and mercy and forgiveness from a different perspective, and they're greater and deeper than I ever imagined. I knew he was right there with me—I *felt him* with me—at the bottom of a forgotten well. His presence has never felt more real to me than it did right then."

I felt tears fill my eyes, knowing these were tears of joy. "God met me there, E.A. It was like he caught me when I jumped, and then brought to mind the verse on Jimmy and Lucille's gravestone—'The Lord" will fight for you; you need only to be still.' It was exactly what my heart needed to hear when I was so frightened, clinging to that ledge." I sat up straighter to look up into E.A.'s eyes, saw them glistening with tears too. Reaching up to brush the stubborn lock of hair from his forehead, I said, my voice husky with emotion, "It's like Jimmy and Lucille sent it directly to *me*. Before, I couldn't figure out in my mind how I could love my adoptive mom and dad and my biological parents all at the same time. But I have this special connection to the Blevins now. And so I do. Love them all, I mean."

"I think we'll need to make those leaps of faith into his arms throughout our lives," E.A. said. "It's what surrendering control looks like, a decision made—being willing to make that jump. Choosing to believe he'll catch us, every time. No matter where life takes us."

"Even to the bottom of a nasty well?" I asked, smiling to myself.

He pulled my chin up and tenderly kissed me. "Well, maybe not *there* ever again. But our hearts have to be willing to go wherever God takes us. That will be our jumping place."

I closed my eyes, took a deep breath and let it out slowly. A cleansing breath, I guess, for a new way of living life. A new start with the man I adored. But when I opened my eyes, E.A. was looking at me like his heart was in his throat again.

"What? What is it?"

"When I realized you had to jump down that well? Jules, I prayed like I've never prayed before. I got to you just in the nick of time when you were shot at. And when Brent tried to drown you. Felt like God coordinated every bit of that and I'm so grateful. But this time? I knew I wasn't going to make it in time and I was nearly panic-stricken with worry. Suddenly realized how totally dependent on God *I* was, too."

"I want to point out that—though you say I'm always dog-determined to do the opposite of what you ask me to do—I did listen that time, didn't I? I jumped—despite all common sense." Positioning myself so that I could look directly into his eyes, I asked, "Know why I came to Collinsville? Because I was convinced I'd find what I'd always been searching for."

"And did you?" he asked, grinning at me.

"Oh, I most certainly did. I found my God at the bottom of that well. And I discovered you at the top."

—

I was still pretty shaky walking back to E.A.'s truck. Everything was taking its toll: The trauma of Brent's betrayal, the lack of food, being in the freezing well and the continuing chill of the now drizzling rain. E.A. supported me with an arm around my waist, but eventually he scooped me up into his arms again, insisting we could move faster that way. For once, I didn't argue with him.

As expected, my car was gone, in Brent's possession now. What we weren't expecting was the blare of sirens, and by the sounds of them, close by. E.A. put me gently on the front seat of his truck, commanding Clancy to jump into the back, grousing about something Clancy had clutched in his mouth. "Typical lab. He's likely got somethin' disgustin'. Clancy's always convinced it's a treasure, though." E.A. gunned the truck and backed out onto the road, sending gravel flying.

"You're worried about the sirens, aren't you? That it could be Brent."

E.A. kept his full attention on the road as the storm had turned it into an obstacle course. Slick from the heavy rain, water standing in large puddles, the pavement was also riddled with tree branches, slippery leaves and loose gravel. "Let's just say in a small town like Collinsville, you never want to hear a siren. Chances are high it's someone you know and love."

The sirens had stilled by the time we got there, but the lights of a fire truck, several police cars, and an emergency vehicle were flashing. Remnants of a violent collision—smeared oil, broken glass, bits of twisted metal and plastic from tail lights—lay spewed across the pavement. The trail of detritus led to my dad's car, on its side in the ditch, the side gouged again. It was barely recognizable.

As we took in the horror of the scene before us, we realized what was so odd: The emergency personnel were standing around, hands in pockets. E.A. and I jumped out of the truck and rushed towards them, E.A. shouting out questions.

They responded with shrugged shoulders and perplexed looks. "E.A., if we knew where Brent was, we'd treat 'im!" an emergency technician explained, frustration apparent in his voice. "But whoever was drivin' this here car? They're long gone."

My stomach lurched when I saw the blood stains on the front seat, and the police pointed out a few spatters staining gravel in the middle of the road. But beyond that, there was nothing. No trail to follow. No other clues. It was as if Brent had vanished into thin air.

The only lead, pointed out by the sheriff, was the obvious black paint embedded in every dent of my dad's Lexus. Deputy Jenkins pushed his hat farther up onto his head and fixed a stare on me. "Didn't you say it was a black SUV what was givin' you trouble?"

I nodded, feeling sick to my stomach again. E.A. moved closer to me and wrapped an arm about me, protectively pulling me to him.

"Don't know I believe anyone was up to mischief, but if they were, could be they thought *you* was drivin'. Still doesn't make a whit of sense why Brent's plum disappeared. Got word a few minutes ago his apartment's been ransacked too. Nobody saw nothin', of course." He sighed, scratching his head and pulling his hat back down. "Don't make no sense atall."

E.A. insisted I get treatment for my wounds, so emergency personnel cleaned and applied bandages to wounds, gave me a tetanus shot, and made sure I'd downed some liquids. Then we set out for A Byrd in the Hand, to explain, as best we could, the entire convoluted story to both Myra and Uncle Oliver. Myra, E.A. and I skirted around the issue of mind talking, not wanting to wade into that with Uncle Ollie right now; everything was confusing enough as it was. I did have a feeling, though, that if I told Uncle Ollie now, he was bound to be more receptive. Especially with Myra's deep-seated belief!

The saddest explanation we needed to give was Brent's part in all this. We assumed he (and Kate, possibly?) had decided to leave town to avoid possible arrest—sparing Myra the shame and humiliation she would undoubtedly feel. Poor Myra was distressed enough already, and no amount of hugs from Uncle Olllie or E.A. removed the shadow of pain from her eyes.

Lastly, we explained our new relationship as best we could, pointing out how surviving a traumatic event together can change perspectives—and drive people closer. Myra grinned knowingly, and winked at me when Uncle Ollie was busy pouring a cup of coffee. As for Uncle Ollie, he was downright smug. Acted like he expected this to happen all along and was quite pleased with himself for his foresight.

We were pulling into the parking lot later when E.A. asked, a note of teasing in his tone, "We do have one more thing we have to settle, you know. And I'm hopin' we won't have to bicker over it."

I looked at him quizzically. "Bicker? You and me—never!"

"My dilemma of worrying about calling you *Jules* instead of *Julia* has come to an end. But can you get used to calling me E.A.? Even when we're mind talking?"

"Oh, I might slip up now 'n then, but I think I can adjust. What's E.A. stand for anyway?"

He rolled his eyes. "*Eavan Andrew*. Mama wanted to honor our Scottish ancestors, so she insisted on spellin' *Evan* the Scottish way—*Eavan*. And ironically it was Brent who originally started callin' me E.A., givin' me the nickname."

"Oh E.A.," I said, suddenly realizing what Brent's poor decisions meant for him. "You've essentially lost your relationship with your brother, haven't you? I'm so sorry."

"To tell you the truth, feels like Brent was lost to me years ago. He's been chasing after dreams of power and riches in a way I couldn't begin to relate to. I'll miss the Brent he used to be, not the one who tried to take from me what I value most in this world." He suddenly reached out to me, pulling me into his embrace while whispering, "Oh, Jules. I *love* being able to do this. I think I could hold you like this forever."

-Eavan Andrew Byrd, *I spoke into his mind, reveling in the pleasure of finally knowing my love.*

-Oh, I like the sound of that being sent from your mind to mine.

-Ummm, I think I like it too, but I need to test it out loud. Just to make sure.

"Eavan Andrew Byrd. I do like how it feels on my tongue too. But now comes the real analysis: Eavan Andrew Byrd, how about you kiss me again? One last test?"

"Oh, this won't be the last. I can guarantee you that," he assured me. Light, tentative, tenderly testing at first touch, he then claimed me as his. This kiss stated firmly, *You belong to me.*

Clancy's barking jolted us back to the realities before us, and reluctantly, we both climbed from the truck to investigate. "Clancy, hush! And what is this treasure you've claimed? Fetch it for me, boy." Obediently retrieving, Clancy dropped his prize at E.A.'s feet.

I let out a whoop of joy: It was the bundle I'd found in the well.

"E.A., I can't believe—it must've dropped on the ground *after* you pulled me out of the well." I hugged Clancy, praising him. "Good boy, Clancy! Oh, E.A., what a miracle that he brought it to us."

"Gotta think it was meant to be, Jules." He carefully pulled away the rotting leather wrapping. Inside we discovered a journal, but only a few decades old by the looks of it. E.A. placed it into my waiting hands, where I just stared at it. "Aren't you gonna open it?"

"Oh, I'm just…disappointed. It can't be what I'd hoped for. I mean, look at it." I turned it over. "Could be from the early twentieth century, but it's certainly not the one Esther was talking about. The one from my ancestor Benjamin's grandfather."

E.A. shrugged his shoulders. "You've certainly learned by now that the outside wrappings of a package can be deceptive." I glanced up at him. Saw the dark eyes glow conspiratorially as he leaned in for another kiss.

Our lips touching, I whispered, "We'll never get anything done if we don't practice some self-restraint."

He kissed me lightly again and whispered back, "I've been practicing self-restraint for the last twenty-four years, biding my time, waiting for you to come to me. This past week? Do you have any idea how many times I wanted to take you in my arms and kiss you?"

"I must admit. In the final tally column for best kisser, the win's definitely on your side."

"Never a doubt in my mind that would be the result. Now, open the journal before we get distracted again."

The book was ugly to look at, disgusting to the touch with slick mold, and the smell was awful. But the first page transformed it into the most beautiful book ever:

I, Elijah Gibbons, do hereby proclaim that the following sheaf of papers has been handed down by generations of the Gibbons family from fifteen eighty-eight to this present day. Though the original cover long ago fell into decay, we Gibbons have faithfully preserved this diary as a testimony to our heritage. You are now the carrier of this sacred trust. To God be the glory.

Elijah Manuel Gibbons, 1935

30 of July, 1587

To You, My Future Children, My Descendants,

If our Merciful and Gracious God deigns to allow this lowly soul's survival, one knows I can merely pretend and hope that you will one day come to be. I only imagine you reading this poor Seaman's attempts to describe what cannot be adequately put into words.

I looked up into my love's eyes. Hiccupped once, and welcomed the joy.

©used by permission only

JUST A FEW MUSINGS FROM CAROLYN

First, a confession: I've been fascinated with Anne Boleyn for decades. The basic facts of her life are incredibly intriguing, including her marriage to another captivating figure of history, King Henry VIII, complete with his own notoriety. Known for having some sort of beguiling spark, Anne wasn't considered beautiful, however. She's pictured as dark complected with olive skin, dark hair and eyes—the opposite of that time period's favored pale skin, blond hair and blue-eyed features. What was it, then, that made her so desirable, and especially to the King of England?

It was rumored that Anne had six fingers on one hand. Was that a trait she somehow used to her advantage, to set herself apart? King Henry described her personality as so enchanting that she "bewitched" him, causing him to fall passionately in love with her. Anne was often painted wearing her signature pendent necklace: The letter *B* with three pearls dangling on the bottom of the *B*. When I discovered the necklace had disappeared after her execution, then I could easily imagine it also being smuggled to her surviving male child, hiding in Spain. And why couldn't it one day journey on a ship to the New World with him, eventually handed down to his descendants? What a find that would be!

I've also wondered about her spiritual life: Was religion simply a mantle she wore when it suited her ends? If Anne fully embraced a gospel of grace as defined by Martin Luther, were all the accusations inflammatory lies by her enemies—lies which would lead to her beheading—merely because she fought as a brave advocate and champion of the Reformation? Whatever the truth, Anne Boleyn makes for an extraordinary historical figure to include in a novel, and a perfect tie to the mysterious Melungeons.

I first came across the ethnic group of people called *Melungeons* while doing research for my novel, *Jordan's Bend*, which takes place in the hills of Tennessee. Settling in Appalachia, this noteworthy race is almost always referred to as the *mysterious* Melungeons because for decades, their origin was a complete mystery. Possessing the common features of olive complexions, dark eyes and hair, and high cheekbones, they were noticeably different than the area's other major residents, the Germans and British, and especially the Scots. Oral tradition delights in other thought-provoking Melungeon abilities and attributes: foresight, healing, animal communication—and most notably, for my story, at least—possessing a sixth finger and telepathy. Those traits matched perfectly with the folklore about Anne Boleyn, and my creative imagination was ignited!

Due to advancements in genetic tracing, we now know the Melungeon descendants have ancestors from Sub-Saharan Africans, American Natives, and Europeans. Therefore, I judge that it's still possible the "Lost Colonists of Roanoke" could have traveled westward, feeding into that genetic strain. And why not Mauro, a secret grandson of Anne Boleyn? What better way for him to escape the on-going peril to his life, should any royals sniff out this threat to the throne?

The New World held great allure of new beginnings and escape from the danger and despair of life in Europe. And though this New World also contained its own unique threats and hazards, the glamour and desire for *what could be* over the *reality of now* meant the Roanoke Colony provided hope for those courageous adventurers who traveled there. Mauro—had he truly existed—would've proved to be a brave survivor in every way. Jules would have been proud to know him, as would I.

Maybe…just maybe these characters are real enough now in your mind's eye that you'd like to meet them too? If so (and I hope that's true)—that, my reader, is a sign of a memorable story.

John 16:22b – "I will see you again and you will rejoice, and no one will take away your joy."

Made in the USA
Coppell, TX
11 February 2026